ORKNEY TWILIGHT

CLARE CARSON

HEAD
&ZEUS

First published in the UK in 2015 by Head of Zeus Ltd. This paperback edition first published in the UK in 2015 by Head of Zeus Ltd.

9 7 5 3 1 2 4 6 8

A catalogue record for this book is available from the British Library.

Paperback ISBN 9781784080969
Ebook ISBN 9781784080938

Typeset by e-type Aintree, Liverpool

Printed and bound in the UK by Clays Ltd, St Ives Plc

Head of Zeus Ltd
Clerkenwell House
45–47 Clerkenwell Green
London EC1R 0HT

WWW.HEADOFZEUS.COM

For Andy, Eva and Rosa

'The sorcerer who sincerely believes in his own extravagant pretensions is in far greater peril and is much more likely to be cut short in his career than the deliberate impostor.'
The Golden Bough: A Study in Magic and Religion, 1922
Sir James George Frazer

CHAPTER 1

21st June 1973

THE DAY SAM realized that her father wasn't quite what he appeared to be was one of those June days when the unexpected heat was making everything shimmer like a mirage. Nothing was quite what it seemed. From where she was standing, Sam could see the gleaming cranes and gantries of Tilbury towering like an industrial Oz above the muddy flatlands of Essex, hoists and winches moving magically as if nudged by some unseen hand, giant rusting containers floating weightlessly in the air and, running through it all, the amber pathway of the Thames heading enticingly towards the far horizon. It was like a belated seventh birthday treat. She hadn't expected all this when she had conjured up the list of vague symptoms carefully calibrated to be too bad for school but not quite bad enough for a doctor's appointment. Liz, for once, had lost her rag.

'She is your daughter too, you know,' Liz had shouted up the stairs. 'I can't take her with me again. I'm lecturing today. She'll have to go with you.'

Jim had shouted back down that there was no way he was going to take her to work with him, it wasn't allowed, it was against the rules. But Liz didn't want to know, she didn't care about him and his stupid work and what was allowed and what wasn't, she had a job to do too and she wanted to get on with it. Liz yelled that as far as she could tell they made their fucking rules up as they went along anyway, and then slammed the door on her way out.

So there she was at Tilbury docks, happily ensconced in Jim's crow's nest office, suspended in the scaffolding high up in the stratospheric blue of the sky.

'Don't touch anything,' Jim had said, pacing the restricted rectangle of grey-marbled linoleum, not bothering to disguise his irritation at her presence. She was sitting on his fancy swivel chair, kicking her legs back and forth, making the seat twist around and around.

He had watched her impatiently with his steely blue eyes, flicked his wrist, checked his watch, and pointed out the window. 'Look. A kestrel. There's a pair of them nesting up on one of the gantries. It must be hunting for voles to feed the chicks. Keep your eyes peeled and you might see it dive. Don't blink or you'll miss it going in for the kill.'

She had followed the point of his finger and located a distant tawny cruciform speck; an angel of death hovering motionless apart from the just perceptible flutter of its gold-flecked wings. As she stared through the glass, she sensed Jim disappearing through the door behind. Alone in his office now, she watched the kestrel abandoning whatever prey had been in its sights and looping and looping on a rising warm thermal and she imagined she was the falcon soaring high above the river, surveying the ant-like dockers patrolling the walkways far below. Seeking out the secrets of Tilbury's hinterland. She glanced down, searching for the distinctive curly black mop-top of Jim's head in the sea of steel and concrete, but he had vanished and, while she searched vainly for traces of her father, she wondered what he was doing here anyway. What was his part in all of this? What exactly was his job? He had come to work that morning in his regular brown suit, his big-collared shirt unbuttoned at the neck and his blue tie knotted at half-mast. He didn't bother with stuffy formalities. He was ready to do business. Yet now she was in his workplace she couldn't quite make sense of it all, couldn't see what his business was, couldn't fathom what it was he did here all day. Nothing quite tallied with the story she had been told. She looked over her shoulder at his tiny office: locked filing cabinets, avocado Olivetti typewriter, piles of envelopes, paper, notebooks, boxes of bulldog clips, rubber bands of assorted sizes. The hard glare of the sun revealed the icing of dust covering all of his accoutrements. She surveyed the room thoughtfully and in her head she itemized what was there, what she had expected to find, what was missing.

'Dad,' she said after he had returned from his forty-minute mystery jaunt, 'What do you do here?'

He cocked one eyebrow. 'A bit of this, a bit of that.'

'But what sort of thing?'

'Keeping an eye on the boats coming in and going out.'

'Why?'

'Why not?'

She tried a different tack. 'Where do the boats come from?'

'All over. North America, Scandinavia. Sometimes Russia.' He put his hands behind his back and stared out of the window. 'The third secretary. It's always the third secretary.'

The third secretary? What was he going on about? She glanced at Jim, but he seemed distracted and she decided she could take a risk, ignore his instruction not to touch anything, reached for the enticingly huge and heavy metal Sellotape dispenser, pulled off a long stretch and scrunched it in her hand. Forming the sticky ribbon into the shape of an ant. She peeked furtively at her father while she worked, half expecting him to shout at her, tell her to stop being so wasteful, to leave his things alone, but he wasn't taking any notice of her craft activities. Jim was still eyeing the horizon, lips moving silently, forming unreadable words, incanting some arcane spell. She pulled off another piece of tape.

The second ant had been completed and she was beginning to think he really would spend the rest of the day doing nothing but staring and pacing when the walkie-talkie lurking on top of a filing cabinet crackled into life. He leaped over, grabbed it, retreated to a corner and proceeded to have a conversation with an unseen person somewhere. It was difficult to make out what he was saying. She could hear a lot of swearing and a lot of laughing and she vaguely recognized some of the strange words he uttered – names, foreign names – but they didn't form understandable sentences. None of it really made any sense. She wondered whether he was just mucking about. He was always mucking about.

'Dad,' she said, when he had replaced the radio and they were standing together by the window, watching the moving dots on the ground, 'who were you talking to?'

'Harry.'

Harry. Of course. It would be. Harry was Jim's mate. Harry had a broken nose, came from Wales and you would have to be a bit of a thicko even to think about crossing him. She liked Harry. She knew him quite well because he had a habit of turning up at their house late with Jim, kipping on their settee, reeking of what she would one day identify as the smoky perfume of the pub.

'Does Harry work here too?'

Jim grunted confirmation before he turned and grinned in his skew-whiff sort of way that told her he was about to embark on one of his extended jokes and she had better look out for her cues if she wanted to keep up with him.

'Harry is the second man at Tilbury,' he said.

She asked the obvious. 'Well, if Harry is the second man, who is the first man?'

'Me, of course. I'm the first man. And Harry is my second man.'

'Is there anybody else?'

'Nope. There are only two of us; it's just Harry and me.'

She frowned; she was sure there should have been more of them.

He glanced at her slyly. 'Although...'

'What?'

'Well... I do sometimes think we could do with the help of an extra set of eyes. A third man.'

She shrugged, reached for the Sellotape dispenser and carried on with her sculpting while he pondered the ceiling.

Eventually he said, 'You know, I think you could be quite good at this game.'

Her pale eyebrows shot up, surprised by his comment. Was this still part of the joke or something else, something serious?

He leaned against a filing cabinet. 'You see, you're not quite as stupid as you look. You sit around hardly saying a word, acting as if you wouldn't harm a fly. Unthreatening. Nobody notices you. Yet you don't miss a thing. You can spot the patterns, the anomalies. Work out what's going on. I suspect you've got a natural talent for it. You must have inherited it from me.'

He tilted his head to one side as if he were making an enquiry rather than issuing a statement.

'But Dad, everybody notices you,' she said, without thinking. He laughed, stood in front of her now, placed the tips of his fingers on the desk.

'Ah. Good point. The thing is, there are two ways of playing

5

this game.' He moved forwards, blocking the window view, shards of sun radiating like a halo around the darkened outline of his head. 'You can make yourself invisible and hide in the shadows or you can do the opposite, make your presence known, dare anybody to challenge you. Hide in the light.'

Uncertain whether a response was required, she half smiled a doubtful sort of smile.

Jim stroked his chin with his thumb and index finger. 'I wonder... could you do it?'

'Do what?'

'Do you think you could be trusted to be the third man?'

She hesitated, running through his question in her head warily, calculating the angles, trying to work out how to join in with his banter, play along.

'Yes,' she said decisively. 'I could be trusted to be the third man.'

'Are you sure about that?' he demanded sharply.

Perhaps she had given the wrong response, made a serious mistake and irritated him with her reply. 'Maybe it's better if I'm not the third man then. I don't think it's a good idea.'

'No, I've made my decision. You are the third man. You can't sit around here all day abusing my stationery supplies. You've got to do something useful. You're the third man whether you like it or not.'

'But Dad—'

'No good getting the heebie-jeebies about it now. Too late.' He guffawed maniacally and suddenly he was off, prancing around the cramped space of the tiny office, a carousing rabble-rouser, whirling his arms, flicking up envelopes and scraps of paper with his outstretched fingertips, creating an unseasonal snowstorm, singing 'Three Men Went to Mow', wildly out of tune.

At first she thought his song-and-dance routine was funny, but he carried on being the madman just a bit too long and she could detect the familiar creeping edge of menace in his tone that made her wonder whether he really was slightly cracked. She began to wish he would stop, calm down, return to normal. Then she knew she had to tread carefully because she didn't want to tip the balance. She sat silently and smiled at his antics.

'And when you've proved yourself as the third man,' he added when he had run out of steam and was standing by the desk again, 'you can graduate to working at the Foreign Office and you can have a stab at being the third secretary.'

He snorted at his own joke. She laughed too, just to be on the safe side.

He stopped snickering and pulled his serious face. 'But you mustn't say anything to anybody. Not a word. Not even to Liz. It's a secret. You must never let on you're part of the team.'

She nodded obediently, noticed he was grinning to himself and decided then it must have been a joke after all, just like everything he ever said was always a bit of a joke, had the touch of a pantomime to it.

And that was the moment when it dawned on her that he wasn't a real policeman at all; it was just another of his funny stories. In that one quick flash, everything – the office, the docks, the sky, the river – had risen up in the air like a disturbed flock of starlings and resettled back on the ground in a completely different formation. Suddenly it was obvious, crystal clear that he had been making it up, having her on. And now she couldn't understand why she had gone along with his line in the first place, why she had told all her friends her dad was a sergeant at some unnamed cop shop, had a truncheon and handcuffs and went around locking up criminals, because now she could see there was absolutely nothing about Jim to show his story might be true. He didn't wear a uniform. He didn't chase robbers. He didn't arrest people. The facts were as bright and as hard as the gleaming cranes of Tilbury. He couldn't possibly be a proper policeman. The doubts in her stomach that must have been sitting there all along, fermenting like the windfall apples left lying in the grass to rot in their back garden, were becoming uncontainable, rising upward, making her want to puke. She felt the tears welling but she blinked them back because she knew crying made Jim cross. She swallowed hard and ripped another piece of tape from the dispenser.

'Oh, I almost forgot,' he said, rummaging in his jacket pocket, 'I've got a present for you.'

He produced a feather, amber and black striped. 'I found it over in the container park. It must be from the kestrel's tail.' He considered its sleek form. 'Funny things, feathers. Who would have thought that something so flimsy and light could be strong enough to keep a bird hovering in mid-air?' He smiled and handed it over. 'Here, take it.'

She smiled back. 'Thank you.'

'It's a souvenir from Tilbury.'

She held it up to the light, admiring the fine vanes, the clean, sharp bars of colour, distracted and soothed by its beauty and, as she twiddled the quill between her finger and thumb, she decided that it didn't really matter what he did. Work wasn't that important after all. Who cared what job a person had, what they did for a living? What really mattered, she thought as she stashed the feather in a trouser pocket, were the birds and the sun and the river and the days off school when you could just read a book or daydream and you didn't have to listen to some dreary teacher telling you things you had learned when you were three.

Later, much later, the touch of a feather would take her back to the day at the docks with Jim, and the delicate strength of the fine barbs able to hold a raptor aloft would remind her that nothing was ever quite as it appeared; reality always had an unsettling habit of turning out to be more like the knot in her stomach, a suppressed feeling, the half-familiar details of a story told once, long ago, and left buried in the drift of discarded memories.

CHAPTER 2

7th June 1984

THE CRACK OF the motorbike's engine made her jump. The beam picked her out in the dusk, its brightness blinding, her frozen silhouette caught in the oncoming glare of the head-light. Jesus wept, was he trying to kill her? At the last possible moment the front tyre swerved and the heat of the beam whipped away. She stared after the dancing red trace of the tail light as the bike roared off, leaving her alone again in the gloom of the oak-shaded road. She shook her head, sniffed, wiped her nose on her sleeve, noticed her right arm was trembling, pressed it against her stomach, trying to stem the flow of fear and breathed in deeply. Her shoulders sagged. What was all that about then? What a wanker. Perhaps he had just lost control of the bike momentarily. Or maybe he was stoned. Jerk either way. Anyway, he'd gone now. Nothing to worry about. Nothing at all. She had overreacted, panicked.

She stepped back on to the kerb cautiously, pulled her second-hand overcoat around her slight frame and listened out for the crack of the bike's engine. But there was nothing to hear now except for the normal suburban soundtrack: a backyard mongrel howling, the bass line of 'Blue Monday' pumping through a Ford's open window, the drone of the traffic chasing south. Above her, a darkening track of sepia sky was just visible through the tangled branches of the trees. She tipped her wrist to the light to check her watch – it was past nine. How long had she been standing there? Ten minutes at least. Becky was late.

'Come on, come on,' she muttered under her breath, feeling edgy and, as she peered down the road again to search for the bus, she heard a low-pitched buzzing coming from behind. She twisted, saw a black bullet hurtling straight at her, raised her hand, ducked too late, felt the sting on the side of her face, half screamed, curtailed her yelp and smiled when she recognized the gross mandibles of a concussed stag beetle lying at her feet. Everything appeared to be targeting her tonight. The humidity must have brought it out from the wood. She hadn't seen one in years. She squatted down on the pavement to admire its branching black antlers, its copper armour plating, its lumbering crawl as it blundered back towards the shadow line of the trees. She was so engrossed in its strange beauty that she almost failed to hear the crescendo crack-crack until the bike was almost on top of her again. Adrenalin hitting, heart racing, she straightened, just had time to tense her muscles for flight before clocking that the beam had swept past her and the bike had swerved off the road into the pub's car park. So he had just been looking for an out-of-town bar after all. He wasn't after her. Stupid. She bit her bottom lip and surreptitiously watched the bike manoeuvre into a space between two cars, caught sight of its black hornet-shaped thorax; off-road night-rider.

He huffed with the effort of hauling his heavy machine on to its stand, sauntered in her direction, leather-clad, helmet on, visor up, the scent of oil greeting her before he was halfway across the car park.

'I'm sorry,' he said as he drew near. Muffled voice. 'I must have scared you just now. I thought I ought to apologize.'

She shrugged, made as if she didn't know what he was talking about, hadn't been scared at all. He removed his helmet, thick black greasy locks plastered against his dirt-streaked face. Mid-twenties she reckoned.

'I was out for a bit of a ride. Not really sure where I was going, just looking for somewhere to have a drink. I saw you standing there, on the kerb.'

A twang was audible now, a lift at the end of his sentences leaving a trail of unanswered questions. Australian possibly.

'I thought you were someone I knew. You look like an ex-girlfriend of mine. She's Dutch. She came to England to train as a nurse. It threw me a bit. The likeness. Are you Dutch?'

'No,' she said. Course she wasn't Dutch; first he nearly runs her over with his mad bike-riding and then he tries to chat her up with some lame bollocks about looking Dutch. She turned and stared down the road pointedly, hoped he would get the message and piss off.

'Well, I'm sorry if I scared you.'

She folded her arms, glanced back at him out of the corner of her eye, caught sight of a hand disappearing inside his leather jacket, a flash, a compact, metallic object in his palm, raised arm. Shoot position. She blinked. It was just a gold box of Benson and Hedges.

'Are you sure I didn't scare you?' he asked. 'You look a little jumpy.' He held the open packet out for her. 'Want one?'

'No thanks.'

He pat-patted his jacket with his spare hand, searching his pockets. 'Do you have a light? I usually have my Zippo on me, but I can't find it. I must have left it somewhere.'

'I might have a box of matches.' She rummaged in her coat pocket, felt the rough edge of a Swan Vesta box, was about to hand it over, remembered she had stashed her hash inside, retracted her offer and instead grasped a single matchstick, pushing its red head against the sandpaper strike. The match flared, licked the thickening dusk air, illuminating the man's hands cupped to shield the flame, revealing the un-etched skin on his fingers. Not a mechanic, then, or a courier like most of her sister's chopper-owning biker mates. He held the fag between his index finger and his thumb, took deep drags, cracked his jaw and sent a trail of smoke rings wobbling skyward. Not impressed. She scanned the road, slowly, deliberately.

'What are you doing out here on your own anyway?' the rider persisted.

It wasn't an Australian accent. Kiwi perhaps.

'I'm waiting for a friend.'

'Are you going in there for a drink?' He nodded his head over his shoulder at the mock Tudor façade of the pub set back among the trees. She nodded a tentative response. The corners of his mouth pulled sideways into the start of an easy smile, lighting up his face, and she thought for a second there was something quite attractive about him. He caught her checking him out. She flushed.

'What's your name anyway, if you don't mind me asking?'

She spotted the bus lumbering down the road. 'Frieda.'

'Frieda what?'

'Frieda People. My friend will be on that one.'

His eyes were on her back as she waved at the driver and waved again to make sure that Becky had seen her, make sure the rider got the message. The double-decker pulled up to the stop. Becky was dangling from the pole on the rear platform, snakes of mahogany hair writhing around her face in the back-draught of the bus's forward movement. Becky Shapiro.

'Am I late?' Becky asked.

'A bit. I thought I'd wait out here for you because I wasn't sure you knew the right stop.'

'Thanks. It's not that easy to tell where you are once you are in the countryside.'

'This isn't the countryside. It's the periphery. It's all bypasses, golf courses and rubbish tips. And boring bikers.'

She flicked her eyes dismissively to indicate the rider standing behind, but the gesture was met with a blank stare from Becky. She turned. No one was there. She scanned the car park; the black machine was shimmering under the sulphurous cone of the solitary car park light. Its rider had vanished. He must have dived into the bar while she was greeting Becky. Odd.

'God, I don't know how you survive this far out,' Becky said. 'Where is everybody else?'

'Inside.'

'Come on, Sam.' Becky grabbed her arm. 'You don't want to be late for your own party.'

The Coney's Tavern was aptly named: a sprawling, airless warren of a pub that had taken to serving food in an attempt to turn a profit. Jim had objected to the venue, of course. He had tried to dissuade her from holding the party there with his usual combination of sarcasm and casual threats, declared he wasn't prepared to eat in a place that catered to the golf-playing classes and specialized in microwaving everything to buggery. It wasn't what he called a bar. She had dug in; insisted it was her birthday so it was her choice. But now, as she peered through the smoke and was confronted by a fug of florid self-satisfied faces, she wondered whether she had made the right call after all. She felt uneasy; she searched for the rider in the crowd, couldn't see him.

'There they are,' said Becky, pointing to a long table in a side dining room around which her friends and family were gathered. The white plastic tablecloth made the scene look like a bargain basement re-enactment of 'The Last Supper'. Becky dragged Sam through the pressing bodies filling the bar and she pushed the rider to the back of her mind.

She had drunk way too much, way too quickly. The table was littered with empty plonk bottles and discarded plates of sludge and chips stubbed with fag butts. She gazed blearily across the debris at Liz, her mother, sitting opposite; tight-lipped, hands clasped tensely in front of her on the table, recusing herself from the party. Even when she was annoyed, Liz had a natural elegance – unruffled, straight chestnut hair that always fell in a sharp-edged bob. Sam ran a remonstrative hand over her own frizzy locks and, in the absence of any engagement from her mum, turned to look at the far end of the table where Becky was holding court among their mates. Becky was recounting in gory detail the afternoon she had spent at the local hospital, watching surgery being performed on various bits of male anatomy: preparation for the start of her medical degree in September, Becky was explaining. Becky knew where she was heading. Becky was the rising star in their crowd.

At the nearer table end, Sam's two sisters sat cawing raucously, snow-white faces and crow-haired heads rocking. The Coyle girls: three of them born at eighteen-month intervals. Sam looked different from her sisters – a smudgy sandy summer to the clarity of their dark and light icy winter – yet you could tell they shared a bond, unable to move as individuals without creating a ripple across the surface of the whole. And now here they were on the verge of going their separate ways. Helen, the eldest, had been desperate to find an excuse to move out of the family home and had been handed it when she landed a job in some shop in Camden selling post-punk, gothic glad-rags to her nightclubbing friends. She had moved out to a bedsit on the north side of the river that April. Jess was working part-time stacking shelves at Iceland, a job that just about paid enough to keep her bike on the road with a bit left over for a pint with her mates. As for Sam, she had surprised herself and everyone else by passing the Oxford entrance exam the previous autumn. Hadn't really taken it seriously at the time. Jim had laughed when she had told him she had been accepted, and proudly explained to anyone within earshot that she had managed to pull a fast one on those old farts in their ivory tower, a girl from a comp no less, sneaking her way into the country's top university. You could tell, he had declared, from which side of the family she had harvested her talents. He was right, she had suspected; she was a fraud, not really cut out for the bright lights, the glittering prizes. A bit of a cowboy when it came to academic endeavour.

She sat silently, caught up in her own doubts, trapped in the space between competing conversations, on the edge of every-thing as always, never at the centre, beginning to think no one would miss her if she weren't there. She poured herself another glass of vinegary white and turned automatically, sensing eyes on her back again. The rider was watching her from the far end of the bar. He lifted his helmet in the air, a half salute, and then he was off, through the door and out.

'Who was that bloke then?' Jess asked – her radar attuned to any man in leather.

Sam shrugged. 'He came over and started talking to me when I was outside waiting for Becky.'

'What kind of bike was he riding?'

'Black.'

Jess rolled her eyes. Sam rolled hers back. Helen laughed, or perhaps it was a sneer.

She drained her glass. Everything was moving in slow

motion now, voices raucous, not quite in sync with mouths, conversations increasingly incoherent. Jess was explaining that she wouldn't fancy being a barmaid in the Coney's Tavern because everybody knew that 'coney' was Anglo-Saxon for 'cunt' and she certainly wouldn't want anybody to get the wrong idea and think there was more on offer than a pint of lager and a packet of crisps.

Liz's head swivelled round. 'Cunny.'

'What?'

'Seventeenth-century. Pepys. He used the form "cunny" in his diary. "His wife caught him with his main in his mistress's cunny."'

Jess frowned at Liz, momentarily perplexed by the reference, then continued to rant about her best mate being a bit of an old slapper. Sam watched Helen half-heartedly chasing a lettuce leaf around the plate with her fork.

Jess reached the end of her diatribe and followed Sam's gaze. 'Why did you order a salad?' she asked. 'Are you going anorexic on us?'

'I'm just not hungry,' Helen snapped.

'We've always used food as a weapon in this family,' said Liz and sighed.

'Food does make good ammunition. It's surprising how painful a roast potato can be if it hits you at speed.'

'I didn't mean it quite so literally.'

Sam chipped in. 'Helen's not anorexic. She's not hungry because she's just shoved a line of speed up her nose.' Helen kicked her under the table and caught her shin with the pointed toe of her buckled stiletto boot. Sam yelped loudly and was about to kick her back when something made her pause – an almost imperceptible disturbance pulsing through the golfing crowd by the bar. A Mexican wave of hackles rising. Jim was standing at the pub's entrance. He pushed through the crowd, his plaid shirt unbuttoned to the point of disreputability – perhaps a deliberate distraction from his burgeoning paunch below – his mouth pulled sideways in that lopsided smirk of his, hinting he had something on everybody sitting in the room. He could have them all if he wanted – one way or another. She cringed. Then felt a stab of anger: it was all his fucking fault she was so jumpy, saw death threats in every passing vehicle. He navigated a winding course between the dining tables, seemingly oblivious to the churning he left in his wake; swivelling faces caught between attraction and disapproval, gritted teeth and pink cheeks as he skimmed sports jackets and pretty waitresses. He pulled up a chair, swung his stocky form into the vacant berth next to hers; didn't even bother to apologize for being late.

'Where have you been?' Liz asked.

'Drink with Harry,' he said. He didn't work with Harry anymore; he just turned to him when he needed back-up. He ordered Sam to pass him the menu, grinned at her conspiratorially, peered theatrically at the plastic-laminated card.

'Tell me what's for dinner,' he said. 'I've forgotten my glasses.'

'You don't wear glasses,' Sam replied. Jim had twenty-twenty vision. 'It might help if you held the menu the right way up.'

He ignored her, rotated his head to gawp at the table behind, pulled a face, hailed a nearby waitress and said he wanted tomato soup. He certainly didn't want what they were having, he added, gesturing his hand in the direction of the surrounding diners.

Jim's soup arrived as everyone else was dispatching slices of sickly sweet cheesecake. He fished around in the bowl for a few minutes with no obvious intention of actually eating anything and then, with an unexpected urgency of movement, he lifted his spoon, waved it in the air and swiped it down on the side of a wine bottle. The resonant chime had the desired effect: all eyes round the table lifted and fixed on Jim. He searched the gathered faces, checked everyone was paying attention. Oh God, what next.

'It is Sam's eighteenth birthday,' Jim said. She frowned at him, willed him to shut up; she could do without the benefit of his maudlin proclamations of the totally bloody obvious.

'Thanks for pointing that out, Dad.'

Liz was trying to catch the eye of the waitress, writing an invisible signature in the air. Good move. Wrap it up. Time to go before Jim had a chance to embarrass her further. Too late.

Jim continued, slurring his words now. 'I didn't think I would make it this far. Still, here I am.' He paused and his eyes swept the corners of the Coney's Tavern as if he were, indeed, genuinely surprised to find himself there. Or perhaps he was searching for someone, she thought with slight alarm.

'But I very much doubt whether I'll live to see Sam's next birthday.'

Helen tutted. Jess yawned ostentatiously. It wasn't the first time their father had announced his impending death, although he'd never done it quite so publicly before. Jim dropped the spoon he had been waving like a sorcerer's wand and let it clatter on the table. Jesus wept. What would her friends make of that performance? She caught them exchanging meaningful glances before Becky carried on talking as if nothing had happened. Sam breathed a sigh of relief. And then she seethed.

'Dad,' she said.

He didn't respond.

'Dad.'

She said it more forcefully this time. He turned towards her with blank eyes, carelessly knocked a bowl with his hand and sent a tsunami of viscous red soup rolling across the table towards Liz. Jess muttered in Sam's ear.

'Well, he might not live to see your next birthday, but I hope he lives to see the bill, because he's the only person here with a credit card.'

Jess turned away and picked up her conversation with Helen again: the perennial debate about why the best-looking blokes in the room always turned out to be gay.

Jim was still staring without seeing. His mouth moved. He mumbled; indistinguishable sounds swallowed up in the clamour of the tavern. She leaned forward to catch his words.

'Asgard.'

'What?'

'Operation Asgard.'

Sam repeated the words in her head. Operation Asgard; it sounded like one of Jim's jokes.

'I'm not sure,' he continued, 'I'm not sure... which side I'm on... I don't even know who I am anymore...'

He really was going for it tonight. Hamming it up. She was about to tell him to stop messing around when she noticed his eyes were damp. She'd never seen the glint of tears before, not in Jim's eyes. She didn't want to see him cry, it didn't seem quite right. Not Jim. She looked away. Looked back. And now all she could see was a half-cut, middle-aged, sweaty face glistening in the heat of the crowd.

'So what's Operation Asgard all about then?' she asked, cheerfully.

He snapped out of his daze, scowled, reached for a napkin, dabbed at his soup-splashed shirt. 'None of your bloody business.' He jabbed his finger towards her face. 'Don't mention it again.'

She was about to protest, point out that he was the one who had mentioned it in the first place, but he didn't give her the chance.

'Where's Liz gone?' he demanded. She glanced across the table, clocked that her mother had disappeared, searched the room and shrugged – the toilet perhaps, or outside for some fresh air.

The waitress appeared with the bill, hovered nervously behind Jim. Helen reached over, snatched the paper and shoved it under Jim's nose.

'Time to cough up, face the damage.'

He examined the bill belligerently. 'Do I really have to pay for this crap as well as eat it?'

The waitress flushed. Jess whispered loudly, 'Cunny's Tavern', and started tittering uncontrollably.

'It's my birthday treat,' Sam said. 'Please just pay the bill so we can go.'

She could hear a wheedling hint of desperation in her voice and caught the beginnings of a sadistic smile playing at the edges of Jim's mouth.

'Oh, for fuck's sake, hand your card over,' Helen snapped.

Jim teetered precariously on the verge of explosion, then subsided just before the point of no return. He must have thought better of it, decided to back down. For once.

'Where do you get it from?' he asked. He addressed his progeny with a look of injured innocence plastered to his face. 'Where did you lot learn to behave like this? Uncouth. That's what you lot are, bloody uncouth.'

Jess leaned over, deftly dipped her hand into his pocket, fished out his wallet, extracted his credit card and handed it to the waitress. The woman walked off and returned a few minutes later with the imprint of his card on a paper slip. Sam shoved the pen into Jim's hand and guided it toward the signature box.

'There,' he said as he handed the paper back to the waitress. 'Tell your boss he can buy a new microwave and a couple more can-openers with that.'

'You're such a berk,' said Helen. 'I'd be surprised if you make it to next week, let alone Sam's next birthday.' She pushed herself up from the table, stalked away, stabbing the floor with her boot heels as she left.

Sam grabbed one of Jim's elbows, Jess grabbed the other, hoisted him out of his chair, giving the golfers something to talk about as they dragged him through the bar and outside into the mugginess, her mates bringing up the rear.

'What was your dad on about? He's so...' Becky muttered as she headed towards the bus stop. Sam strained to hear the end of Becky's sentence but there wasn't one. It wasn't like Becky to be stuck for words.

Liz was waiting in the car, gripping the steering wheel with white-knuckled hands. They bundled the comatose heap of Jim into the passenger seat, strapped him in. Liz turned the ignition in silence, reversed and was about to leave the car park when the black bike appeared out of nowhere, burned up the road, cutting across their exit. Heading north. Back to the city.

'What kind of bike is it then?' Sam asked Jess.

'Yamaha XT500. The noise of the engine is the giveaway; single cylinder. You can hear it firing. Pretty powerful bike; built to handle anything – mud, sand. It's won the Paris–Dakar rally across the Sahara a couple of times.' Jess narrowed her eyes, icy splinters. 'I always think you can tell a lot about a bloke from the type of bike he rides.'

Sam was never quite sure where she stood on her sister's philosophizing about men.

'So what kind of bloke rides a Yamaha XT500?'

Jess pursed her lips, turned to look through the rear-view window. 'The kind of bloke who likes a spot of trouble.'

Sam said nothing, events, faces and words churning in her mind, the spectral trunks of silver birch trees slipping past in the dark outside. Dutch. What did Dutch people look like anyway? Weren't they supposed to be quite tall?

Liz parked the car in the damp garage of their boring forties red-brick and walked off in disgust. Jess and Sam eased Jim's dead weight out of the car and managed to steer him as far as the kitchen where he aimed for the dog's bed and tipped himself on top of the hairy black mutt already lying there. George the dog was a recent acquisition; a sly gift from one of his mates, a rejected bomb-sniffer who snarled and lunged at anyone entering or leaving the house with a bag in their hand, making the weekend supermarket run a bit of a nightmare. Jim was the only one who called the dog by his name and repeatedly excused its behaviour on the grounds that the animal had lost his purpose in life, didn't like being an ordinary family pet. The dog shifted accommodatingly on its bed to allow Jim a bit of space. Jim belched.

'I'm sorry,' Jim said from his resting place on the floor.

It wasn't clear for what or to whom he was apologizing. 'I won't do it again,' he added. Sam sniffed, switched off the light, glanced back as she left. In the darkness of the kitchen, Jim had merged with the dog to become a single, grotesque two-headed beast.

Trudging up the stairs, mulling over the evening's events: the biker, the self-imposed death sentence, the gobbets of secret information dribbling from the corner of Jim's mouth. Operation Asgard. Perhaps it wasn't a joke. Perhaps he was being deadly serious. Perhaps Operation Asgard really was the name of his latest mission. She wondered whether there was anything more than lack of imagination and hubris to the naming of their operations. Some not immediately obvious rationale, an alphabetical ordering perhaps like the naming of hurricanes or a link between title and mission objective. Asgard. It sounded like something out of *Lord of the Rings*. Or was it a name from Norse mythology? That was it. Asgard, home of the Norse gods. They were always raiding the story-books for their stupid mission names: Merlin, Troy, Neptune. Asgard. She lay down on her bed. Asgard, Asgard, Asgard. She chanted the word into meaninglessness as the room around her rocked and the rising moon cast a gilded path across the floor.

A persistent tap-tapping outside the window woke her some-where in the dead hours just before dawn. She panicked: an intruder in the garden. She crept across the thin carpet, care-fully lifted the dilapidated bamboo blind slats an inch and peeked out. A corpulent thrush was posing just below the sill on the flat, leak-prone extension roof and was waving a half-smashed snail in its beak dementedly as if it were trying to flag an SOS message in her direction. She knocked sharply on the pane.

'Go and do that somewhere else. You're giving me a head-ache.'

It fixed her with its beady yellow-ringed eye and shook its head from side to side once more before flitting off into the apple tree. She sighed, relinquished the idea of sleep and opened the window wide, climbing over the sill and slumping on the roof, back against the wall.

The moon was casting a low-down hazy glow now from the far side of the railway line at the bottom of the garden. She shivered, despite the sweatiness of the dark. Jim's words flitted through her consciousness, she couldn't dislodge his voice; he didn't think he'd live to see her next birthday. She tried to dismiss his pronouncement as the usual drunken rambling but she was plagued by the haunted look in his eyes, the tears she might have seen. He didn't know which side he was on. He wasn't even sure who he was anymore. She sat in deep contemplation, listening for early morning bird song, a hint of the dawn chorus. But there was no sound. And in the stillness of the dark she found herself wondering about Jim's real identity, the true self beneath the cover. She hadn't really thought about his identity that way before; his history, where he was coming from, what he was really like. She had always taken it as given that his past was no-go territory. Restricted access. Assumed it was part of the secret policeman deal. The family omertà of silence about Jim. She hadn't really cared; she had her own life to be dealing with. She had grown up casually lying about her father, inventing the details of his history. But now, as she wrapped her arms around her knees, she wondered whether she should know about her own dad, whether she needed to know, whether she could ever know who she was, her own real identity, if she didn't know about Jim. His job. She had a fleeting vision of herself at Freshers' Week: the chatter, the clamour, the new faces, the personal questions, the endless need to provide answers. What could she say about her father? She sighed.

Her eyes followed the arcs of the stars falling towards Heathrow while her mind turned over the fragmented pieces of information she had about Jim, attempting to sift out the basics from the handful of stories he had fed them over the years. The facts were limited. All she really knew was that he was the son of an itinerant publican, born in Glasgow, the youngest of three brothers. He had attended a Jesuit school and had run away at the age of fifteen for undisclosed reasons and joined the army. He served for six years in hot and exotic places. Somewhere, at some point in the army years, he had lost three of his toes from the middle of his left foot. Explosion. Landmine, he had told her, leaving him with what looked like the sign of the devil blasted into his foot. After the army he had drifted to London; he was twenty-two when he joined the Force and was sent out on the beat in the East End where he spent his days dealing with card sharks and his evenings drinking with the Krays. At least, that was Jim's story. But it was always difficult to triangulate his tales: she had never met any of his relatives and he didn't seem to hang on to childhood friends.

And when she checked her own memories, Jim was always in some disguise or another, doing something secret. She was six, in bed, woken by the laughing of strangers, the funny accents. She had crept downstairs, stuck her head through the banisters, curiously assessing the two strangers drinking in their front room: sharp-angled, olive-skinned, exotic faces, incongruously dressed in boring navy pressed trousers, white shirts and ties. One of them was pointing at the fireplace and commenting on their lovely carp. She had shouted down from her hiding place at the top of the stairs that he meant hearth, not carp. Jim had been furious, he didn't want her spying on him, but the two men had thought it was a great joke – having their English corrected by a six-year-old. She had asked Jim the following morning where they were from and he had told her they were Russians. Grunts, he had added quickly. Just a bit of friendly business.

She was eight when Jim had left his post at the docks unexpectedly. Harry had stayed on. No clear reason had been given for Jim's sudden departure and his evident lack of a replacement posting. Not to her at least. Although later she had heard Jim and Liz discussing it in another room, their voices barely audible over the *Magpie* theme tune blaring from the telly. She had listened to their conversation as she sang along with the words of the familiar nursery rhyme; 'five for silver, six for gold, seven for a secret…' They just didn't appreciate his methods, Jim had said, you had to give something away to get something in return. Liz's pointed silence had radiated through the serving hatch.

It was the Commander who had rescued Jim after the docks. The Commander had been in charge of operations at Tilbury and now he had moved his sights, apparently, to another, bigger agenda. It obviously wasn't the Commander, then, who had failed to appreciate Jim's methods because he had invited Jim to move with him, brought him back into the fold. The Diggers, Jim had christened them, his new lot. Then Jim was setting off to work in a fresh disguise: Chairman Mao cap, thick donkey jacket, combat boots and a dirty black Bedford van. The beard had appeared overnight, a prolific growth of his curly sideboards fusing under his chin, transforming him into a wild man, a degenerate hippy in the heartlands of the conservative outer suburbs.

'Dad,' she had asked when she had first seen the fuzz, 'is the beard your disguise?'

'No,' he had replied. 'The disguise is when I shave it off.'

He had laughed when he said it and she had laughed with him, even though she wasn't quite sure why it was funny.

Ten. Eleven. Twelve years old. Sometimes he was away for days before he resurfaced, triumphantly brandishing some substandard item he'd picked up in a bar room deal – the set of kitchen knives that didn't cut, the thin carpets that fell off the back of a lorry and reeked of noxious chemicals. They, Liz and the sisters, would stare perplexedly at his crappy acquisitions. He would shrug off their doubts and lurk in the back garden, nursing a can of lager, huffing and puffing and failing to light the poxy barbecue before he said *fuck it*, poured some petrol on the charcoal, produced the Watneys party pack, and summoned the neighbours. The Smiths, the Hunts and the Drains would huddle by the kitchen door, standing well back from the inferno, gingerly eating the cindered fish that Jim liked to grill whole because he said it tasted better that way and he didn't have time for whingers who were scared of swallowing fish-bones.

'You can always tell when summer is here,' said Mr Hunt with a nervous wink, 'because Jim stops wearing a shirt.'

And now she was eighteen, and earlier that year he had crashed his Bedford. It hadn't seemed significant at the time, but thinking about it now she could see the accident had marked a watershed in many ways; another change in his persona. He had driven the van into the railings running down the hill from Blackheath. He had walked away unscathed, but the Bedford had been a write-off. He had hinted it was brake failure, sabotage. The local paper had suggested something different. The front-page report in the *Southern Advertiser* had appeared a couple of days after the crash and had implied that the thankfully nameless driver had been drinking. Jim had taken one look at the article and stormed off to the pub, muttering that he didn't want the press poking its nose into his business even if was only the local rag that everyone threw into the bin before they read it. The Bedford hadn't been replaced. Two weeks after the crash, he had turned up on the doorstep without his beard, his freshly mown face strangely pale and luminous in the fading evening light. They had tried hard to conceal their shock. The beard had been well past its sell-by-date, but shaving it off had aged him instantly, revealed his jowls, the softening lines between jaw and neck, the flash of wiry silver at his temples. His past was catching up with him.

Sam rested her chin on her knees. The moon had disappeared, leaving a faint trail of brimstone in its wake. She searched for the first signs of the sun. And she wondered whether the most recent Jim – middle-aged, clean-shaven Jim – was his real identity at last: a washed-up, ornery bloke on the run, trying to escape the shadows of his life, fleeing the deceptions, the blowback from a lifetime undercover. Or perhaps it was his final cover. The disguise was when he shaved it off. Operation Asgard. The unlit milk train rattled past the far end of the garden. A slight breeze stirred up out of nowhere, rustled the leaves of the apple tree as it passed and whipped a scrap of newspaper high into the air and over the garden fence. Somewhere down the track a mangy fox screamed and a blackbird shrieked its early morning alarm call.

CHAPTER 3

SHE THREW ON a crumpled T-shirt and fading 501s, stomped down the stairs, dragging her finger along the wall as she descended, pulled at the corner of one of the pictures of far-flung places that Liz had snipped from the Sunday colour supplements and plastered on instead of wallpaper. She noted, with some satisfaction, that she had left a white jagged trail across the blue sky above a palm-fringed, golden beach of some exotic island. Barbados. Or Mauritius perhaps. She slammed open the kitchen door, kicked the empty dog's bed as she passed. No sign of Jim. Liz was rummaging around in a cupboard, dressed for work in her usual carefully uncoordinated smart casuals, brunette bob blow-dried perfectly. Sam glared at her mother's back.

'What was Jim on about last night?'

Liz shrugged indifferently, didn't bother to turn round.

'What makes him think he's about to die this time?' Sam persisted.

Liz picked up a spice pot, examined it. 'I'm not sure,' she said.

'Cowards die many times before their death.'

'You could at least provide the complete quote.'

Sam sometimes thought her parents should swap jobs: Liz would make a deadly undercover cop with her forensic attention to detail and Jim would make a flashy academic with his ability to craft a gripping narrative on the basis of a couple of things he'd picked up from some blokes down the pub.

Liz added, 'And anyway you could call your father many things but I don't think a coward is one of them.'

'Okay then, he's not a coward. He's an ageing undercover cop with a drink problem.'

Liz twisted round now, opened her mouth to speak, paused long enough for Sam to suspect that she was about to say something that wasn't going to sound very convincing.

'I don't know how much longer he's going to be a detective.'

They all had their own ways of relabelling Jim's job when it suited them; detective was Liz's. 'He's thinking of leaving the Force. He told me today that he has arranged a holiday in Orkney. He wants to get away from it all for a while.' Liz was speaking to the back of the cupboard again. 'He knows somebody up there with a holiday cottage. It's sitting empty for the rest of June and he's said Jim can use it. He's going to take the car-train up to Inverness at the end of next week. He wants a chance to think about something other than work.'

Orkney. When was the last time she had been there? 1978 when she was twelve. The last time they had managed a holiday all together, as a family. The ferry crossing from Scrabster to Stromness had been particularly rough that year. It was always bad, because the ferry didn't have any stabilizers. But that year an insistent north-easterly had churned up the sea, and the ferry had pitched and lurched across the turbulent Pentland Firth. Liz and the girls had stayed below, turning green. Sam had remained outside on the deck with Jim, just as she always did, whatever the weather, drenched by sea-spray, searching for the first signs of the Old Man of Hoy. Jim had struck up conversation with an old fisherman, his features etched by saltwater, and she had listened to his tales of island life, uncertain whether he was retelling his own past or the distant history of his ancestors. Long ago, the fisherman had said, Orkney was at the heart, not on the edge. In those days, if you had a good boat, then it was quicker to travel by water than land; water offers less resistance than land, less friction. Jim had nodded in agreement. Orkney was in the backyard of the Norsemen, the fisherman had continued, once they had perfected their oak-timbered longboats, built to bend not break. Beautiful oak boats, he had said, peering into the distance. And then he had pointed. She had thought, for a moment, he had spotted a dragon's head prow advancing through the swell. But he was indicating the dark fins of a pod of porpoises, chasing the warmer waters of the Gulf Stream.

'Seafood paella,' Liz said now, 'I must buy some saffron.'

'Isn't that a bit expensive?'

Liz ignored her comment. 'He's thinking about taking an early retirement deal. Picking up his history degree with the Open University.'

'But the Open University degree was a joke.'

Jim had registered with the Open University in the wilderness weeks after leaving the docks; something to fill the empty hours between lunchtime closing and evening opening, an excuse for getting out of the house and visiting unidentified people in unspecified locations. He had abandoned it as soon as he had joined the Diggers.

'You shouldn't be so dismissive of your father's academic interests.' There was something immensely irritating about the way Liz asserted that Jim was 'your father', when she suspected he was up to no good but didn't want to admit it. 'We should give him a chance, support him if he wants to leave the Force and do something different.'

32

We. Sam glanced out of the window, spotted a sleek black-bird with its head tilted to one side, listening for worms.

'Are you going with him then?' she asked.

'Unfortunately, I can't. Roger has organized a conference on concepts of gender in Marlowe's work and I have a long-standing commitment to present a paper. It's a shame I can't go, but it's too late to do anything about it now.'

Somewhere in another room the dog growled as if it were having a bad dream.

'I thought Roger did modern literature,' Sam said.

'That is his specialism. But as head of the department it's his job to ensure that we maintain our reputation in all areas.'

She was about to make a sarcastic comment about all the areas in which Roger had a reputation, at least according to Helen – Roger the Todger, Helen called him and cackled in a disturbingly knowing fashion whenever she said it – but Liz spoke first.

'I was thinking.' Liz was looking directly at Sam now. 'Maybe you could go and keep an eye on your father. You seem to be getting along with him better than anybody else in the family these days.'

Sam dropped her jaw, mouthed a silent scream like the Munch poster she had bought from Athena and Blu-Tacked to her bedroom wall.

Liz remained unmoved by her daughter's gurning. 'You loved Orkney when you were a child. You and Jim were the ones who insisted on going there every year. You two were always more interested in all those ancient ruins than the rest of us. We always wanted to go to the beach, the Mediterranean, anywhere it didn't rain the whole time.'

Sam was momentarily taken aback by her mother's undertone of accusation, the suggestion that they were on opposing sides.

'So, are you asking me to spy on him?'

'I didn't say spy. I said keep an eye on him.'

'What's the difference?'

Liz didn't answer.

'Why does he need watching if he's just taking a break? What can possibly happen to him if he's doing nothing?'

'Oh, you know what your father is like. He'll probably drink too much and fall over the edge of a cliff.'

'I'm hardly going to be able to stop him from drinking too much. You never have. And anyway, he's not going to want me hanging around any more than I want to be around him.'

'I'm sure he wouldn't mind so long as you don't get in his way.'

She couldn't quite be bothered to point out the flaw in her mother's argument, the inherent contradiction between not getting in Jim's way and keeping an eye on him.

'You haven't got anything else to do for the summer,' Liz said.

Sam folded her arms.

'You could always take a friend.' Liz was heading towards the door, ferreting in her handbag for the car keys, conversation over as far as she was concerned. Deal agreed.

'I'd be surprised if I have any friends left after Jim's performance last night,' Sam yelled at Liz's rapidly disappearing back. There was no reply. She stared out of the kitchen window again, mulling over her conversation with Liz. The dog was out in the garden now, scrabbling away at one of the flowerbeds, digging for buried bones. Or buried bombs. Perhaps it would be a chance to find out more about Jim, a last few days together before she went to college. And, loath as she was to admit it, Liz was right; she had loved their holidays in Orkney, crawling into passage graves, tramping across fields in horizontal rain to investigate the tumbledown walls of ancient brochs, searching stray megaliths for the stick-figure runes of the Vikings. Orkney, islands of the Norsemen, she mused to herself and a wire fizzled in her brain like one of Jim's gaffer-taped electrical repair jobs. Operation Asgard. Asgard, Norse myth. Norsemen, Orkney. Was that it? Was that the rationale for the name – some dodgy connection with Orkney? She slumped on the kitchen floor, rested her head against the kitchen cabinet and gave the dog a dirty look as it moseyed its way disconsolately back into the kitchen.

Sydenham Hill, West Dulwich, Herne Hill – the litany of stops on the commuter line. Sam whispered the names into the still evening air as she left the station, conjuring up the fields and woods beneath the tracks. A foaming-mouthed Alsatian tied to a rubbish bin snarled at her. She eyeballed the dog, straining on its frayed rope lead, tried to resist breaking into a run, swerved down the sandy path to the builder's yard, negotiated her way around the piles of wooden pallets and headed to the warehouse. She put her hand on the door, hesitated, pausing to collect herself, calm her nerves.

This was their regular meeting spot; an empty storeroom in the prefab building that Lee's dad used as a base for his burgeoning construction business. This was the place where she hooked up with Becky, and a handful of others in their tightly-knit cabal, to plan their activities: the CND meetings, the leaflet stall outside the library on Saturday afternoons, the showings of 'The War Game', the marches. And, more frequently now, the trips to the peace camps that were sprouting up all over the countryside outside the British military bases housing American nuclear missiles. Protesting, political activism; it was becoming more like a way of life than an occasional activity, especially since they had all finished their exams. But despite the closeness of her clique, she still had to steel herself to climb the stairs. Just as she had always done. They might be her friends, but they all came from families with a radical pedigree: Aldermaston marchers, trade unionists, card-carrying members of the Labour Party. Hers was a slightly less salubrious heritage. Although, there was a pleasing irony about the fact that she had honed her political views courtesy of the Force and the trail of radical pamphlets left lying around the house by Jim: the Little Red Book, the Communist Manifesto, the Anarchist Cook Book and other guides to the philosophy of revolution and guerrilla warfare. Not that she ever shared that joke with her friends. God, no way. She didn't think anybody else would see the funny side.

They looked up in unison as she entered and she caught a guilty flicker lingering on Becky's features. They had been talking about her. Or Jim. Sam pulled a wonky smile, glanced down at the floor to avoid their gaze and surveyed the coffin at their feet. A replacement for the one that had gone missing after they had parked it outside a pub and had come out an hour or so later to find someone else had walked off with it. It was their prop for the CND march this coming Sunday. Along with the funereal black jackets and top hats purchased cheaply from the local Oxfam shop. Pall-bearers. Coffin carriers for humanity in the event of mass death by superpower exchange of nuclear weapons. Armageddon. They had constructed the coffin mark two out of odd bits of four-by-four that Lee had cadged from his dad. All it needed now was a couple of daubs of black paint to cover the remaining stubborn patches of bare pine. And then it would look almost convincing. She joined in wordlessly with their efforts.

Job done, Paul and Lee sauntered to the offie to buy a packet of Rizlas. Sam slumped on the floorboards next to Becky. 'Do you fancy a free holiday? Do you want to stay in Orkney for a week?'

Becky's pupils expanded, registered interest. 'What, with you?'

'Yes. And Jim.'

Becky pulled a face. 'Not Liz?'

'No. She's busy. She has to write a paper. She's asked me to go with him instead. Come with me – we could have a laugh.'

'Not with Jim there I couldn't. Anyway, I'm going to Greenham.'

Becky went to Greenham regularly to visit the peace camp outside the RAF airbase that was being prepared for the arrival of American's Ground Launched Cruise Missiles. Sam had been with Becky a few times. Sometimes they camped all weekend. Other times they borrowed her mum's car, went up early, stayed for the day, and came home late. In a funny sort of way, it was a lovely place to stay. Greenham was as near to being in the middle of nowhere as it was possible to get in the southern well-heeled Home Counties of England. If you turned your back on the barbed wire, the military paraphernalia, the armed guards and the sinister observation tower, and just gazed out over the ancient common land, it was rather beautiful. Peaceful.

The first time Sam had trekked to Greenham with Becky was December 1982. They had embraced the base. Held hands and joined the chain of women protestors encircling the sprawling perimeter fence. The second time they had sat down in the mud outside the main gate, refused to move when asked to do so by the police, and had been arrested along with twenty or so other women. Charged with obstruction. Brief appearance at Newbury Magistrates' Court. Their appeal to the Geneva Conventions had been dismissed as irrelevant and they had been handed a thirty-pound fine. After that, Sam had lost her enthusiasm for the camp a bit. Becky hadn't. Sam still went with Becky though, every now and then.

Green Gate, the part of the peace camp where they usually stayed, was overlooked by the watchtower and was situated right next to the cruise missile hangars – grass-smothered silos rising ominously from the flat earth. Burial mounds for giants. The camp was a ramshackle collection of flapping tents and smoky fires, watery vegetable soup and meetings where nobody could speak unless they were holding the bloody conch shell. What bugged Sam about Greenham were the women with posh voices who wailed 'take the toys from the boys' and lectured the squaddies about their career choice through the perimeter fence. As if they had a choice. As if they weren't sixteen-year-olds desperate for a job, scrabbling for an escape route. Like Jim must have been. Actually, what really bugged Sam about Greenham was the memory of her most recent trip there with Becky. They had cut the fence and trespassed on the base. Searching for the supposed weak link of the bunker's communication system, the old telephone cable cabinet. They had narrowly missed being caught by the Ministry of Defence police.

Becky was sitting up now, staring down at Sam almost accusingly as she lounged on the floor. 'Why don't you come to Greenham with me?'

'I ought to go with Jim.'

Becky's eyebrows fused above the bridge of her nose. 'You haven't told Jim about cutting the wire, have you?'

'No. Course not. He's not interested in that sort of stuff anyway. He's just a normal plainclothes cop.' Sam smiled briefly, and then glanced away. Paul and Lee returned from the offie. They demolished a spliff. Necked the contents of a cheap white wine box. She was ready to call it a night. Becky had other plans. She wanted to spray-paint the fence around Crystal Palace Park, the starting point of the march. Sam said she felt too stoned and woozy, needed to go home to bed. Becky gave her that slightly suspicious, accusing look again. Sam felt aggrieved. She didn't have anything to prove. But she dragged herself out into the night all the same.

They traipsed to the top of Crystal Palace Park. The sky was inky and star-spangled here, away from the lights of the high street. At the park entrance they decided to split; Becky and Lee trekked off, leaving Sam alone with Paul. Sam tossed a coin, Paul called it and decided to take the easy option – lookout. She left him standing at the corner of the main road as she strolled casually back down the hill, the spray can in her pocket cold against her thigh.

It was quiet along the park boundary, her only company the strange Victorian clay monsters skulking in the shrubbery on the other side of the fence and the deep gurgle of the Effra spring waters bubbling somewhere way below. She reached a section of the fence where the overhanging horse chestnuts camouflaged the pavement, checked over her shoulder, shook the can quickly and started to spray. The whiff of peardrops tickled the back of her throat and the nozzle kept jamming, but she was enjoying herself now, fuelled by the addictive crack of rule-breaking. As she prepared to join the final line, the beam of a headlight swept across her and illuminated her outstretched arm. Startled, she hastily stuffed the spray can in her pocket and backed away. The car's elongated bonnet appeared over the hump, beams arcing across the sky, slowing to a crawl as it passed. She shuddered, sensing eyes peering through the window, locked on her face, checking her features. Rover. Black. She squinted as the dark vehicle accelerated up the hill, trying to read the number plate before it was swallowed up by the shadows. MVF something or other. Enough to tell her it was a south London registration anyway. Jim had taught her how to decode number plates on their occasional strolls through the outer reaches of the suburbs, searching for black-berries, walking the wretched dog. The dubious perks of being the daughter of an undercover cop.

She rubbed her neck, stared up the hill into the darkness. A wave of paranoia threatened to swamp her; fears about her own illegal activities mingling with anxieties about Jim's covert work. Was somebody following her? She was being stupid, surely. Over-reacting. It was just a stuffy stockbroker in a Rover. She retrained her sight on the spot where Paul should have been standing and watching her back: he had disappeared. Thanks a bunch.

She hesitated, dug her hand into her overcoat pocket, fin-gered the metal canister, drummed her fingers on its side, turned back edgily towards her unfinished handiwork and, in the tail of her eye, spotted a panda car cruising down the hill. Shit. He had probably been hanging out on the forecourt of the all-night garage; the coppers often waited there – easy access to the coffee machine and Mars bars. The driver of the Rover must have pulled in and reported her. She considered the possibility of legging it, hesitated, indecisive, left it too late to scarper, gave herself no choice but to stay put and bluff. The panda car pulled up beside her, hazard lights flashing. A hefty copper struggled with the door, levered himself on to the kerb and surveyed her nearly finished peace symbol.

'You've missed one of the arms,' he said.

She shrugged.

'Ban the bomb. I've had my weekend leave cancelled because

of you lot.' She had an urge to tell him to think about the over-time he would be paid.

He pre-empted her train of thought. 'We've been so stretched these last few weeks, what with the miners' strike and half of us having to provide support in the north and everybody else having to play musical chairs to cover the gaps. I've had enough overtime to pay for my summer holiday twice over already. And now we've been landed with you and your bloody march. You ban the bombers.'

He shook his head sadly. 'You know what, I've been on the beat for thirty years and if I've learned one thing, it's this.'

He paused. She smiled expectantly. He pushed the peak of his cap up with one hand and put the other behind his back. 'There are three types of people in this world. You've got your law-abiding citizens, your criminals and your stirrers.'

She contained the urge to smirk.

He raised an eyebrow. 'Harder to tell, of course, with teen-agers. So you're going to have to enlighten me. Law-abiding citizen, criminal or stirrer: which, young lady, do you intend to be when you finally get round to growing up?'

She smiled sweetly again, maintained her silence.

'Well, I can see that you're a nice girl really.' He pulled out his notebook. 'Boyfriend get you into this lot, did he?' She nodded. He flicked the pages until he found a clean sheet. 'Now. What's your name?'

'Sam.'

'Sam, short for Samantha.'

'It's just Sam.' Liz had named her after an unfulfilled wish for a boy and a beloved dead grandfather.

'Sam what?'

'Sam Coyle.'

The copper gave her a look of paternal sternness.

'What are your parents going to think about this then?'

She shrugged.

He narrowed his eyes. Brows drawn. Perturbed. 'Your dad's not a copper is he?'

The alarm must have shown on her face. How had he worked that one out? Had the man in the Rover identified her? Were the Ministry of Defence police on her trail? The blood drained from her head. Her hands were clammy. Legs heavy.

The copper grinned. 'I can always tell,' he said. 'Don't quite know what it is. Perhaps it's the attitude. Quietly cocky. I tell you what though, I wish I had a fiver for every copper's kid I've had to caution. And it's usually the daughters, would you believe.' He shook his head. 'So where's your dad stationed then?'

'He works undercover,' she said. Words tumbling out in her relief that he had just guessed; he hadn't been told that her dad was a cop. 'The Diggers,' she added.

He inhaled sharply. 'The Diggers,' he repeated. 'Oh, I've heard talk about them. Never sure whether they really existed or not.'

He paused. He pointed the butt end of his pen at her. And then he used its tip to scratch the back of his head. His actions were making her feel uneasy again. She tried to inveigle his mind, identify what was disturbing him.

He caught her staring at him. He dropped his jovial copper face back into place. 'Well, I can see I'm going to have to revise my theory now,' he said. 'Let's see: you've got your law-abiding citizens, your criminals, your stirrers. And, in a class all of their own, your policemen's daughters.'

He replaced his notebook in his pocket. 'I'm going to have to sort this out with the Governor. You'd better run along now before you land yourself in any more trouble.'

She knew better than to ignore her exit cue, turned silently and strode rapidly up the hill.

Slouching against the bus stop, attempting to hold the fears at bay, she wondered whether she should say anything to Jim about being caught. He would find out soon enough anyway, the cop would make sure of that. She glanced back down the road and thought she spotted a dark figure outlined against the park fence, a broad-shouldered man standing, waiting among the shifting shadows of the horse chestnuts. But when she peered into the dimness again, there was nothing. She looked up, searching for the comfort of the moon's face, and was greeted instead by the red winking eye of the radio mast peering down. She twiddled her lip between her finger and thumb and hoped the night bus would hurry up.

Jim had been absent and she didn't come face to face with him until the morning after the march. Monday. The pungent tang of his breakfast engulfed her as she ran down the stairs, making her want to retch. Offal. Jim was at the table, wiping up kidney juice on a slice of bread with one hand, holding the *Guardian* up like a shield with the other. She sat down opposite, read the headlines while she waited for the inevitable confrontation. The front page was full of the miners' strike. The creases of Jim's forehead floated above a black-and-white photograph of the picket line, policemen being pelted with fruit and bricks. And she wondered then whether there was a connection between Jim's strange behaviour – mutterings about Operation Asgard – and the strike. Every force in the country was affected by it one way or another, according to the copper who caught her spray-painting.

'Do you think the miners will win?' she asked.

Jim's newspaper stayed firmly in place, his voice floating upward from behind his cover.

'Not a chance.'

'Because the coal stockpiles mean the strike won't have any effect?'

'No. Because the government is determined to crush the unions to buggery.'

'Oh? Is that you as well? Are you involved in crushing the unions to buggery?'

He didn't reply. The furrows on his forehead deepened; an answer of sorts, she decided, as she waited for him to pronounce on her run-in with the local constabulary. She sensed him strategizing behind his screen, trying to unnerve her, picking his moment, taking his time. Cold War tactics.

Eventually he lowered the paper, skewered her with his steely gaze. 'Do me a favour,' he said slowly. 'Next time you have the urge to decorate public property with spray-paint... make sure you don't get caught.'

The biggest crime you could commit in Jim's book, she reckoned, was the inexcusable offense of being stupid enough to get caught.

'I won't do it again,' she said. 'Get caught, that is.'

A flash of concern crossed his face. 'You've got to be more careful, you know.'

What did he mean? Was that a general warning or was he talking about something specific? She half considered mentioning the Rover with the south London registration, but when she thought about it, tried to grasp the concern, there was nothing to say: shadows in the night, paranoid delusions, too much Red Leb.

'You don't tell any of your mates about my work, do you?' It wasn't the first time he had asked that question.

'Of course not. Well, I mean obviously I have to tell them something, so I tell them you are a plainclothes cop. A

44

detective.' One of Jim's tricks: don't lie; just don't reveal the whole truth. Omission rather than commission.

She waited, expecting more; a dig, extraction of penalties at the very least, but there was no further comment. He re-erected his newspaper barrier and flicked it into an impenetrable double-page spread.

She poked at her bowl of muesli. Ate in silence.

Jim folded the paper, placed it on the table, pushed his chair back, stood up to leave. He hesitated. 'So I hear you're coming with me to Orkney,' he said.

'You heard wrong. I'm not.'

'Are you bringing a friend?'

'Definitely not. None of my friends want to spend a week with you.'

He laughed to himself as he left. The dog emerged from under the table, snarled and sauntered off into the kitchen. She picked up the newspaper, had a quick flick through the pages to find the cryptic crossword. Araucaria. Her favourite. She wiped her forehead with the back of her hand and stared at the space where Jim had been standing. It wasn't like Jim to pass up an opportunity to be by himself, escape. The childhood holidays in Orkney had been rare times when she and Jim had hung around together, trekking off to visit the Neolithic ruins that littered the islands while her sisters went elsewhere with Liz. They had pretended they were archaeologists, trying to reconstruct the life of Skara Brae's inhabitants from the debris that the villagers had left behind; a dish of ochre-red pigment, the skull of a bull, fish bones, shells. At Maeshowe she had squirmed with embarrassment when the guide had told them about the Viking's rude runes carved on the stone walls of the burial chamber. 'Thorni fucked. Helgi carved.' Jim had been amused. Funny, he had said, that a bit of mindless graffiti ended up

45

being an important historical record, somebody's off-guard thoughts bringing the past to life. Being an archaeologist, Jim reckoned, was like being a detective, digging down through the layers, sifting through the soil, the rubble, the middens. Searching for clues about long-vanished people. Those trips with Jim had always been interesting. He had, she suspected, found it easier to spend time with her when she was younger, less likely to challenge his commands. She wasn't quite sure now whether she should be flattered or alarmed by his willingness to let her tag along on his trek north.

CHAPTER 4

THEY WERE STOPPING at Ruth's house in a shabby corner of south London on the way to the station. Ruth had phoned that morning; a back-garden fence had collapsed in the night under the weight of an overgrown jasmine. The neighbours had unleashed a torrent of foul-mouthed bilge when she had said the repair might have to wait. Ruth had retreated, locked the doors and phoned Jim. He promised they would drop by that afternoon – the train didn't leave until the evening. He would fix the fence and the neighbours.

Ruth was a Parsi, born in Bombay, exact date unknown, although she was undoubtedly ancient with a face that had been as wrinkled as a walnut for as long as Sam could remember and wispy grey hair that barely covered her scalp. Ruth was Sam's unofficial godmother; she had slipped into the unfilled vacancy through mutual agreement. When Sam had told Liz about the arrangement, she said she wasn't sure it was possible to have a Zoroastrian godmother, but Jim had decreed that religious affiliation was a piffling irrelevance and had waved all objections aside with a flick of his hand. Ruth was a rare window on Jim's past. Ruth had arrived in Stepney decades earlier with a suitcase full of the family silver and an encyclopaedia in her head. She had befriended Jim when he was a rookie cop on the beat in the East End and she was in charge of the local library. Later, when she had saved enough, Ruth had moved south of the river.

The sun was blasting Ruth's treeless street as they pulled up outside her home and had triggered the annual swarm of flying ants. Newly hatched insects were spewing from the cracks in the baking pavement, unfurling translucent wings before launching themselves into the air in a kaleidoscope of dancing dots. Jim swaggered round to sort out the neighbours, unbothered by the insect plague. She made a dash for Ruth's back door, swatting at the irritating critters as she went.

'They are God's creatures too. I suppose,' Ruth said, assessing the black swarm as she motioned Sam inside.

They sat in silence, wilting in the kitchen's heat, rice bubbling on the stovetop, listening for signs of trouble. Sam cringed as she imagined Jim jabbing his finger provocatively. Ten minutes passed, maybe more, before he returned looking pleased with himself. The neighbours had backed off, apologized even. Jim said he would have a word with the governor at the local cop shop and make sure the bobbies on the beat kept an eye out for her. Ruth told him not to bother. She seemed content with the immediate victory, unconcerned about the long-term peace. Perhaps she didn't foresee a long term, Sam speculated as she crunched on grains of pilaf and Ruth talked about her funeral arrangements.

'I want a Zoroastrian funeral.'

The last time Ruth had visited their house she had talked endlessly about the details of her will. The solicitor. The executor. The solicitor again. And now it was her funeral. At least it was more interesting than the paperwork. Jim suggested gleefully that they could build a tower in the back garden and put her body in it so the crows could come and clean the bones. The customary Zoroastrian way.

'That would really please the neighbours,' Jim said.

Ruth laughed. Jim seemed to be the only person who

could say anything to Ruth these days without aggravating her.

'A tower won't be necessary,' Ruth said. 'Lewisham crematorium will be fine.'

The cemetery was visible from the mainline to Charing Cross: row upon row of neat white tombs jammed between Grove Park and Hither Green, a daily reminder of the last stop for all commuters. The idea of a Zoroastrian funeral there seemed incongruous to Sam, although it clearly didn't bother Ruth.

'All the elements have to be present. Fire. Air. Water,' she said. 'Will you sort it out?' She looked at Jim.

He raised an eyebrow. 'If I'm still around.'

God, they were trying to out-compete each other now on the morbidity stakes.

'Sam will see to it,' he said. 'She'll make sure you have a good funeral.'

Sam folded her sweaty arms. 'What if I go before either of you?'

'Don't be ridiculous, child,' Ruth said. Irritable again. Sam wanted to argue, but she couldn't quite be bothered in the soporific heat of the afternoon.

Jim announced he was going to fix the fence, departed to the back garden. Sam grabbed her opportunity in his absence.

'Do you have a book of Norse myths I could borrow?' she asked.

Ruth glared. 'Didn't I give you a book of Norse myths once for a birthday present?'

Ruth was right, she had. Norse myths: typical Ruth present. The volume of Norse myths was the first book that Ruth had ever given Sam and almost the last, because she had mislaid the slim paperback shortly after receiving it and Ruth had judged her carelessness with reading matter to be bordering on sacrilegious. She had been forgiven, eventually. And every June since then some esoteric volume that Ruth considered to be essential reading had materialized: *Legends of Eastern Lands*, *Greek Gods*, *Sir Gawain and the Greene Knight*, *Beowulf*. That year's present hadn't yet arrived. She reminded Ruth that she had mislaid the book of Norse myths a long time ago. Ruth scowled and Sam thought she was about to be re-reprimanded for her carelessness when she was six, but Ruth had something else on her mind.

'*The Golden Bough*. Have you read it?'

Sam shook her head; she had seen the title before in a footnote to one of her A-level English Literature texts. She could name the author, but had only a vague idea what the book was about.

'If you are interested in mythology you should read *The Golden Bough*. James Frazer. He looks at the origins of Western myths. Explains how they have evolved.'

Sam nodded and smiled in what she thought was a congenial manner.

Ruth glared at her through opalescent eyes. 'What's wrong with you anyway?' she demanded.

'What do you mean?'

'You seem anxious. Are you in some kind of trouble?'

Sam hesitated. She could tell Ruth about trespassing at Greenham, her fears that she had been identified, Jim's strange declaration at her birthday dinner that had knocked her off-kilter, made her feel slightly out of control. A moth to the flame. Unable to pull away even though she feared the heat. It would be a relief to tell somebody. Instead she shrugged. 'No. I'm not in any trouble. Not as far as I know.'

Ruth raised an eyebrow, levered herself unsteadily up from the chair, ordered Sam to follow her to the front room.

A shaft of dust-speckled light sliced through the gap in the half-drawn curtains and fell on a forlorn landscape of unwanted household objects: pairs of knotted-together shoes of the black and flat variety that Ruth always wore; battered books; assorted, barely used kitchen appliances. Everything was to be organized and stacked, ready for a local charity collection. Sam sighed. Ruth folded her arms. Sam squatted on the floor, rummaged around among the jumble, poked at the books, picked up a box of paste jewellery, pulled out a ring topped with a gaudy red plastic ruby, rubbed it, put it down again when she realized Ruth was eyeing her with patent irritation.

'You'll miss your train at this rate.'

She left Sam alone to get on with it.

It took Sam half an hour to bring order to Ruth's discarded chattels. She called to her godmother when she had finished the task. Ruth returned, clutching a tatty paperback. She surveyed Sam's work critically. Nodded grudging approval.

'Here, I suppose you can have this,' she said. She held out the volume she had been carrying. 'It bills itself as a history of the Vikings. I'm not entirely convinced. The author doesn't seem to see the need for references. I suspect it might be more fiction than fact.' She sniffed. 'But you can have it if you want.'

'Thanks.' Sam took the book. 'I'll just go and put it in my backpack.' She buried it in among her other belongings quickly before Jim had a chance to spot it. She didn't want to give him any reason to suspect that she was digging around, looking for connections between his outburst about Operation Asgard and their trip to Orkney.

They drove northwest in the glare of the late afternoon sun. The combination of heat and Jim's driving making her feel slightly sick. Jim insisted on throwing the Cortina around the seedy, litter-strewn backstreets of south London, swerving around corners, speeding up, suddenly braking, diving down side turnings at the last minute. Why did Jim always have to drive as if he were in a car-chase? Christ, maybe they were being shadowed. She glanced into the wing mirror, trying to see if there was a suspicious car tailing them. An innocuous dirty green Volvo estate hugged their bumper, four heads of varying heights just visible: a family. Stupid; of course they weren't being trailed.

Around the common, past Mrs Dee's Chinese restaurant where the best spare ribs in south London were to be found, according to Jim, heading for the river. She peered through the iron girders of Battersea Bridge as they crossed the grey smear of the Thames at low tide. The bullhorn handles of a BMX bike poked upwards from the kippled beach of broken glass and plastic pebbles. A solitary figure patrolled the shoreline, waving his metal detector optimistically. The black arrow of a cormorant shot out from under an arch, flying downstream towards St Paul's and the ominous cumulonimbus tower building in the east.

'Which is your favourite bridge?' she asked.

Jim paused to consider. 'Vauxhall. I like Vauxhall best.'

Jim often backed the underdog. Unless there was any danger it might bite his ankle, and then he kicked it.

'What's so great about Vauxhall?'

'It has a particular atmosphere, Vauxhall.'

He jerked his head over his shoulder. 'I reckon Vauxhall has always been a bit of a hot spot, a crossing point. It's where the Effra and the Tyburn dump out into the Thames. Places where rivers meet are always... sacred. Gateways to the other side.' He glanced wistfully over his shoulder at the south bank.

On the north side, the Cortina edged along the polluted streets of Chelsea. She checked the car behind: still the Volvo. The road bent slightly to the left and now the cars behind the Volvo came into view: a navy Renault, a red Peugeot and behind the Peugeot, a black Rover. She peered into the wing mirror but the car was at the wrong angle to make out the numberplate. She glanced at Jim. He was staring straight ahead, keeping his eye on the road now, muttering about the smear of squashed insects on the windscreen. They swung right at a set of traffic lights. The Volvo peeled off to the left. The Peugeot turned right behind them. So did the Rover.

'Is that car following us?' she asked,

'Which car?'

'The one behind the Peugeot. The black Rover.'

He didn't check the mirror. 'Nope,' he said.

Had he clocked it already? Dismissed it? Anyway. Black Rover. There had to be more than one of those in the world.

She faced forwards again, beginning to feel relieved that they had almost made it to the station without engaging in a slanging match.

'So what about this friend of yours, then?' Jim demanded. 'The one that's tagging along.'

'Tom?'

'Yes. Him. What does he do?'

'He's just finished his A-levels; like me.'

'Then he's going to university in September.'

'No. He's taking a year out.'

'A year out? So he's taking it easy in between farting around at school and doing bugger all at college.'

Jim slowed down for an amber light.

'No, he's looking for work experience that might help him with his career.'

'What career is that then?'

'He wants to be a journalist.'

Jim slammed his foot on the accelerator, sped across the junction as the light turned red.

'What did you do that for? You could have killed us.'

Jim ignored her. 'So he's a journalist,' he said. 'A bloody gongfermor. A night-time trawler of cesspits.'

'I said he *wants* to be a journalist,' she replied, backtracking from what, she surmised from his reaction, was not the best career choice for someone he was about to share a holiday cottage with.

'Wants to be – is. Same thing, isn't it?'

'No. It's like me saying I want to be a barrister.'

'You don't want to be a bloody barrister, do you?'

'I was just trying to illustrate the difference between having an aspiration to be a journalist and actually being a journalist,' she said, with exaggerated patience. 'Anyway, what's wrong with being a barrister?'

'Barristers. Bunch of crooks. Masters of pettifoggery.'

'I thought they were on the same side as you.'

Jim puffed out his cheeks and shook his head at the naïveté of his daughter.

'Are there any careers you do approve of?'

He sucked his teeth. 'I'll think about that one.'

'Thanks. Might be useful to know.'

She stared out of the window. Why on earth was she asking a secret policeman for careers advice?

They crawled past the Kensington Olympia exhibition centre. The Mind, Body and Soul experience.

'You won't say anything to your mate about...' Jim said.

'No, I won't say anything.' How the bloody hell did he think they were going to manage a week crammed into a

54

holiday cottage together without anyone talking about what Jim did for a living? She took a deep breath. There was a whiff of hot-weather bad drains in the air.

'Journalist on the make. Now that is bad news,' Jim said. 'You'd better check what he's got in his pockets when we leave.'

She muttered 'piss off' under her breath.

Stuttering down the slip road to the station, she peered in the rear-view mirror and spotted the Rover gliding smoothly past like a shark. Maybe she was just being paranoid after all. They parked.

'Get your bag out the boot,' said Jim. He handed her the car keys, started fiddling with something under the driver's seat.

She hauled herself out of the Cortina, walked around to the back, opened the boot. He had dumped his haversack on top of her bag. She leaned over, reached in, knocked her knuckle against a hard object in the front of his haversack, retracted her hand. Froze. Eyes locked. Half an inch of rag-wrapped dull black metal sticking out from the loosely buckled pocket. Not much. But enough. Pistol. She didn't have to look twice; she'd seen it before. Once. Years ago. She had wandered into her parents' bedroom for no real reason, drawn towards Jim's unlocked cabinet – curious – she'd never seen it unlocked before, and opened a drawer. It had been lying among the rubber bands and envelopes. She had peered over and read the word 'WALTHER' engraved on its side. It looked like a toy, so small and neat with its funny name. Walther. She reached out to touch. And just then Jim had shouted up from the bottom of the stairs. What the fuck was she doing? She knew she wasn't allowed in their room. She had better move her arse out of there pretty bloody quickly. She had legged it, more scared by the threat of a bollocking from Jim than by the danger of a gun. The very next day she had been watching the six o'clock news with her sisters and there was a story about the lead singer of this American pop group. Chicago. Accidentally killed himself with his own shotgun. Don't worry. It's not loaded. So he had said just before he pulled the trigger, according to the newsreader. She had burst into tears and Helen had whacked the back of her head, told her not to be such a big cry-baby, blubbing about nothing. She felt like crying now, although she knew she wouldn't, knew that she could fight down the prickling tears of anger. What was he doing taking a pistol with him? In his haversack. On a journey with her. And one of her mates. Christ, what kind of a trip were they on?

The noise of Jim moving around in the front of the Cortina snapped her back to her senses. She carefully, very carefully, lifted the haversack to one side. Removed her bag. Closed the lid of the boot. Locked it. Double-checked that she had locked it. Jim was standing by the car, scrutinizing the train's trailer waiting for its load.

'Motorail,' he said, talking to the air, 'I reckon it's the only way we'll get from one end of the country to the other at the moment without having our number-plate checked and being stopped on suspicion of travelling to join the picket lines.'

She glanced at him out of the corner of her eye and had a fleeting image of madness; they were outlaws on the run, fleeing north, dodging police surveillance, road blocks, pulling a crafty getaway move by travelling middle-class Motorail. With a lethal weapon. A Walther. Heading to Orkney for a shoot-out in a holiday cottage. Please leave this cottage as you found it and make sure all dead bodies are disposed of in the rubbish bags provided. But that was nuttiness. Even on Jim's sliding scale of undercover cop simmering insanity that had to be crazy. Surely.

'Oh the miners' strike,' she said. Her comment didn't sound quite as casual as she had intended it to be.

Jim raised an eyebrow darkly. 'It's a bloody war zone out there. Chaos.'

He flicked his wrist to check the time, the watch face on the inner side of his left wrist. She had copied his habit, wore her watch on the inside of her wrist too. Just like Jim. He'd learned that one in the army he had once told her, easier for quick time checking when you're driving. Or using a gun.

'There are a couple of things I need to sort out with the guards,' he said.

'Right. See you in a bit then.'

She handed him back his car keys. He headed off towards a huddle of men in blue uniforms, leaving her standing alone by the car. She glared at the Cortina's boot, pictured the Walther, swaddled in its white cloth, nestling in its pocket on the front of Jim's haversack. She shook her head disbelievingly, turned and walked away.

CHAPTER 5

THE PLATFORM WAS humming. Passengers were milling around, climbing on board the train, jumping off again, sticking their heads out of the small gap at the top of the carriage windows, shouting at each other to go and fetch that bag from the car before the guards drove it on to the trailer. She checked the slip road. Perhaps Tom had got cold feet. Perhaps she was better off without a travelling companion anyway. After Becky she had drawn a blank, decided she would tell Liz, definitively, that she couldn't find a friend to accompany her and she certainly was not going with Jim alone. And then Tom had phoned. Tom Spiller; only son of a doctor and a Marxist sociology lecturer at Manchester University. She had met Tom through Becky and Becky had met Tom when he came down from Manchester for a march in London. Becky fancied Tom, invited him down to stay, but it came to nothing because, it turned out, he had a steady girlfriend in Manchester. Let's be friends, he had said and that was the end of it as far as Becky was concerned. It was Sam who stayed in touch with Tom long after Becky's sights had shifted elsewhere. Sam didn't care about the girlfriend. In fact she preferred it that way. She didn't fancy Tom. He wasn't her type. He was too porky and ginger. Although he was tall. And he was a laugh. They had fun together. Which was why she liked him.

He had phoned to find out what she was doing over the summer. His girlfriend had flown to California for a few months to earn some money as an au pair and he was loafing around Manchester looking for an attachment or an internship or a job on a local paper, but he hadn't managed to find anything yet. She hadn't realized before then that he wanted to be a journalist; maybe he had told her and she hadn't really taken any notice. She still wasn't taking much notice when she asked him whether he'd like to come to Orkney with her to keep an eye on Jim. He had said yes instantly, pleased with the offer of a free holiday and the chance to meet Jim because Tom had always been curious about her dad.

'The thing that's interesting about you,' he had said one evening when she was thrashing him at backgammon, 'is that everyone else I know has grown up with liberal parents, but your dad is an authoritarian.' It had rankled, his observation that what was interesting about her was Jim, but she had let it drop.

'It would be more accurate to describe him as an authoritarian liberal,' she had replied.

'How does that work then?'

'He has liberal views about the world. But if anyone disagrees with him, he tells them to fuck off.'

At least Tom knew the score then, when he said yes.

As soon as she had put the phone down she suspected she had made a mistake; she felt breathless, panicked. Tom, she reminded herself too late, asked too many questions, he didn't leave you alone, he didn't let up, she would have to spend the whole week fending him off, losing him. She wanted a sidekick, a supporter, not an inquisitor. She phoned him back to say Jim had cancelled the trip, but he was already out for the evening and the next day she was out with Becky and didn't have time to call. After that it was Thursday. Departure day. And as she stood waiting on the platform she reassured herself with the thought that he might ask lots of searching questions, but he never took much notice of the answers because he was always more interested in forwarding his own theories than listening to anything anybody else had to say. Anyway he lived at the other end of the country, so if it all went wrong she would never have to see him again.

And there he was now, loping self-consciously towards her. Scuffed Adidas trainers, black Peter Storm windcheater, duffle bag slung over sloping shoulder, one hand in pocket. He didn't look like someone who might have hidden ambitions. Although he did look different from the last time they had met up. He seemed taller, sharper, clothes hanging not clinging. He had lost weight.

'Okay?' he said. He sidestepped up to her uncertainly, towering over her.

She shuffled back, feeling small. 'Fine. You?'

'I've lost some weight.'

'I didn't notice.'

'No chocolate or sweets during the week and no biscuits on long journeys.'

'What's that then?' She pointed to the packet of Hobnobs sticking out of his duffle bag.

'Emergency rations.'

She nodded. 'Always good to be prepared. Especially if you're going somewhere with Jim.'

'Where is your dad anyway?' he asked. Nervously perhaps.

'Behind you,' said Jim. Tom turned. Startled. Caught unawares by Jim's sudden appearance from nowhere. He was standing there looking pleased with himself. Victorious. Oh God, he was at it already. Establishing the pecking order. They shook hands, exchanged pleasantries while Jim gave Tom the gimlet eye.

'Shouldn't we be getting on the train?' she asked with pointed exasperation.

Jim shoved a couple of tickets in her hand. 'You're in there. The caboose.' He performed his usual dismissive wave in the direction of the furthest carriage.

'Where are you sleeping?' she asked.

He nodded vaguely at the front of the train. 'I blagged one of the compartments with seats.'

He set off up the platform at a pace with his haversack on his back. She squinted at the flat front pocket as he walked away, wondering what he had done with the pistol.

'See you in Inverness tomorrow morning,' he said over his shoulder before he vanished in the crowd.

'We haven't even left London and he's given us the slip,' said Tom.

Sam's stomach twinged; he was obviously taking the surveillance of Jim seriously then. That really wasn't going to help.

They struggled to negotiate the narrow door into the tiny cabin with its neatly made-up bunks. She felt a sudden flush of awkwardness: too close for comfort. Tom seemed unperturbed by their forced physical intimacy. He dumped his bag carelessly on the bottom bunk. She grappled with the truculent ladder, heaved and pushed herself inelegantly on to the top bunk, tried to sit up, banged her head on the ceiling. Ten minutes ago she had felt too small and now she was too large. She propped herself awkwardly on one elbow and interrogated the reflection of Tom in the mirror as he shuffled around in the cramped space.

The train shuddered to life, jolted, lurched out of the cover of the station into the nicotine-stained evening haze.

'We're off,' said Tom. 'On our journey into the unknown.'

'Your starter for ten,' she said. 'Name the song that begins with a summertime train journey into the unknown and ends with a death.'

He rubbed his chin stubble with a grubby finger, 'Oh, that sounds familiar. Let me think.'

'I can give you a clue.'

'No, no. I've got it. Kenny Rogers. "The Gambler",' he shouted. He started singing the first verse. She joined in the refrain. Loudly. Wildly out of tune. Laughing. There was a thump on the compartment wall.

'The walls must be a bit thin,' said Tom.

'That's us,' she said, still snorting. 'On a train journey to nowhere. Well, not exactly nowhere. Although it is a long way north. Fifty-nine degrees, to be precise.'

'Is it really fifty-nine degrees? That's almost as far north as Leningrad.'

'Yes, and it's too late to turn back now. We're on the run to Orkney.'

Her own words sobered her. She crawled down to the bottom of her bunk, lay on her stomach and peered out of the window, calculating their coordinates. The train was passing Camden. It had swung round from the west and joined the mainline north. She pinpointed Helen's bedsit in relation to the tracks, imagined her sister getting ready for a night out at the Camden Palace. A jagged blue flash illuminated the skinny backsides of the grey terraces. The first fat drops of summer rain blitzed the window, hitting her with an inexplicable anxiety, a need to be with her sisters.

'Jim's good-looking, isn't he?' said Tom, ignoring the lightning streaks outside. 'In a rugged sort of way. That rough look that women always seem to find attractive. But obviously a bit of a difficult old sod,' he added.

'I did warn you.'

'So what exactly does he do anyway? You said he's an undercover cop.'

Sam winced.

'Does he keep an eye on organizations like CND?'

Jesus, he didn't waste time. She caught her reflection in the train window, staring at her with its firmly pressed lips. She was losing it these days though, her self-censorship. Her ability to manage a convincing cover-up for Jim.

'He doesn't talk much about his work,' she said.

'But what do you think Jim is up to in Orkney then? You obviously think he's up to something.'

She shrank back into her bunk so she couldn't be seen in the mirror, grappled with the urge to confide, wondering what she could say that wouldn't give too much away, sound too ridiculous. Too alarming. The proclamation of impending death. Operation Asgard. The Walther.

'Maybe it's something to do with the miners' strike.'

'What, you think he's picking up some information on the strikers from a contact to pass on to the Force or something like that?'

'Maybe.'

'But why would he go all the way to Orkney to do it?'

'I don't know. Maybe that's where his contact lives. Orkney is full of dropout lefty types who might have some information on the strike. Although I suspect it's not quite that straightforward.'

'What do you mean?'

'I'm not sure it's as straightforward as him looking for intelligence on the strike to feed to the Force.'

She shouldn't have said that, should have kept her hunches to herself.

'You mean, you think he's feeding information to someone else?'

'Possibly. I don't know.'

'Who would he be feeding it to?'

'I've no idea really. KGB perhaps.'

'Sounds a bit far-fetched. Why would the Soviets go to a cop for information about the miners' strike? They can probably get it direct.'

He pulled a dismissive face, irritating her instantly. What did he know about anything?

'Actually, he used to hang out with the KGB.'

'Did he? The KGB?'

'He worked at the docks. Tilbury. He checked the boats coming from the Soviet Union and he was mates with some of the KGB agents.'

Well, she had always assumed they were KGB agents. She sensed Tom assessing her disbelievingly; she could tell he thought she was a bit of a fantasist. She tried him with the story about the strange men from the Russia she had seen drinking at their house. Related how she had corrected their English. Tom laughed. She was momentarily chuffed by his reaction.

'But even if they were KGB, they were probably really low level,' he said. 'More like security guards.'

'Yeah, probably.'

'And I really don't see what the connection might be to a trip to Orkney twelve years later.'

She couldn't see a connection either. 'I guess you're right.'

Rain-blurred brown semis rattled past, the dog-end of the periphery. They cracked open a couple of miniature bottles of whiskey, purchased from the buffet car. Jameson's. One of

Jim's pearls of wisdom: if you can't afford a single malt, buy Irish. It'll leave you with less of a headache. Some people's parents steered them through difficult career choices. Jim gave her guidance on what to do when faced with a confusing array of bottles behind the bar.

'What are you thinking?' Tom asked.

Why did anyone ever ask that question? As if they seriously believed they would get an honest answer. She searched for something to say. 'I was thinking that it's a compulsion. It's a way of life he's incapable of giving up. He can't exist with only one identity; he has to have secrets, somewhere else to escape. Sometimes I think undercover work is little more than a professional licence for men who want to avoid any form of domestic obligation. Whenever Jim is asked to do something tedious or time-consuming, he just disappears and nobody can ever ask him about it. Official secrets. Matters of national security. I reckon that's the appeal of the spy story to men; it's not the complexity of the politics that's the pull, it's the fantasy of the man with no commitments. Personal betrayal not political betrayal, that's the draw, that's what people are really interested in.'

She broke off abruptly. She was rambling: one of her feminist diatribes.

'Now there's a possibility,' said Tom.

'What do you mean?'

'I think that's the most likely explanation for the sudden trip to Orkney. He's dodging his domestic responsibilities.'

She frowned.

'He's having an affair,' he said triumphantly.

'I had thought of that,' she said. Of course she had thought of that. 'But he asked Liz to go with him, which sort of rules out that theory.'

'Maybe he knew she wouldn't be able to make it anyway.'

'But if he's having an affair, why would he let us tag along?'

'To give himself an alibi; a cover story to throw your mum off the trail. She obviously suspects he is having an affair and that's why she asked you to keep an eye on him. He must have known that she suspected him, which explains why he agreed to let you go too. The double bluff.'

'But why he would go all the way to Orkney to do it?'

'That's what men are like. Don't like to crap in their own backyard. So they go on holiday without their partners, arrange to meet their bit on the side. Playing away.'

He was checking her reaction in the mirror. She scowled. The train plunged into the darkness of a tunnel, the noise of the wheels on the tracks echoing, making conversation impossible.

'At least, that's what married, middle-aged men do,' he said as they emerged into the dwindling light.

She folded her arms across her chest.

He continued, unperturbed. 'It's the hair.'

She looked blank.

'Older women always go for a bloke who still has all his hair. Do you think it's screwed you up in any way? Having such a difficult dad?'

'No. I don't.'

'You don't think it's stopped you from forming proper relationships with men?'

'No.'

Christ almighty. They had hardly left London, hardly passed the Heinz factory, and now he wanted to talk about relationships. She wasn't sure which was worse – the relationship questions or the questions about Jim. Couldn't quite tell what he was really after. In which direction his sights were set. How did she get herself boxed into this corner?

'Don't you ever worry about the repeat patterns?' he persisted.

'What?'

'The repeat patterns. The cycles you can't break. Ending up like your parents.'

'I'm hardly going to end up like Jim. I'm not going to turn into an undercover cop.'

'Yes, but do you have a clear idea of where you are going? If you want to move forward, you've got to be able to leave the past behind.'

She shivered, worn down already from the effort of keeping the conversation from sliding off track into the undergrowth. 'How many people,' she said, 'do you think Agatha Christie murdered on a train?'

He screwed up his face. 'That's a tough one. I'm not sure I know the answer to that. I'll have to work it out.'

She tried to decipher the black letters of a sign as they steamed through a station. Milton Keynes, she guessed. Milton Keynes: home of the Open University's headquarters.

'Did I tell you his explanation for his sudden urge to return to Orkney?' she asked.

'No.'

'He told Liz he wanted to go somewhere quiet so he could have some space to think about leaving the Force; taking early retirement and doing something else.'

'Is he old enough to retire? He's still in his forties, isn't he?'

'Forty-six. Policemen always find some way of retiring early. Health grounds. Something like that.'

'You said he was thinking of doing something else.'

'History degree with the Open University. He started a course on the early Middle Ages years ago, but never finished.

He's always been interested in all that stuff, the Norsemen. And I suppose Orkney is a good place to go to rekindle an enthusiasm for history. But I still can't really believe the Open University story. It just seems unlikely to me.'

'Perhaps he really is thinking about doing it. It's not that unlikely. It's a bit of a classic, isn't it? Affairs, the Open University, early retirement. It all adds up. Mid-life crisis.'

She shook her head, stuck her hand into her backpack, rummaged, fished out the book of Viking history that Ruth had given her, waved it at Tom. 'I wonder whether he's been doing his homework on the Vikings,' she said. 'We can test him on the drive to Scrabster tomorrow.'

'What's his starter for ten going to be then?'

'Women in the Viking age.' She scanned the index, found what she was looking for and flicked to the page.

'Listen to this. "Women had little formal authority in Norse society, but there is some evidence that they could achieve power and high status by becoming a priestess in the religious cults of the Vanir. Norse mythology contains two, sometimes warring, pantheons of gods. Odin and his descendants formed the Aesir, the gods of war, law and death. The Vanir, to which Freyr and the goddess Freyja originally belonged, were the rulers of the earth, nature and fertility."'

She leaned over the side of the bunk, dangling upside-down, to see if Tom was paying attention. He was fiddling with a hole in the toe of his sock. She hauled herself back up, continued anyway. '"Vanir cults emphasized the importance of veneration of the ancestors and encouraged the living to visit them in their burial mounds, invoke their spirits and ask them to ensure the rebirth of the land and the continuity of the family."'

She glanced in the mirror. Tom was studiously picking at his toenail.

'This next bit is really interesting.'

He reached for another miniature whiskey bottle.

'"Freyja was the High Priestess of the Vanir. She was believed to be able to take on the form of a falcon and travel vast distances. Freyja's name was linked with a kind of witchcraft and prophecy known as seiõr. Female practitioners of seiõr would erect a tall platform on which a seeress would sit, sing spells and fall into trance induced by hallucinogenic drugs. At the close of the ceremony, the seeress would be able to answer questions put to her by others participating in the ritual."'

Tom shrugged indifferently.

'That's what I would have been if I was a Viking,' she said, 'a priestess in the cult of Freyja. A drug-smoking seeress and a practitioner of witchcraft.' She gave Tom's reflection a hard stare.

'I'm not disputing it,' he said.

'Apparently, archaeologists in Scandinavia have unearthed all these graves of women who have been buried with their magic tools. Metal staffs. Animal bones. Pouches with henbane seeds and cannabis.'

He drained the final drops of the last bottle, slumped back against the pillows. She gave up. Closed the book, returned it to her bag.

He yawned and, as he stretched his arms behind his head, she glimpsed a notebook with a mottled yellow cover in his shirt-pocket, a biro stuck through its spiral binding.

'How's your search for work going anyway?' she asked.

He replied groggily, 'I applied for a six-month placement on a local newspaper and I heard yesterday that I've got an interview the week after next.'

'So you'll be speaking truth to power, holding the elected representatives of Manchester to account, exposing their corruption and lies?'

'Something like that.'

She paused. 'How do you get a career in journalism then?'

'There's no real career path. You just have to work at it. Make a bit of a name for yourself. Get noticed. Get a by-line. Get a story on the front page. I might try doing a bit of investigative stuff. See if I can dig up something that might interest one of the nationals.'

'Good plan.' She hoped it wasn't obvious that she didn't have the faintest idea whether it was a good plan or not.

'What do you write in the notebook then?' She nodded at his top-pocket.

'Oh, just bits and pieces. Things people say that interest me or conversations I overhear. Details. It's what writers do. Writers and journalists.'

She was pointedly silent. He didn't seem to notice.

'You know...' His words were running into one another now, the miniature bottles adding up, taking their toll. He stalled. He started again. 'You know, I've often thought that there are a lot of similarities between journalists and cops.'

'Why is that then?'

'Because they're all outsiders. They sit on the sidelines, and watch what other people are doing rather than taking part in the action. Journalists and policemen are observers, note-takers, reporters.'

'So you have to be careful in the presence of either,' she said. 'Because anything you say might be taken down and used in evidence against you later.'

He mumbled something incomprehensible.

Journalists and cops, cops and journalists. She tried to recall who else had made that comparison. Perhaps it was spies and journalists.

'Philby said something like that as well.'

'Kim Philby? Cambridge Five?'

'Yes. In his memoir.'

She had found it among Jim's collection. Essential reading for every spy, lessons in tradecraft from the master double-agent; drop-boxes, coded messages, secret signals. She had noted them in Philby, and ticked them off against the strange scenes and actions she had occasionally witnessed when she was out and about with Jim.

'I should read Philby,' said Tom. 'He was a journalist, wasn't he?'

'Yes. Foreign correspondent. He said something about journalists and spies being separated by a fine and not always visible line when it comes to their methods for obtaining information. Journalists are supposed to use legal methods. Spies, well, they don't bother.'

'Do you read a lot of books about spies?'

'No.' And detectives. Crime fiction. Had a graph in her head: x axis – outward appearance, tics, tradecraft; y axis – inner motivation, beliefs, dysfunctions. She plotted all the fictional coppers and spooks on the graph, mapping them against Jim.

The clunk of the wheels on the tracks rolled through her mind.

'What are you thinking?' he asked. Again.

'Nothing.'

'You must be thinking something.'

She turned to the window and spotted the diamond light of the Dog Star, trailing them across the storm-cleared sky.

'I'm thinking I hope you're not going to write anything about Jim's work in that notebook of yours.'

'Of course I'm not going to write anything about Jim's work. Anyway, I can't see there is much to write about. Where's the story? Undercover cop possibly involved in covert surveillance of unions and left-wing groups. Not exactly a gripping headline. Everybody knows about it anyway.' He pushed his feet under the tightly tucked sheets.

He was right, she thought. No story there, everyone knew about that anyway.

'Do you think,' he said, 'he might be having an affair with one of his contacts?'

She hesitated, something about the tone of his voice set an alarm bell ringing. 'Dunno. Not something I've ever really thought about.'

'I bet he tries it on with some of his contacts.'

'I suppose any cop who was watching a left-wing group would have to try it on with some of his contacts. I mean if he didn't he'd soon be found out, wouldn't he, because he would be the odd-man out. Oh look, there's a bloke not trying to have it off with anything that moves; he must be an undercover cop.'

She was finding it hard to sound jokey. Jesus, she really would have to be more guarded about what she said to Tom.

'That's probably why he's thinking about leaving the Force,' he said. 'He was caught with his trousers down.'

'Don't you ever let up?'

He didn't respond.

'Why did you ask me to come with you anyway?' he asked eventually, a note of sulkiness in his voice. 'Why didn't you ask Becky?'

'I did ask Becky but she couldn't make it. And I couldn't think of anyone else who I could persuade to spend a week with Jim and then you phoned. So I asked you.'

'Thanks.'

'Pleasure.'

'Anyway, I'm going to try and get some sleep now. I need my eight hours.'

He turned his back on her.

The compartment lit up and darkened again as they passed empty stations and plough scarred fields, leaving the south behind. The comforting chunkety-chunk of the train on its tracks was making her eyelids droop when the metallic screech of grinding wheels and the intoxicating scent of brake oil filled the air and yanked her back to consciousness. She heard men shouting, saw torchlight beams sweeping the cabin ceiling. She panicked. She was back at Greenham. Inside the base. By the telephone cable box. The patrol was chasing her.

She had unearthed the secrets of the bunker's communications system almost unintentionally from an off-duty Ministry of Defence policeman in a pub in Newbury. She was on her way back with Becky from one of their day trips to Greenham and had stopped off for a quick drink. He was standing at the bar. Young. Bit laddish. He had started chatting to them while they were waiting to be served. He must have thought they were locals. The smoky atmosphere of the pub must have covered the smell of the campfire in their hair and clothes, because he had told them that he was part of one of the patrols that guarded the exterior of the perimeter fence at the base. He started teasing Sam, guessed she wasn't eighteen. Not that anybody took much notice of the laws about the legal age of drinking. He was digging, trying to find out exactly how old she was. She had told him – just to change the subject – that her dad used to be in the army and now he was a cop. Of course, that had got him going; it was like a masonic hand-shake, a sign that she was one of them. So he had opened up, fed her some of his stories. Boasted about his exploits. Trying to impress.

She had asked him about the bunker, the command and control centre inside the base that was the subject of much feverish speculation among the women around the campfire. He had told her it was an impenetrable fortress that housed the legendary hotline to the White House; the phone line the President used to give the order to light the blue touchpaper of the cruise missiles. Then, without any prompting from her at all, he had revealed the chink in the bunker's armour: the telephone cables. The US officials had installed their own communications system because they didn't trust the assholes at British Telecom. He had laughed when he said that – assholes – and she had laughed too. Although now, he had added, the American military had been forced to revert temporarily to the British system because their imported, high-tech equipment was suffering from too many glitches. Voltage incompatibilities leading to long-term damage apparently. So the American military had closed the US system down for overhaul. Of course, they had radio and other forms of communications too. But the landline, the legendary hotline to the White House, was currently routed through the ageing British Telecom underground telephone cables.

She had smiled. And he had casually added that maybe the Americans did have a point about British Telecom, because the White House hotline was easily accessible in the Crookham Common end of the base via an above-ground telephone junction cabinet. The cables had originally been installed in the sixties, when Greenham was little more than a barracks for RAF personnel. The cabinet was standard practice, in case additional lines were required. It had just been left there. A green metal box, right by the perimeter fence.

Becky had listened in astonishment to the policeman's story, open-mouthed amazement at the ease with which Sam had extracted this ridiculously sensitive piece of information. The policeman had caught sight of Becky's slack jaw and immediately realized he had made a mistake. Given too much away. Much too much. Sam saw his features drop into lockdown as it dawned on him he was chatting up the enemy. He had walked off abruptly, pint glass trembling perceptibly in his grasp.

They had returned to Greenham in May, just after their exams had finished, on a demob high. Becky had suggested they drive round to the Crookham Common end of the base and take a look for the telephone cable cabinet. Sam had been happy to fall in with Becky's plan. She enjoyed roaming the common at night, listening for owls. Didn't think there was much risk of being caught. It was ridiculously easy to break in at the far north-eastern end of the base, where it merged almost seamlessly with the scrappy woodlands. Everybody knew that.

They didn't need a torch; it was a clear night and a waxing moon lit their track across the common to the twelve-foot perimeter fence. It didn't take them long to locate a section that had already been cut by a previous invader from the camp and hastily repaired by the Ministry of Defence police. Pliers were sufficient to reopen the hole. They checked for patrols and crawled through to the other side, hands and knees in the sandy soil and tangled undergrowth. Sam hadn't really expected to find anything, assumed it would be a quick jaunt. In and out. Adrenalin hit. Triumphant high. But Becky had insisted on scouting around and had spotted the refrigerator-sized military green metal cabinet squatting behind the fluorescent yellow of a gorse bush. Easy to find if you knew what you were looking for. It had to be the telephone cable box. What else could it be? Becky had wanted a closer look. They traipsed over the heather. They were standing right in front of the cabinet, scrutinizing the locks on its doors, when they heard the dogs baying.

Torch-beams directed at them. Lights jumping around as the patrol ran along the perimeter. Men shouting. Ordering them to stand away. They had sprinted back to the fence. Scrabbled though. Slipped among the silver birches of the common. Melting into the moon shadows of the night.

Becky had been exhilarated. She was full of plans to return and sabotage the cabinet. Sam had been unnerved. Panic-stricken. She tried to talk Becky down while she silently worried that the policeman would have reported his slip-up to his superiors straight away, recounted his pub meeting with the copper's daughter. The information he had given away was far too sensitive to let it lie. They were probably making enquiries already. Putting two and two together. Trawling through photographs in the police files on the camp. Looking for her face. Alerting all forces. She was plagued by the sense that she had breached some unspoken boundary, abused the fact that she was a copper's daughter. She couldn't contain her anxieties. The crosswire of the fence was making random appearances in her dreams and she would wake, sweating, uncertain whether she had been inside looking out or outside looking in.

She sat up, banged her head, realized it was only night workmen repairing the tracks and lay back on her scratchy pillow. She couldn't get back to sleep. She needed to pee. She tried to ignore the urge but she knew it was useless. She levered herself down over the edge of her bunk, searched with her toe for a safe spot on the bed below, made it to the ground and fumbled her way in the semi-darkness through the compartment door. The overhead bulbs cast a stark, surreal light along the corridor. She stumbled right towards the toilet, glanced back over her shoulder and jumped when she saw a guard leaning against the wall at the end of the carriage; sleeves rolled, arms folded, gazing into space. He looked up, barely acknowledged her through hooded eyes, made her feel uneasy.

She closed the toilet door, double-checked the lock. The stench of urine made her gag. She washed her hands, trying not to step in the piss-puddles covering the floor, and caught sight of her face in the clouded mirror above the sink. Her image had a greenish tinge: a ghoulish doppelgänger. She lurched out in to the corridor again. The guard was still propped up against the carriage wall, gawking at nothing. She noticed a small bare patch on his hairy forearm that made him look like a sick monkey; a shaved spot for a scabby new tattoo of something dark. Scorpion. She pushed her way hurriedly into the compartment, locking the door firmly behind her. She accidentally trod on Tom's overhanging leg as she clambered back into her bunk. He stirred and asked whether they had passed Manchester yet.

'You're on the wrong track,' she whispered.

She stared at the ceiling through whiskey-blurred eyes, saw the outline of a scorpion in its crosshatch patterns and wondered how long the guard been standing outside their compartment. Whether he had been listening to their conversation. Wondered what on earth Jim was doing. How she managed to end up going on holiday with a reprobate undercover cop, a pistol and an aspirant hack on a quest for a headline. She pulled the blanket over her head. The train rattled north. On the run to Orkney.

CHAPTER 6

A SEA OF blue dawn mists hung low over the cutting. She was almost close enough to touch the heather-tufted slopes rising steeply above the single track. Tom wormed his way out of his bunk and stood behind her.

'The Highlands,' he said.

'Aviemore, to be precise,' she replied.

She saw the silhouette of an antlered stag up above them on a spur, poised, ready for flight. 'Look.'

'What?'

'Stag.' She pointed, but it had vanished.

The train strained as it started its descent along the incline, then rolled into the station and stopped shy of the buffers. Passengers swarmed on to the platform in the grey light. Jim appeared from nowhere.

'Follow me,' he said authoritatively as he marched off, puffing dragon breath into the cold morning air, skilfully dodging any early-morning social niceties.

'Good morning, Dad,' she shouted after him. He ignored her, heading along the platform. The Cortina had already been offloaded from the trailer and was in the car park, its decrepit state exaggerated by the two gleaming metallic saloons parked on either side. Jim strolled off to collect the keys from the guard.

'We've got about six hours to reach Scrabster and catch the ferry,' he said on his return, glancing at his watch, 'which should be plenty of time, but we've got to cross Caithness, so I don't want to bugger about. No shilly-shallying.'

She clambered into the passenger seat. He dumped the haversack at her feet, underneath the glove department. She retracted her legs, didn't want her feet to touch the bag, wasn't taking any chances with lethal weapons. She fumbled with the seat belt.

'Look sharpish,' Jim snapped. 'No fannying around.'

Tom clambered clumsily into the back seat. Sam wound down the window a smidgen to let in some fresh air, smiled to herself, enjoying the sense of escape under a vast sky, rolling clouds. Leaving the south far behind.

'Viking country,' said Jim as they set off, heading into the streets of Inverness. It felt like a pre-emptive attack, a challenge to anyone who might be thinking about trying to swing a punch at his cover story.

'Is that what you're going to do your history degree in then – the Dark Ages?'

She caught Tom's eye in the mirror and tried unsuccessfully not to snigger.

Jim said, 'If you are going to take the piss, you really should try and do it without giggling like a three-year-old. What's so funny about the idea of me doing a degree anyway?'

She didn't answer.

'Why shouldn't I try something different? I've had enough of this malarkey. Policing. I've been at it for too long. It grinds you down after a while: all the criticism, the snarky comments. Nobody has a good word to say about coppers. Whatever you do, it's wrong. Damned if you do, damned if you don't. Pisses me off. They've got some early retirement deal going at the moment and I'm eligible. I've done a lot of years; put a lot of dosh into the pension pot, so I'd be a bit of an idiot not to consider it. But then, if I retire now, I'm going to have to find something else to occupy myself.'

'How about golf?' she suggested.

He ignored her. 'I'd like to avoid the private security company trap. I've seen too many of my mates fall into that one. It's not a dignified way to go. I don't want to end up being a private dick.'

'Is being a private dick any worse than being a public dick?'

Tom snorted in the back. Jim scowled and for a moment she thought he was going to lose it, but then his frown softened at the edges. Holiday mood perhaps.

'Yes. I would say it is worse than being a public dick. When you're a private dick, you have to do what the money tells you to do. At least if you're a public dick you have some sense that you're there to do the right thing, whatever the profit margin.'

She squinted at him as he watched the road and noticed his hands feeding the steering wheel round corners. Advanced driving course for policemen. Tics, habits; the signs were there if you knew where to look. Some things were impossible to disguise.

'Bastards,' she said.

'What?' said Jim.

'Vikings. They were bastards. All that raping and pillaging.'

Jim shook his head. 'Everyone thinks they were mindless thugs, but there was more to them than that.'

'What good did they do then?'

'They were explorers, entrepreneurs. They did a lot to open up important trade routes, establish new markets. Early capitalists.'

Sam pulled a dismissive face. 'Yes, but you can't use the economic ends to justify all the violence.'

'I'm not trying to justify it. I'm explaining it, saying the violence wasn't totally gratuitous. They didn't just kick a few heads in. They produced. Traded. Farmed the land. Norsemen settled all over this part of Scotland. Caithness,' he added. 'Orkney too, of course.'

'So when did they arrive in Orkney?'

'The first raids on northern England were in the late eighth century. But the archaeologists reckon they were settling in Orkney before that.'

Tom joined in the conversation from the back. 'Was anybody already living there when they arrived?'

'The Picts. Small-scale farmers. Christians. The Neolithic people who built Skara Brae and the stone circles were long gone. They come from a much earlier time. Nearly four thousand years earlier than the Vikings in fact.'

'Although in some ways,' Sam said, 'the Vikings had more in common with the Neolithic people than with the Christian Picts. They probably had similar beliefs to the stone circle builders – ancestor worship, fertility rites. Magic. Do you think the invading Vikings converted the Picts back to paganism and Odin worship?'

'Some people argue that the Vikings took over Orkney's Neolithic monuments, the stone circles and the burial chambers, and used them for their own religious rituals. They say that's why you find Norse runes all over the ancient stones. But nobody really knows what happened to the Picts when the Vikings arrived. It's one of the great mysteries of Orkney's history. There isn't much evidence to go on. No battle corpses. No signs of fighting. But then there's no mention anywhere of surviving natives either. No written record of cohabitation. Only a few pre-Norse place names to serve as a reminder of the times before the Norsemen arrived. So it's all speculation. Annihilation or assimilation.'

'And which do you think is the most likely theory, war or peace?' Tom asked.

'Well, I don't think the Vikings would have wiped the original inhabitants out because they needed people to work the land for them.' Jim checked Tom in the mirror. 'And maybe they were slightly in awe of the Picts if they thought they were the descendants of the monument builders. So I'm inclined to think—'

His hypothesis was cut short as he jammed his foot on the brake in order to avoid ramming the boot of the car ahead.

'You've got to be kidding.' His irascibility surfaced rapidly. 'It can't be a traffic jam. We're in the middle of bloody nowhere.'

'We're not,' Sam said. 'We're in the middle of Inverness.'

He wound his window down and leaned out to find out what was happening. Nothing. The Cortina inched forward. Jim swore under his breath. Someone was taking the mickey. It was a total bloody shambles. She was afraid of catching Tom's eye in the mirror in case it set her off.

Ten minutes of crawling and cursing brought them to a crossroads. An out-of-order set of traffic lights. Two traffic cops, young and female, were mismanaging the junction, ineffectually waving their white-gloved hands in the air and miserably failing to keep the cars moving.

'Fucking amateurs,' Jim muttered.

The Cortina stuttered up to the lights and stopped in front of an outstretched hand attached to the arm of a frazzled looking WPC. Jim ferreted in the glove compartment, found what he was looking for, thrust his police identity card out of the window. She'd never seen him do that before. She watched him waving the card around; it almost seemed as if he were trying to act the part of a cop.

Jim jabbed a finger menacingly at the WPCs. 'What the fuck do you think you're playing at?'

Passing pedestrians turned and stared. Sam attempted to disappear, hunched her shoulders and buried herself in the front seat. She could sense Tom behind, observing the scene with detached interest. The WPCs froze, unable to speak, caught on the barbed wire of Jim's temper, faces reddened with humiliation, glassy eyes. Sam willed them not to cry.

Jim yelled. 'You've got as much intelligence as two piles of shit.' He gripped the wheel angrily, put his foot on the accelerator, spun the wheels and sped across the junction. Tom was silent in the rear.

'Do two piles of shit have more or less intelligence than one pile of shit?' she asked.

'Will you do something useful instead of making smart-arse comments? Have a look for the sodding road map; see if you can give me some directions to Scrabster.'

She rummaged under the seat, pulled out a battered AA guide to Britain. 'How did the Vikings navigate the seas? They couldn't have used the sun because half the time it's too cloudy up here.'

Nobody answered. She gazed wearily out of the window; a shaft of light illuminated a road sign to Thurso along the A9, the route across Caithness.

She absorbed the passing scenery and found a strange comfort in the desolate landscape of the Flow Country. It was less dramatic than the mountains and glens of the Highlands, but the endless brown moors and the vast leaden skies had an alluring bleakness. The Cortina, though, was struggling with the plateau, buffeted by the crosswinds, growling in response to Jim's angry foot on the accelerator. Jim was oblivious to the car's protestations. A never-ending stretch of fast, straight road was punctuated by a clank of metal on tarmac. Tom enquired politely from the back, 'Did something just drop off the car?'

Jim grunted dismissively. The car's rear emitted an alarming wet farting sound. Sam glanced over her shoulder, pulled a face at Tom. Jim ignored them, ignored the noise, pushed his foot down harder. The futtering became more insistent. Bemused sheep lifted their heads from their incessant nibbling and bleated as the Cortina passed.

'Shit.' Jim swerved the car towards the heather lapping the roadside, squealed to an emergency stop, threw off his seat belt, grabbed his haversack, leaped out of the car, slammed the door, stomped off at speed over the peaty soil into the damp emptiness. Sam and Tom peered through the car windows out over the moorland and watched the small dot of Jim, disappearing into nowhere.

'What was that all about?' Tom asked.

'He's always bad in the mornings. I suppose he's annoyed because there's something wrong with the car and he doesn't know what to do about it.'

'He's not going to solve the problem by storming off like that.' She shrugged.

'Where do you think he's going?' Tom asked.

'Maybe he's gone to look for a Viking burial site.'

'He was certainly putting up a good show on the old early Middle Ages. I thought he was quite convincing back there with his theories about the Vikings.'

'Did you? I thought he was overdoing it a bit with his revisionist history lecturer act.' She wrinkled her nose. 'What are we going to do, then?'

'Well, the car is still moving even if it is making an

embarrassing noise. So, if Jim doesn't come back soon, I can drive us back down to Inverness.'

She clocked the ignition. 'You can't. He's taken the keys with him.'

'Bastard.'

They tumbled out of the car on to the heather. The wind tugged at Sam's coat. She stretched out her arms, leaned into the gusts, a kestrel soaring over the moor, searching the hollows for shadows and movements, waiting to dive. She felt Tom staring at her quizzically. She put her arms back down at her sides, returned to earth.

She said, 'Have you ever been hanging around in a pub and had some dodgy-looking bloke sidle up and tell you he's an ex-member of the SAS?'

Tom nodded.

'And he says he's done that thing where they drop you in the middle of nowhere without any food or equipment and then they come back three days later to see if you're still alive?'

Tom nodded again.

'Well, Jim once told me his lot trained with the SAS and he passed the three-day survival test.'

'So is he a dodgy-looking bloke who hangs around in bars making up stories or do you think he was telling the truth?'

She poked the heather with her toe. 'Possibly both. But if he was telling the truth, we could be here for a long time.'

'We could test our own survival skills. Head off into the wilderness and see if we can make it back to civilization before we die from lack of caffeine. He who dares wins. Or she,' he added quickly. 'They who dare win. We'd make it. We've got a map.'

'We've got your emergency rations as well. We could crack open the Hobnobs.'

'I've eaten them all already.'

'What? The whole packet? When?'

'In Inverness, when we were in the traffic jam. I was hungry. I wasn't sure we'd make it out alive and I thought it was a pity to waste them.'

She had noticed he was being suspiciously quiet in the back seat.

'In that case, we're stuffed.' She gave him a reproachful glare. 'Whatever happened to comradeship? Solidarity?'

'It's all about survival of the fittest. You've got to be tough to make it. You've got to be able to compete if you want to win the prizes.'

She tutted disparagingly.

'That's the trouble with us lefties,' he said. 'We're not competitive enough. Not ambitious enough. We wouldn't last a day in the city.' He fixed his sight on the horizon. 'Jim would be okay in the survival stakes. He's obviously pretty fit, judging by the speed he managed to keep up when he stormed off. Was he ever in the army?'

'Yes. But I've never been quite sure what he did. He's a bit fuzzy about the details. All I know is he signed up when he was sixteen and was sent off somewhere hot, Africa I think, where he learned how to make do with little more than a couple of sheets of hard toilet paper and some dry biscuits. And his toes were blown off when he trod on a landmine.'

'His toes? Wouldn't he have lost his whole leg in a landmine explosion?'

'Landmine,' she repeated. 'That's what he's always said anyway. Landmine.'

'That's an unlikely story.'

She felt herself tumbling, hitting an unexpected dip, engulfed by greyness, uncertainty, the fear that there was nothing solid, no roots touching soil, nothing living, nothing genuine about her life. Nothing to hold to break the fall. They lapsed into silence, both of them staring across the moorland, lost in their own thoughts.

Ten minutes. Twenty. Half an hour. It was beyond a joke. A small speck appeared on a ridge out on the edge of the world. Sam watched, hypnotized by the fuzzy form gliding over the boglands in a seemingly effortless forward movement, growing larger and larger.

'Silencer,' Jim announced as he climbed back into the car.

'What?' she demanded.

'It's the silencer,' he repeated. Impatient. As if he'd just nipped round the rear of the car for a couple of minutes to have a look and hadn't actually stormed off in the middle of nowhere without explanation.

'Must have dropped off. But we'll make it to Scrabster without it anyway.'

He pulled away from the heather, pushed his foot down. She caught a faint whiff of whisky.

'I'll take it to a garage when we get to Orkney,' Jim continued. 'See if a mechanic can do anything about the noise. Can you drive, Tom?' Jim made eye contact with Tom in the mirror. Tom smiled, clearly relieved to be addressed in a straightforward manner with no obvious sneer.

'I passed my test when I was seventeen.'

'Not as useless as Sam then.'

'Well, maybe if you'd offered to help pay for the lessons,' she said, 'like everybody else's dads, I might have learned by now.'

Jim ignored her. He said to Tom, 'Why don't you use this car while we're in Orkney? That'll give you two a bit of independence. I can borrow another car from my mate in Stromness.'

Jim and Tom started chatting about problems with cars as if they were both expert mechanics. She watched in the mirror and noticed that Tom appeared to be taking it at face value, this man-to-man chat. She glanced sideways at Jim and spotted the corner of Jim's mouth forming a sly smile that made her wonder why he was so keen to offload the Cortina. Was he setting them up as a decoy? Allowing them to drive around in the hard-to-miss noisy old Cortina while he slipped off silently in a less conspicuous vehicle? She sighed. You couldn't even take his kind offers at face value; he really was a bastard.

Jim slung the car around the hairpin bends, feeding the wheel furiously, zigzagging down to the coast. 'Don't want to miss the ferry,' he said.

She clung to the door handle, reluctant to upset the delicate balance of Jim's fragile temper again, closed her eyes as they swerved around an acutely sharp loop in the road, barely hanging on to the corner. 'Dad. Do you have a licence to kill?'

He fed the wheel aggressively. 'Yes. Do you have a licence to be totally bloody irritating?'

'Actually I do.'

'Well it's been revoked. So you'd better watch it.'

A ray of sun pierced the cloud blanket and lit up the Cortina as they advanced noisily over the final stretch of the headland and descended to Scrabster, its granite harbour walls like fingers clutching at the outflowing tide. A line of vehicles was already waiting to drive on to the ferry. The rickety old *St Ola* that had ferried them across the Pentland Firth every summer of her childhood had been replaced with a larger, roll-on roll-off of the same name. She felt a wave of nostalgia; it had always been a bit of a thrill watching the cars being hoisted on to the boat by crane, the exciting touch-and-go tension as the Cortina was lifted up in the air like a toy and swung over the quay into the hold.

'Pity. I wouldn't have minded if they'd dropped it in the water this time,' Jim said, as he surveyed the new ferry. 'At least I could have claimed the insurance. Still, the old banger might prove to be useful while we're here.' He smiled to no one in particular.

Despite Jim's disappearing act out on the moors, they still had more than an hour to spare. Jim announced he wanted to talk to a man about a dog so Tom and Sam headed to a café built up against the rocky headland, pounding across the flagstones, pushing against the strengthening wind that was whipping anything light and loose into horizontal lines, thrumming the cables of tightly moored lobster boats. They reached an oilskin-clad fisherman pulling the slack out of a wrack-covered rope, feeding it into a neat coil on the quayside.

Tom stopped. 'Is it rough out there today?'

The fisherman didn't bother to look up from his task.

She elbowed Tom in the ribs. 'It's always rough in the Pentland Firth,' she whispered. 'Didn't you know?'

She ran off, smirking as she climbed the wooden stairs to the café; her black overcoat flapped behind her like a witch's cape. At the top she turned, stared commandingly at the sea beyond the harbour walls and conjured up the sun and the waves and the wind. A herring gull squawked aggressively and a splat of green shit strafed the plank next to her foot. 'Missed,' she shouted into the air. It squawked again.

Tom joined her at a table by the window.

'That's how the professional does it,' she said indistinctly, her mouth thick with oozing crab sandwich. She nodded her head in the direction of the harbour. Jim was visible in the distance, distinct yet blending in with his surroundings, always at home in the hinterlands, the places between land and sea, weaving his way around the ropes and the fishermen; talking, listening, laughing. She wondered whether it was the product of being in the army, his ability to conjure up an instant camaraderie with strangers.

'It must be his Scottish accent,' said Tom, echoing her thoughts.

'Do you think Jim has a Scottish accent?'

'Actually, no. He uses short vowels, so he's obviously not southern, but it would be hard to pinpoint exactly where he came from on the basis of his accent. Are you sure he's from Glasgow?'

'That's what I've always been told.' In the corner of her eye she spotted a massive bonxie high up in the sky being hectored by a flock of terns.

'Haven't you ever met any of Jim's relatives?'

'No.'

'Don't you think that's odd?'

'Not really.'

'So you've never seen a picture of any of them?'

She hesitated. In fact, she had seen a picture of one of Jim's brothers. It was in a newspaper of all places, years ago when she was about nine, and she had come downstairs one Friday morning and spotted a redtop lying open on the kitchen table. It only caught her attention because Liz didn't usually allow tabloids in the house. BUST UP! the headline declared. Beneath the bold type was a small blurry picture of a man who looked a bit like Jim, and below that was a large clear picture of a topless woman and two paragraphs explaining that Ian Coyle had been sentenced to do time at Her Majesty's Pleasure for his part in a fracas involving bars, booze and birds. Including the one in the picture who worked as a topless model for the *Sun*. Liz had pointed at the fuzzy image of the man. 'That's your uncle, in case anybody asks,' Liz had said. As if they would. 'Your other uncle is just as bad,' she had added when she passed through again, fussing around, getting ready for work. Sam recounted the story to Tom through a spluttering of breadcrumbs. And as she did so, the picture of Jim's crashed van on the front page of the *Southern Advertiser* appeared in her mind. Her stomach churned slightly, for no clearly discernible reason, except the vague sense that there was something of a repeat pattern here that she hadn't noticed before.

The snippet amused Tom. 'So you come from a long line of bar-brawlers. I suppose that might explain why he doesn't stay in touch with his relatives if half of them have got criminal records. But if it were my family I think I would just be open about it all. I can't see the point of keeping secrets.'

She licked a blob of mayonnaise from her finger. 'All families have secrets. I'm just more aware of the secrets than most people. At least I know there are lots of things I don't know about my dad.'

Tom pulled his sceptical expression. It had been appearing with increasing frequency. The investigative journalist look, she decided. Question everything.

She said, 'Did you know that every time there's a major plane crash they always find the body of at least one man whose partner had no idea he was on the flight?'

He raised an eyebrow. 'Who told you that?'

'Jim.'

He laughed and they slurped their coffee in amiable silence, watching Jim going about his business. She noticed him tilt his hand to check his watch on the inside of his wrist; she was about to point out the almost imperceptible action to Tom, tell him it was a sure sign of military training, when Jim turned towards the café window and beckoned them down. As if he had known all along they were watching him perform.

They sat in the Cortina, waiting for the man in the fluorescent jacket to direct them on to the ferry. She put her foot on a black plastic bag lying next to the haversack on the floor under her seat, prodded it with her heel. It twitched. She emitted the first note of a scream, cut it abruptly when she caught sight of Jim smirking.

'What's in that bag?' she demanded. 'It moved.'

'Crab. What did you think I was talking to the fishermen about?'

She frowned. 'Is it still alive?'

'Of course.'

'Won't it die if you leave it in that bag?'

'Should be okay until we get to Orkney. I've put a damp cloth over it. That normally helps.'

'Seafood paella,' she suggested.

'Nah,' he said. 'No point messing about with seafood. If it's fresh, eat it straight. And if it isn't fresh, don't bother eating it.'

She nodded slowly. The rear lights of the car in front glowed red and the line moved forwards.

'Are you going to boil it alive?' she asked.

'Yes.'

'That's cruel.'

'It doesn't hurt.'

'How do you know?'

He huffed, exasperated, and steered the car towards the gaping mouth of the ferry.

'Only a cop would claim it doesn't hurt to be plunged in boiling water,' she said.

Jim gave her a filthy glare and she feared for a moment he was about to wallop her, but the man in the yellow jacket was gesticulating, making urgent turning signs in the air with his finger and he had to keep both hands on the wheel. They clanked over the metal flaps bridging the gap between harbour and ferry, a glimpse of roiling green sea churned by propellers below.

'If you have to be a smart-arse,' he said, 'I'd try not to do it while you're sitting next to open water.'

She peered down at the narrow boarding bridge. 'You're closer to the edge than me.'

'Possibly. But I'm professionally trained. I'm prepared to deal with the consequences of my smart-arsery and I'm not sure you are.'

She shrugged and, as she did so, some instinct, a bristle, made her look back. She glimpsed a movement in the furthest edge of her vision; a dim blur advancing across the headland. A car? Or was it just the shadow of a scudding cloud? She craned her neck, trying to get a better view. But it was too late; the Cortina was swallowed down into the cavernous belly of the *St Ola*, engulfed by the miasma of engine oil and darkness.

CHAPTER 7

Stromness filled the view, the gable ends of sombre houses hiding their faces from the wind. The Cortina breached the peace as Jim rolled off the ferry, steered around the quayside, through the narrow streets and out into the farmland beyond. Sam was surprised by how much was familiar, how easily she could navigate the green and grey contours without conscious effort. Past and present, living and dead, woven together in fields and hills; ghosts of summer holidays past playing among the standing stones, whalebone arches, burial mounds. Around every bend, the sea appeared. She licked the salt from her lips, stole a sideways peek at Jim and wondered whether he was happy to be revisiting old haunts. His mouth was set in a grim slash across his face, his eyes fixed on the road. She checked the wing mirror; the road stretched away behind emptily to the straggling edges of Stromness. The backward glance; it was becoming a bit of a nervous tic.

They found Nethergate halfway up a hill behind Tirlsay, a crofter's dwelling long and low, perpendicular to the road. It exuded melancholia, a sense of abandonment. Although, as they stood in the gravel courtyard waiting for Jim to locate the keys, she noticed small signs of life everywhere: a manky donkey looking sorry for itself in the thistle-filled meadow behind the croft; a sleek black cat patrolling the garden perimeter; a dumpy bird with a black executioner's hood glaring malevolently from its rooftop perch. The bird cawed as Jim returned, waving the key he had retrieved from one of the outhouses clustered at the far side of the courtyard.

'Hooded crow,' he said. 'You have to be careful here. There are eyes everywhere. Corvids: rooks, crows, ravens. Intelligent birds. But a bit mischievous. Not to be trusted.'

Jim grinned and the crow cocked its head on one side, as if it were taking the measure of him.

She asked, 'Who owns the cottage?'

'Bill.'

'Who is Bill?'

'Don't think you ever met him. He only moved up here a couple of years ago. He used to be a policeman. Uniform. Sergeant.'

Of course.

'This is his grandmother's cottage. He inherited it when she died and decided to give up policing, move here, see if he could scrape a living as a smallholder. Then he decided to buy another place over by Stromness. Flatter. More usable land. Kept this place on as a holiday let. Luckily for us, he doesn't get much business before the start of the school holidays.'

'So you know him from the police.' she said.

Jim paused. 'He comes from Glasgow. I went to school with him.' He glanced up at the crow before walking briskly towards the croft, leaving her standing open-mouthed, gobsmacked by his straightforward divulgence about a person from his past.

They followed him into the cramped galley kitchen. Jim opened the window to let in fresh air; the donkey's snout appeared, snuffling hopefully. He offered it one of the apples they had purchased at a corner shop on their way over. It crunched in time to the insistent ticking of a wall clock.

'God, that's really irritating,' she said.

'What?' said Jim.

'That clock. Ticking.'

'Doesn't bother me. I've made my peace with the passing of time.'

He pushed open the door leading off from the kitchen and assessed the adjacent bedroom.

'I'd better take this room then. You two can have the far end.'

Up three concrete steps to a homely sitting room: fraying forest-green cord sofa, two mismatching armchairs with crocheted antimacassars. She picked up the handset of the dirty cream Bakelite telephone sitting on a nest of side-tables. No dial tone on the line; incoming calls only. The shelves on one side of the chimneybreast held the usual holiday cottage odds and sods: a couple of board games, a row of read and discarded paperbacks, a pile of well-thumbed copies of the *Reader's Digest* and something more unusual – an ivory whale's tooth, finely etched with a three-mast ship sailing towards a sea-serpent rearing up from the water.

'Scrimshaw,' said Tom, peering over her shoulder.

She nodded, edged away, sliding along the tiled edge of the hearth to get a closer view of the print hanging above the mantelpiece. It looked like an illustration from a children's book, *Grimm's Fairy Tales* perhaps. It had that sinister edge: a shadowy streak of horses, hounds and birds chasing across an indigo night sky – a phantom hunt led by a cloaked rider, brimmed hat shielding his face, horn in hand. The image seemed out of place among the conservative homeliness of the rest of the room, a reminder of stormy nights pressing in, the wildness of the wind. She checked Tom; he was examining the reading matter. She backed quietly out of the room, through a short hallway with a door that opened on to the garden. She claimed the dim gable-end room with its one front-facing window, a moth-eaten candlewick-covered bed and a tatty wardrobe. A small mirror hung at an awkward height on one of its doors. She stood on her toes to look at her face, saw her khaki eye staring back at her unblinkingly and, behind her, another mirror on the wall. She shifted position slightly until she found the spot from which she could see a line of faces, reflections of her eye watching into infinity.

Squatting, knees up by her armpits, in a dark, wind-free corner of the furthest barn, next to a rusty Qualcast lawn-mower, she fumbled with a couple of Rizlas, licked the glue strips, pressed them together, ripped open the white stomach of a Silk Cut and disembowelled its contents on to the carefully crafted paper shroud. Balancing her efforts in the palm of one hand, she dug around in her overcoat pocket with the other, pulled out the matchbox and removed the cling film wrapped resinous lump.

Tom screwed his nose as she heated and crumbled. 'Whacky backy. Won't Jim smell it?'

'No. And even if he did, he wouldn't care. It's only a bit of dope.' She struck another Swan Vesta, held it under her hash.

'Does he ever actually arrest anybody for anything?'

She looked up. 'Ow, shit.' The acrid tang of burned skin momentarily filled the air.

'You should be more careful with your drug habits,' Tom said.

*

She blinked in the surreal pink light as they returned outside, lay on her back on the coarse grass of the lawn, searching for the last warmth of the evening sun, extremities tingling. She was sinking into the earth. She was atoms, dust, sediment, sandwiched between sky and sea, nothing more than a thin layer of history. Tom lifted his binoculars and focused over the stunted rose bushes at the panoramic sweep of the Bay of Firth beyond. The mournful notes of a bird's song drifted through the air.

'Curlew,' said Sam.

'You're good on wildlife. That's why you always win Trivial Pursuit, because you can do the green questions,' he said. Accusingly.

'Knowledge of science and nature is not normally considered a form of cheating.'

'Where did you learn all that stuff anyway?'

She was going to tell him that Darwin had been her first crush, filled her with a lifelong desire, compulsion, to classify the flora and fauna around her. She had collected beetles when she was younger; asphyxiated them in a jam jar with torn-up laurel leaves, their corpses kept in a neatly labelled matchbox morgue. She decided against giving him that bit of information.

'Jim used to tell me the names of the birds when we were here every year for our summer holiday. He loves nature, wildlife. He's an instinctive environmentalist. I reckon it's something to do with his Jesuit education. He's been taught to appreciate the order and beauty in all things; he sees the spiritual in nature, he looks beyond the physical reality. I sometimes think that's what makes him a good cop. He sees the shadows and the ghosts.'

Tom snorted derisively. 'Is there anything to look at here other than birds?' he asked.

'You could see if there's anything going on in Tirlsay.'

He swung the bins in the direction of the village, nestling in a coastal dip.

'There's absolutely nothing happening. Oh, hang on. I'm wrong. Someone's just got out of a silver Merc and walked into the post office.'

She tried to lever her head up without moving her body from its comfortable horizontal position, decided it was not worth the effort and lay back on her grass mattress again.

'Does it get dark here at midsummer?' he asked.

'Not really. The sun sets at ten, but it doesn't drop very far below the horizon. There are about six hours of crimson before it reappears. Like a drawn-out sunset. Eternal twilight.'

'So you can see clearly all night.'

'Well, I remember people playing golf at midnight on midsummer's day, but I think it's harder to see clearly in the half-light than in the dark. Eyes can adapt to the dark. In the twilight it's like trying to watch television with a broken aerial; nothing is clear.'

She glanced back at the magenta cloudland building behind the darkening purple hills.

'Still, it's very pretty.'

The clank of pans spilled out through the open kitchen door into the evening air; the gushing of a tap, Jim filling a pot with water.

'Dad, will you shut the door,' she yelled. 'I don't want to hear the crab scream.'

'That's a bloody old wives' tale, you big eejit,' he shouted back. 'Of course they don't scream.'

There was a pause in the pot bashing. A click. The twang of an acoustic guitar wafted around the courtyard – a lament for the lost bones of Tom Paine. Jim's favourite folk song. Hers too.

'Folk music? He likes folk music?' Tom asked.

She nodded.

'Don't you think it's a bit funny?'

'What? The song?'

'No. I didn't mean the song. I meant, don't you think it's funny that an undercover cop likes listening to lefty folk music?'

'Oh. No. Not really. Maybe I'm just used to it.'

She was more than used to it; she was inured to it. She'd had to put up with years of the playground taunts, the snotty-nosed looks from the stockbrokers' kids. 'My mum says your dad is a dirty hippy. So I can't come round to play at your house.' And all she could do was shrug her shoulders and say so what with carefully practised indifference. Always covering for Jim. She gazed down the hill at the shifting light on the bay below, casting dark shadows among the waves like bobbing seals' heads. Or maybe they actually were seals' heads, it was hard to tell in the dusk. A thin scream emanated from the kitchen.

'Did you hear that?' she asked. 'That must be the crab.'

'It was the tape. Why do folk singers have to wail like that? They always sound as if they are suffering from indigestion. Which bit of the Force did you say he worked for anyway?'

'I didn't.'

He focused the binoculars on her. She raised her arm in front of her face to avoid his scrutiny, heaved herself half up and crawled over to the scrubby roses. She scrabbled around among the thorny stalks, examining the sandstone rocks that marked the bed's border and identified a flat-bottomed stone that satisfied her requirements, lifted it, brushed away the millipedes, lugged it over to the centre of the lawn and attempted to balance it upright. It remained standing. She identified another, carried it over, placed it carefully next to the first and sat back on her heels to admire her handiwork.

'What are you doing?'

'Building a stone circle.'

'Oh God. Why?'

Because she was fed up with dodging his bloody questions about Jim.

'It's a shrine to the dead.' She grubbed around the flower-bed, selecting more rocks. 'I'm going to light a bonfire here on midsummer's night to celebrate the solstice and appease the ancestors.'

'You don't even know who half your ancestors are. You wouldn't even recognize most of your nearest relatives if you bumped into them in the street.'

She ignored his sneering tone, stood upright facing the dis-appearing sun and flung her arms open wide. 'I am the High Priestess.'

'You are the queen of the potheads.'

'I am the High Priestess,' she repeated. 'Seeress and wor-shipper of Freyja.'

The sun dipped behind the ridge of the hills, drenching the garden in a sepia wash. Goose pimples formed on her bare flesh, her shoulders hunched instinctively.

She dropped her arms to her sides. 'Midsummer is more depressing than midwinter. It's darker in December, but at least the days are bound to get lighter. Midsummer is like a long goodbye. You can sense in your stomach that it's all down-hill from here, when the nights start to stretch out after the high point of June.'

She shivered, uneasy, suddenly aware that she was exposed out here on the flank of the hill. She felt a prickle in the back of her neck. 'Here, give me the bins a moment.'

'No. I've just spotted a very nice curlew.'

'Seriously. Let me have them. It feels like someone is watching us. I want to check.'

He puffed his cheeks as he handed her the binoculars. 'Here you are then.'

She scanned the coastline, swept the hills behind them.

'Well? Can you see anyone spying on us?'

'No.' She paused. A movement in the corner of her vision drew her head towards Tirlsay. She locked on a flicker, a gleam, focused, steadying her hands, trying to distinguish shadows from solid objects. She half expected to spot the black Rover. But there was nothing. She swung the lenses back towards the post office. The Merc was still parked outside, no sign of its driver.

'Too much pot makes you paranoid,' said Tom.

'Just because you're paranoid… Let's go in,' she added. 'I'm getting cold out here.'

The resident crow cawed and cackled as they trekked back to the kitchen.

A half-empty glass of Jameson's and a plate of broken crab limbs sat on the mottled carpet. Jim was fiddling with the television.

'No reception. Must be the hills. Shame. I wouldn't mind watching something mindless for half an hour or so. I'm knackered after all that driving.'

'The video might work,' said Tom. They riffled through the cassettes stacked under the television and Jim selected one labelled 'The Sweeney'. The video player refused to co-operate. Jim threatened the machine and Tom offered helpful comments about connections while she surreptitiously unwrapped the bar of Cadbury's Dairy Milk which Tom had left lounging on the sofa. She stuffed a couple of squares in her mouth, squashed them against her palate. Savoured her sweet revenge for the unshared Hobnobs.

Jim was about to give up when the video player sprang into life of its own volition.

'First series,' said Jim. 'The best one. Gone downhill a bit since then, though. It's always the way. Still my favourite cop series though.'

'It must be every cop's favourite cop series,' she said.

'Inspector Regan is a great character,' said Tom. He turned to Jim. 'Do you think *The Sweeney* is realistic?'

Jim paused. She cringed. They had only been at Nethergate a couple of hours and already Tom was quizzing Jim. He would flip. She counted to five.

'Well, there's an element of truth there,' said Jim. 'In the characters more than the plot, though. And, in fact, the writers talked to a lot of cops. In the bar, of course. Best place to get stories out of cops.' He laughed. She watched him curiously. What was his game? 'I spoke to them a couple of times,' he added.

Tom looked impressed. Sam rolled her eyes.

'So did they base Regan on you?' Tom asked.

'Better ask the scriptwriters that.'

'I bet every detective in Scotland Yard would like to think they were the inspiration for Regan,' she said.

Jim and Tom stared at the television, laughing chummily at the banter between Regan and his sidekick Carter.

She was feeling bored. 'Isn't it funny that everyone loves a fictional detective but nobody likes a real-life copper?'

Jim and Tom ignored her.

She continued anyway. 'Why do you think that is? What is it about policemen that makes them so popular on television yet so unpopular in real life?'

Jim lobbed a crochet-covered cushion at her. 'Belt up.'

She bit into another square of the chocolate bar, regarded the paltry remains slyly and decided she might as well polish off the lot.

'Have you ever noticed that television cops are never happily married?' she said.

No answer.

'Why is it that in cop shows policemen's daughters always end up being kidnapped or murdered?'

'Maybe it's because they don't know how to keep their mouths shut,' Jim said, then clenched his jaw.

She pulled her knees up to her chest, hugged them, glared at the screen angrily.

'*The Sweeney* is about the Flying Squad anyway,' she said in Jim's direction. 'You don't have anything to do with the Flying Squad. That's Harry's lot, isn't it? Wasn't he trying to move to the Flying Squad? Maybe the scriptwriters based Regan on Harry.' She knew that would get his goat.

'Harry?' said Jim. 'Harry? I doubt it. And anyway, the Flying Squad's not his lot.'

'Who is his lot now, then?'

'Well, after he left Tilbury he went to the drugs squad, but he couldn't put up with the early morning raids. So then he tried to get a transfer to the Flying Squad and they wouldn't have him.'

'Why not?'

''Cos he's a lazy bloody bugger; likes to sit around. He'll do anything to avoid getting off his fat arse.'

'What's he doing now then, if the Flying Squad wouldn't have him?'

'He's on diplomatic duties. Managed to finagle a good sitting-down position.' Jim laughed, for some reason. 'That reminds me,' he added swiftly. 'I'd better send him a postcard.'

'Why?' She tried to remember whether she had ever received any kind of card from Jim. He didn't even sign her birthday cards. It was always Liz who wrote his name on them. And now he was sending postcards to Harry.

'You don't usually send postcards.'

'I won't see him before he heads off to the Algarve for his summer holiday. He's going in August.'

'So?'

He stared fixedly at the television. Regan and Carter were searching for something to pin on the bank robber because he'd nobbled half the jury and walked away from the court scot-free.

The credits rolled and the theme music died away.

'But don't the plots have some element of truth?' Tom asked. 'I mean coppers do fit people up, try and get them sent down for crimes they haven't committed, don't they?'

Jim's eyes sparked. God, thought Sam, Tom had better watch it; he had better not push his luck. If he wanted to survive the week. But Jim was still in a question-answering mood.

'Well, of course there are plenty of cops who go in for fixing and fitting. But the thing all these television scriptwriters don't seem to realize is that it's actually quite difficult to fit someone up, create a watertight case that will stand up in court. Some of the shit always floats to the surface. So I tend to think it's easier to look for the real evidence: the facts.' He paused long enough to allow Tom and Sam a silent sceptical exchange.

'Of course, if you can't get at the facts, then it's always possible just to spread the muck a bit. Tell a few stories, put somebody out of action for a while by ruining their reputation. That's easier. Smear campaign.'

She heard an undertone of self-pity in Jim's voice, a hint that he was speaking as a victim not a perpetrator, and wondered whether it was the Jameson's talking. Or an act. Or something different. She watched as he turned and trained his eye on Tom, locked him in his sights.

'Mind you, it's not just policemen who spread the crap. They don't work by themselves. It helps if they have a tame hack to help do the dirty work. You'll soon find out. Reporters trying to fill the pages. Stringing together a few stories they've heard from someone down the bar, concocting some old cobblers to fill the columns. Preferably some old cobblers that allows them to plaster a picture of a woman with big tits on the front page.'

She grimaced, conjured up an image of the tabloid spread about Jim's brother, Ian Coyle; the lurid story with its extra-large photo of the topless Page Three model.

Tom crossed his arms. 'Maybe some reporters are happy to pump out crap,' he said. 'Especially if they work for the tabloids. But most journalists want to get at the facts because their credibility depends on it.'

She wasn't convinced Tom really knew what he was talking about, but she had to admire his bottle, refusing to be bulldozed by Jim.

'Serious journalists have standards,' Tom continued. 'Codes of professional ethics they have to follow.'

'Professional ethics my arse,' said Jim. 'Only standards most hacks follow are the ones they think will get their name recognized, push up the circulation figures.' He drained the last of the whiskey before pushing his hands down on the antimacassars and levering himself up from the soft depths of the armchair.

'Anyway, I'm just going to drive down to Tirlsay. Use the

phone; see if I can arrange for the Cortina to be fixed tomorrow and call Bill to see about borrowing a car. See you later.'

They listened to the crunch and splutter of the Cortina pulling away across the courtyard.

Tom scanned the room. 'Where's my Cadbury's Dairy Milk?'

'Sorry. Was that yours? You could always have a bit of crab.' She nodded at the dismembered body lying next to them.

He eyed the hacked-off claws suspiciously. 'I'll give it a miss.'

She swiped a leg, crunched it, nipped at the shreds of meat inside, picked the strands of white meat from her front-teeth gap with a fingernail while she scoured the shelves.

'Hey look – there's a box of Trivial Pursuit. That's lucky. I can beat you with my superior knowledge of science and nature.' She stood up to reach for the game. Her movement was accompanied by a sudden scrabbling up on the roof above the fireplace, as if she had disturbed the crow from its post by the chimney.

'He doesn't like journalists much, does he?' said Tom.

No, she thought, he doesn't. 'He doesn't think too much of television scriptwriters either,' she said. 'There aren't many professions he does admire. He always thinks he can do everybody else's job better than they can.'

Tom gave her a sidelong look. She could sense him lining up more questions. She took out the Trivial Pursuit board, fiddled about with the pieces of coloured plastic, reached for the dice, threw it quickly.

'Green question, please.'

CHAPTER 8

THEY LEFT THE mechanic staring sorrowfully at the Cortina. Jim said he was going to find Bill and pick up the car. He headed off with his haversack. Sam and Tom ambled into the centre of Stromness, following narrow side passages hemmed in by thick granite walls. They stumbled across the museum by the water's edge, meandered through its rooms holding a mish-mash of stuffed birds, Neolithic pots, telescopes, chronometers from ships of the Hudson's Bay Company. Tom was drawn to an exhibition about Scapa Flow, the stretch of sheltered water between Mainland and Hoy, used as a harbour by the Vikings and then the British navy in the First and Second World Wars.

Sam examined the photos of old battleships. 'Scapa Flow is a bit of a watery graveyard.'

An accidental fire had caused an explosion on board HMS *Vanguard*, anchored there in 1917, killing eight hundred and four men. And then in 1939, a German U47 had penetrated the eastern end and torpedoed HMS *Royal Oak*, killing eight hundred and thirty-three men. Tom seemed unmoved by the loss of life, more gripped by the fear of diving below the waves in a U-boat. He said there was no way he could be part of a submarine crew because he was afraid of drowning; he had toppled over the side of a dinghy into the sea when he was four, but fortunately his mum had managed to hoik him out of the water and saved him, and now she regularly recounted the story of seeing his little white face staring up at her pleadingly from below the waves. Sam said that the idea of being in a submarine freaked her out as well.

'I thought you loved the sea.'

'Claustrophobia. I can't go in lifts. The tube is fairly difficult too. The Northern line is the worst. It's deeper than the others.'

'What do you think that's all about, then?'

'No idea. I think it's pretty common. All those people standing for hours at bus stops in London; I reckon they are all just there to avoid the tube. There's no other reason to wait for a bus in London.'

'Phobias,' he pressed the tips of his fingers into a steeple, 'usually have their root in childhood.'

She checked her watch. 'Let's go and look at the boats.'

She peered into the oil-filmed water slapping against the quayside, her pale face peered back imploringly, pulling her down, drowning in bleak thoughts about Jim and his shadowy life. And his death. Operation Asgard. The pistol. Uncertain whether she was anxious. Or sad. Resentful perhaps. Angry. A shoal of tiny fish shattered her image, darting this way and that, flashing silver as they twisted.

'What kind of fish do you think those are?'

Tom wasn't listening. He had spotted a gang of men, early twenties, joshing, swearing, unloading creels from a string of gently rocking boats. He strolled towards them, hands in pockets. She left him to it, meandered off in the other direction, wandering along the harbour wall, eyeballing the ranks of honking black-backed gulls. She found herself at the top of a slipway, close to a boatshed with its rusty metal sliding door pulled half-open, the gap filled with a curtain of thick black plastic strips. She poked her head through without thinking and almost as quickly pulled it back when she glimpsed yellow oilskins inside. She heard a shout as she sidled away.

'Come back!'

She wavered, unsure which way to jump. A sinewy arm appeared through the flaps followed by a head of coarse curls, forget-me-not eyes and a fat-lipped smile. He seemed sad, despite the smile.

'Do you want something?' he asked. Not aggressively.

'I was just being nosy.'

'Yes. That's okay to be nosy. Come in, take a look around.'

He spoke with an offbeat grammar, the hint of a foreign accent. He held the curtain aside to reveal a gloomy interior. She hesitated, caught between wariness and curiosity. He smiled again. What the hell.

She breathed in the whiff of old fish and diesel as he waved his hand proudly around: plastic crates neatly stacked, blue polypropylene ropes coiled in a corner and an array of dirty engine parts spread out on an oily floorsheet, like a school-child's frog dissection. She suddenly felt a bit coy, grinned inanely.

'What are you doing?' she asked.

'A bit of repair work.'

She guessed now he was Scandinavian with his near-perfect English.

'A boat engine?'

'Part of a trawler.'

'You are a fisherman,' she suggested.

'Very good. Almost correct. In fact I am the skipper of a trawler. I'm not going out again until the beginning of next week, so I'm just taking some time to make sure everything is in order. And you are...'

'Sam. I'm on holiday here.'

'Nils.' He wiped his hand on his oilskins and then gripped her hand, shook it, his flesh warm and firm.

'So, Sam. What do you think?' He nodded at his domain.

'It's great, very neat.' Searching for appropriate compliments. 'It must be hard work being a fisherman, though. Sorry, I mean it must be hard work being a skipper.'

'Of course. Hard work, yes. But I enjoy it. It's my vocation. It's what I was born to do.'

She kinked her head to one side. 'Are there many fishermen in Stromness?'

'Not as many as there used to be. There are a few offshore trawlers based here, like mine, after the whitefish. And then there are the smaller fishing boats that put out the creels around the coast and catch the crabs.'

'Do you catch a lot of fish?'

'Nobody catches huge amounts of fish here these days. Fish are nearly as rare as mermaids in these waters. I catch more than most, though. Fish that is, not mermaids.'

'Why is that?'

'Because I am Norwegian.'

She couldn't quite tell whether he was being serious or not.

'What difference does being Norwegian make?'

Grief, she was picking up bad habits from Tom. Still, he seemed happy enough to answer her questions.

'Norwegians are born to the sea.' He flourished his hand dramatically. 'It is in my genes, seafaring. I can read the flow of the tides, the pulse of the currents and I know where to find the fish. That is why I always land the biggest catch in Stromness. Because I am a skilled skipper.'

She tugged her earring, smiled, bemused by his boasting.

'I lead the way to the fish grounds. Wherever I go, the other boats come behind and they get the fish I haven't managed to catch.'

'That's probably why you catch the most. Because if the others come behind you, they have to make do with your leftovers.'

She hunched her shoulders awkwardly, realizing too late that her comment was too critical, not the kind of thing she should say to somebody she had only just met. He smiled. He obviously didn't mind her odd mix of shyness and directness.

'Well, maybe you are correct. But I don't ask them to follow me. They could go elsewhere, find other places to trawl. It is their choice to come behind. That's part of the skill of being a good skipper, leading the pack, knowing how to do a bit of magic: change fish into money.'

He stepped towards her, stood so close she could smell the salt on his skin and see the dark hairs lying flat on the back of his hand.

'Are you really a tourist?' he asked.

'Yes. What else would I be?'

He assessed her in a way that made her turn pink. 'You ask a lot of questions for a tourist. And you say some sharp things. Are you a tax inspector perhaps?'

She laughed nervously, assuming he was joking. Then she wondered whether there was an edgy undertone to his voice. 'Course not,' she said.

'A researcher?'

'No, I'm not a researcher. What would I be researching anyway?'

'Scotland's declining fishing industry perhaps. There are plenty of researchers hanging round Stromness these days. I let one of them come on a couple of trips with me last year as an extra pair of hands. I thought he was very nice. Funny.

Interesting to talk to. But he unsettled the crew a bit with all his odd questions; they began to think he was bringing us bad luck. So I've steered clear of researchers since then.'

'Well, I'm not a researcher. I'm just a nosy tourist.'

'That's okay then.' He wiped his brow, an exaggerated swipe with the back of his hand and, as he did so, he revealed a pattern on the underside of his forearm; a ray-haloed red-and-orange sun inked on to his skin.

'I like your tattoo.' Her cheeks reddened again as she said it.

'It's a Viking symbol. A blessing from Thor, patron saint of sailors. It's an ancient protection against the perils of the oceans. If you can see the sun then you are safe, you can find your way home.'

'I've got a tattoo too.' The words came out before she could stop herself. She hadn't told anyone else about the tattoo and here she was revealing her secret to a total stranger. She had planned it with Becky for months; they had wasted hours agonizing over what image they would have needled into their skin. Becky had come up with her own design, the Hebrew words *tikkun olam*, combined with various carefully crafted abstract patterns which, she had explained, symbolized her Russian-Jewish ancestry as well as her liberal humanist beliefs. *Tikkun olam*: repairing the world. Making it a better place. Sam had tried to follow suit and had come up with a variation on a swirly Celtic design, but had failed to find anything that even halfway matched the cachet of *tikkun olam*. The Wednesday after her birthday dinner they had gone up to London on the train to get it done. Dennis Cockell's on the Finchley Road. As soon as she stepped inside though, and saw all the photos of tattooed body parts everywhere, she realized she couldn't live with the ersatz Celtic guff. It really wasn't her, she'd never been to Glasgow, she didn't feel even remotely

Scottish. In an indecisive flap, she scanned the pictures on the wall and chose the first image that caught her eye.

'What do you have a tattoo of then?' Nils asked. He took a step closer.

'A bird.'

'What kind?'

'Swallow.'

'Hah. A quick flyer. Let me see.' He moved his arm towards her playfully. She stepped back defensively, dodged his out-stretched hand, glanced over her shoulder to check the position of her nearest exit and saw Tom's head poking through the plastic strips. She wasn't entirely relieved to see him.

'I thought I heard your voice,' he said. 'I wondered where you had gone.'

She smiled half-heartedly, introduced Nils. Tom turned his back on her and proceeded to interrogate Nils about the finances of deep-sea trawling: crew numbers, costs, prices, profits. She cringed inwardly, fearing Tom's questioning would rile Nils, make him suspect they really were from the Inland Revenue, trying to nose out any undeclared income. She jumped in and asked Nils to show them his boat.

He pointed across the harbour. 'The trawler is over there, the large one moored near the ice tower.'

It loomed out of the water like Noah's ark, square and top-heavy. Ugly. He must have gauged her reaction.

'I have another one just there.' He pointed to a smaller boat that was tied up to the quayside; a boat-in-a-bottle boat with its red clinker sides, white wheelhouse and a cloud of seagulls hopping around its bows.

'Oh, that's really pretty,' she said.

'The *Marie-Jean*. Named after my wife. Her father owned the boat. She was his only child. He died shortly after we were married. Marie-Jean inherited it and she gave it to me. It's the kind of fishing I like best – inshore, lines. Small-scale. But it's not really possible to make a living like that.'

Nils turned to her now, his face lighting up. 'Would you like to come out on the *Marie-Jean*? A quick trip round the harbour? Yes?'

She hesitated, flicked a sly look at Tom.

'When?'

'Now. Why not now? Half an hour out, half an hour back.'

Maybe she shouldn't. But why not? Anyway, he was interesting to talk to with his knowledge of the sea and his Viking ancestry.

'I'd love to. We haven't got anything planned. What about you, Tom? Do you want to come too?'

'No thanks.' He stuck his hands in his trouser pockets.

'Come on. It looks calm. No chance of sinking today.'

He glared at her reproachfully. 'You go. I'll just wander around the town.'

'Okay. Meet you back here in about an hour then.'

Tom sloped off in the direction of the High Street.

She followed Nils, cutting a path across the piers, skipping over ropes, heading to the *Marie-Jean*. Something occurred to her; she halted, called after Tom. 'Can I borrow your binoculars?'

He dug in his anorak pocket, walked over and reluctantly handed her his bins.

'Thanks,' she said.

He didn't respond. Sulky bugger. She caught up with Nils. He was studying the boat moored behind his: dull grey, enclosed, low in the water, shark-like, predatory with its pointed prow poking her lovely rose-red stern, giving her unwanted attention.

'I haven't seen that one here before,' he said. 'Cruiser.'

She peered at the neat white letters almost completely concealed underneath its prow. '*The Inquisitor*. That's a creepy name for a boat. What do you think they are searching for?'

'Not for fish, that's for sure. I couldn't tell you what it is kitted out for though,' He nodded towards the antennae bristling from the cabin. She stood on tiptoes and tried to peer through the cabin windows.

'Leave it,' Nils said warily. 'None of our business anyway.'

He studied *The Inquisitor* pensively as he clambered aboard his boat.

The *Marie-Jean* pulled away from its mooring, followed by a phalanx of raucous seagulls as they retraced the *St Ola*'s path across the harbour. Nils stood square in the wheelhouse, steering their course. She sat at the stern, watching the receding slipways of Stromness, the wake fanning out behind as they skimmed along between wind and water.

'How about east to Scapa Flow?' he asked.

'No thanks. Too many dead bodies. All those drowned sailors. I'd like to avoid the ghosts.'

'Hah. It's not possible to avoid ghosts here. There are strange spirits everywhere on these islands. Drowned sailors all around these shores. We could go west if you like. But there's another wreck that way. The HMS *Hampshire*. Lord Kitchener's ship. Lots of bodies there.'

'Isn't that the one that hit a mine,' said Sam, 'and sank with all its men on board in the First World War?'

'Well, that's the official explanation,' Nils said. 'Although, of course, there are all sorts of stories about what really happened. Conspiracy theories. Tales about the involvement of Russian agents.'

He was staring at her face. She flushed. Was he getting at something? A nagging anxiety tweaked her stomach. Perhaps she had been rash, accepting a boat trip alone with this stranger.

'Anyway, I thought his ship went down further round the island,' she said. 'Kitchener's Memorial is up by Marwick Head. Isn't that quite a long way to go?'

He grinned. He was definitely sizing her up, testing her a bit, but she wasn't quite sure why. Still not convinced that she was just a tourist perhaps.

'Just round the Ness then,' he said. 'Along by the Battery and back.'

'Okay. What's the Battery?'

'Second World War lookout post. The buildings are used by the scouts these days.'

She hung over the side of the boat, stretched her arm out to see if she could touch the water, felt her centre of gravity slipping, saw a sheer green wall rising above her, panicked, hauled herself back in. Even on the calmest of days, the waters around here seemed treacherous.

'How do you navigate the sea?' she asked. 'Do you have a map?'

'I don't need one. I know these waters: the rocks, the sandbars, the smell of the beach, the winds. I have a chart in my head. And when I'm in open water, I can navigate by the sun.'

'Like a Viking. What happens when the sun isn't visible?'

'Then I use the radar,' he said.

The desolate buildings of the Battery came into view; black slits of concrete sentry posts and bleak windows of wooden huts louring over the water, forever searching for the traces of German submarines. She fished in her pocket for the binoculars, lifted her sight to the citadel above the sentry posts and latched on to the dark outline of a solitary figure breaking the smooth lines of the mound. The sunlight was shining from behind, shadowing his face. But he was still instantly recognizable. Startled, she dropped the bins, let them dangle and twist. She saw him turning towards the sea, focusing in their direction. She ducked, crouching low, pushing herself against the larch planks of the boat's hull. Squatting in the damp, she wondered why she hadn't simply waved and shouted hello. That would have been the normal thing to do. And she realized then that it was an instinct, the vanishing act. She just did what she had always done – slipped below the radar, reassured herself that he wouldn't be able to see her hiding among the ropes, not even with his twenty-twenty vision.

She waited a minute, dared to lift her head slightly, peeked cautiously, up and over the boat's side. His unmistakable silhouette was still outlined against the sky, the King of the Castle, surveying his surroundings. And then he was off, striding briskly down the hillside in the direction of the Battery, making a beeline for the nearest hut. At the door he hesitated, peered at the frame, checking for some kind of a sign, she assumed. He gave the door a sharp shove with his shoulder, pushed it open. Disappeared inside for just a moment. He reappeared and closed the door carefully as he left. She almost missed the slight hand movement, marking the frame with what – a piece of chalk? – before he was striding briskly back up the slope, vanishing over the far side of the mound.

She remained crouching, clasping her knees, her legs trembling with the tension and the cold. Oh God. Well, at least he was on his own. At least she could console herself with the fact that he wasn't meeting some woman in a scout hut. Be thankful for small mercies. She let her head flop, staring down at the *Marie-Jean*'s wet planks. She sighed. She knew what he was doing there anyway; it wasn't difficult to work that one out. Kim Philby and his book of tradecraft tips: dead-letter box. Someone must have left a message for Jim, some kind of instruction perhaps, a location, a pick-up or a drop-off point maybe. And then she sighed again. She hated that moment, the point when the lurching feelings in her stomach surfaced, her suspicions became observable fact and she realized she wasn't just telling herself stories. It happened quite a lot with Jim. She levered herself upright, searching for her balance in the rocking boat.

Nils was concentrating on the pattern of the waves and the rip tides underneath, steering the boat with his inbuilt compass, more mechanical than man, caught up in his own world, not noticing hers. He glanced over his shoulder. 'Are you okay?'

'Yes, fine thanks.' She clambered around the ropes and baskets to join him in the cabin.

'Not seasick?'

'No. I don't get seasick.'

He looked at her curiously. 'You remind me of Marie-Jean.'

Remind. The word was spoken wistfully. As if his wife was in the past. No longer there. A shadow.

'I don't know what it is about you,' Nils continued. 'Nothing obvious. Not your appearance. Maybe it's just the sense that there is something slightly unreachable about you, that you are forever wanting to escape. That you like to keep your secrets to yourself.'

She felt her stomach flip again, uncertain whether she was flattered or worried by his interest in her.

'Everybody likes to keeps their secrets to themselves,' she said. 'Otherwise they wouldn't be secrets.'

'But some people are no good at keeping secrets. They wear

their thoughts and their feelings on their skin. I don't think that's you; I guess you keep secrets without thinking about it. I suspect you are very good at keeping secrets.'

'Not quite as good as I used to be.'

She gazed at the green slopes rising gently from the shore, the neat cottages dotting the hillside and she wondered what it would be like to live there all year round, through the long darkness and storms of winter. She could be happy up here, scraping together an existence, doing a bit of this, a bit of that. Fishing trips with Nils. It seemed more appealing than going to university and trying to work out what sort of career she should have, competing with all the sharp elbows.

'Time to turn round,' he said. 'Catch the tide. We could go further next time.'

She didn't reply.

'Where did you say you were staying?' he asked.

'Just beyond Tirlsay. In an old croft that belongs to a mate of my dad's.'

'What's it called?'

She hesitated. He smiled.

'Nethergate,' she said.

'Nethergate. That's the one all by itself halfway up the hill. Right by the roadside.'

She nodded. 'How do you know it?'

'I went there with Marie-Jean a few years ago. The old lady who owned it was a friend of her father's. She died in her sleep. I took Marie-Jean to pay her respects. I remember her body was laid out very peacefully in the room at the end of the cottage.'

'Oh,' said Sam. 'She must have died in the bed I'm sleeping in. That feels a bit odd.'

'But everybody has to die somewhere, no? It is good that she died in her home.' Nils concentrated on the sea as he swung the boat round, heading back to Stromness.

The mechanic had done what he said he would: fitted a temporary silencer, reduced the noise and left the car with a burbling at its rear end that probably wasn't audible from a great distance, but was still loud enough to make people stare when they drove past. Inside the Cortina, on the road out of Stromness, there was an uncomfortable silence. Tom was still grumpy about her sea trip with Nils. She was staring out of the window, trying to work out how much she should tell Tom. A raptor hovered overhead, the sun gilding its tail feathers.

'Look,' she said.

'What?'

'Hawk.'

She was about to tell him it was a kestral when she caught sight of an advancing silver streak, bearing down on them, growing rapidly larger. It decelerated momentarily as it passed, giving Sam just enough time to register a woman with short brunette hair who, even at a distance, was obviously attractive; she had the confident posture of somebody who was used to being admired.

'Dangerous driving,' Sam said.

'It's a Merc. What do you expect? We're lucky he didn't rear-end us. Stockbroker on holiday.'

'It was a woman.'

'Was it? That's interesting. The City: soon it'll be the only game left in town,' said Tom.

'If Thatcher has her way and the pits are closed,' she joined in, waving her arms around. 'And the unions are destroyed and our manufacturing base disintegrates, there'll be nothing left except financial companies and shopping centres.'

'The service economy. And there goes its outrider in the northern reaches. Tearing up the highway.'

She heard the admiration in his voice and wondered whether he had always been like that, a bit in awe of the money-makers. Maybe she just hadn't noticed before. The silver glint vanished in the distance, merging with the hills. She peered up, searching for the kestrel again. It had disappeared.

They had already started a game of Trivial Pursuit when Jim returned in the inconspicuous black Renault he had borrowed from Bill. She eyed him suspiciously as he hovered in the doorway, filling out the frame. He was obviously feeling edgy; he couldn't stand still. He walked over to the table, deposited a newspaper, went to the kitchen to fetch a glass, poured himself a drink from the half-empty whiskey bottle he had left on the mantelpiece, knocked it back, returned to the table, picked up his paper again. She caught sight of a book lying underneath. It was hard to miss with its front-cover photo of a bulging-eyed ivory chess piece biting his shield, staring up maniacally at her. Lewis chessman, a berserker.

She stretched out her hand to pick up the book. Jim moved to intercept, tried to grab it, but she was quicker and swiped it away from his reach. 'The Orkneyinga Saga,' she read. 'Is it yours?'

'Give it back.'

The book felt warm in her hand. She held it up to her face, studied the berserker with his mad eyes. That was Jim. He was like that; wound up, waiting to let rip. Maybe that was what all the Coyles were like.

'Give it back,' Jim said again. 'I'm reading it for the history degree. It's on the Open University coursebook list.'

'Let me just have a quick look at it.'

He let his arms slide down to his sides, but his left fist was clenched. She smiled. Liar. He hadn't brought that book with him; she could guess where he had found it.

'Liz will be pleased to hear that you are being so studious,' she said.

'So you're reporting on me to your mother.'

She clucked dismissively, sensed Tom turning red, kept her eyes on the book and thumbed through the pages, ignoring Jim's blazing stare, casually searching for what – pencil jottings, inserts? Nothing. She flicked the pages again, double-checking. Still she couldn't see anything unusual. She was just being silly after all, imagining spooks and plots where none existed. Taking Philby too seriously. Just because she hadn't seen the book before didn't mean he was fabricating. The idea that he might have collected it from the Battery that afternoon, that it might contain some kind of coded message, was just plain ridiculous. She studied the pale, luminous image of the berserker, chewing his shield with frustration, trying to convey some message to her, desperate to share his secret. Unable to speak. A voiceless informer. She gave the book a final flick, spotted a page with a creased corner that had obviously been folded over at some point and then unfolded again. She flipped through to the dog-eared page. Chapter 13, Earl Sigurd's Sons. She made a mental note of the page number. Thirty-eight.

'It's not history,' she said to Jim. 'It's a saga. Story. Myth.'

'History is always part myth. Anyway, it's a great book.'

'Is it?' asked Tom.

'No,' she said. 'It might be a classic of Norse literature. But I borrowed a copy from the library once and I couldn't finish it; it's just a liturgy of Viking murder and revenge. The Earls of Orkney killing each other. It was too boring for me. I just don't understand the point of revenge.'

'Who would have thought,' said Jim testily, 'that I could have produced such a pious daughter.'

Tom snorted. She glanced at the book again. Now she knew what to look for, she quickly located another page with a creased corner. This one had been folded and unfolded twice, like an abandoned origami attempt. Page seventy. She etched the numbers in her brain, filed them away for future reference: thirty-eight, seventy.

'Well, I'm right about it being nothing but killing,' she said, skimming the contents of the double-folded page. 'I mean, take Chapter 29 for example. The Death of Rognvald. It's all about his murder. Of course. He was trying to escape from his enemy, Thorfinn. So he took his lapdog and hid among the rocks on the shore. But his dog barked and betrayed him. Then Rognvald gets killed. And so do all his mates.'

'But I quite like that,' said Tom. 'Viking dies because of barking lapdog. Man betrayed by best friend.'

'Exactly,' said Jim. 'It's full of great stories. Your problem is you don't know a good book when you read one.'

'It's not a good book. It's bollocks.'

'That's your attitude to everything,' said Jim, with a sudden flash of aggression that took her by surprise and, as he spoke, he stretched over, twisted her arm and snatched the book from her hand.

'Everything is bollocks as far as you're concerned. You know what you're against but you've got no idea what you're for. You think you know everything, you and your smug middle-class mates who sit around all day smoking dope and criticizing everybody and everything without ever shifting off your lazy arses to help anyone or anything apart from yourselves. But the fact is, you and your lot know bugger all about anything. You haven't got a clue. It's all slogans with you. You're a bunch of bleating whingers. I reckon my lot know more about politics than you—'

'Your lot?' she interrupted. 'Your lot is just the same as all the other lots of boot-boys in the bloody Force.'

'Oh, right. So now you're an expert on policing, are you? Well, I reckon half the time my lot is saving your lot from your own bloody naïvety. There are dark forces out there you know nothing about—' he stopped abruptly. He must have realized he had momentarily let his guard down, forgotten that Tom was in the room.

'What are you on about, Dad?' she demanded. 'What dark forces?'

Jim glowered. She almost laughed; he looked more comic than menacing. He was definitely losing it these days. He just wasn't that intimidating any more.

Jim carried on with his rant. 'You know what your problem is? You've got no...' he paused, searching for the right word. 'Soul. No soul at all.'

'I have got a soul. I just don't feel the need to say I appreciate boring Norse sagas to prove it. You're the one who has sold his soul to the devil.'

'At least I had something worthwhile to barter with in the first place.'

'Well, at least I'm actually going to do a real history degree and I'm not just pretending.'

She realized she had gone too far as soon as the words left her mouth.

Jim's lip curled. 'Ha bloody ha. I suppose you think that coppers are too thick for university. I suppose you think that you and Liz are the only ones in this family capable of completing a degree. I suppose you think that the Open University is a joke and Oxford is the only place worth going to.'

Her face burned. Tom shifted uncomfortably on his feet.

'I suppose you think I'm not as smart as Roger the bloody plonker and his fancy shirts.'

'I didn't mention Roger. I've never noticed his shirts.'

'He wears orange shirts.' Jim flicked his hand as if he were brushing away an irritating midge. 'He thinks that makes him interesting. Daring.'

She didn't know how to respond. They stood awkwardly for a moment, all three of them, unspeaking, deafened by the embarrassed silence.

Jim broke it first. 'Well, I'm going to bed to read.'

He strode towards his room with *The Orkneyinga Saga* gripped firmly under his arm, the front-cover crackpot berserker peering out crazily above the crook of his arm.

'He has a point,' Tom said. 'You are a bit of a snob sometimes. What's so ridiculous about the idea of him doing a degree?'

'I'm not being a snob. For God's sake, he's an undercover cop. He tells lies for a living. That's why I find it hard to buy his history degree story.'

'Who is Roger the plonker anyway?'

'He's the head of the English department where Liz works. She's known him for ages. They met at University in fact.'

Tom nodded knowingly. 'And Jim doesn't get on with him.'

'That's putting it mildly. They're at each other's throats given half a chance. Jim nearly decked him at Mum's last New Year's party because he quoted something from *Ulysses* and Roger scoffed and made a comment implying Jim couldn't really have read such an abstruse piece of literature.'

'Has Jim read *Ulysses*?'

'It's one of his favourite books, best approached after half a bottle of whisky, he says.'

'Has he still got all his hair?'

'Roger?' She paused. 'Actually he has. He's very bouffant. Lots of strawberry-blond hair. Helen calls him Roger the Todger.'

Tom laughed. She joined in. He gave her a furtive glance.

She stopped laughing. 'Let's carry on with the Triv,' she said.

Thirty-eight, seventy, she chanted to herself while Tom asked her questions. Thirty-eight, seventy. Thirty-eight, seventy. And she wondered what the numbers signified and who had passed Jim his coded message.

CHAPTER 9

SUNDAY EVENING, THE day frittered away; cups of coffee, holiday cottage pursuits.

'I'm just going to drive down to the phone box in Tirlsay to call Liz,' Jim announced, poking his head into the front room. 'I shan't be long.'

The tyres churned the gravel as he pulled away.

'Do you think he's really going to call your mum?' Tom asked.

'Yes.'

Jim was away for an hour perhaps, maybe more. On his return he clanked around in the kitchen for ten minutes before he entered the front room, hovered in front of the fireplace, making her prickly with his looming presence.

'How was she?' Sam asked.

'Who?'

'How was Mum?'

'Oh, I couldn't get through.'

She could tell Tom was smirking without having to look at him.

'Maybe we'll walk down to Tirlsay,' she said. 'And I'll see if I can make the phone box function for me.'

'Good idea.' Jim filled his tumbler and settled down in an armchair, opened the paper he had bought in Stromness, disappeared behind the front page: oil workers boost local economy, bike stolen, ferry delayed by mechanical fault.

Nine. The sun was sliding slowly towards the rim of hills behind. They trotted briskly down the valley, sheltered from the nagging wind by the high hedgerows on either side, their shadows leading the way.

'I'm right about your dad,' Tom said.

'What do you mean?'

'He clearly didn't try to phone your mum.'

She snatched at a bobbing grass head, scraped its seeds off between her finger and thumb, threw them up into the air.

'Maybe he didn't try and phone Liz. But that doesn't mean to say he was phoning another woman.'

They had reached the straggling edge of Tirlsay and the phone box now. She stepped inside and pulled the door shut behind her so Tom couldn't hear her conversation, turned her back to the door, dialled her home number.

Almost immediately, Liz picked up at the other end. 'Hello,' said the disembodied voice.

Sam pushed the coins in the slot.

'I wondered when anybody would remember to call,' said Liz. 'How is Orkney? Has it changed?'

'No, it's pretty much the same as it was last time we were here. Lots of birds, lots of wind.'

'And what about Jim? What is he up to?'

She wondered how much she was obliged to report, how bound she was by their unspoken contract. 'Oh, the usual – a lot of drinking, a lot of swearing, a lot of arranging things with his mate.'

'Has he said anything about the Open University?' A touch of desperation in her voice, Sam thought, a touch of delusion.

'Not exactly. We've only been here a couple of days.' Why

was she making excuses for Jim? 'We've not had any major arguments and he mentioned something earlier about an outing together tomorrow morning. So he must be relatively happy.'

'Well, that's good, I suppose. Nice for you to spend a bit of time with him.'

Awkward pause.

'He didn't say anything about mushroom picking, did he?' asked Liz, a sudden note of alarm in her voice.

'Mushroom picking. What about it?'

'Don't let him take you. When you were little, he used to take you mushroom picking along the cliffs. It was his idea of fun: taking all three of you over the edge and down the sheep paths, even in a force eight gale. I used to wait at the top, terrified, and wonder what I would do if you were all blown away.'

Sam said nothing. She didn't recognize that scene. In her head there was another image – cliff, sheep paths, but she was laughing in the wind, carefree, messing about with her sisters. No danger.

Liz continued, 'I tried to stop him, but you know what your father's like. He never listens to anything I say. He never listens to anything anybody says.'

'But Mum, why—' Sam started to say. The phone beeped. She dug around in her overcoat pockets; they were empty.

'Please, avoid the mushrooms,' said Liz. 'If you survive the cliff, you'll probably end up being poisoned because I'm not sure he really knows what he's looking for. I sometimes think he's his own worst enemy. Call me from Inverness station,' Liz commanded. 'Let me know when you've made it back across Caithness.'

The phone line cut out. She slammed the handset down on to its cradle, uncertain whether she was angry with herself or with Liz. Or Jim.

'Okay?' said Tom as he opened the door with a satisfied grin. 'Sounded like you were having an argument with your mum.'

'Just normal mother–daughter stuff.'

'Jim didn't try to call her, did he?'

'Probably not.'

'Do you think he was calling someone else, then?'

'I'm not sure I really care what he was doing, right at this moment.' She strode off down the road without looking where she was going.

He caught up easily with his lanky strides. 'Happy families are all alike,' he said. 'Every unhappy family is unhappy in its own way.'

'Arguing is different from being unhappy. God, I'm beginning to sound like Liz. Do you know what she told me? She said Jim used to take us looking for mushrooms over the cliff edge when we were kids. How dangerous is that?'

'Sounds fairly harmless to me.'

'Well, that shows how little you know then.'

'Do you think there's a pub here?'

She didn't reply, continued her angry march along the road. Fed up with him and his smug observations about her family.

'I could do with a drink,' he said.

She relented. 'There must be a pub here somewhere. Jim reeked of the boozer when he came back from Tirlsay yesterday evening. Let's just try at the end of this road.'

They hung a right down a narrow lane enclosed by dry stone walls and spears of rosebay willowherb towering over their heads. Not exactly promising pub territory, but they carried on anyway, enjoying the stroll now, away from the sea and the breeze, air heavy with humidity, pollen, dancing midges glinting in the sun's low rays. They rounded a blind bend and were confronted by a herd of swaying cows; an unstoppable tide of steaming flesh and flies. Tom nodded, indicating a wooden stile in the hedgerow. They dived towards it; he clambered over and she perched on the top bar, inhaled the sweet-sour smell of milk and shit as the herd flowed past.

'What's up here anyway?' Tom asked. The footpath cut across a field in the direction of a small copse, treetops angled from too much bowing and scraping to the prevailing wind. She assessed the trees from the stile, a flock of rooks rose in the air, circling in the coral-pink sky above the low canopy, alarm calls rasping. Something about the suddenness of their cries made her nervous.

'Crows,' said Tom. 'A murder of crows.'

'Rooks. A crow in a crowd is a rook. A rook on its own is a crow.' Where had she learned that?

'What's the collective noun for a flock of rooks?' he asked.

'Storytelling.'

'That's a good one. I like that. Storytelling.'

He raised his hand to his shirt pocket as if he were about to scribble something in his notebook about collective nouns for birds, had second thoughts, let his hand slip back to his side again.

'It couldn't have been us that disturbed them.' She squinted up at the agitated birds, still cawing their warning. 'We're not close enough. There must be somebody else in the wood.' She hadn't thought of that possibility until she said it.

'It is a public footpath. People are allowed to walk through here.' He was so prosaic. She stared at the boundary, where the copse engulfed the daylight.

'Somebody was standing there, watching us walking up the road. They scarpered when they saw us coming over the stile. That's why the rooks flew up so suddenly.' She twitched, unnerved now by her own logic. 'Let's go. I don't like it here.'

'Don't be girly. Come on, let's have a walk in the wood anyway. See if we can find anything. Or anyone.'

He set off across the meadow; she trailed reluctantly behind, single file through the long grass. A huge black bird took off from just underneath their feet, lazily flapping its ragged wings as if it really wasn't that bothered whether it remained airborne or nose-dived into the end of the runway.

'Crow,' said Tom. 'It's on its own. A rook on its own is a crow.'

She squinted up as the bird gained height, noted the wedge shape of its tail.

'No. It's not a crow. It's a raven.'

'I can't spot the difference. I wouldn't be able to identify a raven in a murder. Or a storytelling come to that. What's the collective—'

'Unkindness,' she said.

She spotted a feather the bird must have dropped on the path, bent down to pick it up: lustrous, shimmering blue-black barbs.

'It's a sign,' she said.

'It's a feather,' said Tom.

She held it aloft, twiddled the dark quill between her fingers. She stared at her treasure for a second and then slipped it into her coat pocket.

The wood was small but dense; twisted branches of hazel, oak and birch pleading to the light, the earthy scent of damp moss and rotting wood trapped in the stagnant air below. She listened for the snap of twigs, the swishing of bracken, soft footsteps on dropped leaves. Nothing. They followed a stony path wending through the brambles, across a shallow ditch and out on the far side of the wood by a field that swept the hillside. There, beyond a long barrow and along the contours of the fields to the right stood Nethergate. Distant but distinct. Grey against green. Jim was standing like a megalith in the elevated garden. Scanning the horizon. Just as she had done the evening of their arrival when she was the High Priestess, carefully constructing her stone temple. She tried to visualize the spot where they were standing now from the vantage point of the croft's front garden. Was it possible for Jim to see them, standing there watching him? She stared, but he did not turn to look their way and she concluded the tangled branches and a wrinkle in the landscape must obscure their hiding place. She felt a prickling sensation in the back of her neck.

'God, this place gives me the creeps.' She looked down and saw a flattened patch of undergrowth by her feet, straddling the border between the wood and the field. 'Someone's been lying on the ground just there.'

She knelt and examined the compressed foliage. It revealed the imprint of a body: quite long, quite broad. Male, she guessed. A shrine of fag butts lay half-concealed among the bent stems. A smoker. He had been lying among the brambles and bracken, she surmised, waiting, watching. Hunting. She thought of the Ministry of Defence police. The shadowy Rover. Was somebody after her? Had she been trailed here, to Orkney? Or maybe they were chasing Jim. She shuddered. Tom squatted down beside her. Close enough for her to feel the heat of his body.

'We are being watched,' she whispered.

He inspected the patch of flattened grass, glanced at her. 'Could be any number of reasons why someone might want to lie down out of sight on the edge of a wood. Probably just a couple out for a quick shag.'

'Is that your explanation for everything? Is that always your angle? Sex?'

The words came out more prudishly than she had intended. He shrugged. She turned away, knew he was smiling, bemused behind her back. She half smiled as well before turning back with her puritanical face in place. He stared at her, unblinking. A susurrus in the bushes behind cut short their silent battle.

'Fox,' he said. 'Must be a fox.'

'There aren't any in Orkney.'

'A rabbit then. Or the wind.'

'It's a watcher.'

She peered between the tree trunks: no movement, no sign of life.

'Forget it,' he said. 'You are spooking yourself out. Let's see if we can find this pub.'

The pub turned out to be at the far end of the village. Whitewashed walls and slate roof outside; inside, old men huddled around the bar, curved backs interspersed with the upright handles of the beer pumps. The locals broke their conversations as they entered, assessed the foreigners in their midst before returning to their own business. She sat at a small table in a secluded corner, played nervously with the raven's feather, twiddling the quill again between finger and thumb. He placed the frothing pints between them, sat down opposite her, pushed himself back in his chair as if to get a better view, said nothing. She let the silence run, waiting to see how long it would last before he cracked.

'It's that slight twilight zone thing that I just don't quite get about you,' Tom said eventually. 'All the signs and ancient mysteries and dope smoking.'

'And the thing I don't quite get about you,' she snapped, 'is all this flirting with capitalism.'

'Flirting with capitalism? What, because I want to have a

career? Because I bother to think about how I'm going to earn a living?'

'It's not that. It's this interest in making money, the awe you have when you talk about the City.'

She picked up a pile of beer mats, tried to balance one across two uprights in an attempt to construct a miniature Stonehenge.

'Maybe you're right,' he said. 'I am getting a bit fed up with the lefty knee-jerk rejection of anything to do with making money. And I do find it a relief talking to people who run a business, because at least you can have a conversation about something practical, tangible. Prices, supply and demand. Straightforward rational stuff.'

She winced – an inexplicable twinge of rejection – and focused on her beer mat monument, searching for a suitable riposte. She retrieved her conversation with Nils, recalled him saying he had to use magic to turn fish into money.

'I'm not sure business is that rational and straightforward. Markets. Trade. It's not all practical and tangible. A lot of it is hocus-pocus.'

He pulled his sceptical face, his cynical journalist look. It egged her on.

'I mean, what about economics, what about the invisible hand.' She waved her arm dramatically, sent her beer mats scudding across the table. 'It's straight out of the twilight zone. It's a myth, it's a fairy tale.'

'The invisible hand isn't a myth.'

'What is it then?'

'The invisible hand is a...' he paused. 'It's a model, a metaphor, used to explain how markets work. You could say it's an ideological device, but I don't think you could call it a myth.'

'What's the difference between a myth and an ideology?'

'Well, I think a myth...' He stalled.

She looked through the pub window, spotted the Dog Star shining in the crepuscular sky. 'Myths are just ideologies from other times and places that we no longer believe,' she said.

'I don't think it's as—' The clang of the barman's bell cut him short. There was a flurry of activity around the bar as last orders were shouted.

'Shall we go,' she said.

She pushed her chair back and as she did so a twinge – hairs rising on her neck – made her turn. A stranger was standing by the bar, slightly apart from the old men, cigarette smoke writhing around his arm, coiling upwards, gathering in a particle cloud above his head. Her stomach knotted. Gut feeling. He must have trailed them to the bar. She assessed his appearance: mid-forties, mid-height, square shoulders, once black now salt-and-pepper hair brushed back revealing a widow's peak, blunt moustache, royal blue fine-knit Pringle jumper – a thin veneer of respectability pulled down over his shirt. He would have blended in at the Coney's Tavern. Almost. Something about his outfit jarred, wasn't quite in character. She glanced down at his shoes: burgundy mock croc slip-ons. No self-respecting suburban golfer would be seen dead in a pair of mock croc slip-ons; they were more seedy Soho than self-satisfied Surrey. Maybe he wasn't trying too hard. Maybe he wanted her to know he was shadowing her. Maybe he wanted to unnerve her. She looked up from his shoes and he caught her in his glare. He passed his hand in front of his face in a slow motion movement of cigarette from mouth to ashtray and his unblinking black eyes momentarily mesmerized her. What was he after?

'Come on,' said Tom. 'What are you waiting for?'

Tom pulled her to the door, breaking her free from his hypnotic stare. She felt his eyes following her back as they left.

They walked the road in silence, past the shut-up post office, the solitary telephone box, beyond the straggle of village houses, the burial mound, up the dimming hillside.

'That was him,' she said, his gaze playing on her mind.

'Who?'

'The man standing at the bar, the one who was dressed like a golfer from Surbiton.'

'What about him?'

'He is the spy in the woods.'

'How do you work that one out? If he was dressed like a golfer, maybe he is a golfer. You said people come to Orkney to play golf in the midnight sun.'

'He's the Watcher. I know he is. I can sense it.'

'Twilight zone,' he said dismissively.

'Maybe he's after me.'

'Why would he be after you?'

'Because I broke into the base at Greenham with Becky.'

'Did you? But so what? Loads of people have done that. Nobody's going to follow you to Orkney because you trespassed on an RAF base. That's a ridiculous idea.'

'I know. But...' She fell back into herself. Tried to unpick the knot in her stomach. He was right, she thought. The Watcher in the woods wasn't after her. He was after Jim. This wasn't anything to do with Greenham. This was something more serious. Darker. Somewhere in the distance an owl hooted.

'Short-eared,' she said.

'I reckon you make it up as you go along.'

The owl hooted again, closer this time. Behind them.

'It's hunting. Come on. Let's get home.'

Jim had the Ordnance Survey map spread out on the living-room table. He narrowed his eyes as they entered, registered her nervousness. She wondered whether she should mention the Watcher. Warn him that somebody was on his trail. But she couldn't speak then anyway, not with Tom listening.

'Okay was she?' he asked.

'Yes.'

'Good.'

He leaned over the chart again.

'What are you looking for?' she asked

'Somewhere we can visit tomorrow. How about Marwick Head?' He pointed to the northwestern edge of the island, a ruffle of cliffs marking the border between land and sea. She felt the memories stirring, heard Liz's warning in her head. Ignored it. No point in trying to avoid the ghosts. They were everywhere.

'Great. Kitchener's Memorial. That's near to the place where you used to pick mushrooms.'

'Yes. That's right. Funny, the tastiest mushrooms always grow near cliffs. Must be something to do with the salt in the air. I'll drive the Renault and you two can take the Cortina. That way, I can leave when I get pissed off.'

He picked up the map, folded it carefully along its concertina creases. Maps, he was fond of his maps she noted. Outside an owl hooted again. It was in the field behind the house; it must have followed them up the hill.

She was drifting, deep sleep eluding her in the gloaming. She heard a voice calling her name. She sat up. Listened. No sound. She must have imagined it. Ghosts plaguing her. Or else it was the owl calling. She glanced at her watch. Just past midnight. She turned to face the wall, trying to block out the revenants of the night. And then she heard the voice again. Clearer this time. Soft and sad. A man's voice.

'Sam. Sam. Are you there?'

Somebody was calling to her from the front garden. She walked over to the window, tweaked the curtain and saw the silhouette of a tall man standing by the rose bushes. He was swaying slightly, as if he were at sea. She peered into the gloom, saw the blue of his eyes turning violet in the lingering rays of the summer sun. It was Nils. It was a relief more than a surprise to see him there; an unexpected midnight visit from a melancholic Norwegian skipper was hardly the worst event she could have imagined. She pulled the curtain further back, waved. He smiled and beckoned her outside.

She grabbed her overcoat, slipped quietly out of her room and through the front door in the hallway into the garden, the grass damp beneath her bare feet, the air perfumed with the sweet scent of dusky roses and the sour trace of beer. Not that it bothered her. The alcohol.

He opened his mouth, but said nothing, his eyes flitting past her.

'What are you doing here?' she asked. 'Are you okay?'

He nodded, his sight finally settling on her face.

She couldn't quite tell whether his hesitation was caused by embarrassment or alcohol.

'Do you want to come in? I could make you a cup of coffee.'

'No. No. I have to tell you something,' he managed to say.

She shrugged, bemused. 'What?'

'The boat. *The Inquisitor.*'

The name caught her unawares. She was half hoping for a drunken declaration of attraction. 'What about it?' she asked, almost curtly.

He stalled again. 'I was worried about it. It wasn't right. I asked the harbour master. He's a friend of mine. He said it hadn't been here before. He checked it out. Made some enquiries. It sailed from Scrabster a couple of days ago. Changed hands in Scrabster, different man sailed it out from the one who brought it in. Harbour master said he didn't like the look of the skipper. He thought there was something not pleasant about him. Shifty.'

Her mouth drooped, downhearted as much as concerned.

'Did he say what he looked like?'

She didn't really have to ask. She could guess what was coming.

'Dark. Said he was dark. Black holes for eyes.'

The Watcher.

'I wanted to tell you,' Nils said. 'Thought he might be after you for some reason. Thought you might be in some kind of trouble. Because you... because you seemed sad. Anxious. As if you were carrying some secret burden perhaps. I'm sorry. This is stupid of me. Shouldn't have come here at this time. I stopped for a drink in Tirlsay. I'm sorry.'

He lurched towards her. She reached out to steady him.

'It's okay,' she said. 'Thank you for telling me about the boat.'

'No. I'm sorry about the drinking.'

'Oh, that's okay.'

He slumped down heavily on the grass, stared over at the bay.

'Are you sure you wouldn't like a cup of coffee?'

He shook his head morosely. 'All fishermen drink, yes?'

She wasn't sure whether he was asking her a question or stating a fact.

'It goes with the life,' he continued. 'It is part of the rhythm of fishing. The sea and the land. The peaks and the troughs. I promised her I would control it. But it didn't make any difference. She still left me.'

'Marie-Jean?' Sam asked. She sat down beside him.

'She went nearly a year ago now.' He nudged one of the stones of her ancestor memorial with his boot. 'She moved down to Edinburgh with a writer. He came here for a summer break without his wife to finish his book. Then he ran off with mine. I couldn't understand it. She was younger than me. He was old and a bit fat.'

She nodded sympathetically.

'She said she couldn't put up with my drinking,' Nils said. 'I'm not sure the drink had anything to do with it in the end. This is an excuse. She just wanted to escape.'

'And you decided to stay here in Orkney anyway.'

'Yes. I moved here to be with Marie-Jean but, in the end, I fell in love with the islands. I miss her though. I hope she will come back to Stromness. And to me. She loves the sea.'

'I'm sure she will get fed up with the writer and come back.'

'I don't think so.'

He rested his forehead on his knees, eyes down at the ground. She wanted to comfort him, put her arm round him, but couldn't quite summon the courage. He lifted his head sharply, taking in his surroundings. He glanced back at Nethergate, looked at her.

'Well, I just came to tell you about *The Inquisitor*.' He sounded suddenly sober. 'I had better go now.'

She wanted to prolong the conversation. 'How are you going to get back to Stromness?'

'I left my car in Tirlsay.'

'Are you sure you're okay to drive?'

'Of course.'

He heaved himself to his feet. 'Come and see me in Stromness,' he said. He smiled. 'And we can go out on the boat again.'

She wondered if he always ended his conversations like that, with an invitation to accompany him on a sea voyage, or whether he really meant it.

'Okay,' she said. 'I'll come and find you again before we go.'

He was already heading to the road, loping down the hill, swallowed up by the twilight. She peered into the valley, searching the borderline of the wood for the giveaway amber flare of the Watcher's cigarette. But there was nothing. As she turned back to the house, a shadow flitted across her vision and the owl called its haunting note.

CHAPTER 10

SAM CHECKED NERVOUSLY over her shoulder as they drove away from Nethergate. Jim raced ahead in the Renault. They tried to keep up in the Cortina, ploughing noisily through sheep-splattered hills while above them clouds scudded across the sky. By the time they reached the car park below Marwick Head the strengthening wind was making it difficult to open the car doors. Jim was waiting, propped against the Renault, assessing the rolling fields through his binoculars.

'That's why it takes longer to fly to the States than it does to fly back. It's the prevailing winds,' Jim yelled as they struggled to join him. 'The Jet Stream. I'm the first person that's stood up to this lot since it left the east coast of North America.'

He put his face up against the gale and prodded the air with his finger. 'Back off. Don't mess with me,' he shouted.

She exchanged sidelong glances with Tom as they shivered in their flapping thin coats and she wondered what they were doing here alone with this madman attempting to bully the elements into submission.

'What a couple of namby-pambies,' yelled Jim, intercepting their unspoken communication. 'Race you to the memorial.'

He head-butted the wind as he pounded up the path towards the square tower standing guard over the island.

'That's not fair. You've had a head start,' she shouted.

'That's not fair,' Jim echoed in a mocking squeaky voice as he turned and ran backwards, waggling his hands in the air. She set off after him, bent over by the assault and battery of the gusts, hair lashing her face, calves aching with the effort of running up the hill. When was the last time she played this game with Jim? Greenwich when she was eight. 1974. He was still at the docks with Harry. Just. Still watching the ships sailing between Tilbury and Russia. She had spent the day with Liz and her sisters, jumping the meridian, running around the Observatory and admiring the cloud-topped spires of the city. Jim did not rendez-vous at the prearranged meeting spot. They had given up waiting for him, walked down to the *Cutty Sark* as the sun was setting, Liz biting her lip angrily. A cool breeze was blowing off the water, carrying the chime of distant church bells and far-off voices. A familiar figure was leaning on the railings, staring out over the Thames, mesmerized by the oily tide sweeping its secrets past Deptford and Gravesend and out to the sea. That was their man. What was he doing there? He dragged his eyes away from the water and grinned with what he hoped was boyish charm.

'Who is coming to the Isle of Dogs? Who wants to look for the secret passage under the river?' Jim shouted.

'Me,' Sam yelled. 'I'll go.'

Liz sat with regal disdain on a bench by the clipper and Helen and Jess, her ladies in waiting, slumped by her side. They were not amused.

'We'll have to be quick,' said Jim, 'or Liz will have our heads chopped off.' Jim led the way to the crystal dome glowing irresistibly against the violet sky.

'If we're lucky, we might catch Charlie the lift-man.'

Charlie was pulling the concertina lift-gate shut as they arrived and he shook his head and tapped his watch. 'You're too late. You'll have to use the stairs.'

'Do us a favour,' said Jim.

Charlie folded his arms. 'I'm always doing you favours.'

'Official business.' Jim winked and nodded his head in Sam's direction. Charlie laughed.

'Come on then, jump in, princess,' he said to Sam. 'Last ride of the night. It's been a busy evening.' He gave Jim a meaningful look as the old-fashioned lift descended to the white-tiled foot tunnel buried beneath the Thames. At the bottom, Charlie sang a sad song as he watched them go.

'Let's face the music,' he warbled and the words pursued them as they walked.

'Why is he singing that song?' she asked.

Jim quickened his pace. 'Charlie makes a song and a dance out of everything. Race you to the Isle of Dogs.'

She chased Jim and her short legs failed to match his adult strides even though he was running backwards and shouting profanities that passed over her head and echoed round the tiles. Halfway across he stopped, abruptly, and walked over to the side of the tunnel and, as she caught up with him, she saw he had pushed one of the white tiles with his finger and lifted it away from the wall.

'Stop it.' Horrified. 'You'll let the water in.'

'Not me,' he said. 'I'm not going to let the water in. I'm the one who makes sure there aren't any leaks. I'm the bloody plumber.' He laughed. And she laughed too. For some reason. She watched him curiously as he peered into the dark space in the white wall, stuck his hand in quickly, retracted it, pushed the tile back into place. In the strange silence of the tunnel she thought she could hear the river water rushing past above her head. She felt a wave of panic engulfing her.

'The walls are caving in.'

'Don't be silly. Hold my hand and we'll run back together. You're safe underground with me.'

She wouldn't be there in the first place, she thought, if it wasn't for him. But she did what she was told and held his hand and felt the strength of his grip. Together they paced through London's red clay while Jim marvelled at the magic of the Victorian's underground engineering. Charlie was waiting for them when they reached the south side and he whistled his mournful tune all the way back to the surface. Let's face the music. Later, when she tried to recall that evening, it took on the hazy quality of a haunting dream and she could no longer be certain whether Jim really had taken something out from a drop-box behind the tile and slipped it into his pocket or whether she had just imagined it. All she had to hold on to with any certainty was the feeling of sickness in her stomach, the tightness in her chest, the rising panic. And even then, she wasn't sure whether the fear was reaching out to her or she was clinging on to it.

She wiped an unexpected tear from her eye with the back of her hand, took a deep breath as she steamed against the wind, towards the memorial. More oxygen plus red blood cells equals stamina, she chanted and felt the power surging around her body. As she caught up with Jim, she veered to the right to overtake but he barged her, hard, making her stumble and he ran on to reach Kitchener's brick memorial first.

'I won,' he shouted.

She yelled, breathlessly, 'You cheated.'

'I still won.'

'You're past it, Dad.'

He winced and she regretted her words.

She slumped down with her back anchored against the tower, watching the skerry-strewn coastline beyond the sheer drop of the sandstone cliff, and ran through the Beaufort scale in her mind, the roaring wind paining her ears. High waves,

breaking crests, white foam: force eight. Tom strode noncha-
lantly up the hill to join them, anorak pulling against his frame.
He read the memorial plaque.

'So this marks the spot where Kitchener and his crew went
down with the HMS *Hampshire*,' he said.

They were respectfully silent for a moment as the breakers
pounded the cliff way down below. A furiously flapping puffin
cut across the headland and set a course for the open sea.

Tom sat down on the grass next to her. 'I wonder how many
men drowned here.'

'Hundreds.'

'How long do you think anybody could survive in that
water?'

'About two minutes I should think. Your country needs
you,' she said, pointing at Tom, 'to waste your life for a completely unnecessary cause.'

'What do you know?' Jim said scornfully.

'The First World War was a total waste of life,' she retorted.
'Everyone knows that.'

'Hindsight always gives you easy answers. The certainty of
the armchair perspective. Right and wrong are not so clear
when you're in the middle of it, out there patrolling in the dark.
Then it's harder to make judgements. Then there's no time for
riding moral high-horses. Sometimes you don't even know
where you are. You might think you're fighting for one side,
put your head down and get on with it, and when you finally
have a chance to breathe, you stand up and realize you're in a
completely different battlefield. Somewhere else entirely.'

Tom looked as if he was about to say something, but he kept
his mouth shut. She couldn't quite bear the reverence, the
brotherhood, the respect for all things macho and bloody. Take
the toys from the boys.

'Anyway, wasn't Kitchener on his way to fix up a dodgy deal with the Russians when his ship went down?' she said. 'Wasn't there some story about a Russian agent being involved? Somebody wanted Kitchener out of the way for some reason or another.'

She felt the heat of Jim's glare.

'Conspiracy theory,' he said dismissively. He clenched his jaw as he shifted his sight to the far horizon, the vanishing point, the place where the *Hampshire* was swallowed up by the sea. She tried to see what he could see, stared at the chopping waves and the dark spaces, let them fall into a pattern. Seals. Submarines. Shadows. And then she spotted the anomaly, the hard grey outline: the pointed prow of a boat. *The Inquisitor.*

'Let's move it,' said Jim.

Southbound along the narrow path that clung to the cliff edge, the fulmars bobbing along beside their feet, inches away from being blasted against the hard rock, skuas making them duck and shield their heads with their arms. Kitchener's Memorial shrank behind them, nothing but a chess piece now. The cliff face eased out marginally into a more forgiving angle, scars of sheep tracks zigzagging the slopes.

'Now this is the place,' said Jim, 'where I used to pick mushrooms. Look.' He pointed toward a narrow gulley running off into oblivion. 'I can see some down there. Who's coming with me to pick them?'

'Not me,' she said. 'I'll wait here.'

'Afraid of heights, are you?'

'Yes.'

'I'll go with you,' said Tom.

'That's your funeral,' she said. 'It's that way.' She nodded her head towards the cliff edge.

She flumped on the springy grass mattress. A stream trying to find its course along a small gully nearby caught her attention; the wind was so strong now it was blowing the water vertically into the air as it hit the edge of the cliff. She considered the meandering creek denying gravity and thought of Liz watching her husband and daughters disappearing over the edge at the same spot ten years earlier. For a moment, she was eight again, laughing at the wind with her sisters. And in her head the wind was tugging at Jim, pulling his fingers back from the rocks, flinging him to feed the waves below. She sat up, tipped on to her hands and knees and crawled towards the brink, lichen-starred stone rasping her palms. Jim and Tom were nowhere. But beyond the lines of curling waves, she spotted the dark shape of *The Inquisitor* again, visible for a few seconds in the spindrift before vanishing down a trough and reappearing further along the horizon, pursuing a dogged course parallel to the coast, shadowing their path. She pictured Jim and Tom, two dark dots moving across the pale cliff face like nits crawling across a forehead. They would be clearly visible even from a distance. What was Jim doing? Signalling his presence? Creating a diversion?

The black crescent moon of Jim's head emerged above the cliff's edge, followed by his triumphant smirk. Tom straggled behind and collapsed on the ground beside her, his face taut and wan. Jim opened his cupped hands to reveal a pile of white fungus.

'Mushrooms,' he said.

'Puffballs,' she replied, giving the stuff a dirty look.

'Mushrooms. Anyway, puffballs are edible.'

'Well you'd probably eat babies' brains if somebody offered them to you with a nice bit of bread to mop up the juice. I'm certainly not going to have any.'

'I wasn't offering you any.'

He retrieved his Swiss Army Knife from his windcheater pocket, wiped the malingering slivers off the blade with his hanky, folded it lovingly, slipped it into his haversack. And she wondered whether he had brought the Walther with him, whether it was in there too, nestling at the bottom of his bag.

'Okay then,' he said abruptly. 'I've had enough of you lot. I'm off. If you're hungry, turn left out of the car park and there's a café just down the road. Proper coffee. None of your gnat's piss. See you back at the house.'

He hoofed away inland, diagonally across the slope in the direction of the car park.

'Where are you going?' she shouted after him. 'I need to know in case you don't come back and I have to send the old bill out to search for your body. Are you going to see a man about a dog?'

He turned, shouted back, the wind trying to snatch away his words. 'Not a dog. I'm going bird-watching.' He waved the back of his hand dismissively and headed off over the fields at a cracking speed.

'He's given us the slip again,' said Tom. His face had reverted to its normal shade of pale now. 'He's led us on a merry song and dance up and down the cliffs and tired us out with his mushrooms and now he's disappeared. Anyway, do you think that was a sort of confession?'

'What?'

'Bird-watching. A bad joke. He was telling you he's going to meet a woman.'

'Don't be ridiculous.'

'Men sometimes ask to be found out,' he said undeterred. 'Usually when they get fed up with the other woman because she wants more commitment. That's when they need a get-out, so they start dropping huge hints, hoping to be found out by their wives. And possibly daughters.'

She didn't respond.

'So what do you think he's going to do?' Tom needled.

'I've no idea.'

'Have a guess.'

She stuck her hands in her pockets, put her head on one side, glanced at Tom; he wasn't what you would call good-looking, but he was quite attractive in an unconventional sort of way, now that he was more angular.

'Well, he probably was telling the truth in a funny kind of way,' she said. 'Because he does sometimes, tell the truth. Just not all of the truth. So maybe he is heading to a bird-watching place, a reserve or something like that. Although God only knows what he is going to do when he gets there.'

'Maybe we should try and follow him and find out?'

She hesitated. 'Why?'

'Why not? It could be fun. Come on. Let's find out what he's really up to.'

She glanced over Tom's shoulder to the ocean, saw the distant predatory form of *The Inquisitor* chasing through the waves and felt a twinge of fear for Jim.

'Okay, but we'll have to move quickly; otherwise we'll lose track of him.'

They raced down the hill, a tailwind harrying them along now. She pushed her arms down straight and held her hands out horizontally to the ground, gliding effortlessly, feet hardly touching the ground, floating over red clover, white clover, ragged robin, heart's ease. 'The prevailing winds,' she shouted, 'are carrying me away. I'm flying.'

'What makes you so sure that you won't turn out like your dad?'

'Half of my DNA may come from him, but I reckon all his genes are recessive. That's why I don't look anything like him.'

She tried without success to barge Tom and knock him over. He stuck his foot out to trip her up. She jumped over his trainer, escaped, running down the hill laughing, just in time to catch sight of the roof of the Renault as it slid along the hedgerow and sped down the road.

'He's travelling south,' she shouted.

'We'll have to see if we can work out where he's heading,' said Tom.

They sat in the car with the map spread out between them.

'I wouldn't know where to start,' said Tom. 'You'll have to make an educated guess.'

She pondered for a second, pictured *The Inquisitor* drawn away by Jim's mushroom-picking escapade to the northwest of the island.

'This is the way I see it. Jim's going to a bird reserve. Probably somewhere to the southeast, and I would imagine it's a place I will recognize, somewhere we went to together when I was young, because he seems to be revisiting old haunts. So we have to look for one of those bird symbols somewhere on the other side of the island in a place that sounds familiar to me.'

'Good deduction.'

'Elementary, my dear Watson.'

She studied the map through the shimmer of her eyelashes and felt light-headed: contour lines, roads and grid marks twirled, kaleidoscope patterns formed in front of her face and dropped like dust on the paper, the day trips of childhood summers danced across the map's creases. And suddenly she realized everything was a bluff for Jim, nothing was what it appeared to be, even their bloody summer holidays. She felt a fermenting anger in her stomach, swallowed it down and told herself to concentrate; she searched the map coldly this time, a geomancer reading the landscape, ruling out various places because they were too close or because they didn't ring any bells. Something clicked.

'I know that beach.' She prodded the map. 'Waulkmill Bay. There's a bird reserve there. That's the one, I'm sure. Jim used to take us there to look for mussels. I still have a scar on my knee from tripping on the rocks because we had to scramble back when Liz pointed out the tide was coming in.'

The corners of Tom's mouth sagged. 'God, I nearly got more than a scarred knee out there on the cliff face just now. I thought at one point the wind was trying to rip me away from the rock. Jim is a bit...' he started to say.

'I did warn you,' she shouted. 'Anyway you're eighteen. You are an adult. You didn't have to follow him over the edge of a cliff in a force nine gale. It was your stupid choice.' She reached for the car door, about to flounce away and tramp off over the cliffs, when she caught sight of herself in the wing mirror, realized she was on the verge of acting like a nutter. Like her dad. She fastened her seat belt.

'Why are you getting angry with me?' Tom asked.

She couldn't answer. She had no idea. She saw herself momentarily through his eyes: Sam Coyle, a bar-brawler in a pub called Emotion, flinging random punches at no apparent target before making a dive for the saloon door and legging it off into the night. She let her temper subside and fizzle out. Smiled sheepishly.

The wind dropped as they drove and was almost non-existent by the time they reached Waulkmill Bay. They crawled around the tyre-rutted car park of the bird reserve a couple of times, but there was no trace of the Renault or of Jim. She was beginning to think her instincts were wrong, she couldn't read the signs after all. They agreed they had better give up the chase, call it a day, and head back to Nethergate. Driving along the main road, it was Tom who spotted the Renault parked outside an ugly breeze-block building, a tacky reproduction of a crofter's cottage that had ended up looking like a public toilet. A salt-rusted board by the road clanked in the breeze: the Oyster Catcher Café.

'That was where we used to go for tea after we'd collected the mussels.' She yelled with the relief of being right after all. 'Do you think he would have heard the Cortina go past?'

'Doubt it. The café's too far from the road. What shall we do then? Turn around and drive back to the café?'

'No.' She wrestled frantically with the folds of the map. 'Turn up here. Left. Park there, behind that hedge.'

They pulled in at the side of the road by a stile and a footpath, hidden from sight by a stubby hawthorn.

Standing by the car, debating what to do next, she felt uneasy. She scanned the hill ridge behind, searching for the brief flare of a match, the warning cry of a crow. Nothing. It must have been the breeze. She was imagining things; Jim had lured the Watcher out on the seas beyond Marwick Head, shaken the shadows.

'Perhaps we should run back to the café and look inside,' Tom said. 'We can peer in through the windows.'

'What if he spots us?'

'We'll just say we were driving past, saw the Renault and thought we'd take a peek in to see if he was there because we fancied joining him for a cake and a cuppa. Okay, let's get moving,' he said. Taking charge. Enjoying the chase. 'Zero hour. We're going over, men.' He set off down the road at an officer-like clip before she had time to object.

She caught up with him at the café car park, crouching behind a mud-splattered Land Rover.

'Down,' Tom hissed. 'You might be seen. We have to rethink,' he added as she squatted next to him. 'The windows are too high to look in.'

She stuck her head up above the bonnet of the Land Rover, took in the narrow windows pushed up against the eaves.

'You could hold on to a windowsill and pull yourself up,' she said. 'If we go round the back, no one will be able to see us.'

They trampled through the nettles, inspecting the windows.

'See if you can lift your head above the ledge.'

He stretched, clutched on to the windowsill, hauled himself up, pushing his feet against the wall for leverage, momentarily raising his chin above the sill before dropping back to the ground.

'What did you see?'

'Jim. He's with a woman.' He sounded smug. 'They are sitting alone at a table in the corner talking.'

'What did she look like?'

'Late twenties, I would guess. Long blonde hair. It's hard to see clearly through the net curtains.'

'You're making it up.'

'I'm not. It's what I saw.'

'I have to look.'

'You'll never reach up there.'

She cast around for a solid object to stand on, an old milk crate perhaps, but couldn't locate anything that would hold her weight.

'You'll have to lift me. I can sit on your shoulders.'

Tom crouched down while she clambered on; he swayed and grunted with the effort as he stood up, staggered the few steps to the window. She steadied herself by holding on to the sill as she peeked through the mucky netting. The interior of the café was the same as it had been eight years before: flustered teenage girls in too-tight black skirts, three-tiered cake-stands, dour couples in drab hiking gear scouring the room irritably to see if their food was on its way. Jim was sitting in a corner, leaning in close to a woman with straggly dirty-blonde hair. She couldn't quite make sense of it all. She blinked and the scene shimmered and danced, everything solid seemed to melt into air and just for that moment she doubted her own existence; her whole life was a cover. She was the shadow, a figment of Jim's imagination, conjured up to provide a bit of depth to his fake backstory and the true reality, the solid Jim and the relationship that meant something to him were there in front of her eyes, on the other side of the window.

Her eyes were watering. She took in a gulp of air, told herself to get a grip, to concentrate. The molecules rained down around her and settled into an understandable order. She wondered then how Jim managed this life, shifting from one identity to another, one world to another, without everything colliding. But of course, he wasn't managing; he was letting things slip and slide. She wouldn't be here watching him play this part if he were still in control. He was losing his grip. Or maybe he was tightening it in some perverse way that she didn't quite understand. She brushed her eyes with her hand, scrutinized the scene in front of her, concentrated on identifying the key to this meeting: the give-away detail, the anomaly, the piece out of place. Her vision locked on to a biscuit-brown rectangle. An A5 envelope. It was lying on the red-and-white checked plastic tablecloth, halfway between Jim and the woman. She watched as Jim's hand moved to cover it, then paused momentarily before sliding it off the table and into his open haversack, ready and waiting by his feet. That was it; that had to be the key. He had arranged to meet this woman here to pick up whatever information was in that manila envelope.

'What's going on in there?' said Tom.

'Nothing,' she said.

'Let me have another look.'

'Okay.'

She pushed herself back from the windowsill. Tom swayed with the sudden movement. She leaned the wrong way and he lost his balance and stumbled as she moved the wrong way again and they fell down to the ground in a heap. They lay still for a moment, limbs tangled, winded among the nettles.

'What happened there?' Tom asked. 'What made us fall?'

'I don't know. I lost my balance somehow. We'd better get back to the car,' she said, with a sense of urgency in her voice. 'Jim was getting ready to leave. Let's go back up the hill and watch what he does from there.'

Tom plucked at the strands of goose-grass sticking to his jeans, still slightly befuddled.

'Come on,' she said. 'We have to skedaddle.'

He looked at her, thoughtfully.

'Come on.' She said it more firmly this time, grabbed hold of his arm.

They jogged across the car park. She checked nervously over her shoulder to see if Jim was coming out of the café door, but they made it back along the road before there was any sign of movement behind them. They followed the footpath up the side of the field along the hedgerow, halted in its lee, and surveyed the café through the tangle of hawthorn and wild roses. Jim emerged alone through the café door, lingering in the shadow of the doorway, scanning the low hills, sniffing the air like a hunted animal before making a quick dash for the Renault. He drove right, headed down the main road, back towards Nethergate.

'Here comes Jim's friend,' said Tom.

The woman walked nervously across the car park: black combat trousers, green-and-black striped mohair jumper, army issue canvas bag slung across her chest. She looked, Sam could see now, like a woman who might go to Greenham. She wondered whether she might even have met her there, and couldn't work out whether that possibility made her feel better or worse. What if she was an informant from the peace camp? Filling Jim in on the activities of his errant daughter. Letting him know that Sam was the enemy within, the home-grown domestic subversive who had unearthed the top secret information about the hotline to the White House and had very nearly been caught investigating the critical cable. She was over-dramatizing. Tom was right. Nobody would care about a couple of teenage girls breaking into Greenham.

The woman clambered into a beaten-up red 2CV and reversed out on to the main road.

'She's put her indicator on,' said Tom. 'She's turning left, up the road that runs by the side of this field. We'd better duck. She might see us.'

They dropped to the ground. The car passed below the hedge. Sam quivered. Whoever this woman was, whatever information she had passed to Jim in that envelope, her secrets were so sensitive that Jim had trekked to Orkney to obtain them. Fifty-nine degrees north. And he had taken a pistol with him to protect the intelligence.

Back in the Cortina, Tom spread the map out again so they could identify the road the car had taken.

'Well, it shouldn't be difficult to find out where she was heading,' Tom said. 'Look, that road is a dead-end and there are only a couple of houses anywhere near it.' He grinned. 'I could enjoy this surveillance business. I'd make a good spy. Let's drive down, take a look.'

She felt panicked by Tom's interest in this woman. 'No. Let's drive back to Nethergate,' she said. 'I'm hungry. We could stop in Kirkwall on the way back and pick up something to eat.'

'Okay. But we could come back tomorrow and work out where she lives. See if we can find out anything else about her.'

She was torn now between wanting to find out more about Jim's contact, and keeping Tom from finding out too much; grappling with her need to know about Jim, and being afraid to find out.

'Okay. Let's come back tomorrow,' she said. 'We could always go to the beach and the Oyster Catcher if we get bored.' She checked the map again. Something clicked in her head. Thirty-eight, seventy.

'Eastings and northings,' she said.

'What about them?'

'Nothing. Great words, that's all.'

CHAPTER 11

BACK AT NETHERGATE, the fungi were sitting in a conspicuous pile on the kitchen counter. Sam picked up a ball, inhaled its musty scent, snapped it in half, rubbed the dense flesh on her lips, hesitated, opened the kitchen window and held the white matter out in the flat of her hand. The donkey advanced, sniffed and turned away. Very wise. She fished around at the back of the fridge for a bendy carrot to offer to him instead.

'Who is going to eat mushrooms with me?' shouted Jim from his room.

'Not me, thanks. I'm too young to die.'

'What about you, Tom? You helped pick them after all. Don't let her put you off.' Jim appeared in the kitchen. 'Doesn't know her arse from her elbow.'

'Thanks, but we ate on the way back,' Tom replied. He smiled in a strained sort of way.

'Don't know what you're missing. Fresh mushrooms on toast. My favourite. Bit of butter, bit of parsley.'

'Bit of poison,' she said.

He squeezed past them to the far end of the kitchen, scrabbled in a drawer for a knife. He whiffed of whisky. He stopped mid-chop, knife in the air, shuffling his feet, squirming as if he was suffering from some kind of pain. She wondered whether the information he had found in the envelope was making him uncomfortable.

They left Jim to his frying, trudged into the front room. She spotted Jim's Ordnance Survey map lying on the living room table. Eastings and northings. She unfolded it, narrowed her eyes, screened out the contours, the green, the grey, the coastline and focused on the grid. She reminded herself of the numbers of the turned-down pages in *The Orkneyinga Saga*: thirty-eight, seventy. Eastings first, northings second. She held her breath as she studied the map.

Stab of disappointment. The numbers didn't work; it couldn't be a grid reference because there wasn't a seventy along the bottom or along the side. Her mind was creating codes to crack where they didn't exist; so much for the Death of Rognvald. And then she thought of another possibility. Chapters. The single dog-ear: Death of Rognvald, chapter 29. The double dog-ear: Earl Sigurd's Sons, Chapter 13. She flattened the folds of the map, located the twenty-ninth easting, traced the grid-line with her finger to the thirteenth northing. She almost yelped triumphantly. The lines intersected just below the Ring of Brodgar.

Tom glanced up from the book he had picked up from the shelf. 'What are you looking for?'

'Nothing in particular. What are you reading?' The Sicilian Defence, mirror his move.

'One of those Freemasonry conspiracy books that people always leave in holiday cottages. Jesus wasn't killed on the cross. He married, had a load of children, fled to the south of France. The Freemasons have protected the lineage and evidence of its origins. Pile of crap.'

'So what's your theory about the Freemasons then?' She glanced down at the map again.

'My theory is that no theory is necessary. The Freemasons are a bunch of middle-class blokes who hang out together and protect each other's interests; you scratch my back and I'll scratch yours. It's a white-collar club. The secret signs, the rituals, they're all meaningless claptrap.'

'Jim would probably be on your side on that one.' She was half listening as she discreetly rechecked the grid reference. Lord. She had read it correctly. What was he going to do at the Ring of Brodgar of all places?

'But Jim must be a Freemason,' said Tom. 'He's an inspector, isn't he? I thought you more or less had to be a Freemason to get on in the Force.'

'No, he's not a Freemason.' She looked up. 'It's not his kind of thing at all. I remember overhearing him tell his mate Harry that the Commander had invited him to join a couple of times. And Jim said he wasn't interested in poncing around in a pinafore and acting like a twerp just to keep in with a bunch of boring accountants and bloody lawyers.'

'The exception that proves the rule.'

'Maybe. Let's play Triv.'

Jim walked into the room, belched, made the air reek of rotten eggs, loomed over them as they played.

'I've got a Trivial question for you,' he said eventually.

They raised their heads in unison.

'Where is Shinkolobwe?'

'Don't know,' Sam said.

'I don't think I've heard of it,' said Tom.

'Really? I'm surprised that you two haven't heard of Shinkolobwe.'

'Why should we have heard of it?' she asked.

He shrugged. 'Thought it was the kind of thing all you sandalistas knew.'

'Where is it, then?'

'Guess.'

'Africa?' said Tom.

'Good start. Right continent at least.'

She was about to take a stab at a country, but Tom slipped in one of his intrusive questions first.

'Is that where you served when you were in the Army? Africa?'

'Yes. Africa. Among other places.'

Jim closed the conversation down with a yawn, announced he was tired so he was going to read in his room, retreated. She wondered then whether Tom had hit on a connection, a link between Shinkolobwe and Jim's spell in the army, whether that could somehow be tied up with whatever he had found out from the woman in the café, the information in the manila envelope. But it didn't make much sense. Then again, the lines of Jim's strange existence never made much sense. She twiddled a stray strand of hair. She couldn't concentrate on the game, distracted by Jim and his own trivial pursuits. Shinkolobwe. She flicked her wrist – seven – suggested they go for a stroll, make the most of the calmer weather.

They climbed up behind the house, away from Tirlsay, past a field of bullocks swatting clouds of flies with their tails. The fields petered out, replaced with bracken, heather, deserted crumbling crofters' cottages and tumuli. More ghosts. No escaping the phantoms. Even up here, exposed on the hillside, the wind was hardly even a gentle pressure. She swiped inef- fectually at the midges dancing in irritating patterns around her head, breaking up her vision, and wondered whether it was an unnatural calm before the storm. At the hill's crest, they paused to take in the view.

'Look up there.' She pointed to a single standing stone, grey on the ridge. And then she spotted another solitary finger, further along to her left. They were at a crossroads; the hill's ridge marked the intersection of two paths: tarmac and ley-line.

'Signposts. Markers,' she said.

'Markers of what?'

'The path for pilgrims. The spiritual highway.'

'To where?

'The Ring of Brodgar.' She stretched her arms out and up to the sky.

'Oh God, please spare us the bloody High Priestess again.' She smiled. Tom smiled back.

'Go on then,' he said. 'Tell me about the Ring of Brodgar.'

'It's a Neolithic stone circle to the west of here. It's a strange place. It radiates ancient powers. Even you will be bewitched by its mysterious magic. We'll have to visit it before we leave.'

'Okay. I'll give it a go.' He looked down, seemingly engrossed in harassing a long, black beetle with the toe of his trainer, forcing its abdomen to curl upwards like a scorpion.

'Sam. There's something I want to say to you.'

Something about the tone of his voice made her want to pretend she hadn't heard him. 'Let's carry on along the road for a bit longer,' she said.

The beetle made a dash for the heather, tail still curled.

'Hang on a minute. I want to talk.'

She wasn't listening. She took a step, one foot on the ley-line, one foot on the road. The warning tweet of a passerine made her look up. The flecked grey underside of the raptor was just visible high in the stratosphere, hovering, resisting the upward pull of the warm thermal. Suddenly it folded its wings and dived, screaming downwards, sending out an electric shockwave as it swooped. It vanished. She checked over her shoulder. Nothing. Forwards again: face to face with the yellow blazing eyes. Glaring. Perched on a fence post on the far side of a track running out across the moorland. She blinked. It was up in the air again. Flying above the track, head down, searching.

'Peregrine. Let's follow it.' She swerved off the road, down the trail, catching her feet in the coarse grass, switching between ridges and ruts, the falcon hanging in the air a few yards ahead. Feet pounding, out of breath as the track curved round a sharp corner. She came to a sudden halt, confronted by an incongruent metallic glint. The silver gleam became a recognizable shape: a silver Merc superimposed on the landscape.

'Oh my God, it's that car again,' she whispered as Tom caught up with her. 'The one that nearly rammed us on the road out of Stromness. What on earth is it doing here?'

'Let's find out.'

'No. Let's scarper.'

'Don't be stupid.'

He strode confidently over to the car.

The Merc's driver was leaning over the bonnet, hands either side of a map spread out below her. She was wearing a leather biker jacket and her hair was cropped quite short. But, Sam noted resentfully, her red lipsticked mouth gave her an edge of seductiveness, a clear signal of intent. A glamorous tomboy. How old was she? Late twenties possibly. She turned her large smile on Tom, almost expectantly. He smiled back.

'Are you lost?' Tom asked. What a ridiculous question. As if she might have inadvertently taken a wrong turning down a barely used track and driven for quarter of a mile before she realized what she had done. Anyway, she hardly looked helpless. Not to Sam anyway. Tom was obviously too stupid to see beyond her make-up.

'I just pulled off the road to take in the view.' She had a hint of an American accent, not the brashness of the northern states but the drawl of the south. It sounded slightly overdone to Sam, as if she was deliberately trying to soften her persona, knew that she had to disguise her hard edges.

'I'm just trying to get my bearings.' She gestured – the hills, the valleys, the bay, the road to Nethergate clearly visible, winding its way through the bracken moor-grass. Her explanation was about as likely as Jim's history degree.

'I'm Avis, by the way.'

Avis – what sort of a stupid name was that? Avis held her hand out to Tom without a glance at Sam.

'Tom.' He gripped her hand.

'Let me help. I'm good with maps.' He was standing right next to her now. Sam said nothing, fuming at Tom's willingness to buy her obviously implausible story. She assessed Avis slyly, searching for clues to her identity, chinks in her annoyingly attractive exterior. She stared at Avis's hands for a moment, hoping, perhaps, to catch sight of a sixth finger. There wasn't one. She let her eyes travel up from Avis's elegant hand to a slender wrist encircled by a silver-strapped watch. She blinked and double-checked the evidently expensive watch.

'We're here,' Tom said, pointing at the map, lining it up. 'That's the Bay down there.'

'Oh of course,' said Avis. 'Thank you.'

Tom smiled again. Like a prize idiot.

'Are you on holiday here?' Avis asked.

Sam assumed he would have the sense not to answer the question honestly.

'Well, a sort of holiday,' he said. She attempted to tread on his toe discreetly to stop him from talking but he moved his foot while hers was in mid-air and she missed, managed to crunch her own toe instead.

'Actually, we're here to keep her dad company.' He nodded dismissively in Sam's direction. 'He wanted to take a break in Orkney and we are just trying to keep him on the straight and narrow while he works out whether or not to do a history degree.'

'How interesting,' she said. 'History. And what about you? What do you do, Tom?'

Avis asked more questions than Tom did, she noted.

'I'm a writer.'

Sam raised one eyebrow in an attempt to convey the delusional nature of Tom's claims.

'Well, journalist actually,' he added.

Well, not actually.

'Journalism? That's my field too,' Avis said.

'Is it?' Tom's eyes glistened with interest. 'Journalism? Which paper do you work for?'

Sam kicked her foot impatiently against a tussock of cotton grass.

'I'm freelance. I write a lot of features for magazines – the colour supplements, women's glossies.'

'What are you doing here then?' Sam said, pointedly.

Avis narrowed her glinting green cat's eyes. 'I have a contract with a travel writing publisher to cover the Highlands and Islands for a series of guides they are producing. So I'm doing a tour, visiting all the attractions, checking out the hotels.'

Sam had an urge to point out that it was a bit stupid to employ someone who couldn't read a map to write a travel guide.

'You must be doing well to be able to afford a Merc,' Sam said, not even trying to hide her incredulity now. 'I didn't think freelance writers earned that much.'

'It's my boyfriend's car.'

Avis turned to Tom.

'Who are you working for at the moment?'

'I've just been taken on by a local paper. I'll be starting in a couple of weeks.'

'For Christ's sake,' Sam muttered under her breath.

Tom glared at her.

'Come on,' she said, tugging on Tom's arm, 'we should go.'

He pulled his arm free. 'Will you be okay driving back along that track?' he asked.

'Yes. Don't worry. This car can deal with anything. I'm fine now I know where I am.'

'Maybe we'll bump into each other again.'

'Yes. It's a small island.'

Sam yanked Tom away by the hem of his windcheater. He turned and waved goodbye to Avis as they rounded the corner.

'What did you tell her about Jim for?' she demanded when they were back on the road, out of earshot. 'I could kill you.'

'I only said we were here with your dad. It's not as if I gave away any official secrets. Anyway, she wasn't interested in Jim.'

'She was staring at bloody Nethergate.'

'Sam, she was interested in my writing.'

'What writing? You aren't doing any writing.' And as she said it, she remembered that Tom was doing some writing: his notebook. She took a deep breath of air and narrowly avoided swallowing a midge.

'She'd have your guts for garters,' she said.

'You're just jealous.'

'No I'm not.' Her voice sounded shriller than she had meant it to.

'You don't really believe she's a freelance writer, do you?' she said.

'Why not?'

'The car for a start.'

'She said it was her boyfriend's.'

'I don't believe it.'

'Why not? Attractive, intelligent woman. Rich boyfriend. Makes sense to me.'

She shook her head, exasperated. 'You don't think it's strange to drive your Merc quarter of a mile off the road down a tractor track?'

'Not necessarily. And anyway it wasn't quarter of a mile. It was more like an eighth.'

'Okay. Don't you think it's strange to drive your Merc an eighth of a mile down a tractor track? You really think she's just hanging out in an off-the-road hidden spot in the middle of nowhere, doing a bit of background research for a tourist guide?'

'No. I reckon it's far more likely that she's working for the KGB and she's on a secret mission to monitor your dad and report his movements back to Moscow.'

She tried to kick him, but he dodged her foot. He prodded her in the ribs. She knocked his hand away.

'Did you see her watch?' she said.

'No. What about it?'

She paused. 'Oh nothing. It just looked very posh; a lady's version of one of those expensive diving watches, a Tag or something like that.'

'There we go,' he said. 'Gift from rich boyfriend.'

They walked on in silence, round the curve in the road, past the standing stones, across the ley-line, down the hill, back to Nethergate. The hooded crow was squatting on the roof tiles. She gave the bird a dirty look. It squawked at her.

'Anyway. We're evens now,' Tom said.

'Evens? What do you mean?'

'Oh forget it. I can't be bothered. It's too much like hard work.'

Jim was in his room. Tom wanted to finish the abandoned game of Triv. She played but her mind was absent. Elsewhere, trying to make the connections. She glanced down at her watch on the inside of her wrist. Just like Jim's.

'Decider,' Tom said. He rubbed his hands together. 'Science and nature.'

'Okay. Here goes.' She picked up a card, read the question silently, groaned. Easy-peasy; even he would be able to answer this one.

'What is a devil's coach-horse?'

He searched her face for clues. He knew she knew the answer. She tried to keep her mind blank, but she couldn't keep up the resistance.

'Tick-tock, tick-tock,' she said. 'Your time is running out.'

She pictured Tom's trainer chasing a small black object across the tarmac, tail above its head.

'Beetle,' said Tom.

'Damn. I gave that one away.'

'I've won,' shouted Tom. 'I'm on an upward curve. The trend is my friend.'

'One victory hardly counts as a trend. Anyway, I only let you win because I thought you might sulk otherwise.'

She stood up, walked away and left Tom looking smug.

She could hear Jim moving around in his bedroom. She knocked gently on his door.

'Go away,' he said.

'Are you feeling okay, Dad?'

'Yes.'

She hesitated, wondering whether she should mention Avis:

her feeble explanations, her overplayed American accent, her knack for wheedling information out of Tom. Her expensive watch. The one she wore on the inside of her wrist, like Sam. Like Jim. Like somebody who had military training. Somebody who knew how to use a gun.

'Are you sure you're okay?'

'Yes. Now piss off and leave me alone.'

She opened her mouth. Closed it. Retreated to her room.

CHAPTER 12

She had a bad night, dreaming that there had been a mistake, somebody had put her name on the wrong list, and she didn't have a place at Oxford after all. She woke feeling uncertain, unconfident, miserable. She dressed, crept out of bed and peered at Tom through the hinge-crack in the door. He was asleep, his bed bordered by a mosaic of dirty teacups, casually strewn clothing, snotty tissues and a pile of *Reader's Digests* sequestered from the front room. He had, she reckoned, been testing himself with the it-pays-to-increase-your-word-power page. She wandered through to the kitchen, searched the back of a cupboard for a clean cup, brewed herself a cup of tea to the metronome beat of the clock. No sight nor sound of Jim. Strange, she was rarely up before him.

Tom emerged, bleary-eyed.

'We're running out of mugs,' she said.

'What do you want me to do about it?'

'You could try taking the large collection that's littering the floor of your room to the kitchen, washing them up and putting them back in the cupboard.'

Jim always cleared up after himself, she thought, wiped away the traces, never left a trail.

'Sounds a bit drastic. What's wrong with that one?' he said pointing at her teacup.

'Oh forget it.'

'You're grumpy this morning. Where's Jim anyway?'

'Lying in bed dying from toadstool poisoning probably. Serves him right. I reckon he'd have eaten them even if they were stamped with a skull and cross-bones. Just to prove a point.'

'Shouldn't you check he's okay?'

'I suppose so.'

She knocked on Jim's door. There was no response. She pushed the door open cautiously; a shaft of grey light had inveigled its way through the curtain and was falling on the indistinct form of Jim rolled up in the bedclothes, his haversack next to him, wedged between his body and the far wall.

'Morning,' she said.

The sheets shifted.

'Leave me alone,' he said. 'I've got a cold.'

'That's okay then. I thought for a moment you might have food poisoning. Can I fetch you anything?'

'No. Bugger off.'

'Really, Dad. Let me fetch you a drink.'

There was no response from Jim. She cast her eye down, spotted an empty Jameson's bottle lying under his bed.

'Water perhaps?'

Silence.

'We are going out for the day so this is your last chance if you want me to bring you something.'

No answer.

'I'm going.'

'Good.'

She retreated back through the doorway, pulled the door shut behind her.

Outside, a thick mist draped the courtyard, muffling all sounds, making everything indistinct and flimsy. The black cat appeared from nowhere, stared at her with amber eyes fizzling, before padding off silently, swallowed by the brume.

Tom appeared at her elbow. 'So how is he?'

'As well as could be expected for a man who has single-handedly polished off a plateful of poisonous toadstools and the contents of a whiskey bottle.' She shrugged. 'Doesn't want any help from me anyway.'

'Might as well go to Waulkmill Bay then,' he said. 'If we can find it in this fog. Do a bit of detective work.'

The Cortina's headlights carved out a hazy cone in the dripping vapour.

'It's getting worse,' said Tom. 'I'm sure it's following us.'

The fuzzy lights of an oncoming car appeared out of nowhere, briefly lit up the road and passed by silently, leaving them sealed in their own world again. It was hard to tell whether they were moving let alone where they were. She checked the map, trying to identify passing shapes as they loomed and disappeared, listening for the dampened bleats of sheep.

'We should be coming up to the café now. So you need to turn right.'

He turned, pulled on to the verge when the headlights caught a gap in the hedgerow, a track running away from a gate. 'Assuming we are where you think we are,' he said, 'this footpath runs round the back of the houses that Jim's friend was heading for. We could walk along, see if we can spot her car.'

She sighed. 'Okay.'

The path curved inwards around the edge of a field, hugging the lower contours of the hill that rose behind and disappeared in dense nothingness. She trailed after Tom, feet soaking, ankles crosshatched with thistle scratches, shoulders hunched against the cold drizzle.

'We should be more or less directly behind the houses now,' he said.

'I can't see anything.'

At least no one could see them either.

'Let's just climb up here and rest a moment,' he said. 'See if the fog lifts.'

They sat on their coats, backs against a clammy outcrop of rock, peering down. She idly picked up a feather that was resting lightly on top of a clump of grass at her feet: white with a black tip as if someone had dipped the wrong end of the quill in the bottle of ink. A lapwing perhaps. She peered through the mist, thought she spotted an amber flare above them in the distance, glowing momentarily before it vanished. Perhaps it was an animal's eyes. Or nothing. They gazed vacantly into the void, both lost in their own thoughts.

A warm breath of wind lifted the fog to reveal a purple thistle-spiked meadow dripping with water-jewelled cobwebs. Beyond the field at the bottom of the slope the back of a dour farmhouse was visible, lording it over the crofts of the hillsides with its two-storeyed grandeur.

Tom pointed. 'That's the red 2CV she was driving.'

It was parked on the grass behind the house, next to a hatchback. Blue.

'I wonder who owns the other car,' Tom mused.

His interest was niggling her again. 'This isn't going to get us anywhere. It's pointless sitting here staring at cars. Let's go to the café and find something to eat.'

Tom folded his arms stubbornly. The air was suddenly filled with peewit cries as a black cloud of lapwings rose, swirling, flapping, and then descended, landing in a nearby field on the other side of a dry stone wall. The disturbance unnerved her.

'I'm hungry,' she said.

He pursed his lips.

'The Oyster Catcher it is then,' he said.

'It always makes me laugh,' Tom said through a mouthful of bacon butty, 'how easy it is to spot the undercover cops on a demonstration or at a peace camp.'

She nodded.

Tom continued. 'They just give themselves away with their brand new leather jackets and the wires of their radios poking out the bottom. And there are always four of them who turn up together in a red Ford Fiesta. Why do they bother? Everybody knows they're cops. They might as well stick a blue flashing light on top of their heads.'

'Jim told me once that they let all the rookies loose on what he calls the moaning minnies, so that when it comes to something really important, they've acquired a bit of experience.' She cringed. She sometimes felt that the activist daughter of an undercover cop couldn't be anything other than an informer. A tout. Whichever way you cut it. She lifted the top slice of her sarnie and squeezed a glob of tomato ketchup on to the bacon beneath.

'If you saw Jim in a meeting or on a demonstration,' Tom said, 'do you think you would guess he was an undercover cop?'

She took a bite of butty, let the ketchup squelch out, chewed before answering.

'Well, there's definitely something of the copper in his mannerisms. The way he walks and talks. And I think the military training comes through in small but significant ways. But then I'm probably more alert to the signs than the average person. Do you think you would guess?'

He rubbed his neck. 'I'm not sure. If I walked into a meeting

– you know, your typical CND meeting at the Friends Meeting House with the whole spectrum of lefty types – I wouldn't immediately look at Jim and think he must be a cop. But he definitely has the manner of a man who is used to getting his own way. So I might mark him down as somebody who could be difficult, someone who isn't going to back down. A bit of a nutter possibly. And I would steer clear.'

'You're right. It's the military thing, the authoritarian edge. I'd think the same thing too. Potential headcase. Steer clear.'

'I'm not sure you would steer clear. I think you're drawn to potential headcases.'

'No, I'm not.'

He shrugged. 'It's just an observation.'

'Well, I've observed you're drawn to cod psychology.' She crammed the last of the bacon into her gob, wiped the excess tomato ketchup from her lips with a finger, licked it. 'Beach,' she said.

'Let's just go back and check the house one more time.'

'What for?'

'Just to see if anybody is out and about. It's clearer now, so we might have a better view of what's going on.'

Her gut lurched. She knew it was a bad idea, but somehow she couldn't resist the pull, let herself be dragged along.

The sky was duck-egg blue as they reached the rocky outcrop and surveyed the back of the house again, clearer in its solid drabness now it was bathed in afternoon light.

'There's nobody at home,' said Tom. 'Both the cars have disappeared.'

'That doesn't mean there's nobody there though.'

He set off across the meadow. She ran after him. She had to

stay with him, try and keep him on a short lead. He walked straight up to the back door.

'Hello. Anyone at home?'

There was no reply.

'What are you playing at?' she whispered.

He ignored her, knocked sharply on the back door. No response. He knocked again, louder this time. Nothing happened.

'See,' he said. 'Nobody home.'

'What would you have done if someone had answered?'

'I would have asked if it was possible to have a glass of water because you were feeling faint and we didn't bring anything to drink with us.'

He tried the handle of the back door.

'Don't,' she said.

'Just testing.'

The handle moved down freely, the door swung inwards.

'There must be somebody inside if the door is unlocked. Maybe they are dozing upstairs,' she said.

'Course not. They would have heard us by now and come down. People leave their doors unlocked around here when they go out.'

She frowned. A dark image flitted across her brain, a fleeting impression; the first bat in a fading summer evening.

'Let's take a quick look inside,' he said.

'What if someone comes back?'

'We'll hear them coming.'

'What if we don't have time to get away?'

'We'll use the glass of water excuse. One of us was feeling faint, we knocked, nobody replied but we were desperate so we tried the handle, found the door was unlocked and we came in to the kitchen for a glass of water.'

'We need a fall-back position.'

'The glass of water is the fall-back position.'

'No. That's the first line of defence.'

'You're quibbling,'

'You're crazy.'

'You're scared.'

'I'm not. I'm sensible.'

'Since when? Come on, Sam. Quick shufti round the ground floor, then we're out.'

'Okay,' she said. 'Five minutes.'

Inside, she felt the exhilaration of cold sweat, the adrenalin kick of rule-breaking. Policeman's daughter. She surveyed the scruffy kitchen, looking for giveaway signs that might reveal the identity of the inhabitants, but there were no obvious clues: no photos, no notes. Only a pile of dirty crockery left in the sink. Tom walked over to the far door.

'Wait.'

He didn't. She skipped after him. Out of the kitchen and into a gloomy hallway, a room on either side.

'Let's try this one,' said Tom, diving through the nearest door. She followed. It was homely, familiar even, like a student's den; as if they were hanging around at a mate's house waiting for them to turn up. Book-lined shelves covered the walls and stalactites of cassette-tapes reached up from floor. A worn leather armchair was sitting comfortably in a corner with an acoustic guitar – a Taylor – propped against one arm and lying across the other, an atlas open at a map of North America. Her eye was drawn to the land spit of Baja California. It reminded her of Tom's girlfriend, au-pairing on the west coast of the States. She had almost forgotten he had a girlfriend. She picked up the atlas, flicked to the index and searched for Shinkolobwe. It wasn't there.

She pulled a book down from the shelf. An etching of a gothic tombstone filled its front cover. *Death and the regeneration of life*. She read the back. The common connection between funerals and fertility rites was, apparently, a classic paradox of anthropology. Interesting. She turned to Tom, intending to ask him what he knew about funerals. He was over by the desk, rummaging through books and more papers.

'He's a researcher of some sort or another,' he said. He poked a heavyweight tome lying open on the desk.

'Listen to this. "The expert skipper effect: fact, fiction or self-fulfilling prophecy? Folk models of catch success among the fishermen of Orkney. An anthropology thesis based on ethnographic fieldwork in Stromness. Submitted by Mark Greenaway to the University of London, December 1983." Anthropology: sociology in peripheral places,' he added dismissively. 'Well, anyway, at least it gives us a name. Nobody ever reads anyone else's doctoral thesis. So Mark Greenaway must be the person who lives here and, judging by the title of this,' he said as he flipped the cover shut, 'he's a bit… wacko.'

'Expert skippers?' Sam said. 'That's funny. Nils mentioned something about a researcher. I wonder whether Mark Greenaway is the bloke he took with him on the trawler. That would be a bit of a coincidence.'

'Maybe. Dunno. But he must be the owner of the blue car.'

He crossed to the bookshelf, scanned the spines. She edged over to the desk.

'Don't you think it would be fun to be an anthropologist?' she asked as she pulled the thesis towards her.

'Not really. I mean, what does an anthropologist actually do for a living? Not great career potential unless you want to end up as a waffly academic.'

She flicked her eye over the abstract, read that Mark

Greenaway had spent a year with the fishing crews of Stromness, accompanying skippers and their crews on trips to the open sea.

'He must be the bloke Nils took out on his trawler,' she said. 'I wonder if Nils knows he has written up his research.'

Tom didn't respond. She shrugged, was about to push the thesis back to its original position on the desk when she noticed the edge of a card being used as a bookmark sticking out between the pages. She tugged it free, examined the watercolour violets on the front, opened it and read.

'My dear Anne, I hope this card reaches you before you set off to see Mark. Happy Birthday and here is a small contribution so you can celebrate in style when you are in Orkney. Give Mark a hug from me and make sure he doesn't sit up too late working on his book. See you when you are back in London, love Dad.'

She stared at the words, trying to work out what the inscription could tell her, apart from the fact that not all dads were mad dictators who never wrote in their daughters' birthday cards. Was Anne the woman with the straggly blonde hair? Possibly. Probably. She must live in London. Her dad must have mailed the card to her home address because he assumed it would be quicker than posting it to Orkney, and she carried it with her on the journey north. She momentarily considered the possibility that Anne was Mark's girlfriend, wife even. Then she dismissed the idea: the message from Anne's dad was too caring and paternal towards him. So Mark must be Anne's brother, she decided.

'I reckon the woman in the café is called Anne and she is Mark Greenaway's sister.' She threw the card over to Tom. She turned back to the desk, and glimpsed a purple flash of paper in a woven raffia waste-paper bin. Jim's first rule of detective work – always check the rubbish bin. She swooped, grasped the envelope, straightened, noted the name and address: Anne Greenaway, 24 Milton House, Railton Road, Brixton. South London. She shuddered. Brixton. Not so very far from their home. She knew Brixton quite well; she sometimes went to the market with Becky. There was a shop under the railway arches that sold cheap monkey boots. She stuffed the purple envelope in her coat pocket.

'Maybe we should just have a quick look round upstairs,' said Tom.

She was about to say no, enough, let's leave now while the going is good, but there was no time for the words to form in her mouth. Above their heads the floorboards creaked. Footsteps. Her mouth turned dry. There was somebody upstairs. They must have been up there all along. She stared at Tom. He stared at her. Unable to move. They were about to be caught intruding in someone's house, rifling through somebody's possessions with only a feeble story about a glass of water as an alibi. Another creak. She wondered whether it was possible to be done for breaking and entering if the door was already unlocked. Footfall on the stairs. She collected herself, came to her senses.

'Run.'

They chased down the hall. Shot through the kitchen. Out the back door. Cutting bishop-wise across the meadow. Forcing their legs to move faster. Battling the coarse grass. Pulling their feet from the mud sucking at their shoes. Straining every muscle. They reached the stile at the corner of the field, hearts pounding, wheezing. She paused. Don't look back. Don't turn around. But she couldn't help herself. She twisted and saw the dark face in the upstairs window. The moustache. The sweep of his widow's peak. The Watcher. She recognized now the fleeting image she had failed to identify earlier, realized she had guessed the Watcher had reached the house before them, saw now that she had known, in the pit of her stomach, that he had broken in and left the door unlocked. He was searching for something. The manila envelope.

Tom clocked the face in the window, froze for a second before he yanked her arm, pulling her back to the Cortina. He turned the ignition key, still panting and gasping for breath.

'That was exciting,' he said.

'It was totally bloody stupid.' He might have been carrying a gun, she realized now.

'We weren't caught,' Tom said. 'So no problem. Who do you think that was upstairs then?'

'The Watcher from the woods.'

He sucked his top lip and she thought he was about to dismiss her assertion.

'You know what, I think you could be right. It was the man we saw in the bar. The golfer. What do you think he was doing there?'

'Same as us,' she said. 'Snooping.'

'Hmm...' He left his thought hanging, concentrated on reversing the Cortina.

'Hmm what?'

'Do you reckon he could be a private dick?'

She pulled an incredulous face.

He persisted. 'Maybe your mum has hired an investigator to get the low-down on your dad, trying to find out whether he has another woman on the go, pulling together a divorce case. Maybe he was in there rummaging around for some evidence to give her the upper hand in the court proceedings.'

She hesitated, caught between letting Tom run with his

irritatingly ridiculous story and having to provide him with another angle if she disputed his.

'I don't think he's a private investigator,' she said.

'Why not? It makes sense to me.'

'That's because you don't know Liz. She wouldn't go out of her way to dig for dirt on Jim. She does the opposite; she avoids it. She gets on with her own life. She sticks her head in the greats of English Literature and turns a blind eye to as much of Jim's stuff as she possibly can. It's her survival strategy. And anyway, she asked me to keep an eye on him. She doesn't need to hire somebody.'

He lifted his shoulders. 'You don't buy my theory. But you haven't given me a more convincing one to take its place.'

He put his foot down, pulled away. A green car passed in the opposite direction, its male driver gawking at their rear-end as they accelerated noisily down the road.

'What's your survival strategy for dealing with Jim anyway?' he asked.

She paused. 'I take the piss.'

'Really?'

'Let's go to the beach now,' she said.

The sun was incandescent on the turquoise sea, the beach golden; a colour supplement photograph. She ran shoeless over the damp sand, leaving a trail of dark footprints behind her, sending dunlins and godwits fluttering. They trawled the tide's edge searching for cockle shells, driftwood, strips of red kelp to hang outside Nethergate and forecast rain. The incoming tide filled the moats of their sandcastles, cracked and toppled the water-browned battlements. For the first time since they had arrived she felt relaxed, straightforwardly happy. Like a kid, messing around on the beach. In the Oyster

Catcher café they scarfed scones. Then they dawdled on the drive back to Nethergate, looking for excuses to stop. She spotted a bird of prey. Tom didn't need much persuasion to pull over.

'Definitely a merlin,' she said.

'Falconry,' said Tom. 'I don't know about bird-watching but I could enjoy falconry.'

'You couldn't keep a merlin.'

'Why not?'

'Because merlins are for ladies.'

'Oh that's right. And kestrels are for knaves. How does the rest of it go?'

'An eagle for an emperor, a saker for a knight, a merlin for a lady, a kestrel for a knave. Something like that anyway. So which would you choose, a saker or a kestrel? Knight or knave?'

'I'd be happy with a kestrel. I don't even know what a saker is.'

She took a sharp intake of breath. 'So you're a Knave,' she said.

He shrugged. 'Maybe. Maybe not.'

The sunlight caught the bright trail of the merlin arcing across the sky. She made a wish and crossed her fingers as it faded.

In Tirlsay they parked the car by the phone box, ambled to the pub where they were greeted by the fug of smoke and the sly glances of the old men at the bar. They took their drinks and settled at the corner table. She stuck her hand in her pocket, twiddled the raven's feather she had picked up in Tirlsay. The possibility that the Watcher had been carrying a gun was playing on her mind. The disaster scenario. She had been so stupid to allow Tom to lead her on. It wasn't worth it. She didn't have to do it. She didn't need to know what Jim was up to. She just wanted to have a normal summer holiday, a bit of fun with her mate.

'I just want to forget about Jim and what he's up to,' she said. 'I'm fed up with all his crap; he can keep his secrets, I don't want to know. Let's just go out tomorrow and enjoy ourselves again.'

'Agreed,' he said. 'Two,' he added.

'Two what?'

'I can think of two people Agatha Christie murdered on a train.'

She looked blank.

'It's what you asked me on the way up to Inverness.'

'Oh right. Go on then. Tell me what you know.'

'One bloke with multiple stab wounds in *Murder on the Orient Express* and one woman being strangled on a train travelling in the opposite direction to an old lady who is on her way to see Miss Marple.'

'There's a third. American heiress murdered on the way to the French Riviera in *The Mystery of the Blue Train*. I think she was strangled too. Poirot solved that one.'

'Actually, I've never really liked Agatha Christie. Her books are too formulaic for me. I prefer a detective story when it's a bit messier, a bit more realistic.'

'Detective stories are never realistic. I mean, in the real world most cops never deal with a murder at all. Especially if they are stationed somewhere like Orkney.'

'Or if they work for some peculiar part of the Force like your dad. Which bit of the Force does he work for anyway?'

'It's just an undercover thing that was set up ages ago,' she said. Fuck it. Why shouldn't she tell him? She was so fed up with all the secrecy rubbish. Just tell him and forget it. No big deal. He'd already guessed most of it anyway. 'It's run by this

Commander bloke. I've never met him. I've just heard stories from Jim. Apparently he used to be in Intelligence. And then he moved and set up this funny lot. Half spies, half cops. Policemen who use spy tradecraft: fake ID, secret messages, that sort of thing. Jim calls them the Diggers.'

'Diggers? What you mean like the seventeenth-century radicals? Why?'

'Because they go underground, I suppose. Maybe because they are always trying to pass themselves off as road workers or builders. Easy identities to adopt. Deep cover. Drop the agent behind enemy lines and leave them there to work their way in. Except that in this case the enemy lines are domestic. The enemy within.'

She regretted telling him as soon as she had stopped talking, saw his eyes had registered interest, realized she'd said too much, given him too many juicy details. She felt slightly sick.

'Half cop. Half spy. Now that could make quite a good story,' Tom said.

Jesus. Good story? Her stomach churned. 'I don't see that there's much of a story there,' she said too quickly. 'I mean, like you said, everybody knows already. Where's the news? Undercover cops watching loony lefties. Nothing you couldn't have guessed anyway. Cops with delusions of grandeur. Policemen with beards and dark glasses. Silly disguises.'

She told herself to shut up, she was making it worse. She turned her wrist slightly, checked the time. 'We have to go.'

Jim was in the kitchen hovering by the kettle, still a little bit grey, a little bit hunched.

'Feeling any better?' she asked.

He nodded. 'I've been listening to the radio most of the day,' he said. 'Nothing but the miners' strike. Sounds like it's a bit of a mess at Orgreave. Violent clashes between the police and pickets. Injuries on both sides. Glad I'm up here.' He winced. 'So what have you two been up to while I've been lying on my deathbed?' He eyed Tom suspiciously over her shoulder. She could sense Tom fidgeting, flicking his thumb against his finger.

'Oh this and that,' she said. 'We weren't short of things to do.'

'No. I'm sure you weren't.'

Jim glugged some milk into his mug of tea. 'I'm going back to bed. I'll be out and about tomorrow, if I survive the night.'

She asked casually, 'Where are you going?'

He narrowed his eyes until they were little more than splinters.

'I'm going to visit Bill, follow up on a couple of other people I need to see, find out what crimes and misdemeanours have been committed in my absence.'

She smiled, willed herself not to redden. 'We'll be out all day tomorrow as well.'

'Will you now. And where are you going?'

'Haven't decided yet.'

'Well, I'll see you tomorrow then. At some point.'

'If you survive the night, that is,' she replied.

He stared at her, hard. 'I've reviewed the situation. And I've decided that I'm going to make it after all. I'll be alive tomorrow all day.'

'That's good news. I won't have to waste any time making funeral arrangements for you then.'

'No. You won't.' He paused. 'I've made my own arrangements for that eventuality anyway. Or should I say inevitability. But you won't have to do much when it comes to it. Not that much anyway. No more than a loyal and dutiful daughter should have to do.'

He disappeared into his room leaving her to listen to the clock ticking. She wondered whether he was serious about the funeral arrangements.

They sat huddled over their tea in the living room, the night's silence punctuated only by the crow scrabbling on the roof, and the stiffening gusts of wind whispering down the chimney.

Tom leaned forward, 'What was that all about? Do you think he suspects something is up?'

'He always suspects something is up.'

'Do you think we should say something to him about the man in the house?'

'What, you mean like, Jim, we found out where that woman you were talking to in the café lived, we broke into her house and there was a strange man upstairs snooping?'

'I see your point. Best not say anything then.' He yawned. 'I'm dropping off. I'm going to bed. See you in the morning.'

As he stretched, the metal spiral of his shirt-pocket notebook glinted.

'See you.'

She wasn't tired. She went outside. Everything was quiet. The amber eyes of a cat glowed from the far side of the courtyard. She crossed to the garden, inhaled the perfume of the roses, circled her miniature stone monument glowing in the half-light, feeling comforted to be near it, her own shrine to the happily ever before and after. She gazed down at Tirlsay, followed the hill's contours to the wood, searching for an amber flare, a movement, shadow. Nothing.

She stood quietly in the hall outside Tom's bedroom. The door was open a crack, the light was still on. She caught a glimpse of him sitting in bed, writing in his notebook. She pulled back and waited silently for a moment, pondering. Knight or knave. Knave or knight. And then she pushed open the door, swung suddenly into the room. A real Jim manoeuvre. He looked up, startled, and jammed his notebook under the blankets.

'Just thought I'd say good night,' she said. 'See you in the morning.'

She pulled the door shut again, left him looking guilty. Shit. That was a stupid slip-up. What an idiot she had been. Telling him about the Diggers. She was going to have to find out what was in his notebook. She retreated to her room, stretched out on the candlewick bedspread. In the distance she heard the low call of an owl. It was answered by another call, nearer. Then another. Up on the roof.

CHAPTER 13

SHE SAT UP, startled awake by, what? It sounded like the blast of a horn. Perhaps it was the wind. It must have been the wind, surging out of nowhere, rolling in waves down the hillside, crashing on to Nethergate, howling, making the gale at Kitchener's Memorial feel like a taster, a forewarning of the worse storm to come. Another blast, fusing with the growing rumble of approaching thunder, made her duck instinctively. A wailing rush of air pulled at the eaves of the croft as it hounded past. Debris hurled on to the slates. Clattering like hooves. Cries of crows caught up in the mayhem. And then she heard something else, closer, softer, almost drowned out by the raging of the sudden summer storm. She held her breath, trying to identify the sound below the turbulence. There it was again. Faint brushing. Not above but outside. Just beyond her window. The careful tread of a footstep. Nils? Had Nils come back to visit her again? It didn't seem likely. This was somebody trying to disguise their presence, not attract her attention. An intruder. Her brain seized up. Stupefied with fear. Flat for an eternity of thirty seconds before her mind flipped into overdrive. Panicking. Flailing around inside her skull. Sending her brain spinning into frenetic activity, shooting urgent messages out to her limbs. She had to stay calm, be sensible. She needed to wake Jim. He could deal with it. He would know what to do.

She edged herself off the bed. Crept towards the door. Peered into the gloomy hallway. The door handle to the front garden glinted as it moved. The intruder was trying to break in. She froze again. Inside her petrified body the panic was rising. No air drawing into her lungs. Her eyes locked on the door handle as it was forced down and up, down and up. She willed the external presence away with her mind. The handle stopped, horizontal, released from the pressure of the outside force. Footsteps retreated along the side of the house, eaten up by the wildness of the wind. She sidled along the hallway, listening to Tom's stertorous breathing. She considered waking him, rejected that course of action, peeled away from the wall and put one foot over the entrance to the sitting room. She stopped. A distant flash of lightning illuminated the menacing clouds and outlined a shadow against the window, the gleam of a handgun arcing through the air. She would have screamed if she could have found her voice. She pushed herself back into the darkness. Hardly breathing. Another lightning flash. And then another. Jagged electric bolts flared above the sea, turning the sky blue, outlining the square-shouldered figure of the Watcher retreating.

She flung herself across the sitting room. Down the steps. Hurtled into the kitchen. Jim was already standing there. Filling the doorframe. Dull black metal in his hand. Walther. Licensed? Or not.

'Back,' he snarled. 'Get back in there. Behind the sofa. Don't move until I tell you.'

She hesitated, eyes frozen on the gun's barrel.

'For fuck's sake, just do what you're told for once.'

She noticed a sheen on his upper lip.

'Where's your mate?' he asked.

'Asleep.'

He grunted, headed to the kitchen door and out. She charged back into the sitting room, crouched down, jammed herself between the sofa and the back wall, the gale booming as it gusted down the chimney, rattling the windows, determined to enter one way or another. The force of the thunderbolts shaking ornaments, rocking the floorboards. How did Tom manage to sleep through this? He could sleep through a bloody revolution.

She cowered behind the sofa, waiting for the crack of gunshot. Holiday cottage shoot-out. In the terror of anticipation, she imagined Jim lying in the courtyard with a wave of blood seeping from his body. A tsunami rolling towards her. Tomato soup not blood, she told herself. It was just Heinz tomato soup spilling across the table. She pushed the image of Jim's oozing corpse out of her mind. But all she could see now was the round end of a gun barrel. She lay still, squeezing her eyes shut, reciting the comforting litany of the stations on the line to Victoria: Sydenham Hill, West Dulwich, Herne Hill; and there she was back on the train heading for Dennis Cockell's tattoo parlour, yakking to Becky, blathering on about being a wrinkly seventy-year-old with a tattoo, a life-long inked sign which, she had added, would still be there if and when she died, and Becky had laughed, pointed out there was no 'if' about it. Halfway between West Dulwich and Herne Hill she had realized she was mortal. She was going to die. But please Lord, not there and then, curled up below a game of Trivial Pursuit and a pile of well-thumbed copies of the *Reader's Digest*.

A clattering on the roof made her look up. Christ, what was that? It sounded as if somebody, or something, was running across the slates. Scrabbling. Slithering down the tiles. Was it Jim? The hooded crow? She heard a bird craw. Another answered. And then the screech of an owl, carried along in the baying wind. A flash of lightning turned the room white. Almost immediately thunder cracked. Deafening. The storm must be right overhead now. She caught sight of the print above the fireplace. The black horses were moving, galloping across the night sky, animated by the lightning strikes, the malicious spirits of the night. She had a sudden urge to follow, a deep pull luring her out from her hiding place, calling her, telling her to do something, anything. Stop playing the part of the secret policeman's daughter. Forever doing what she was told. Shut up. See, don't say. Head down, keep quiet, be invisible, stay below the radar. Or else. Or else what? Or else she'd had it. A lifetime of crouching behind sofas in case she was caught in the crossfire.

From somewhere faraway Jim's voice floated in on a gust. 'And don't fucking come back.'

A crack? A shot? Or wind slamming a door shut. Rain peppering the window like a burst of machine-gun fire. Heavy footsteps on the gravel.

Jim reappeared in the doorway. Breathless. Puffing. Drenched by the summer night downpour, a watery trail behind him. 'You can come out. I've seen him off.'

She hesitated, reluctant to move.

'Out now,' he ordered.

She crawled out from behind the shelter of the sofa.

'I need a cup of tea,' she said. She stumbled wearily into the kitchen, reached for the kettle, let the gushing tap water splash over her wrists, its coldness making her skin tingle, reminding her she was alive. The storm was still raging, but not as violently now; blowing itself out in the valley, not tearing across their roof. She could sense Jim standing there behind her, arms folded.

'Have you seen him before?' he demanded.

She concentrated on filling the kettle. Remained silent, uncertain of the best response.

'Well?'

She turned and saw the bead of sweat on Jim's upper lip still. At least he didn't have the pistol in his hand. He must have returned it to his haversack.

'It was the Watcher, wasn't it?' she said.

'The Watcher?'

She momentarily considered telling him about the murky face in the window of Mark Greenaway's house. Decided against it. There was too much to explain. He would kill her if he knew what she had been doing with Tom.

'There was a man with black hair and a moustache watching Nethergate from the woods in Tirlsay.'

'Why didn't you tell me you saw him there?'

'I wasn't really sure what he was doing.' She looked down at her feet. 'And anyway, I didn't have a chance,' she added. 'I didn't want Tom to overhear.'

'I told you not to be a smartarse. I told you there were dark forces at work.'

She seethed. What right had he to be angry with her? No one had ever asked her if she wanted to be the daughter of an undercover cop. She wasn't the one who had signed up to the fucking Force. She folded her arms, mimicking his body posture, staring at him truculently, resenting him and his questions, his stupid bloody job.

'Anything else you should have told me?' Jim asked.

She tried to avoid his gaze, but she could feel the daggers of his eyes needling her. 'There was a woman,' she said. 'Short brown hair. Drives a Merc.'

'You've seen her, have you?'

She nodded.

'Where?'

'Up on the hill behind Nethergate.'

He paused, puzzled perhaps, the half-light exaggerating the deepening lines on his forehead. 'I know about her,' he said. She wasn't sure what that meant.

She tried to turn the tables, pose the questions. 'So who is the Watcher?'

No answer. He stepped over to the window, opened it, the red underbelly of the clouds announcing the sun's return from its brief dip below the horizon, the passing of the storm. And when he turned to face her again, he had his skew-whiff smile in place.

'Good name that, the Watcher,' he said. 'Suits him.'

She studied his expression sceptically.

'Maybe I should tell you about the Watcher,' he continued. 'So then you'll know to steer clear.'

'Go on then, tell me.'

'The Watcher does odd jobs for Intelligence.'

'Intelligence?'

God, she had thought of lots of possibilities, but Intelligence wasn't one of them.

'Keep your voice down. I don't want your mate waking up.'

'The Watcher works for Intelligence?'

'On an arm's-length basis. He used to be a security clearance fact-checker. But he had a nasty habit of finding out more than Intelligence needed to know. So they moved him down a notch or two. Put him on a contract basis. And then a very occasional contract basis. Only use him when they are up to something really dodgy and want to deny any knowledge. A floater.'

'Floater?'

'Somebody they can cut loose quickly. A middleman.

Intelligence set him up to hire the blokes who carry out the dirty work. He's the one who makes sure orders are carried out. And cops it if they aren't.'

He walked over to the kitchen door, opened it. A damp gust muscled in, carrying the mews of distant seagulls. He stood on the threshold, surveying the courtyard, lingering for a moment before he shut the door again and returned inside. His face clouded.

'Not good news that he's involved in this,' he said. 'Not great that Intelligence have put him on my tail. They must know that he's got it in for me, that he has his own reasons for wanting me out of the way. Typical manoeuvre, letting loose a nutter with a gun and a grudge. Muddies the waters a bit, makes it less obvious that it's them that are after me.'

'Intelligence is after you?'

He shrugged. She took that as a yes. And almost smiled, nearly gave away her relief to hear Jim confirm that the Watcher was after him not her. Nothing to do with her trespassing at Greenham after all.

'But why? Why is Intelligence after you? Aren't you on the same side as Intelligence? Doesn't your lot work with them?'

He snorted with exasperation. 'You're so bloody green sometimes. It worries me. You have to wise up. Of course we're on the same fucking side as Intelligence, but that doesn't mean we fall in with everything they bloody do. Doesn't mean we just say yes sir, no sir, three bloody bags full sir. This isn't some happy-clappy fairy tale. We're not in sodding Wonderland. We're not all sitting round at one big bloody tea party. Pass your cup, why don't you, duchess. Here, have one of my fucking jammy dodgers. It doesn't work like that. Everybody is out to protect their own slice of the cake. Their seat at the table. You have to watch your back in this game. You can't afford to trust anybody. Not even the people you think are on your side.'

The cawing of the crow back on its chimney-top perch broke his flow.

'Especially not the people you think are on your side,' he added.

She scowled, trying to fathom what was going on. 'But I thought Intelligence was only interested in Russian spies. I still don't see why they are after you.'

'Intelligence is branching out,' he said. 'The spooks have territorial ambitions. They're expanding their reach, finding new ways to keep themselves employed.'

'Why?'

'They can see the writing on the wall; they know the Cold War can't last forever. And the miners' strike has meant they've been given the wink from the top, the blind eye to their methods, the political licence to expand their remit on domestic subversives.' He glowered at her knowingly. 'And they are moving pretty bloody quickly. So you and your mates had better watch it.'

'But do they know anything about domestic...' She stopped herself from saying subversives. She was beginning to sound like a member of the security forces.

'Intelligence? Know about domestic subversives?' Jim spluttered. 'All they really know about is their bloody Whitehall dining clubs and their embassy dinners. Intelligence is run by a bunch of bloody public school boys. They haven't learned anything over the years. They still think a posh education is a guarantee of reliability. Still can't quite bring themselves to trust the hoi polloi. Although, of course, the ones they contract to do the dirty work – the arm's-length floaters like the Watcher, the quickly disowned night-trawlers and shit fixers – they're from a different class altogether. They're all from the scummier end of the spectrum. Riff-raff. And worse.'

The kettle rattled on the stove. She lifted it hastily to stop it whistling and waking Tom, poured the water into her mug, left it to stew.

'That's why the Commander started our lot,' Jim continued. 'He used to work for Intelligence for a while. So he knows what they're like. He could see the need for ordinary men on the ground, men who understood what was going on in their own backyard. Normal men. The Commander's not stupid. Did Classics at Cambridge of course.' He laughed. Sourly perhaps. 'Latin. That's what impressed him about me. I can read Latin. Suppose I have to thank the Jesuits for something. But he's a practical man. Despite the education. He did a spell in the city before his stint with Intelligence. He's quick at doing the sums, keeping a clear eye on the books. That's what makes him a good manager of cops. Doesn't lose the thread, doesn't waste time on sentimentality; it costs too much. But of course he doesn't like to see his investments undermined, his assets going to waste. All that training and experience. Doesn't want his lot pushed out of the way by his one-time mates in Intelligence. So he tasked me with finding out what they are up to. Get the gen on Intelligence.'

He stared fixedly at the floor. The tick of the clock punctuated the silence; it had a backbeat she noticed now, an after-tick like the deadly murmur of a sticky heart-valve, a silent killer.

He shook his head wearily, his mouth a grim slash. 'You think our lot is bad, you should see what Intelligence gets up to. There's something a bit reckless about this outfit that's operating on our turf. I don't like their methods.'

Jesus, what was a bit reckless by Jim's standards? Or was he was pulling the old trick; pointing at somebody else in order to distract from his own activities, sending her running in the wrong direction so he could nip out the back door and over the garden wall. She tried to pull together the information he had given her.

'So Intelligence is involved in the miners' strike in some way,' she asserted. 'And Intelligence is after you because—'

He didn't let her finish her conjecture. 'Intelligence tried to shove me out of the way. Ordered me to hand over the names of my contacts. I refused, but I knew they were shadowing me, watching the people I met. Targeting the people I knew. So I had to lie low. I guessed they wanted to use my contacts for their own ends. I thought they might try and plant somebody into my turf. But it's backfired, because my contact decided to give me the dirt on them.'

His contact; that was Anne. So the manila envelope that Anne had handed to Jim must contain information about Intelligence. Their involvement in the miners' strike. The Watcher was following Jim to try and retrieve the information, hand it back to Intelligence. She scratched the back of her neck. Agency rivalries, turf warfare, office politics. She wasn't sure it all added up. What exactly was in the envelope that made Intelligence so keen to retrieve it? They must be doing something fairly dodgy if they were prepared to send the Watcher north to Orkney to track Jim and the envelope.

'So Operation Asgard is a sort of secret services in-fight,' she said.

His face darkened. She thought he was about to lose it. 'I told you not to mention Operation Asgard.'

For a moment she was back at the Coney's Tavern, Jim's drunken declaration of doom, his finger jabbing in her face, telling her not to mention Operation Asgard again. She closed her eyes briefly, confused by Jim and his orders of silence that so often seemed to be mixed in with his dropped hints and revelations. She tried again to clarify. 'This information on Intelligence you've picked up; you are going to hand it over to the Commander,' she asserted.

He rubbed his mouth with the tips of his fingers, nodded slowly, eyes fixed on the mid-distance. Her mind kept churning. She pictured Jim at the Battery, the folded pages of *The Orkneyinga Saga*, the grid reference for the Ring of Brodgar. What was that all about? Was the Ring of Brodgar a meeting point? Or a drop-box perhaps. A place where he could leave the envelope for somebody else to collect so Jim didn't have to hand the information over to the Commander himself? A courier who could slip past the Watcher's surveillance undetected.

Jim cut in, interrupting her line of thought. 'You have to keep on your toes in this game. Keep three moves ahead. If you want to stay alive, that is.'

The donkey's nose nuzzled against the kitchen window. Jim picked up a hunk of bread from the counter, walked over, opened the window, fed the sodden beast. She stared at his back. Sensed his mind working overtime; fighting the fatigue. Sorting out his strategy perhaps. His next three moves.

He waited for the donkey to finish before he turned back to face her. 'I should have guessed it was him,' he said. 'Should have known it was the Watcher when I saw that picture of my van in the local rag.'

She blinked, trying to grasp the relevance of the newspaper report, but Jim was moving on, not waiting for her to test the undercurrents.

'We go back a long way,' he continued. 'Slimy piece of shit. He's been after me for years. He disappears for a while. Goes off to do his dirty business elsewhere. Then he reappears again. Finds new ways to aggravate me.'

'Why does the Watcher want to aggravate you?'

'Long story,' he said. He looked up at the clock.

'Go on,' she said. 'Tell me. I'm not going to be able to go back to sleep now.'

Jim hesitated. And then he grinned. 'Okay. Nothing like a good spook story for a stormy night.'

He paused again to collect his thoughts, check his lines were straight.

'Tilbury,' he said. 'It all goes back to the docks. When I was there with Harry. Before I moved on to the Diggers. Back then, at Tilbury, it was all about the Soviets. We were watching the comings and goings from the Russian Embassy. Keeping an eye out for any diplomatic bags leaving Tilbury on the ships heading to the Baltic.'

He leaned back on the kitchen counter, his features relaxing. Enjoying, perhaps, the chance to talk about more distant dangers. Past enemies. The good old days with Harry.

'Why did you have to watch out for the diplomatic bags?'

'Everyone knows the diplomatic bags are a channel for the spooks. It's an open secret. It's part of the game. But there are rules – limits to what you can and can't do. Harry and me, we were the tradesmen, the plumbers; our job was to make sure the system was running smoothly. Maintenance. No unexpected leaks. No overheating. That sort of thing. If we had any concerns, major problems, then we passed them on to Intelligence. So we were just doing our job.'

'Why did you end up in a fight with the Watcher, then, if you were just doing your job?'

He gave her a withering look. 'I was too good at my job. They didn't appreciate my methods.'

She'd heard that line somewhere before. 'What did you do?'

'I nailed the Soviet spook. Intelligence knew there was an

agent in the Russian Embassy, a handler, a middleman passing too much information back to Moscow. But they didn't know exactly who it was.'

'The third secretary,' she said.

He looked momentarily nonplussed. 'How did you know that?'

'You told me.'

'Well, anyway, it's always the third secretary.'

'That's what you told me.'

'When?'

'Tilbury. When I was seven. I remember. You said it's always the third secretary.'

He laughed. 'It is.'

'Why?'

'Because the third secretary in an Embassy isn't very important. Usually in charge of cultural affairs. Something like that. They don't have anything to do except go to the theatre. Watch the ballet. Officially. So what are they doing with all that spare time?'

'Spying?'

'Exactly.'

'Haven't Intelligence worked that one out yet?'

'Well, you can't just point the finger.' There was a slight huffiness to his tone.

'You need some kind of lead, evidence to identify the agent. And I was the one who found it. I was mates with the grunts on the other side, the KGB bottom plodders, the ones that Intelligence couldn't be bothered with because they thought they were too low down to know anything. But I went out drinking with them. God, those Russians can drink; it's always straight to the hard stuff. That's why I used to bring them back to our house – they were too much of a liability out on the town, running amok in the West End, lifting Levis to sell in Moscow. Anyway, it took a bit of time and a lot of vodka, but in the end they let something useful slip that pointed to the third secretary. Cultural attaché. Like I said, nothing to do but watch the ballet. So I passed the information on to the top brass on our side and they passed it on to Intelligence.'

'What's wrong with that?'

'It showed them up. Showed him up in particular. The Watcher. The agent in the Russian Embassy was his brief and he was going nowhere with it. He was trying to work his way back up the greasy pole, shorten the length of the rope that Intelligence had him dangling from. Make himself more of a permanent fixture. But I put paid to his plans because I nailed the identity of the Soviet agent before he had a chance to demonstrate his worth. That really pissed him off: shown up by some oik from the Force. He likes to think he's smarter than a mere plod. He went to university after all. He has a degree.'

She briefly wondered whether he checked up on everybody's academic qualifications.

'So the Watcher kicked up a fuss with his bosses in Intelligence. He implied that I was too close to my KGB contacts. Insinuated that I was double-dealing.'

'Oh, now I see,' she said. 'That was that why you left Tilbury and started the Open University course. You were suspended because Intelligence thought you were a double agent.'

His face clouded. 'I wasn't suspended. I took a break from the Force while Intelligence kicked up a fuss about nothing. They were just upset because I did their job better than they did. Fortunately the Commander wasn't interested in their whinging.'

She exhaled heavily.

'Will you stop sighing,' he said. 'You're as bad as your mother. It's like living with Darth bloody Vader.'

'God, I hope this doesn't have anything to do with the Russians.'

'Don't be daft. Anyway, I've moved on. You know I don't deal with the Russians any more. Thank God. Now they really are serious, the bloody Bolshies. Although—' He stopped.

'Although what?'

'Just thinking,' he said. 'You have to be careful with the Russians. Wouldn't want to end up looking the wrong way down one of their poison-tipped umbrellas. Stay three steps ahead.'

He guffawed. She wasn't sure why he thought the Russians were so funny, but she joined in too. Then pulled herself together abruptly when she felt him glaring, flashing her a warning signal. She twisted and saw the somnambulant figure looming in the doorway. Tom. She glanced back at Jim, scowling. Looked again at Tom, yawning. Lord. Her adrenalin level crashed. Energy drained away. Wedged between her maverick secret cop of a father and her dozy wannabe hack of a friend. Trapped in a holiday cottage kitchen that was drowning in the rising grey light of a lacklustre dawn.

'What's going on?' asked Tom.

Jim jumped in. 'It's Sam and her vivid imagination. She thought she heard someone prowling in the garden. She's always doing that. Imagining things. I reckon she smokes too much dope. Makes her paranoid. Thinks people are following her.'

He smirked. 'Anyway, I've had a good look around outside and I couldn't find anybody. So I'm going back to bed. I could do with another couple of hours' kip. Night. Or should I say morning.' He retreated to his room and pulled the door shut behind him.

Tom regarded her quizzically.

'I was sure I heard something,' she said. 'Somebody walking

around outside. Obviously I was wrong. Must have been the crow. Or the storm.'

'Storm?'

'Didn't you hear it? It was a wild night.'

'No.'

'Sleeping Beauty.'

'Oh well.' He rubbed his eyes. 'I might as well see if I can get a bit more kip as well.'

'I need a cup of tea.'

'Too early for me,' he replied over his shoulder as he padded away.

She waited until he had closed his bedroom door before she tiptoed out into the courtyard. The wind had dropped; a skiff of rain and the dampened notes of a curlew's song hung in the early morning air. The cat was licking its paws fastidiously in a far corner. She clambered over the low brick wall through the shrubs into the garden. The torrential downpour had flattened the grass, blasted ravines through the soft soil of the rose beds. Her monument, at least, was still standing. Although now she could see that one stone had been moved and was lying on its side outside the ring. The Watcher must have accidentally kicked it. She squinted at the dislodged rock, spotted a glint of orange poking out from underneath. Rubbish. She bent down, nudged it with her hand, letting a centipede scurry away, removed the Sainsbury's plastic bag. Shook it. A folded piece of paper fluttered out, landed on the damp grass at her feet. The bag had protected it from the worst of the rain; the blue letters of the biro message were smeared but still legible.

'The pub in Tirlsay. 19:00 tonight; 20th June '84. Come by yourself. I have some information for you.' The last sentence was underlined twice. She read the message again. It wasn't addressed to anyone, but it had to be for her. The Watcher knew it was her monument, he had watched her build it that first afternoon at Nethergate; he would have guessed that she would spot the plastic bag under the displaced stone. She read the note a third time, irritated by its directive tone, stuffed it in her back pocket. He had some information for her. About Jim, she assumed. Chickenfeed probably. Or possibly not. What was he playing at anyway, trying to make contact with her? He had to be kidding.

CHAPTER 14

JIM'S HEAD APPEARED round the door.

'I'm off. I've a few things to sort out. I won't be back until late.'

'Right.'

'What are you going to do? Looks like a miserable day.' His voice was edgy. Haggard eyes. Hangover from the night before.

'No plans,' she said. 'Play Triv, I suppose.'

'Zaire.'

'You what?'

'Shinkolobwe. It's in Zaire. Katanga.'

His head disappeared. Why was he telling her that? She was fed up with his stupid stories. His hints and half-truths. The back door creaked open, slammed shut. The Renault pulled out of the courtyard.

She joined Tom in the front room, stared disconsolately out of the window at the mizzle drifting across the bay, blurring the line between sea and sky, joining them in one vast, dreary backdrop.

'I've had enough of Triv,' Sam said. 'I want to go out. Let's go to Stromness. Nils offered me another trip on his boat before we leave.'

Tom stuck his hands in his pockets.

'The wind has dropped. It would be fine out on the sea today.'

Tom shrugged indifferently.

*

The sea was still heaving though, thrashed into white-foamed peaks by the fierceness of the storm. The *Marie-Jean* was bobbing up and down at the quayside, tugging at the ropes holding her to the wall. The slipways were strewn with rubbish regurgitated by the agitated ocean: putrefying kelp, plastic bottles, dead starfish with upwards curling arms. Nils was skulking in his boatshed. He smiled wanly when they entered. Sam wondered whether he was embarrassed by the memory of his alcohol-fuelled appearance at Nethergate.

'Are you okay?' she asked.

He shook his head. 'I received a letter from Marie-Jean yesterday. She wants a divorce.'

'I'm sorry.'

'Sometimes you just have to let the bleakness wash over you,' said Nils. 'There's nothing else you can do.'

'Would it cheer you up to take another quick boat trip round the harbour?' she asked. 'We could go to Scapa Flow perhaps?'

She knew it didn't sound quite right. Insufficiently sympathetic to his bad news. Nils shook his head wearily. 'I'm too tired to take the boat out today.'

She tried to disguise her disappointment.

'I couldn't sleep last night,' he said. 'It was a bad night for me. Very bad. Probably not a good night for anybody. I doubt anybody had much sleep last night with that storm. The wild hunt on the loose.'

His words caught her interest. 'The wild hunt?'

'Odin's Hunt. The Asgardreia. Didn't you hear the wind? The racket. When a sudden storm arrives out of nowhere like that, people here say it is Odin hunting with his wild pack;

hounds, horses, dead souls, berserkers. And when it passes, you had better hide. Nobody can see the hunt and survive. Not when Odin is out for the kill.'

Tom turned to face the plastic strips of the boatshed door, muttering under his breath about new-age nutcases.

'I wasn't expecting it last night.' Nils continued. 'It's more common to hear it pass in midwinter. Strange for the Odin and his ghostly huntsmen to appear in the middle of summer. A bad omen.'

'Well, it certainly felt like some terrible phantom force was chasing us when the wind was trying to pull the roof off last night,' Sam said. 'What does Odin hunt anyway?'

'His enemies. Traitors. Once the hunt is on the run, it doesn't stop until the horde has found its quarry. They say the hoot of the owl is the first sign the hunt is stirring – Odin's horn. And then Odin's ravens, Hugin and Munin, mark the path, lead the way to the victim.'

His words sparked an unexpected jolt of recognition. In a corner of her mind she heard the crackle of a walkie-talkie. Tilbury. She was seven, up in Jim's crow's nest office, high above the mudflats. Jim was speaking into his radio as he retreated to a corner. She was eavesdropping, trying to make sense of his conversation. Attempting to decipher Jim's cryptic messages. He had used odd names. Foreign names. Hugin, he had said, and he had laughed. Munin here, he had added. And he had laughed some more. She had sort of recognized the words; she must have read them in her book of Norse myths. But it hadn't made any sense at the time. Nothing had made much sense at the time. Jim and his games. Why was her father using those names when he was speaking to Harry? Why was he talking about fairy tales and legends?

'So Hugin and Munin were Odin's pet ravens?' she asked Nils.

'Not really pets,' he said. 'More like spies.'

She willed her features to remain motionless. Blank.

'Odin's ravens fly from his shoulders every day,' Nils said. 'They report back on the dead bodies they have found, the souls of the slain. So the story goes.'

She smiled, but inside her gut flipped. It couldn't have been anything more than one of Jim's stupid jokes, using the names of Odin's raven spies when he talked to Harry. Just banter. Jim and his pantomimes. And yet the coincidences, the patterns, jarred and made her anxious. Spooked her. The storm, the events of the night, were like a repeat story, a refraction of the original. Odin's wild hunt for his enemies. Traitors. Except in this tale, the raven Munin wasn't at the head of the hunt. Last night he had appeared to be the quarry.

'There is a verse in the old Norse poems,' Nils continued. 'Odin says Munin is the one he worries about most. "Hugin and Munin fly every day over the wide world; I fear for Hugin that he will not come back, yet I tremble more for Munin."'

'Why does Odin worry that his ravens won't come back?' she asked.

'I suppose he is afraid they might have been killed. Or lost. I'm not sure. Why else might he worry about his ravens?'

She hunched her shoulders, realized Nils and Tom were both looking at her quizzically now; she was saying odd things, she needed to change the subject. She started prattling. 'Oh by the way, I think someone has written an anthropological thesis about you,' she said to Nils. 'It was all about the expert skipper and the beliefs of the fishing crews in Stromness. It looked really interesting. It must have been written by the researcher you were telling me about; the useless one you took out on your trawler.'

Nils' bemusement morphed into suspicion, the barometer needle dropped sharply. She shouldn't have been so jumpy. She had made a tactical error.

'Somebody has written about me, have they? Who is that, then? Was it Mark Greenaway?'

She went red. 'I can't remember the name now.'

'Mark Greenaway. So he has written his report?' His accent was more obvious now he was agitated. 'How did you come to read it?'

She inspected her hands, searching for a convincing answer. Tom smirked, enjoying her embarassment.

'A friend of my dad's mentioned it and I was curious. I thought it sounded interesting, so they showed me the summary.'

'Is he still here? In Orkney? Orphir. He was renting a house in Orphir, near Waulkmill Bay. The old farmhouse. Is he still there?'

'I'm not sure,' she said. God, she was useless.

Nils was fuming now. 'He said he would let me read what he was writing. He said he wouldn't use any names. Did he use my name? I hope he didn't include any details. No numbers.'

'No. No, I don't think so.' He was concerned about the Inland Revenue again, she guessed, the possibility of the tax inspectors finding a written record of his fishing activities.

She tried to reassure. 'I wouldn't worry about it, though.'

It didn't work.

'Why shouldn't I worry about it? Everybody has a right to privacy. Everybody likes to keep their secrets. Yes? You have your secrets too, Sam. I think.'

Her cheeks were burning. She could sense Tom dissecting her reactions. Nils seemed to calm down, smiled apologetically. Still she edged towards the door, desperate to remove herself now. She had totally messed up the farewell conversation. She had hoped she could keep the friendship going.

'Anyway, we're leaving on Friday. So we came to say goodbye. Perhaps I will come back again one day,' she added.

'Well, come and visit me if you do.' He didn't sound as if he really meant it; his voice was scratchy. He accompanied them into the daylight, stared broodingly across the harbour. She smiled at him one last time and saw the clouds reflected in his eyes.

She put her book down, flicked her wrist. Six-thirty. She cast a cursory glance at the sofa, the spot where she had cowered helplessly in the night, sheltering from the maelstrom that seemed to be following her father. The disturbance that accompanied him everywhere. She looked up at the print on the wall, the ghostly horde. Odin's hunt. And wondered whether she would ever know the truth about her father or whether the doubts, the nagging questions, would always be there. She stuck her hand in the back pocket of her jeans, played with a corner of the Watcher's biro-scrawled note. He had some information for her.

'I'm going for a walk,' she announced to Tom.

He looked up from his pages. 'Good idea. I'll come with you.'

'No. I need a bit of head-space.'

His face registered offence, then suspicion.

'I'm sorry. I just need to be on my own for a bit.'

He didn't respond.

'Tell you what. I'll go out now for a walk and I'll meet you at the pub in Tirlsay at seven-thirty.'

'Okay. Meet you there.'

'Synchronize watches.'

'Six thirty-five.'

'Check.'

She grabbed her overcoat from the armchair, headed out the door.

She dived into the pub, scanned the room, peering into corners through the fug of smoke. The Watcher wasn't there. She checked her watch again. Three minutes past seven. She sighed with what – relief? Disappointment? She glanced towards the bar, wondering whether she should buy herself a drink. The portly barman was checking her from underneath bushy eyebrows as he tipped a glass and pulled a pint.

He placed the foam-topped beer on the bar and beckoned her with a pudgy finger. 'Are you the young lady staying up at Nethergate?'

She hesitated before nodding faintly. He produced a scrap of paper from his pocket, handed it to her. 'Message for you.'

He turned away to reach for a bottle of Drambuie from a shelf behind the bar. She unfolded the paper. Familiar blue biro. 'By the woods in five minutes.' She read the note again. The Watcher was luring her away from the safety of the pub, out of sight, into the shadow of the trees. Stuff it. Forget it. It wasn't worth it. What if he had the gun with him? But why would he bring a gun? The Watcher wasn't after her. He was after Jim. She wavered. She was just trying to find out what was going on. Get the Watcher's information. She had a right to know about her own father.

The midges swarmed round her head in the still air of the valley. She swung her leg over the wooden bar of the stile and stared at the boundary line of the tree trunks, searching for shapes among the shadows, listening for the warning cries of the birds. The rooks were silent. She marched towards the penumbra of the copse, determined not to give away her apprehension. She spotted the red glow of a cigarette tip a second before a hand shot out of the darkness and clasped her arm, held it tight, surprised her with his strength. She gasped and immediately knew she had made a bad mistake. Too late now. He pulled her closer until her face was almost touching his. She could smell his breath. His skin. Stale smoke and Dettol oozing from his pores, as if he had regular antiseptic baths to clean away the dirt. She tried to shrug loose his hand, but her efforts only made him tighten his grip, digging his hard fingers into the tender flesh between her bone and her bicep. She willed herself not to show the pain. He pulled her up against his body. The cigarette in his mouth almost brushing her hair. The smoke choking her. She thought she might puke. She tried to smile.

'Don't bother,' he said, fag clamped between his lips, poking out below his topiary, vowels squashed meanly out of the side of his mouth. 'I'm not some fucking small-town plod. Now then, let's see what you've got in your pockets.' He thrust his spare hand into her right-side coat pocket, groped around, pushing his hand against the top of her thigh. She wanted to scream. She swallowed her revulsion. Scrambling to retain a grip on the situation.

'Nothing? Not even a spray can?'

Bastard. Fucking bastard. So it was him who had reported her to the cop at Crystal Palace. Why hadn't she worked out that it was the Watcher driving the black Rover? She had been complacent. Failed to make the link and seen that he must have driven up to Scrabster in the Rover to pick up *The Inquisitor*. It was so obvious. She was so dumb.

'Quite the little subversive, aren't you? What with the

graffiti and the marches and the arrest for obstruction with all your Greenham friends.'

She willed herself not to react, not to reveal the fact that she was startled that he knew so much about her. Dismayed that the information he had seemed to be all about her, not about Jim. She felt his hand again, searching, and tried to shrink from the press of his fingers through the thin material of her coat. He pulled out a used paper tissue, held it gingerly between finger and thumb, let it drop and land just beyond the tip of his mock croc slip-on. He jammed his hand forcefully into her other pocket, poked and probed; dug out her black raven's feather.

'What's this?'

'Feather.'

He sneered, jammed the feather back in her pocket with one hand, squeezed her arm again with the other. She squirmed. He smiled, pinched harder. She swung her free arm over, tried to push him away but he caught her hand, crushed and twisted her fingers. She felt a searing pain in her wrist, smelled acrid burning flesh, saw the instant excitement in his enlarged pupils as he watched her writhe. She screeched. Like an owl. The rooks picked up her cry, screamed their alarm, cawing and circling the trees in a seething black cloud of agitated wings and open beaks.

'Quiet,' he said with a hint of desperation. 'Keep quiet. Stop that noise.'

'You're hurting my arm.'

He loosened his pincer-grip. The racket abated as the birds settled back on their stick nests.

'Now we can have a little chat,' he said.

She cagily assessed his façade, his attempt to pass himself off as a squeaky clean suburban golfer. Every cover tells a story, reveals what a person wants to be, their inner desires, their weaknesses. She glanced down at his mock crocs. He couldn't quite obtain the acceptability he was chasing, couldn't quite wipe out the air of seediness.

'Now my little friend,' he said 'I want you to do something for me.'

She felt his eyes examining her chest. Her mind raced, flesh crawling. He raised an eyebrow, smiled sadistically, leering, enjoying her discomfort. 'I think you can guess what I'm after.'

She shook her head, scowled in an attempt to disguise her panic, wondering whether she should just try and fight him off now. Make a run for it. He wasn't about to let her escape. He pushed her back against a tree trunk.

'You know what your father does for a living,' he said. 'You know who he works for.'

She shrugged.

'The Commander's a smart man. You can see his rationale, but, really, a bunch of coppers is never going to be competent at this line of work.'

His accent didn't give much away; he had the vocal smorgasbord of a person who had spent too much time in too many places trying to blend in with the natives, but there was something about his appearance – the cut of his cheekbones, the slight slant of his eyes – that made her think that he came from Slavic stock.

'Plods. You can't expect them to know what they are doing,' he sneered.

He grabbed her chin, trying to force her to stare into his eyes. She wrenched her head away.

'And so, it's been decided at the most senior level,' the Watcher continued, 'to develop more effective ways of operating, a more… joined-up approach. Leave the deep intelligence work to the agents who have been thoroughly trained in intelligence matters. Put in place some proper operating procedures. The Commander's men have to be reined in, moved on to more appropriate operations. It's all been agreed. Unfortunately,' he added, 'Jim has been a bit slow coming to terms with the decision. He seems determined to carry on operating as if nothing has changed, picking up information from his old contacts. He always did have odd ideas. Always thought he was a bit superior. Always liked to cultivate his reputation for being a bit of a hero.'

She shrugged. 'I don't really think your office politics are any of my business.'

He jabbed the glowing red fag end towards her face. 'Don't play dumb with me. You're going to find yourself in deep shit if you're not careful. Breaking into people's houses. That's serious stuff, you know. You could go down for that. Prison sentence. They know how to deal with girls like you in Holloway.'

He paused, eyed her, checking to see the point of his sentence had sunk in. She fixed her sight away from him, over the field, towards the stile. God, she couldn't quite believe she had walked straight into this one.

'So I'm sure you can see it's in your interest to co-operate with me and bring Jim back into line.'

She hesitated, trying to work out how she could wriggle her way free.

'I don't see what I could do anyway.'

'Let me spell it out for you, then. If you come across any information, any papers, an envelope that Jim might have picked up from one of his contacts, you hand them over to me.'

'Yes, but it's beside the point because I haven't found anything anyway.'

'No?'

'No.'

'Well, if you do – you will hand it over.'

She folded her arms defensively.

'Now then.' He removed a death stick from a Marlboro packet, tapped it on the box, poked it in his mouth, lit it with a blue plastic Ronson, dragged, pointed the burning tip at her face. 'This is about helping yourself. This is about your future. You're going to university. Oxford. You don't want to have a bad reputation before you've even arrived. You want to start off on the right foot.'

She attempted to appear unconcerned about his vague threats, didn't believe they were real anyway; what could he do to harm her reputation? He leaned close to her again, almost whispered in her ear.

'I can think of a couple of papers that would love the story.'

She floundered, tried to pull away, hearing the hardening in his tone, not quite sure whether she entirely understood the new twist in the conversation.

'Undercover cop's daughter caught in break-in drama. I doubt whether your college authorities would be very impressed by that headline. They are good enough to give you a place and how do you repay them? By behaving like a common criminal. Bringing their college into disrepute. You do understand what I'm saying, don't you?'

She nodded almost imperceptibly. She didn't particularly care what the university authorities thought about her, but the idea that her college peers might find out she was a secret policeman's daughter was unnerving. She sensed him reading her reaction.

'You,' he said, 'are a little bit careless with your policeman's daughter line.' He smirked. 'According to my contacts in the Ministry of Defence.'

She willed her mouth not to twitch, not to reveal her despair, her numbness at the realization that he had chased every lead. He had followed the trail that she had so carelessly left. Gathered the information so that he could use it as a way of trapping Jim. It hadn't just been her paranoia.

He gave her a triumphant glare. 'So you will hand over anything that you find before you go to university in September.'

She didn't answer.

'Well?'

She would just have to agree to get him off her back, escape. 'But how can I contact you if I find something anyway?'

'I will contact you when you have something to give me. I will be keeping an eye on you.'

Her flesh puckered. He pushed his face against hers. 'I'm glad we understand each other, my little friend.'

She tried to pull away. 'I have to go,' she said. 'I'm meeting someone at the pub in a minute.'

He puffed a plume of smoke in her face. 'What does he do anyway, your mate?'

'He's taking a year out before he goes to university.'

'Well, if I were you, I wouldn't tell him about any of this. I wouldn't mention our conversation to anyone. This is our little secret. Right?'

She glared at him resentfully, eyes smarting from the smoke, managed a smile. Nodded.

'Good,' he said.

He gripped her arm tighter yanked her closer to him again, made a grab for her jeans, tried to stick his hand down her waistband. She didn't resist; powerless, passive, sensing that a bit of groping might be an accepted part of the deal. A tax the secret services had a right to claim on any dodgy transaction. The price she had to pay for her stupidity. A rook rasped above her head and brought her to her senses.

'Fuck you.' Her sudden shout sent the rooks into a cloud of frenzied squawking above the canopy again. She elbowed him in the balls sharply, levered herself away and ran into the field, out of the shadows. Fear driving her on.

There was a shout from behind. 'You know what I think?'

She could hear agitation in his voice. She didn't break her stride.

'Jim. He's not a hero. He's just a playground bully.'

She reached the stile, clambered over, pelted down the shaded lane, the screech of the rooks fading, her heart thumping now with the release of tension. Playground bully. She turned the phrase over in her mind. Playground bully.

CHAPTER 15

MIDSUMMER DAY: THE sky clear blue, the sun scattering the
sea with crystals. Jim had already departed, to do what she
didn't know. Anxiety gnawed at her stomach; the events of the
previous day eating away, the shadow of the Watcher hanging
over her, the nagging, painful mistrust of Tom, the ever-pres-
ent ticking of the clock audible through the doorway, marking
off the seconds, minutes, hours. The crow cawed from its
rooftop perch, shook its executioner's hood with mock pity.
Tom emerged, groggy as ever at that time in the morning.

'It's midsummer's day,' she said. 'It's all downhill from here.'

'Oh God. Are you going to be like this all day?'

'Let's go and look at some ancient monuments.'

She needed a distraction.

They drove restlessly, going nowhere. She spotted a sign for a
cairn she had visited years ago with Jim and persuaded Tom to
stop. They followed the directions, collected the key and torch
from a farmhouse, trekked along the stony track winding over
a hill spur with the sea behind them, taste of rotting seaweed
in the air, and there was the tumulus above, its swelling round-
ness pressing against the sky.

'It was built nearly five thousand years ago,' she read from
the noticeboard at the perimeter. 'Time runs differently here,'
she mused. 'It piles up in layers. Sediment. It doesn't flow like

a river.' Tom wasn't listening. She continued reading anyway. 'When they excavated it in 1901 they found eight human skeletons. And the skeletons of twenty-four dogs.'

Hounds. An ancient hunting pack.

'How do we get in?' Tom asked.

'Through that hole.' She pointed at the dark gash in the green. 'There's a fourteen-foot tunnel. We have to crawl. It's a passage grave.'

She shuddered slightly as she said it. She had blanked out the fact that entering the cairn was like being an oversized rabbit burrowing into its warren.

'And what's in the middle?'

'A chamber. You can stand up in the middle.'

'That's funny. It makes me think of...' He trailed off.

'Of what?'

'Well, it's a bit womb-like isn't it?'

She sized up the entrance. 'You're right. Fancy you making that connection. *Death and the Regeneration of Life*. Funerals and fertility rites are closely associated in many cultures.'

'What?'

'Something I read on the back of a book in Mark Greenaway's study.'

He sniffed dismissively. 'Are you worried you will feel claustrophobic?' he asked.

'I'll be fine. As long as I know there is an exit.'

'So what do you think it's all about, then? The claustrophobia?'

She twisted her head, caught his eye. 'Nothing much,' she replied. 'Maybe it goes back to being under the Thames with Jim in the Greenwich foot tunnel when I was a child. It's pretty creepy down there. You can hear the river rushing past over your head.'

'I didn't even know there was a foot tunnel at Greenwich.'

'Jim knows all the capital's underground secrets.'

Tom raised an eyebrow. 'Well, that's it then. That's the explanation. Fear of being trapped by Jim's secrets. Suffocated by his undercover activities.'

She shook her head. 'No, I don't think so. Come on,' she said, avoiding Tom's gaze. 'Let's get on with this.'

The cairn's entrance was blocked by an iron-grilled sheep gate. Tom fiddled with the key in the padlock, dragged the gate open across the uneven ground, left the padlock and chain dangling and clanking against the metal bars.

'Over the threshold. Into the underworld,' she said. 'You first.'

He ducked below the lintel.

'It's a tight squeeze. It would be difficult to turn around in here.'

'We have to go all the way in to come back out,' she said. 'We have to die before we can be reborn.'

They stooped and crawled along the low, narrow passage, hemmed in by the rock, touching the cold stone with hands and knees, scraping along the ground. He shone the torch up and around, throwing a thin beam of grudging light into the gloom ahead, darkness closing in behind.

'It looks like one unbroken piece.' His voice was muffled in the enclosed space. 'A rock coffin,' he added.

She inhaled the stench of damp soil, mould, decay, sensed the pressure of the stone and clay and earth pressing down on her.

'Do you think the roof could cave in?'

'It's been here for three thousand years, so I don't see why it should collapse now. Although it must be carrying a lot of weight.'

'Oh Christ. Get a move on, please.'

She pushed him forwards. He stumbled, caught himself with his hand, stood up, and she tumbled out behind into a reservoir of pitch darkness.

'We're in the womb,' he said.

'The charnel.'

He cast the pin-beam of light around, picking out the architecture of the central chamber: the corbelled layers of rough-hewn damp rocks curving above their heads, the void of the side chambers.

'God, it's dark,' Tom said.

'What did you expect?'

'It's a deeper dark than I imagined. Not like a dark night. It's more dense, like being in a black hole.'

'It is a black hole. We are in the house of the dead, the edge of oblivion. It takes twenty minutes for your eyes to fully adjust,' she said, searching for comfort in science.

'I'm not sure I'm prepared to wait that long. Do you think this is what it's like to be buried alive?'

'No.' Her voice trembled slightly.

They were silent; listening to the chinks in the emptiness, the amplified rasp of their breath, the regular drip, drip of water coming from, where? Possibly one of the side chambers. She strained her ears, searching for audible signs of the external world. Somewhere in the distance there was a sharp metallic clink. She listened again, tried to pick out the note above the whispers of their breath in the damp air. But now there was nothing except the murmuring of the phantoms.

Tom handed her the torch. She shone it upward from under his chin, illuminating his face: a disembodied, ghostly head suspended in the dark.

'We are gathered here,' he intoned, 'to bury the dead.'

His voice was eaten up, engulfed. And then it bounced back out of nowhere, a delayed echo: *'Bury the dead. Bury the dead.'*

Tom tried again, shouting this time. 'Bury the dead.'

'Bury the dead, the dead.'

Sam joined in, yelling at the shadows. 'We are here to bury the dead.'

'Bury the dead, the dead, the dead.'

They cupped their hands around their mouths and hollered into the blackness.

'Tom.'

'Sam.'

'Bury the dead.'

Voices filled the tomb, reverberating around the stones, bouncing back at unexpected angles, noise from every side: clammy walls, cold slab roof, side chambers. A cacophony of voices chanted in her head. *Bury the dead. Bury the dead. Bury the dead.* She turned this way, that, trying to catch the direction of the cries. Her head started spinning. Giddy. Disoriented in the noisy darkness. The voices calling her. Pulling her down. Reaching out to drag her to their under-world. Damp fingers clutching at her neck, clasping her mouth with their silt-filled hands. She tried to catch her breath but the reek of claggy soil filled her lungs, the pungent stench of putrid kidneys, piss, fungus, decay, death choking her. She opened her mouth wider. She couldn't pull in any air. She was suffocating. Her chest was tight. Her stomach ready to heave.

'Stop,' she screamed. 'Stop.'

'Stop, stop, stop,' the echo said.

'Please,' she whispered.

'Please, please,' mocked the tomb.

The voices subsided. She listened for her own breathing, felt her rib cage expanding, forcing dank oxygen into her nostrils, through her trachea.

'Are you okay?' asked Tom.

'Not really.'

'The torch is flickering.'

'I have to get out of here.'

She cast the fading torch beam around the walls and locked it on the passage, dived, crouched on all fours, ducked her head under the lintel, pushing forward to the square of silver light, crawling towards the day. She reached the end of the tunnel, pushed against the metal grill. It gave an inch, then resisted. She pushed again. It didn't budge. The chain was wrapped around the gate and post, joined in a loop by the closed hoop of the padlock. She reached through the bars, grabbed the padlock and tried to yank it open. No movement. It was locked.

'Give me the key,' she commanded, trying to suppress the panic.

'What?'

'Give me the key. I want to unlock the padlock.'

He paused. 'I don't have it. I left the key in the padlock. It isn't locked though.'

'It is locked.'

'Well, take the key out and unlock it.'

'The key isn't there.'

'It must be.'

'It's not.' She felt the tears welling.

'Look on the ground. It must have fallen out.'

Her eyes searched, flitting around frantically. She spotted a metallic gleam, the key lying on the grass three feet in front of the gate. She pushed her arm through the sheep grille, stretched her hand out but she still failed to touch it with her fingertips.

'Shit. I can't reach it.'

'Let me try.'

He squeezed past her, jamming her painfully against the wall, stuck his arm awkwardly through the bars of the gate, stretched, pushing his shoulder against the metal, just managed to reach the key with the tips of his fingers, scrabbled, slowly drew it towards the cairn's entrance, picked it up and unlocked the padlock.

Sitting on the sheep-shortened grass in front of the cairn, she breathed deeply, gladly gulping brackish air.

'It must have been a kid mucking around,' said Tom.

The Watcher, she thought miserably, a reminder, in case she needed one, that she was under surveillance. The shadow of a high-flying bird slid across her face, raced along the sunlit ground; she looked up and saw a hen harrier gliding low over the hillside, searching for a creature to kill. She shuddered. Impending death everywhere. She looked back at the cairn, their prison, their rock coffin, feeling the long entrance tunnel drawing her in. Down. She blinked. Shook her head.

'I wonder whether the passage is aligned with the midwinter sun,' she said.

'Is that likely?'

'Well, the entrance passage at Maeshowe ,' she said, 'is positioned so that the rays of the dying midwinter sun shine through the tunnel and illuminate the central burial chamber.'

'So?'

'So, midwinter is the point of rebirth. Midsummer is the time of death.'

'And?'

'And nothing.'

Nothing except the obvious, she realized then. The really obvious. The obvious time to visit the Ring of Brodgar was midsummer's night, when the final rays of the longest day hovered on the horizon, in the endless twilight.

Later that day, much later, she stood in the kitchen slurping tea, listening to the backbeat of the ticking clock. Nearly eleven; it was late already. They were heading out the door as the Renault appeared in the courtyard. The car door slammed. Jim seemed agitated, over-animated.

'Had a good day?' he asked.

'Yes thanks,' she said.

'Going out again to celebrate the solstice?'

She nodded.

'Good idea,' he said. 'Make the most of the midnight sun.' But he wasn't looking at her as he spoke. He was focusing far away.

The Cortina pulled out of Nethergate, up the hill.

'Where are we going then?' Tom asked.

'The Ring of Brodgar.'

He sighed. 'Haven't you had enough of ancient monuments?'

'It's a stone circle. Nobody can lock us in.'

She directed the Cortina on a noisy loop round the top of the hill before doubling back on to the main road and heading west, chasing the sinking sun. She checked in the rearview mirror at the road stretching away behind them. No other cars in sight. Nothing but sun-bronzed fleeces on the golden hillsides.

'This way.' She signalled right with her hand. Northwest. And then they were surrounded by water, floating on a bridge of land between two lochs stretching away on either side, waves rippling silver.

Twenty-nine, thirteen: the Ring of Brodgar, its stones peaked in an ancient weathered crown. The car park was deserted. The southerly wind buffeted them from behind, pushing them across the springy turf through the ditch, skylarks rising as they passed between two megaliths. The sun was balanced on the horizon now, its rays a dazzling starburst blasting through the stones. A black streak caught her eye; a raven arcing and wheeling, turning somersaults in the air before it dived and disappeared among the heather. At the circle's centre she was calmer, forgetting the melancholia, the anxiety, the anger. Absorbing the eternal present.

'What do you think they used this for then?' Tom asked.

'Marking the seasons I reckon. Asking the ancestors to make sure the sun returned.'

She pivoted slowly around on her heel, scanning the purple hills. She checked the stones in her head as she rotated.

Tom asked, 'How many?'

'Count them.'

She had performed exactly the same ritual ten years before with Jim. It had been supernaturally bright then too; the clarity that comes after the storm. They had skived off together to avoid a day shopping with her sisters and Liz in Stromness. He had told her the stones were sleeping giants, ancient guardians of the islands. And on clear nights, when the moon and the stars bathed the earth in silvery light, they woke and danced, and if you looked out of the corner of your eye, sometimes you could catch them moving. She had twirled around, counting the strange stones while Jim distracted her with his stories. She couldn't reach the same number twice. 'See,' said Jim. 'What did I tell you? They are alive, they dance when you're not looking.' They had strolled around the ring and she had spotted a stone with dark lines etched on its face. Strange runes. She had traced their twiggy arms with her fingers and felt a connection with their carver, the long dead rune-maker.

'Nobody knows what these runes mean,' Jim had said.

'Indecipherable.' He had gazed wistfully at the rock and then he had added, 'The dead like to hold on to their secrets.'

She surveyed the ring now looking for the rune stone and, as she searched, she wondered whether Jim believed the stories he told, whether all spies ended up believing the stories that they told, whether he could see the dark forces rising as he patrolled the desolate borderlands between life and death. Or perhaps the dark forces really did exist. She closed her eyes and conjured up an image of a towering magus, brim of his hat shadowing his face, cloak wrapped around his shoulders, hunting horn clenched in his hand. Odin, his dark presence haunting her. She opened her eyes again and stared at the unmoving stones and there, in the distance at the point where the sun had dazzled five minutes previously, she discerned a tiny amber flame flaring and writhing before it fizzled away. The Watcher: he must have followed them; he was lying in the heather waiting, smoking, surveying. But then another flame appeared, and another, reaching higher and brighter, licking the sky, and she realized it wasn't the Watcher after all. It was a midsummer fire.

'Twenty-seven,' Tom said. 'It's trickier than you might think.'

'That's because they move. They dance.'

'Of course. They would.'

He slumped down on the turf and she squatted next to him, feeling the damp grass beneath her palm, tasting the acrid scent of burning wood blowing in the wind, watching the swirling patterns of bonfire smoke.

'Maybe we should be lighting a fire in the circle's centre and dancing naked around it to mark midsummer,' she said into the breeze. She waited for the withering riposte.

'I'll give it a go if you fancy it,' he said. 'Might be a laugh.'

It might, she thought, and she almost forgot why she was there, almost let go of her reasons for distrusting him. A gust of wind brushed her face with its iciness and reminded her that she was waiting.

'It's too cold,' she said.

He shrugged. 'Don't say I didn't offer.'

She wanted to reply, say something. What? She wasn't sure. She said nothing instead. Let the moment slip. She glanced at her watch. 'Eleven-fifty. Nearly midnight.'

As she spoke, she caught sight of a movement through the stones on the north side of the ring, a shadow flitting across the heather, growing larger, solidifying. She blinked – surprised as she recognized the figure.

'It's Avis,' said Tom.

Of course, it would be. Now she understood. Avis was Jim's courier. It was Avis who had left the book with its coded directions in the Battery, and now she had come to the meeting spot: twenty-nine, thirteen, midsummer's eve. Timed drop. Philby's guide to twilight tradecraft. Avis was here to pick up the envelope and deliver it to the Commander.

'We keep bumping into her,' observed Tom, unperturbed by the coincidence, obviously pleased in fact, that their paths had crossed again.

They walked towards her, met at the northern side of the ring. Sam glared at Avis and Avis glared back. Avis couldn't quite hide her edginess.

'What are you doing here?' Avis asked Sam, bluntly.

'The same as you, I would imagine,' Sam replied. Avis's mouth twitched. Sam watched her making a rapid assessment, repositioning herself in this unexpected situation.

'We were just making the most of the midnight sun,' said Tom.

'Yes, the solstice is quite an event here,' Avis said.

Sam watched Avis's eyes flitting around the ring.

'Twenty-seven,' Sam said.

Avis wasn't listening. Her face had frozen. Her eyes were fixed on the far side of the circle. Sam followed her gaze and saw that Avis was staring at a broken megalith, cracked and lightning-burned. The slipping rays of the sun exaggerated the shadows of the branched carvings on the stone's flat surface.

'The rune stone,' Sam said. 'Viking graffiti.'

She ran over, stooped, traced the lines with her finger, felt again the connection with the carver as she tried to crack the secret code. The age-softened edges of the runes filled her with a strange melancholy; the passing of so many years.

'Winter trees,' Sam said. 'They are not letters at all. They are pictures of midwinter trees. Reminders that life springs out of death. Signs of hope in the face of bleakness.'

But even as the speculation filled her with an inward calm, she felt Avis standing over her, scouring the ground just beyond the ring. Sam automatically searched too, and quickly pinpointed the focus of Avis's fury. Near the foot of the rune stone, a neat rectangular slab lay oddly out of place. It was resting on top of the grass, as if someone had accidentally dropped it on the way to do a bit of crazy paving. And on its rough surface, the faint scrawl of chalk was visible. A tiny zero. She pictured Jim at the Battery, chalking a sign on the doorframe of the scout hut. She stared at the cipher on the stone at her feet. It had to be a message from Jim. His sign for a failed drop. An empty dead-letter box. He was supposed to pass his information on, but for some reason he had aborted the operation. Sam recalled Jim's odd edginess as she had left Nethergate earlier that evening. Did he know that she had clocked the folded pages of *The Orkneyinga Saga*? Had Jim realized she

234

had worked out the coordinates of his drop? Had he decided it was safer, after all, to deliver the envelope to the Commander himself? And then she wondered what she would have done if Jim had left something under the stone. If the envelope had been lying there, would she have taken it?

'Well, I don't want to interrupt your celebrations.' Avis said briskly, a touch of iciness slipping into the deep south of her tone. She gave Sam a toxic glare, turned to face Tom. 'We should stay in touch. Perhaps you could help me out with this travel guide I'm writing. Draft one of the introductory chapters. Here, take my contact details.'

She dug in the back pocket of her jeans, handed him a business card. Sam craned her neck, checking out the address before Tom had time to snatch it away. Avis Chance. Ventura Enterprises, 196 Westminster Bridge Road, London SE1.

'Ventura Enterprises?' said Sam. She knew she should keep quiet, but she couldn't stop herself. 'I thought you said you were a freelance writer.'

'Ventura Enterprises is a company I set up with a couple of other freelancers,' Avis replied coldly. 'For tax purposes.'

Tom nodded. 'That's what freelancers usually do.'

She felt an urge to kick him and his stupid bluffing.

Avis flashed a final smile at Tom. 'Please do get in touch,' she said. And then she retreated, gliding away through the stones, across the ditch, over the heather, south towards the car park, the wind caressing her diminishing form. Sam stared at Tom, trying to catch his attention, but his foggy eyes were glazed, indifferent to her. He yawned.

'You don't know enough about Orkney to do a travel guide,' she said.

'That's not the point. It's about the writing skills.'

'Let's go home.'

'Fine by me.'

They marched back to the car park in silence.

Jim wasn't there when they reached Nethergate. It was almost two. Tom went straight to his room; he needed his eight hours. She stretched out on top of the candlewick bedspread and closed her eyes.

She heard a noise, checked her watch in the gloom. Four. She must have been asleep. There was the noise again, a rustling of fabric perhaps, coming from the other end of the cottage. She sat up. Jim? Unlikely. He had said he wouldn't be back until the morning. Now she heard a scrape, the scrunch of a drawer being closed carelessly. Not very professional. She exhaled slowly, stealthily paced across the floor, peered circumspectly into the dimness of the hall. Tom's door was ajar. His bed was empty. She entered his room. The beige rectangle of his notebook was lying open provocatively on the pillow. What a jerk. She grabbed it, jammed it into the back pocket of her jeans, turned and accidentally kicked a mug dumped on the floor by the bed. Half empty. She picked that up too and quietly crossed the front room carpet, pressed herself against the wall by the entrance to the kitchen and waited.

The bedroom door creaked. Footsteps crossed the tiled kitchen floor. A toe touched the bottom step from the kitchen to the front room.

'Gotcha!'

She chucked the cold tea dregs down into his upturned face. He spluttered. Yelled. Thrashed. Arms flailing wildly around. She stepped backwards, avoided his uncontrolled punches. He recognized his attacker. Folded his arms. Mouth still gawping, chin and shirt dripping with brown tea.

'What the hell are you doing?' she demanded.

'Nothing.'

'What do you mean, nothing? You were ferreting around in Jim's room.'

'I wanted to help you find out what he was up to.'

'Bullshit.'

He pulled his dismissive expression, tried to push past her. She jabbed him hard in the chest. He stumbled down the steps.

'Well? Did you find anything?'

'No'

'Are you sure?'

'Yes, of course I'm sure.'

'What's in your pockets?'

'Nothing.'

'Turn them out.'

'Don't be ridiculous.'

'Turn them out or I'll tell Jim you've been snooping in his room and he'll make you do it.'

He glared at her, incredulously.

'Do it,' she said.

'You've cracked. You're a nutter. You're as bad as Jim.'

'Do it.'

He sulkily emptied his trouser pockets on the floor. Pocket litter. Folded five-pound note, pencil stub, jagged Hobnob fragment, an 'It-pays-to-increase your-wordpower' page ripped out from the *Reader's Digest*.

'Is that it?'

'Yes.'

She reached over to check. He pre-empted her move and stuck his hand into his shirt pocket, produced a torn scrap of paper, shoved it into her outstretched hand.

'There, have it,' he said. 'It was sticking out of an empty Jameson's bottle under his bed.'

She quickly inspected the scrap: an 01 London telephone number was scrawled across the paper in Jim's spidery handwriting. Message in a bottle. She stuffed it into her pocket.

'You're a dickhead,' she said. 'A fucking gongfermor.'

'Fuck off.'

'You fuck off.'

'Okay. I will.'

He skulked away to his room. Fuck him, she thought. She stalked off in the other direction, through the kitchen and out into the fresh air of the courtyard, breathed deeply, leaned against the wall, on the verge of tears but no water in her eyes. The sky was brighter now, the thick bank of horizon clouds coloured salmon pink. Red sky in the morning, shepherd's warning. Too late, she thought. Too late for bloody warnings now. She sniffed and wiped her nose on the back of her hand. Fuck him, she thought again. She meant it this time. She pulled Tom's notebook out of her back pocket and flicked through it. Jim Coyle, Jim Coyle, Jim Coyle, his name was written on nearly every page. What a tosser; him and his poxy journalism, his shitty writing skills, his fucking ambition. She stuck her hand in her front pocket and her fingers rasped the rough strike of her Swan Vestas. She marched across the front lawn, stood above her stone circle, ripped the pages out of the notebook, built a satisfying paper pyramid in the centre of the stones, placed a fat twig on top to pin them down, crouched with her back to the wind, used her hand to shield the matchbox. The flames flared, fizzled and died. She persisted, reigniting, puffing on the embers, striking and blowing until she had reduced the notebook to a pile of scorched paper and ash. She sat back on her heels and sighed. Wiped her forehead with her forearm, looked up to see Tom leaning against the kitchen door, watching her.

'Is that my notebook?' he asked. Quite calmly, given the circumstances.

'Yes.'

'It's just a bloody journal. A diary. That's all. I wasn't going to do anything with it.'

He shook his head, retreated to the kitchen door.

'You'd better get ready to go,' she shouted after him angrily. 'Jim will be home soon and then we'll have to leave to catch the ferry.' No reply.

She sat on the grass with her arms around her knees and gazed over the bay as an early morning curlew keened.

Her trance was broken by the low hum of a car. She stood. Hurriedly dismantled her stone circle, lobbed the sandstone rocks back into the rose bed, kicked and trampled the ashes, ruffled the grass with her plimsoll in an attempt to wipe away the scorch marks. The last remains of the notebook – a few yellow-edged papers – fluttered away in the wind. The rooftop crow cawed as the Renault steered into the courtyard. Jim bounded from the car, followed by the Renault's driver. He was stocky with the same, dark-haired, pale-skinned colouring as Jim. But his warm smile and relaxed manner made him look completely different from her father. An easy-going version of Jim. It had to be Bill. He greeted her with a friendly handshake, said he hoped she had enjoyed her stay at Nethergate.

'Hang on a moment,' Jim said to Bill. 'I've left the tank nearly empty. I want to give you some money for the petrol. I'll go and dig out some cash.'

'It doesn't matter,' said Bill.

'It does. Wait. I shan't be long.'

Jim dived into the kitchen. Sam smiled shyly at Bill, noticed again the warmth in his mouth and it dawned on her that she had an unexpected opportunity to find out about her dad. His past. His childhood. Her gut tightened. She wondered whether she should ask. It was a perfectly normal question; it wasn't about state secrets. She struggled to break the taboo, the silence surrounding Jim.

'You went to school with Jim, didn't you?' she blurted.

She managed to make the perfectly normal sound odd. Bill frowned slightly, with puzzlement more than anything. 'Yes. I did.'

Go on. Don't back out now. Don't lose the chance. 'He was chucked out, wasn't he,' she stated.

'Yes, he was.' Bill clasped his wrist awkwardly in front of his stomach.

'Why?'

'Hasn't Jim told you?'

'He doesn't really talk much about his past,' she said, trying hard to keep the conversation casual, her mouth dry. She sensed Bill's shrewd stare, digging below the surface of her expression.

'You shouldn't be too judgemental about your father,' he said. 'It's difficult for men of our generation to talk about personal things. It's not that Jim has anything to be ashamed of, he didn't do anything wrong. He just stuck his neck out, that's all.'

'What did he do?'

'Oh, it was a Jesuit school. The usual stuff went on. You know.'

She shook her head. He reddened slightly.

'Please tell me,' she said.

He must have felt sorry for her, having to ask a stranger for information about her own father. He heaved a sigh. Hesitated. Eyed the far corner of the courtyard.

'There's really not a lot to tell,' he said at last. 'There was a lot of abuse of one kind or another. We just assumed it was normal. Open secret. Unspoken. It was what we expected. We were generally relieved if it amounted to nothing more than a beating. There wasn't anything we could have done about it anyway; nobody would have taken any notice of us complaining. Just a bunch of schoolboys. So we put up with it mostly. But there was one priest who was a total sadist. He had it in for Jim. Took pleasure in humiliating him one way or another. He pushed Jim too far, made him realize he had nothing to lose, and so he went out one night and painted a message on the school wall. He wrote the name of the priest, said he was a boy-beater. That was all.'

She blinked, absorbing the details of the story: the abuse, the priest, the protest. 'Jim was expelled because he was a whistleblower?'

Bill nodded.

'What happened to the priest?'

'Nothing. That's the way it is with the church. Same old story. The victim gets the blame. Damned for affronting the church. That's how it goes.'

A plip-plop-plip made Sam look up. A pebble bounced down the tiles, hit the edge of the guttering, arced and landed at her feet in the courtyard. The rooftop culprit cawed and hopped behind the chimneypot.

'How did they find out it was Jim who wrote the message?' she asked.

'One of the other boys grassed on him.'

She gasped indignantly. 'Why would another boy do that?'

Bill shrugged. 'Because he wanted to curry favour with the priests,' he said. He inhaled. 'Probably because he didn't like us, and none of us really liked him. He was a bit different, an outsider. Lone wolf. Jarek Crawley. Creepy Crawley we used to call him.'

Jarek. Odd name. Polish mother perhaps. The wires in her brain touched, sparked, gave her an electric shock. Playground bully.

'What did Crawley do when he left school?'

Bill's eyes flickered away and back. She was unnerving him with her questions, digging too deep, cutting too close to the bone. His voice definitely sounded warier. 'Crawley went to university and managed to land himself a stint as a trainee reporter on a national paper.'

She closed her eyes briefly, saw the repeat pattern dancing across her eyelids. Journalist. The report about Ian Coyle in *The Sun*. Jim's Bedford on the front page of the *Southern Advertiser*. The Watcher's threat to sell her story to the press.

'Could have done really well for himself,' Bill continued. 'But somewhere along the way he wandered into another line of business.'

'Security fact-checker for Intelligence,' she said.

Bill jumped, startled, caught unawares by her assertion. She assumed from his reaction she had scored a direct hit. His face darkened and she realized that he might appear amiable, but you wouldn't want to find yourself on the wrong side of him.

'Look,' he said. 'I didn't realize you knew... I hope you're not getting yourself... You have to steer well clear.'

He caught her eye. 'You are like Jim in some ways. You don't back off even when you would be better off well out of it.' He rubbed his wedding ring with his thumb, searched her face intently again. 'I don't know how you found out about Crawley and I don't want to know, but I'm warning you, if Jim hasn't already done so,' he said. 'Keep out of his way.'

She nodded.

He wrinkled his nose. 'He has a reputation for being fairly dogged when it comes to unearthing the dirt. Tenacious.'

She didn't need Bill to tell her that.

'Some would say it's a bit of a compulsion of his. Can't help himself. He has his own peculiar peccadilloes. Voyeur. Bit of a sadist.'

Give me the child, she thought, and I will mould the man.

'We had complaints about him years ago. When I was still working for the police. When I was stationed in Glasgow. Nasty complaints. But we couldn't ever make anything stick. Everybody knows he still keep his contacts with the press, uses them when it suits him. Sells his surplus information when he's short of cash. Everybody knows, but nobody can do anything about it.' He folded his arms. 'Stay away from Crawley. He's dangerous. Men who have nothing to lose are always dangerous. Leave Crawley for Jim to sort out.'

The scrape of the kitchen door on the hard floor tiles made them both turn towards the croft. She could see Bill taking a mental note; the hinge must have dropped, repair needed.

Jim emerged, waving a bunch of green notes in his hand. 'Sorry I took so long. Just looking for a piece of paper I left somewhere. Had a phone number on it. Seems to have disappeared.'

Sam scuffed the courtyard gravel with her plimsoll.

'Doesn't matter,' Jim continued. 'I'm sure it will turn up somewhere.'

She could sense him scrutinizing her. She kept her eyes down.

'Been having a good old chin-wag have you?' he asked Bill.

'Yes. It's nice to catch up with your brood.'

'What were you talking about then?' Jim demanded as he handed over the wodge of cash.

Bill didn't miss a beat. 'Oh, the usual. Families. I was just trying to work out whether Sam had inherited any of the

Coyles' fine features. It's odd, isn't it, the way family resemblances work. Strange how the genes play out. I can't see any real likeness between you and Sam. Sometimes the physical traits seem to skip a generation, jump a few squares on the chessboard.'

'Oh, she's a Coyle all right,' said Jim. 'Can't judge a book by its cover.'

Bill laughed. 'You're an odd clan. You Coyles.'

Jim grimaced, flicked his wrist. 'Time to leave if we're going to catch this ferry.'

The crow on the roof cawed.

'I'm going to have to do something about that bird,' Bill said. 'It's buggering up the rendering on the chimney.'

'It's a bit of a smart-arse,' Sam said as she walked towards the kitchen door to collect her bag. It made sense now though – Jim's views on journalists. She should have paid more heed to his allergic reaction, worked out sooner that it was connected to the Watcher.

CHAPTER 16

THE RETURN JOURNEY across the Flow country had been painful. She had avoided speaking to Tom. Jim had avoided speaking to anyone. Tom had made some joke or other about silencers as they passed the point where Jim had stormed off over the moorlands on the way up. Nobody had laughed. Now here they were, back at Inverness station, Cortina on trailer, killing time before they had to board the train heading south. She had said in the vague direction of Tom that she needed to phone Liz. She was walking away when Jim called after her.

'Do you have a spare stamp on you?'

Sam shook her head.

'Shit,' he said. 'I've left it too late to look for a post office.'

'What do you need it for anyway?'

'Harry's postcard. I'll just have to hope it gets there on the stamp I've got.'

She gave him an exasperated look; not Harry's bloody postcard again.

Jim grinned. 'Harry's always been my second man,' he said.

'I'm sure he won't cry if he doesn't get a postcard.' She couldn't quite contain the seeping resentment.

'I have to go and find a guard,' he continued. 'Need to see if I can arrange my sleeping quarters for the night. Twist a few arms.'

They went their separate ways.

*

Inside the phone box outside Inverness station, she fumbled around for loose change in the bottom of her coat pocket. Liz's voice crackled down the line.

'Hello. Hello.'

The phone beeped like a juvenile herring gull demanding food from its mother. She rammed the coins she had finally located down its gullet.

'Hello. Is that you?' said Liz.

'Yes, it's me.'

'Are you on your way home?'

'Yes, we're at Inverness Station.'

'You don't have to get a lift back with Jim from the station tomorrow, do you? You're not in any hurry.'

'I don't know. I hadn't really thought about it. Why?'

'I want you to go to Foyles and pick up a book on the way home.'

'Mum, Foyles isn't on the way home.'

'The book is for you anyway. It's from Ruth. She phoned this morning. She said she'd ordered a book for your birthday. She has an account there. All you have to do is go and pick it up.'

'Oh, okay. I'll see how I feel in the morning.'

'Sam, just go to Foyles. For Ruth's sake, show her you appreciate her efforts. It won't take you very long. And Sam, there's one other thing you could do for me. Could you just nip down to the theatre department and see if you can pick up a couple of copies of Marlowe's...'

'Beep, beep, beep. I'm out of coins, Mum. See you tomorrow.'

She pushed her way out of the phone box, ambled slowly back across the station concourse, noticed a man standing in a newsagent holding a copy of *Private Eye*, watching her over the top of the pages.

She managed thirty minutes in the sleeper with Tom, fending off any attempt at conversation with her pointedly monosyllabic replies before even she, the mistress of the prickly silence, could take it no longer and had to abandon him on the muttered pretext of needing to check up on Jim. She swayed along the corridor as the train wended through the green and purple cutting, its butt kissing Inverness goodbye, its face squinting up at Aviemore. Dusk, proper dusk; the darkness was rising behind the jagged peaks of the mountains. Somewhere in the distance she thought she saw a stag.

Jim was in the saloon carriage, stretching back in the seat he had claimed as his own for the night. He had leaned on the guard, but had failed to secure a berth. The haversack was slumped on the table in front of him. The bright overhead light bleached his features, smoothing over the boozer's blemishes, tinting his face with a chalky pallor. His mottled hands clutched a tumbler of whisky. The translucent amber disc slithered and slipped around its glass casket with the movement of the train; or perhaps it was the tremor in his fingers. His puffy extremities alarmed her. Forty-six. He was only forty-six. In her mind he was going to age disgracefully, not waste and wither. He caught her scrutinizing him. She glanced away. She didn't want him to see that she had noticed his failing strength, the parting of image and reality, shadow and substance.

He placed the tumbler carefully on the table and tilted back in his seat.

'Where's your journalist friend?' he asked.

'In the sleeper.'

'He was very quiet on the drive back. Something up?'

'No.'

'Did you check his pockets before we left then, like I told you to?'

She nodded.

'Find anything?'

She raised her shoulders into a semi-shrug, half expecting him to demand she hand over anything she had confiscated from Tom. He didn't. He smiled and changed the subject.

'Anyway I've been thinking,' he said.

'About what?'

'About what you asked me.'

'What did I ask you?'

'What I thought you should do with your life.'

'Oh.' That conversation. 'And?'

'I think you should be an archaeologist. Do your history degree, then go and train as an archaeologist.'

'Archaeologist?' She'd had her fill of ancient ruins. 'God, I'm not sure I want a job sitting in a hole in the middle of nowhere digging up skeletons.'

'You'll have to deal with skeletons, whatever job you do.' He laughed cynically. 'One week in an office and I reckon you'd be pleading to be sent to a hole in the middle of nowhere with a couple of skeletons for company. If I had my life over again, I reckon that's what I would do. Archaeology. Has to be more rewarding than my bloody job.'

'I don't really see the point of being an archaeologist. They don't exactly do anybody any good.'

'Good? What do you mean good?'

'*Tikkun olam*,' she said.

'Ah. *Tikkun Olam*. Repairing the world. Leave the world a better place than you found it. Doing good. I'm not sure I'd

248

worry about that too much. Doing good is a bit of a mug's game. No one will thank you for doing good. You might think you're doing good but everybody else will think you're serving the enemy.'

He stared morosely into the bottom of his glass. Oh God, he was on the downward slope.

'Okay,' she said. 'I will think about archaeology.'

She paused. 'But you could still do it.'

'What?'

'Archaeology. You could finish the history degree and do an archaeology course.'

He studied the remains of his drink. 'I'd like to think it's possible,' he said. 'I suspect I've left it too late now though.'

A spit of rain splattered and rolled catawampus down the pane and then another and another, tearing across the glass. Maudlin. He was being maudlin. Or plain bloody stubborn. Selfish, buggering up everybody's life with his sheer pig-headedness, unwillingness to let go of his lot, his other lives. He turned to face her, but his eyes were focused somewhere far away.

'You know I've always felt I've been lucky,' he said, 'privi-leged to see so many sights and places that other people never have the chance to see. The desert. I remember the silence of the desert, and I remember the earthy smell of the first rains in the savannah, the vastness of the night skies, the Milky Way overhead and the Southern Cross just visible above the horizon. And I can still hear the whisper of the hippos grazing in the night.'

He stalled. Jim and his other worlds, faraway places.

'Where did you hear the hippos?' she asked.

'The Pungwe, far end of Honde Valley – the borderland between Rhodesia and Mozambique. Out in the bush, black mamba country. We came in through the back door, up from Beira, through the forests of Mozambique. Crossed the Pungwe in canoes hollowed out from tree trunks, and trekked northwest. Overland all the way.'

'What were you doing?'

'Gun-running.' He pointed under the table to his foot; the withered stumps of his half toes, the sign of the devil blasted into his digits.

'Explosion,' she asserted. 'Landmine.'

He pulled a wry sort of smile. 'I was a rookie then,' he said. 'Out for the crack. Chance was in control.'

She thought for a moment he was saying his life was in the hands of fate, a soldier of fortune, live or die, in the end it is all down to chance. Then she realized he was talking about a person.

'Chance?'

'Yes, Don Chance. He had all the contacts, he always did. Still does. He was the fixer. Chance. American. In fact, he ended up marrying an English woman. But she left him, couldn't put up with his ways, never spoke to him again after she walked out the door. They had a daughter though,' he added. 'And he kept in touch with her.' Yes of course, she thought as she glanced down at her watch, she had read the signs correctly: Avis Chance was the daughter of a military man.

'Fathers and their daughters...' he said, as if she had spoken out loud. He rested his head against the fuzzy fabric of the seat, icy blue glinting through the creases of his face. She waited.

'Funnily enough I bumped into him not so long ago,' he continued eventually. 'Not an entirely coincidental meeting. The Commander suggested I contact him, in fact.'

'The Commander knows Don Chance as well?' Her brain couldn't quite comprehend the spider's web.

'Military connections. It was Chance who introduced me to the Commander in the first place. Long time ago. Once upon a time.' He paused, took a deep breath. 'Anyway, the Commander thought I might need a bit of assistance with the job I'm doing at the moment. He suggested Chance might be able to help. So we met up in a bar for a chat. Of course, he's running a private security company these days; managed to turn the mercenary adventures into a successful business.'

Ventura Enterprises, she thought. It had to be.

'What do private security companies actually do anyway?'

'Bit of this. Bit of that. Bit of the other. In Chance's case, not much in the way of keeping things secure. More like oiling wheels, greasing palms. Digging around for information.' Jim rubbed his silver-stubbled chin. 'Delivering documents. Taking things to other people for you when it might prove tricky to take them there yourself.'

'Courier services.'

'Exactly. That sort of thing. That's why the Commander suggested Chance might be able to help me. Wanted me to use a safe pair of hands for a delivery.'

Her guess had been correct. So much for freelance journalism: Avis Chance was working for her father's private security company. She had been employed as a courier to pick up the manila envelope from the Ring of Brodgar and take it back to the Commander. But her services hadn't been used. Jim had failed to make the drop at the assigned location because he guessed that Sam had sussed it. Or was there another reason for his reluctance to leave the envelope? Had something happened to make him suspect Avis? She opened her mouth to ask about the drop, but she couldn't formulate her questions correctly in time.

'Interesting talking to Chance about his business,' Jim said.

'Chance always did have grand ambitions. He told me he was expanding his portfolio, concentrating on the international side of things. That's where it's at these days apparently: international enterprise.'

'What does international enterprise have to do with security?'

'What doesn't it have to do with security, more like. Or at least, in Chance's case. When he talks about international enterprise, he means commercial operations in difficult environments. Hot spots. War zones. He's attracted to them. Fly to shit. He likes the thrill of doing slightly dodgy business in sticky situations. Exploiting the chink between the legal and not yet legislated for, poking a jemmy in the crack and levering it open. Expanding his portfolio, as he puts it, into unchartered territories. That's his natural habitat: places where angels fear to tread. He told me his latest business had taken him back to some of the spots we had worked in together when we were young. 1960, that was the last time I worked with Chance. And now he's come full circle.'

His eyes lost focus momentarily and then he collected himself. 'Things fall apart,' he said. 'If you want to know where the centre is heading, watch the edges, the shifting borderlines. Look straight ahead but keep track of the shadows moving in the corner of your eye.'

'The twilight,' she said.

'The twilight?' he laughed. 'Yes. That's where you're most likely to find Chance. In the twilight. Of course, when he began telling me about his latest business ventures, I buttered him up, played to his ego. Not that he needed much buttering. Chance has a weak point: showing off. Storytelling. Maybe that's the Achilles' heel of all of us old soldiers. We love an audience – especially if it's made up of our mates. So I asked him about the places and people he had revisited – the shebeens, the witch doctors, the dodgy priests. He told me his stories. None of them were particularly surprising; some of them may even have been true. And then, when we could see the world through the bottom of our glasses, I asked him whether he had been back to the place where he and I had parted company all those years ago, the place where I teetered on the edge of the abyss and knew I had to walk away. While I still could.'

He stared out of the window, assessing the shadows of the night through the rain-splattered glass. She listened to the chunkety-chunk of the train on the track, always so comforting. Why was he telling her all this anyway? What sort of manoeuvre was he pulling now? She waited to see if there was more to come, but he didn't speak.

'Shinkolobwe,' she said, filling the silence. The word had slipped out, appearing from nowhere, bubbling under, waiting for the right moment to drop into place. 'Had Chance been back to Shinkolobwe?'

He nodded slowly. 'Shinkolobwe. That's right.'

So Tom had guessed correctly on that one, come up with the right answer; Shinkolobwe was connected to Jim's time in the army. Shinkolobwe; a place not marked in the atlas.

'What happens in Shinkolobwe then?' she asked.

'Mining,' he said.

'Mining what?'

He tipped forwards. Opened his mouth to speak. She could see his un-cavitied molars. He was near enough thirty years older than her and yet he had fewer fillings. How strange, she thought, that on the small things – the daily routines like cleaning your teeth – his habits were beyond question. Discipline. Control. Military precision. No stepping over the lines when it comes to the quotidian she noted, as she waited for him to enlighten her, reveal more about Shinkolobwe. He pressed himself back into the carriage seat again.

'The locals told a story,' he said. 'They said that Shinkolobwe was haunted by a malevolent spirit, the ghost of a woman who had lived there long ago and had many children before she died. She was buried there in the land of her ancestors, and had slept peacefully underground for centuries. When the Europeans came and dug the mine, they disturbed her. Made her restless. At first she was sad and lonely without her children. Then she became bitter. And she found the only way she could satisfy the gnawing hunger for the comfort of her children was to eat the souls of men. So she stalked the mineshafts seeking out her victims.'

He sighed.

'The mine owners encouraged the ghost story. It suited their purposes because there were so many deaths at Shinkolobwe. Some of them quick, some of them long and lingering. But none of them required a supernatural explanation; it was fairly obvious just from looking at the creaking timbers supporting the underground galleries that there was very little attention to the basics.'

He picked his tumbler up again, tilted it, double-checking it was completely drained before replacing it on the table heavily.

'The mine foreman was a conniving shit of a man. A trigger-happy drunkard. I managed to get in a fight with him in the bar about something or other unimportant.' He glanced under the table at his right foot. 'I lost three toes that night. I was lucky he didn't aim higher. And that was when I decided I had to leave Shinkolobwe. Didn't want any more to do with it. Leave the mining business to Chance.'

So his missing toes weren't the result of a landmine explosion after all. Jesus, why couldn't he just tell the truth? Why did he have to turn everything into a half-baked story?

'So what were they mining at Shinkolobwe then?' she demanded.

He smiled. She thought he was about to give her a straightforward answer.

'Look it up when you get home.'

God, he was so irritating.

He put his hands behind his head. 'Shinkolobwe. When Chance let slip he had been back there, all these years later, I noted it down. Interesting but probably not significant. Filed it away for future reference. And then oddly enough,' Jim continued, 'this week, something turned up in Orkney that made me think about Shinkolobwe again. Funny connection.'

He folded his arms. She waited. But he didn't speak, lapsed into silence. Was that it? Was he just going to leave the conversation hanging? Incomplete? Egg her on with a few cryptic clues about Shinkolobwe, indicate that there was some deep dark mystery, some strange connection with Orkney, and then shut up. That was the story of her life, the script for the undercover cop's daughter. A knowing silence. A warning eye not to dig too deep or say too much. Sod that. She'd had enough of his pointless secrets.

She put her forearm on the table and rested her cheek on her palm. His eye latched on to the patch of bubbly, shiny pink skin on her forearm, the scar from the Watcher's cigarette.

'What's that mark?' he asked sharply.

'It's a burn. An accident. I did it when I was striking a match.'

'It's on your right arm. You are right-handed. Must have been a bit difficult.'

She hesitated, wondering whether she should tell him about her meeting with the Watcher. It seemed like a good moment. She glanced out of the window; the blurred outline of a waxing moon was just visible behind the thinning clouds.

'I ought to go and see if I can get some sleep in a minute,' she said.

'Hang on,' he replied. 'I need to use the karzi. Wait here until I'm back and keep an eye on my stuff.'

He shuffled laboriously along the bench, levered himself up, teetered momentarily before he lumbered away along the carriage. Left her alone with his haversack. Almost inviting her to investigate. She checked behind; saw the illuminated toilet-engaged sign. She stretched out her arm, grabbed the bag, opened its buckles, loosened its drawstring mouth, stuck her hand inside and rummaged, flinched when her fingertips touched the cold metal of the Walther sitting at the bottom of the bag in its casual rag wrapping, hastily moved her hand and located the object she was after. The corner of a book. She pulled it out. *The Orkneyinga Saga*. She held it upside-down, flapped it. The manila envelope dislodged, fell on to the table. She gasped, puzzled. Somebody had doodled a picture on the front of the envelope. A black-barred feather. It reminded her of something, but she couldn't quite fathom what. She had only been intending to take a quick flick through the envelope's contents, see if she could find anything about Shinkolobwe, but the sight of the doodled feather confused her, triggered a strange surge of adrenalin, almost a compulsion to swipe it. She hesitated, glanced over her shoulder, saw the toilet light extinguish, scooped up the envelope, stuffed it quickly in her overcoat pocket, replaced the book in the haversack, pulled tight the gape, refastened the buckles, shoved it back in its original place on the far side of the table, leaned her head against the shiny surface of the carriage wall and traced the curves of the moon in her mind.

She looked up as Jim returned, wondered whether guilt was written all over her features. He sat down opposite again, made himself comfortable in the seat, leaned forwards, took a deep breath, eyes locked on her face. He must have guessed she had taken the envelope. She felt sick as she counted to five in her head, waiting for the explosion.

'I know I've never been a very good dad,' he said.

She was taken by surprise, unsure how to react. She wondered what he was driving at, assumed he was trying to work an angle, unnerve her, trip her up. But when she met his eyes she saw an unfamiliar frankness in his gaze and was startled to find herself considering the possibility that he was making an honest statement, giving her an open invitation to respond. She tried to conjure up a reply. She thought about contradicting him; no, she could say, he hadn't been all that bad, he certainly wasn't the worst father in the world. But she couldn't bring herself to mouth the words. He wasn't the worst father in the world, but he was nowhere near the best. What was the point of starting off an honest conversation with a fatuous politeness? Anyway, she didn't want a conversation with Jim about their relationship. She didn't want to talk about their feelings, her feelings. God, no. She didn't even really know what her feelings about him were; it depended on the day of the week, who she was talking to, what angle she had chosen to look at him from, how much he had drunk, how much she had smoked. She twisted around, searching for the right thing to say.

'You'll be okay,' he said.

What was he talking about? She would be okay? He was staring at her. She thought for a moment there was a tear in his eye.

'Yes,' she said. 'I'll be okay.'

She was aiming for bright cheeriness. Her voice cracked as she spoke. Oh God. She looked away, chin trembling. She turned back to him.

'Dad.'

'Yes?'

'Why did you want me to come to Orkney with you?' She was surprised by her own question, had no idea where it sprang from.

He seemed momentarily taken aback too. He blinked, forehead furrowed. 'Because I thought it would be nice. I thought you would enjoy it. We always had a good time in Orkney when you were young. You and me.'

As simple as that. And it was true – they did have a good time in Orkney when she was young. But that was ages ago. She wasn't sure she could believe it was still that straightforward. Wasn't sure it had ever been that straightforward. Perhaps he did mean it though. Why shouldn't he mean it? She was his daughter. Perhaps he had simply asked her to come along because he thought they would enjoy the break together.

'I did enjoy it,' she said. 'Thank you for inviting me.'

He smiled, warmly almost. 'I don't think we'll have another chance.'

'You never know.'

He shook his head.

She was hit by a crashing wave of desperation, a sudden shifting of the ground beneath her feet, the need to make things right, say something, anything, before it was too late. 'Dad.'

He raised his eyebrow. She hesitated. Unsure what she was trying to say.

'You might not always have been the best dad in the world,' she said eventually. 'But it doesn't really matter.'

'Thanks,' he said. Was that a sarcastic thanks? She couldn't be certain.

'I mean...' She stalled. 'What I mean is; I wouldn't be the way I am without you.'

It had come out badly. She had mangled it. She hadn't said what she meant to say, the way she meant to say it. It sounded almost like an accusation, an apportioning of blame.

'That's what I think as well,' he replied slowly. 'You wouldn't be the way you are without me.'

She bit her lip, wondered whether she should give it another go, try and express what she really meant, but Jim was elsewhere, travelling to distant lands, crossing empty savannah, following the star-lit path of the Southern Cross. She gave up.

'I'm going back to the compartment now.'

He shrugged. And then, as she squirmed her way between the seat and the table, he said, 'You and me, we have our differences, but we are alike in many ways. We can both be a bit pig-headed. We're both smart-arses. But you do things because you think they are the right things to do, not because somebody tells you to do it, or because you are too scared to say what you think. When there are difficult choices to be made, you don't just opt for the easiest route. Whatever anybody else says about you, whatever you end up doing, I'm proud of that.'

She nodded, turned away too quickly, stumbled down the carriage. She didn't look back as she crossed from the dining car to the sleepers, pushed her way into the toilet at the end of the carriage, locked the door, dropped the lid on the seat, sat down on top of it, put her head in her hands and cried. Howled. Shoulders heaving. Crying for Jim. For herself. For their relationship. Ten minutes perhaps or more. Lost track of time. A sharp rap on the toilet door roused her from the morass.

'Are you okay in there?' It was the guard.

'Yes. I'm fine. I'll be out in a minute.'

She heard him moving away. She wondered whether she should return to see if Jim was asleep so she could replace the manila envelope. She regretted taking it already. She should just slip it back into his haversack. She decided against: it was unlikely to work, he would wake up. She would hand it back in the morning, tell him she took it for safekeeping because he'd seemed a bit out of it. That was the best plan. She opened the toilet door, walked unsteadily along the corridor, back to her sleeper. And she noticed that the sky was darkening now, the further south they travelled.

The reek of brake oil heralded their early morning arrival at Kensington Olympia. She stood awkwardly on the platform with Tom, slightly further apart than when they had stood awkwardly a week ago, waiting to board the train. Jim materialized. There was something odd about his appearance; he didn't seem quite solid, he was blurred at the edges, misty. Or perhaps it was her eyes. Jim was looking over Tom's shoulder as he held out his hand to say goodbye. Sam spotted a guard heading towards them. She glanced at the forearm below his rolled-up sleeve and noticed the slightly grown back shaved patch, the dark lines of the tattoo underneath; the guard with the scorpion on his arm.

'Inspector Coyle, there's a phone call for you. It came through to our office.'

Jim raised one eyebrow, followed the guard down the platform and disappeared through a doorway. Her stomach churned. Hands clammy. She faced Tom, unsure how to end their holiday, no longer certain of the terms of their friendship. Too anxious to care.

'I'd better go,' he said.

'Sure.'

'I'll give you a call.'

'Right.'

He pitched towards her. She leaned back. She smiled faintly before she turned away. She didn't look over her shoulder, didn't watch him leave. Anyway, he lived at the other end of the country so she would never have to see him again.

Everything was running in slow motion now. Down the track a red light stopped a northbound train. A double-decker crawled over a traffic-jammed bridge. Behind her, car doors slammed. Engines revved as people reclaimed their keys, returned to their vehicles, drove away. A single cylinder motorbike fired somewhere near the station, struck an odd nerve. She flicked her wrist. Five forty-five: how long had Jim been gone? Her gut lurched again. She panicked. Some instinct made her run to the car park. It was half empty. She scanned the remaining rows of cars, located the Cortina. Something wasn't right. She blinked; she couldn't clear her mind, couldn't think straight, couldn't spot the anomalies. Tired teary eyes not focusing properly. Maybe there was nothing to see. She ran back into the station, sweaty, nauseated, spotted Jim emerging from the office at the far end.

'Dad,' she said as he approached.

'I have to go. Business. Something has come up. You'll have to make your own way back.'

'It's okay. I'm going into town anyway. Mum asked me to... but Dad...' He wasn't listening. He never listened to a word anyone said. He was his own worst enemy. He strode towards the car park with his haversack slung over one shoulder.

'Dad!' she shouted after him.

He turned briefly, smiled, waved his hand, not dismissively this time, a friendly shake, a warm gesture, walked off to collect the car keys from the guard.

'Bye Dad,' she said quietly.

CHAPTER 17

THE SENSE OF foreboding engulfed her as the southbound train halted above the leaden path of the Thames. A cormorant shot upstream and landed on the rusty rails separating the high-tide waters from Battersea Power station. Downstream, the far end of Vauxhall Bridge was just visible against the pewter sky. She removed Ruth's birthday present from its Foyles' bag, hoping for a little light relief. *The Golden Bough* by James Frazer. She flicked through the pages and listlessly skimmed the introduction. *The Golden Bough*: a classic study of the beliefs of mankind from the ancient Greeks to the modern day, from the ages of magic and religion to the rationality of the scientific age. An exploration of the mythical figures woven through the folk stories and fertility myths, disappearing and reappearing in different forms and guises throughout the centuries and the continents; a reassurance that life is born from death and the cycle of the years is never-ending. In her sleep-deprived haze, she struggled to understand what Frazer meant, sensed that somehow *The Golden Bough* held a truth about Jim, about her life, a significance for her that was tantalizingly just beyond her fingertips. Stories told, retold and transformed with every telling. Different characters, different settings. Hugin and Munin. Ravens. Spies. Harry and Jim. As the train pulled away from Herne Hill, she tried to cast her mind back to that day at Tilbury and replay Jim's walkie-talkie conversation in her head. Hugin.

Munin here, he had said. He had laughed. Was there something else? Was she missing something? Had she overlooked some crucial part of the story? She couldn't think, too tired. Head heavy. She left *The Golden Bough* lying open on her lap, shut her eyes, weary, drifting, being pulled down by the undercurrents: the repeat patterns, the lies, half-lies and cover-ups, the predictions and the self-fulfilling prophecies.

A solitary magpie crossed her path. She turned the corner into her street and saw the panda car sitting outside the house. She opened the door and stepped into a bedlam of grief. Liz was teetering above a scattergram of broken household objects littering the kitchen floor. Closer inspection revealed them to be a selection of Jim's finest bar-room deals: the perpetually incorrect clock, the lamp that only worked when its wire was jiggled, and the American emergency transistor radio for which no batteries could be found. Liz must have culled them from dusty corners of the house and thrown them, with some force, against the hard tiles. She was shouting wildly at the inanimate objects, cursing them for being a pile of worthless crap. The dog was in a corner, growling menacingly at Jim's empty sports bag. Two WPCs were hovering around Liz, trying hard to look sympathetic, but managing only to fill the room with faint embarrassment. She assessed the scene, decided it was best to leave Liz to her own devices, and picked her way through the rubble to the back garden.

Jess was sitting beneath the Bramley, staring into space. Her eyes were red, puffy.

'What's going on?' Sam asked. As if she didn't know. As if Jim hadn't foretold his own demise. As if she hadn't sensed that she was saying her final farewell to him when he left her at the station.

Jess didn't reply, just shook her head. Sam squatted down beside her sister among the premature windfalls and the wasps.

Jess tried to smile, crack a joke. 'Well, he wasn't being over-dramatic this time: he's not going to see your next birthday.'

A tear rolled down Jess's face. She didn't bother to wipe it away.

Sam poked an apple with her foot, smashed its maggot-eaten flesh with the back of her heel. Jim had always loved baked Bramleys; he wouldn't taste that year's crop. The thought filled her with desolation. Bleak sadness for Jim and the shadows that had darkened his life and overwhelmed the everyday small pleasures. But she couldn't cry. Not then. Her eyes were dry. She'd already cried herself out on the train back from Inverness.

'How did it happen?' Sam asked. Eventually. When Jess had swallowed down the sobs.

'Car crash,' Jess said. 'Vauxhall.'

Vauxhall. His favourite bridge. Always a bit of a hotspot. Gateway to the other side.

Jess sniffed, dug in her pocket, removed a Rizla packet. 'I could do with a spliff.'

She licked the gluey edge of a paper, attached it at an angle to a second, struck a match and set fire to the vertical seam. The flame flared for a second, dimmed and curled through the paper, extinguished itself at the licked line, leaving in its wake a perfect white winding sheet.

'So what happened with that friend of yours then?' Jess asked after a couple of puffs, searching for a distraction. Trivial pursuits to take her mind off Jim.

'What, the one who came to Orkney with us?'

'Yes. What was his name?'

'Tom.'

'Yes, him. What happened?'

'Nothing.'

Jess tugged on the roach. 'Men.' A cloud of blue smoke drifted from her mouth. 'Men are like a tin of Quality Street. You have to keep going until you find the one you fancy.'

'But you can't be too choosy,' Sam added, 'or you'll end up left with nothing but the nutty ones.'

Jess exploded with manic laughter. Sam too. Sudden release of pent-up emotion. Cackling wildly, lost in the no-man's land between life and death. Uncharted territory. No signposts here. And then Sam stopped laughing, as suddenly as she had started, sensing she was being watched. One of the WPCs was standing by the kitchen door staring at a spot just above their heads, trying to avoid looking directly at the reefer Jess was waving ostentatiously in her hand.

'Could you come with your mother to identify the body?'

'Hang on a minute,' said Sam. She raced upstairs to her room, emptied the contents of her coat pockets – her Orkney findings – into a shoebox and shoved the cardboard sarcophagus under her bed. Although she kept hold of the raven's feather she had picked up from the wood in Tirlsay, stuffed it back in her coat pocket. She wanted that close to hand. For comfort.

The green-tinged light of the subterranean morgue made even the living look half-dead. Surreal. Jim's body was lying on a silver gurney, covered with a pristine white cloth that came up to his chin. She couldn't connect the corpse in front of her with the living being she had said farewell to five hours previously at Kensington Olympia Station. It was him but not him, exactly the same and yet different in an absolute and unquantifiable way. Lifeless. He seemed calm, seraphic, his skin pallid but glowing with an unearthly radiance, the cynical creases around his mouth had softened, the habitual sneer of his lips had loosened. Almost angelic.

Liz glared angrily at her dead husband. 'That's an imposter.' She started to cry. The WPC looked baffled.

'I'd better take her out,' Jess said. She put her arm around Liz's shoulder, steered her towards the door, the WPC behind uttering soothing phrases mechanically.

Sam was alone now with Jim and the tall white-coated mortuary assistant. An administrator of death. He was young yet gaunt, dark rings round his cavernous eye sockets. He gave her a questioning sideways glance.

'Mum didn't mean it literally,' she said. 'That was an emotional response.'

The mortuary assistant nodded, seemingly satisfied with her explanation. She stared down at Jim. It was, she thought, the first dead body she had ever seen. Then she remembered that it wasn't. The first corpse she had ever seen belonged to Lenin: school trip to Moscow the previous year. She had queued in Red Square for hours to see him, traipsed into the darkened mausoleum, filed slowly past the recumbent Snow White figure on its plinth, trying not to giggle in case one of the guards poked her in the kidneys with his baton for being disrespectful. Jim looked less waxy than Lenin. And yet. She stared again at Jim draped in his white cloth; something niggled about his appearance but she couldn't quite articulate her concern.

'That is Jim. But he looks very...' she searched for the right word, 'smooth.'

'That often happens. Before rigor mortis has set in completely.'

The mortuary assistant spoke with an Essex drawl. She also

detected a hint of nervousness in his voice. Perplexed, she closed her eyes for a moment and tried to clarify her thoughts.

'It's odd,' she said, 'I was expecting him to be more beaten up than that. He doesn't look as if he died in a car crash.'

'That's because…' He stalled. Shot an anxious glance over his shoulder at the door behind. 'He didn't.'

Her stomach dropped. 'But we were told.'

He put a fleshless index finger to his thin lips. 'Car crash. Drink driving. That's what they say,' he whispered, 'when it's a hit job.'

She flicked her head nervously. She couldn't quite make sense of it all. 'But how?' she started to ask.

'Wet-worker,' the assistant hissed. 'If you know what I mean.'

'No,' she said. 'I don't.'

'Contract killer. Someone with military training. Technical capability. The old trick, hiding in the back of the car. Low-calibre weapon. Two bullets. Lodged in his brain.'

Too much information.

'Faked the car crash,' he continued.

'Faked the crash? But—' She stole a suspicious glance at the assistant. He was clenching his hands in the pockets of his lab coat. Why was he telling her all this?

'Are you sure?' she started to ask.

'Jim used to keep a lookout for me,' he interjected. 'Watched my back. I always promised him I'd return the favour. So that's what I'm doing. Returning the favour. Just letting you know. Don't ask me any more questions. Don't tell anyone I told you.'

He raised a warning eyebrow. 'Somebody somewhere has been doing a lot of fixing,' he said. 'That's all I'm saying. Wouldn't want to have my name on their list, that's for sure.'

The room was starting to spin. She inhaled deeply and the smell of formaldehyde mingled with the taste of vomit in her throat, black and orange dots swimming in front of her eyes, cormorants flying at her, the amber flare of fags being lit, swirling. Through the thickness in her head she heard the WPC returning, asking if everything was in order. She put her hand to her mouth, barged past the blue uniform, pushed her way through the door, made it to the corridor and barfed a three-dimensional Jackson Pollock splatter on the clinical whiteness of the tiled floor. She puked and puked some more, head hanging down, hands on knees, carrot lumps coming out of mouth and nostrils.

Liz sat upright, unspeaking, in the passenger seat of the panda car next to the WPC, while Jess and Sam slumped in the back. Her life was passing before her eyes as her mind rummaged desperately among her old files, looking for a map, a clue, a sign, anything that pointed to an escape route.

Jess interrupted her racing thoughts with a sharp nudge in the ribs, leaned close and whispered. 'He didn't look that bad.' She paused and then she added, 'for a man who drove into a brick wall at fifty miles an hour.'

'No, not bad.'

Jess hissed. 'It wasn't anything to do with you, was it?'

'No. Nothing,' Sam blurted. 'I don't have the technical capability to do that kind of thing anyway.'

'Technical capability?'

'You know. Military training. Guns. Faking a crash.'

Jess nodded sagely. She whispered, 'Roger.'

'Roger?'

'He used to be in the SAS.'

'No way.'

'That's what he told me.'

'That's what they all say.' Sam snorted, suppressed a giggle, pulled herself together again when she noticed the WPC eyeing her cagily in the rear-view mirror and turned to stare out of the window.

Jess nudged her in the ribs again. 'Are you okay?'

'Yes.' She bit her lip. Felt something warm and wet on her cheek. Realized it was a tear.

Later, as a dull dusk was falling, she disinterred the shoebox from its safehouse under the bed, spread its contents out on the thin carpet, sat back on her heels, wiped her forehead and surveyed disconsolately the objects arrayed before her. Jim's remains. The purple envelope addressed to Anne, the scrap of paper with a London phone number scribbled on it, the A5 manila envelope with its doodled feather. Relics. They seemed to be imbued with a peculiar aura, physical reminders of Jim's disconcerting presence. She gazed at the biro drawing of the black-barred feather, digging into her mind, trying to unearth the fragment of a memory, and it gave her the strangest feeling, a nagging sense that Jim had set her up somehow, contrived to leave her with his mess to sort out; the information he had let slip, the trip to Orkney, the warnings, the conspiratorial glances, the half-revealed histories. It felt as if he were provoking her in some way. Testing her loyalty.

She picked up the manila envelope and held it warily. It contained, if Jim's hints and stories were anything to go by, information that Anne had somehow managed to acquire about Intelligence activities, their attempts to fix the miners' strike. Perhaps it was better not to know the details. But she couldn't quite resist. She removed its contents piece by piece. First – a photocopy of a British passport in the name of Anthony

Baines, showing a grainy shot of a close-cropped, dark-haired man with a big mouth. Scowling. Born 1960 in Carlisle. It had to be a fake ID. She squinted at the image and thought that he looked vaguely familiar – couldn't quite put her finger on the face. It was hard to tell much anyway from a photocopy of a photobooth snap. Next – a till receipt itemizing electrical wire and a circuit board from a hardware shop in Brixton's Water Lane. What did that signify? She conjured up a page from Jim's dilapidated copy of the *Anarchist Cook Book*, a recipe for making an incendiary device in your own kitchen. Ingredients: electrical wire, switches, circuit board, fertilizer. Probably a couple of other things too that she couldn't remember, but it was sufficient for her to suppose that the till receipt was a pointer to amateur bomb-making efforts. The next scrap confirmed her suspicion. It was a hand-scribbled shopping list of ticked-off items: timers, traps, detonators. Mercury fulminate had a question mark after it. Finally, a piece of lined A4 paper with a hand-drawn map of an unnamed British Rail station and attached car park with a registration number written below: MVF 476X. Well, she certainly recognized the first part of that: MVF. Those were the first three letters on the numberplate of the dark car heading up the hill at Crystal Palace. The Watcher's Rover. She shivered, disturbed more than surprised to find traces of his repellent presence here.

Was that it? She had half hoped to find a more damning piece of evidence, pointing to the shadows of the secret state. The smoking gun. It wasn't there. If she made an effort, she could just about string together a story from the information in front of her and the fragments Jim had revealed in Orkney: a conspiracy theory involving Intelligence, the Watcher as middleman, and some other agent using the fake identity of Anthony Baines, explosives and the miners' strike. But there wasn't sufficient evidence to convert the theory into fact. And what about Shinkolobwe? Where did that fit in? There was nothing in front of her that made any sense of that.

She upended the envelope and caught a final scrap of flimsy paper as it fluttered out. A ripped-out page, she reckoned, from a book of receipts – the kind that had a removable piece of carbon paper for producing a duplicate copy behind. The uneven pattern of the diagonally torn edge reminded her of an indentured contract, the two halves cut together so they could later be matched up to prove they were related parts of a whole. A company name was printed across its top: Shaba Security Limited. Below this a scribble of handwriting – a sentence without a beginning because of the tear – something about payment for contracted services rendered. At the bottom of the paper, two lines of very small print indicated that Shaba Security Limited was a subsidiary of – and then there was a word missing – Asset Management. Shaba. Sounded African.

She stuffed all the bits of paper back in the envelope, glanced at the doodled feather, looked over her shoulder involuntarily and tasted stale vomit in her mouth. For the love of God, why had she swiped the envelope from Jim's haversack? She might as well have picked up a live hand-grenade. She might not think its contents were particularly revealing, but someone had been prepared to kill for it. Wet-worker. Hitman. She should have just left it where it was. Maybe Jim would still be alive if she hadn't taken it. She certainly wouldn't be in this mess. She'd really dropped herself in it, one way or another. She had to dispose of the information, pass the package on before some pistol-toting secret agent came creeping into her room in the darkness. Before Odin and his wild hunt chased her down. Jim had been right; she wasn't professionally trained to deal with the consequences of her smart-arsery. She shoved the manila envelope, the purple envelope and the scrap of paper back inside the shoebox. Wiped her clammy hands on her jeans. Tried to formulate a plan. She had to hand the package over to the Commander. That was obvious. It was what Jim had been intending to do. If she passed the package to the Commander, then he could deal with the Watcher. The problem was she had no idea how to contact him. She didn't even know his name. She would have to locate him, make discreet enquiries, without drawing attention to herself and giving herself away to the Watcher. Easier said than done. She needed a clear head to think about it and at the moment her brain was numbed with grief. Exhaustion. Fear. She would have to deal with it after the funeral. Once she had buried the dead.

Time dragged. Sleep eluded her. Kept awake by noises, bangings in the house, footsteps in the garden. Dark and light, day and night, merging. Turned upside down. She hung around the house. Listless. Uneasy. Fearful of going out. Unable to settle indoors. Incapable of making decisions. Jumping every time the doorbell or the phone rang. Haunted by images of the morgue. Jim's face staring up from the slab, hands reaching out to clutch at her, pull her down, underground, ghosts whispering in her ear. Bury the dead. Bury the dead. The mortuary assistant's words playing on her mind. Wouldn't want my name on their list. That's for sure.

Monday. Two days after the crash, the solicitor phoned and informed Liz that he had recently received a letter from Jim containing a sealed envelope with instructions to open it in the event of his death. The envelope turned out to contain notes for his funeral. Sam recalled, with a start, Jim telling her that he had already made his own funeral arrangements. So he hadn't been joking then. It was, the solicitor observed, quite a coincidence that the letter had arrived shortly before his unexpected and untimely death. Jim; always three moves ahead. Liz had gripped the receiver tightly and calmly asked the solicitor to relay Jim's wishes. Jim had, his notes revealed, already reserved a burial plot in an out-of-the-way graveyard on the edge of the periphery. According to the solicitor, Jim's letter indicated that he wanted a small and informal ceremony. Family and friends only. He definitely did not want any coppers, current or ex, to attend. Liz shook her head despairingly as she repeated Jim's strange instructions. He had always had such odd ideas about death, she said. Odd ideas about everything, in fact. Still, she wasn't going to question his last wishes.

Tuesday. The day after the solicitor phoned, a welfare officer from the Force pitched up to return Jim's belongings, recovered from the scene of the accident, and to deliver the official explanation for Jim's death. According to the officer, the fast-tracked coroner's report indicated that Jim had been driving south over Vauxhall Bridge in the early hours of the morning. Too late for the straggle of all-night revellers wending their way home from the Royal Vauxhall Tavern. Too early for the thin stream of commuters spewed up daily by the tube on the hard embankment slabs. No witnesses then, apart from the cormorants plying the river for fish. Nonetheless, the crash investigators were able to surmise the events leading up to Jim's demise. There had been a momentary lapse of attention, apparently, as he drove across Vauxhall Bridge, during which he jumped a red light and swerved into a brick wall on the far side of the junction underneath the railway arches carrying the trains to Waterloo. By the mouth of the Effra, Sam noted. Right next to the last remnant of the old Vauxhall pleasure gardens, a desolate void on the edge of north Lambeth. A place where no one would be around to hear the shot of a pistol. Or linger too long even if they had. The welfare officer droned on: the Cortina had been completely trashed. How? Sam thought. By whom? Somebody, somewhere had been doing a lot of fixing, she heard the mortuary assistant saying.

The explanation whispered by the welfare officer, as he looked over Liz's shoulder and eyed Sam warily, was that Jim had been drunk at the wheel. The pathologist had recorded a high level of alcohol in his blood. Jim was a car crash waiting to happen, the welfare officer said. Drink driving, the mortuary assistant's voice interjected in Sam's head; that's what they always say when it's a hit job. The welfare officer added, in sympathetic tones, that they would of course do everything possible to ensure that Inspector Jim Coyle was buried in a manner appropriate to his rank and standing, albeit a bit quicker and a bit quieter, just to have it all done and dusted without any embarrassment or undue attention from the local press. Liz told him, politely, to get stuffed. There was no reason, she said firmly, to sweep anything under the carpet. She intended to proceed with the funeral arrangements herself, exactly in accordance with Jim's final wishes.

After the welfare officer had been shown the door, Liz and Sam had emptied the contents of Jim's haversack onto the kitchen table: his beloved Swiss Army Knife, clean and ready for use, binoculars, a smutty cotton snot rag that reeked of musky fungus, and a short piece of white chalk. Sam didn't bother to tell Liz that his rag-wrapped Walther and his dog-eared copy of *The Orkneyinga Saga* were missing. She did suggest that they should place Jim's Swiss Army Knife in the coffin alongside his body. Just in case. Liz agreed it was appropriate. Always good to be prepared.

Wednesday, and there was an unexpected kerfuffle. The phone had rung. Yet again. Liz had picked it up and had a heated conversation with the unidentified person on the other end.

'The Commander,' she had announced after she had replaced the receiver.

Sam's heart had raced – she saw her lifeboat passing. Was the Commander trying to contact her? Had he surmised that she might know something about the information Jim had been sent to collect from Orkney? Was this her opportunity to hand over the envelope? Dump her burden. Liz relayed the details of the exchange peevishly. The Commander had asked if he could attend the funeral in an unofficial capacity, as a friend, not a fellow police officer. He had been quite insistent. But Liz had been equally unwilling to budge. Jim's last orders were clear: nobody from the Force to attend. Frankly, Liz said, she thought he had a cheek. In all those years of absence and anxiety he hadn't bothered to call. Not even once. There had been absolutely no reassurance, no concern for their welfare, no offers of help, no support whatsoever. Nothing. So she wasn't about to do him any favours now.

Sam's heart sank as she saw her chance drifting away, just out of reach.

'But the Commander was a good friend of Jim's,' Sam asserted. 'Perhaps he should be at the funeral.'

Liz, though, wasn't having it.

'Did he leave his number?' Sam enquired.

'No.'

'A name?'

'I didn't ask. I'm surprised that you, of all people, are so keen to have a policeman breathing down your neck at your father's funeral.'

Her, of all people. What was that supposed to mean? Liz didn't give Sam a chance to contest. She left Sam feeling dismal as she went out and closed the door behind her.

Thursday. The day before the funeral. Sam was in the kitchen killing time with Jess. The phone rang. Jess picked up the receiver. Asked who it was, pulled a face when she heard the reply. Jess put her hand over the mouthpiece. 'Tom,' she mouthed silently.

Sam shook her head furiously, made chopping signs in the air with her hands.

'She's out,' Jess said into the phone. 'All day.'

Jess nodded as Tom said something on the other end. 'I'll tell her. Yes. I promise.' She replaced the receiver. 'He was a bit insistent.' Jess eyed her little sister quizzically. 'He said he had something to tell you. Maybe you should phone him. Find out what he wants.'

Sam tutted.

'Sounded intense,' said Jess. 'He said it was really important and you should call him back.'

'I'm sure it can't be that important.'

'What did you do to him,' Jess said, 'to make him so desperate?'

'Nothing,' said Sam. She walked away.

CHAPTER 18

FRIDAY AT LAST, and the relentless sun was giving everything a hard edge and a dark shadow. They had followed Jim's instructions and had located his burial plot in a yew-bordered graveyard attached to a squat Norman flint church in the furthermost reaches of the suburbs. The dirty tidemark of the metropolis. No weeping statues here. No service either. The coffin, lid tightly nailed, had been carried from hearse to churchyard and lowered straight into the freshly dug grave on two beige webbing straps. Without ceremony. There were, however, selected ritual trimmings: a Tupperware pot of dust held by a shifty-looking vicar. Lord only knew, Jess had whispered loudly when she saw him, how Jim had persuaded a Church of England Reverend to comply with his unconventional funeral arrangements.

As Jim had wished, there was only a small congregation – Liz, Ruth, Sam and her sisters, and a smattering of their close friends. What's more, Sam noted as Becky and Paul stepped up to the graveside to release their handfuls of dust, his ban on coppers had left him with a motley crew of left field mourners – pinko academics, bikers, night-clubbing outlaws, pot-smoking suburban rebels. The enemy within, she said to Jim in her head. Somewhere in the distance she heard somebody scoff – your lot, call yourselves subversives? What a bloody shambles. Bunch of buffoons. She instinctively glanced over her shoulder, checking to see whether Jim was lurking behind a gravestone, taking notes. But he wasn't there.

There was a slight pause in the proceedings, a respectful gap between friends and family. In the ensuing heavy silence, the soft brushing of beating wings made Sam look up to see the dark streak of two advancing heavy-billed ravens. As they passed overhead, the pair flipped in unison, flew upside-down momentarily before rolling and righting themselves again.

'The birds,' she whispered to Helen, 'they've come to pay their last respects to Jim.'

'Or crap on his coffin,' Helen muttered.

Jess moved closer to the grave, holding her crash helmet in one hand, wiping her eye with the other, head bowed in silent contemplation for a moment before she scattered her dust on the coffin and moved back to join the congregation. Helen's turn next, her spiked heels sinking down in the loose graveside earth as she briskly chucked a fistful of dirt at Jim.

'What a bastard,' Helen muttered as she returned.

Liz threw her eldest daughter a reproachful look.

'But we loved him,' Helen added quickly.

Uncouth. That's what you lot are, said Jim's voice in Sam's head. Bloody uncouth. Sam sniggered nervously. Helen jabbed her in the ribs with a sharp elbow. Sam stepped back and trod on Jess's boot.

'Ow,' said Jess, caught unawares because she had her eyes down to glance at her watch, checking whether there was time for a swift round before lunchtime last orders. Liz frowned.

'It's what Jim would have wanted,' Jess said. 'A quick drink.'

Liz almost smiled.

Sam offered her godmother an arm and helped her shuffle over the uneven earth. The vicar held out his Tupperware pot nervously, and rapidly removed himself when they had both dipped in. They stood silently on the lip of the pit together. The skittish breeze rippled the gold embroidered edging of Ruth's sari, flicked Sam's hair around her face.

'One, two, three, four, five, six, seven,' Ruth said softly. 'All good children go to heaven.'

'Eenie, meenie, miny, moe,' Sam said, completing the familiar verse. 'I wonder where the others go.'

Ruth jabbed her curved thumb decisively heavenwards. 'He was never passive in the face of evil. He's going up,' she said.

'Maybe. But I'm not convinced they'll let him in when he gets there.'

'Well, he's bound to have arranged for someone to leave the back window open a crack,' Ruth retorted. She peered cautiously down into the chasm. 'I find the idea of burial quite disturbing.'

Sam looked over the edge of the pit now too, shuddered at the sight of the varnished lid of the coffin and imagined Jim lying just below.

'I know what you mean. It does seem quite callous leaving him down there alone, while he's still...' she couldn't think of a fitting word, 'whole.'

Ruth nodded. 'Cremation would have been better; it shortens the period of limbo. The danger,' she added.

'What do you mean?'

'When a person dies, their flesh becomes contaminated with the evil of death. And that means the corpse is polluted. It is wise to keep it away from the sacred natural elements – earth, fire, water – in case the evil spreads. That is why it is Zoroastrian custom to leave corpses in the open for the carrion birds, the vultures, the crows, to take away the flesh. They are the birds that have been created by God for this purpose, to deal with the evil of death.'

Sam stuck a hand in her coat pocket and felt the barbs of the raven's feather she had carried with her from Orkney. Raven. Carrion bird. Dealer with death. Odin's companion.

'But where open burial is not permitted,' Ruth continued, 'then cremation is better than burial, because the fire consumes the flesh quickly and reduces the dangerous time of contamination. Still, I suppose it can't be helped. But you will have to be careful.'

She dug her flat, black lace-up into the graveside earth, drew a circle with its tip. 'In the end we all return to dust, one way or another. We come from the elements and we return to the elements. We may have a second of consciousness, but even that vanishes in the gentlest gust of wind.'

Ruth uncurled her arthritic hand as she spoke and let the breeze whip the particles away. Sam followed suit and broadcast the grains she was holding. Ashes to ashes. Dust to dust. Death and the regeneration of life.

She watched the last specks fall back to earth, and was about to retreat from the graveside when Ruth seemed to stumble. Sam reached out an arm to steady her. Ruth clutched at Sam's coat, pulled at her for support. Sam leaned in to prop up her godmother.

With an unexpected swiftness of movement, Ruth stretched up and whispered in Sam's ear. 'By the way, that day the other week when you came round with Jim, I had a quick word with him while you were sorting through my things. I said I was worried about you, thought you might be in some kind of trouble, putting yourself at more risk than you realized with all your protesting. He said that he thought you were smart enough to keep yourself out of difficulties, but he promised he would make sure you had a number to call anyway. Just in case you needed help.'

Sam nearly choked. 'What? What was he talking about? What number?'

'It's no good spluttering at me,' Ruth hissed crossly. 'I'm only repeating what Jim said. I've no idea what number he was talking about. I'm just passing on the message.'

Liz interrupted impatiently from behind. 'Have you two finished yet?'

Sam tried to catch Ruth's eye, but Liz tugged her back, away from the grave. Ruth kept sight fixed firmly on the green sward of the distant golf course.

Liz was the last to step up. She heaved a final sigh in the presence of her husband before brushing her hands together over the coffin, wiping away the lingering motes. 'All over.' She turned to leave the graveside.

The vicar picked up her cue and scuttled off like a cockroach back to the sanctuary of his church.

'To the pub,' said Jess.

'I'll catch you up in a minute,' Sam said.

Liz led the strange procession of mourners away, winding between the angels with their prayer books and the greening jam jars of wilting flowers. Out through the lychgate. Roger was the last in the line, his bouffant quiff lifting in the wind like a billowing sail propelling his large frame forwards. What was he doing here anyway, Sam thought to herself crossly. He wasn't a friend of Jim's. Jim thought he was a tosser. Full of bullshit. Telling people he had been in the SAS. He wished. She glared at his back as he strode breezily down the path, passed under the shade of a wilting rowan, turned and pulled what she presumed was supposed to be a sympathetic face, a drooping lettuce leaf of a smile. Prat. He could piss off. She gave him the evil eye. He recoiled from her stare, disappeared down the lane.

Alone now in the lengthening shadows of the advancing afternoon, she felt uneasy. A black moth flitted past her face, brushing her skin, making her shudder. The back of her neck bristled. She checked the corners of the graveyard through the swaying branches of the yew trees. Searching for Watchers. Spooks. Crackpots. Psychos bearing grudges or firearms. Nobody visible. She gazed down at the coffin in its muddy hole, straining her eyes, as if she might still be able to see through the solid lid of the wooden box and commune with Jim, ask for his forgiveness for pilfering his information, solicit his guidance about passing on the poisoned chalice now she had it in her possession, find out the meaning of his peculiar parting message to Ruth. But Jim was silent. And the sight of the freshly dug gash in the wet soil made her think of rotting corpses, slow putrefaction, worm-eaten flesh. Ruth was right, Jim's death was incomplete, unfinished. Dangerous. She had an urge to pull out the nails, wrench the lid free, open the coffin so the crows and the rooks could clean his bones and hasten the process of decay. She leaned over the edge of the pit. A rustle in the undergrowth behind, the snap of branches, made her panic. She twisted. Heard the soft tread of shoe on earth. Turned again too quickly. Head spinning. Eyes darkening. Nothing but blackness and warm breath behind. She jabbed her elbow blindly in an effort to fend off her attacker. Too late. Her foot moved the wrong way. She was slipping over the edge. A split-second plunge into paralytic fear. The dank pit reaching up to engulf her, to bury her in its earthy embrace.

'Gotcha.'

She yelped with pain as her arm was grabbed and yanked backwards.

'Saved you,' said her captor.

She recognized the voice. 'Becky,' she said, attempting to control the quaver in her throat. 'What are you doing?'

'Coming to check up on you. Make sure you're okay. You looked as if you were preparing to throw yourself on top of your father's coffin.'

'I wouldn't do that.'

'I should bloody well hope not.'

'I am feeling a bit wobbly though. I could do with a spliff before I go to the pub.'

They wandered down the path to the south side of the graveyard, through a wooden gate into a meadow beyond; heifers idly loafing in a far corner, the air humming with bees and the cat-pee whiff of Queen Anne's Lace. They perched on the rotting planks of a moss-covered bench, hidden from the churchyard by a hedgerow of hawthorns.

'What was all that chucking dust about anyway?' Becky asked. 'Why do you think he insisted on that? It felt like a scene from a film about the Mafia.'

Sam attempted a smile. 'I will show you fear, perhaps,' she said.

'What?'

'I will show you fear in a handful of dust.'

'Oh, that bloody misogynist Eliot. *The Waste Land*.'

Sam shrugged. 'Look,' she said. 'Jess taught me a great new way to roll a reefer.'

She removed two Rizla papers from the red packet, delicately licked their gummy edges with the tip of her tongue, stuck them together carefully at an angle, struck a match and held it to the side of the surplus seam. Just as Jess had done. The thin paper instantly burst into flames, whipped into the air, narrowly missing her hair, transformed into a puffball of

284

grey ash and floated away. Becky snorted, laughing. Sam laughed too. Manically.

'You idiot,' Becky said.

She snatched the Rizla packet and nimbly rolled a joint. They puffed contentedly in the late afternoon sun. Sam found herself mesmerized by the gleam of a dazzling emerald jewel in a fresh cow pat; a green dung beetle frantically waving its clubbed antennae. Swimming through the shit. Or perhaps it was drowning.

Ambling back through the graveyard, weaving around the grassy mounds covering long-forgotten bones, she automatically glanced across at Jim's plot. A small black plaque marked the head of the pit. Strange. She couldn't remember anybody leaving a plaque. Somebody must have returned to the grave while they were having a spliff. She darted off the path, picked up the etched marble stone. In one corner, there was a pair of ghostly hands pressed together in prayer. In the opposite, Sam identified the familiar crowned badge of the Force. Becky stepped over to join her as she read out the words carved diagonally across the plaque's face.

'*Ars longa, vita brevis.*'

Latin.

'Art is long, life is short,' said Becky. 'Hippocrates. He was talking about medicine, his professional skills. There's a lot to learn and not much time to do it.' She hesitated. 'Odd thing to put on a memorial.'

Becky was right; it was a peculiar sentiment.

'Who do you think left that then?' Becky asked.

'I don't know.'

Sam stood up and returned Becky's hard brown gaze unblinkingly.

'You're not very good at lying,' Becky said.

'I'm not lying. I don't know.'

But she could guess. Only one of Jim's companions was big on Latin. She screwed up her eyes, squinted along the path leading under the lychgate, searching for movement, a figure, a stranger. The Commander must have found out where the funeral was being held and left the plaque on Jim's grave. *Ars longa, vita brevis*.

'Don't,' Becky said.

'Don't what?'

'Leave it alone. Stop digging. Jim's dead and buried.'

Sam lifted a small pebble distractedly with her foot and sent it arcing over the edge of the grave in a neat parabola. It curved down and bounced on the coffin's lid, making a hollow drum-like plop as it landed.

Becky folded her arms, shook her head. 'If you don't go chasing him,' she said, 'he's not going to come after you.'

'I wouldn't bet on it.' Sam smiled wanly. 'Let's go and join the wake.'

Along the sunken lane, dappled light playing around the twisting trunks and gnarly roots, the leaves rustling in the breeze. *Ars longa, vita brevis*, the oak trees whispered. Taunting her with the hidden meaning of the Commander's message. There is a lot to learn and life is short. Was it a warning? Don't be a smart-arse if you don't have the tradecraft. Or else you'll cop it. She instinctively reached for the feather in her pocket, hoping to gain comfort from its touch. But, instead, it made her think of Odin and his ravens. The wild hunt. Searching out the traitors. Hunting them down. She silently cursed her mother's insistence on banning the Commander from attending Jim's funeral, rueing again her lost opportunity to get rid of the envelope.

They reached the turning point for the double-deckers at the end of their route out of London; a triangular patch of tarmac covering what had once been the village duck pond. She scanned the parked cars and driveways, hoping for some evidence of the Commander's presence, but the village was deserted. All was silent, apart from a pub sign clanking in the wind. The Green Man. The yellow eyes of the strange foliage-entwined creature followed her as the sign swung to and fro, pushed by the strengthening gusts. Odin, master of the winds, she thought. King of the underworld. Lord of the dead. Sam shivered in the rapidly cooling air of the late afternoon, plagued by the nagging sense that now Jim was gone, she had become the hunt's main quarry. The object of the chase.

CHAPTER 19

THE DAY AFTER the funeral, everyone was hanging around the house aimlessly. The phone rang as Sam brushed past it on the way to the kitchen to make another cup of coffee. She picked it up without thinking. It was Tom. Just the sound of his voice put her on edge, her brain searching for a way of cutting him off quickly while she politely said hello.

'I have to talk to you,' he said.

'Okay. I'll call you back later. I'm about to go out,' she lied effortlessly.

'Sam. It's important.'

'This afternoon. I'll call you then.'

'Listen. I've found out about Shinkolobwe.'

The name gave her a start, a painful reminder of her unfinished business. She checked over her shoulder, heard Liz clanking about, busy in the kitchen.

'I know about Shinkolobwe,' she said. 'Shinkolobwe is a mine in Zaire. Katanga.'

'Yes, but do you know what kind of mine it is?'

She dug the fingers of her free hand into her thigh. 'Tell me then,' she said. 'What kind of mine is it?'

'Uranium.'

Uranium. Her legs suddenly felt heavy, tingly. She collapsed on to the floor, back against the wall, the receiver pressed to her ear.

'It was the world's richest bloody deposit of uranium,' Tom continued. 'Shinkolobwe is the mine that supplied the uranium for the Manhattan Project, which developed the Hiroshima and Nagasaki atom bombs. But it's officially closed,' he added. 'It's been abandoned.'

An abandoned uranium mine. No wonder it wasn't marked in the atlas.

'I asked this mate of my mum's – weirdy-beardy, department of development studies, specializes in Africa – his eyes just lit up when I mentioned the name. Set him off. Shinkolobwe is a hell-hole of capitalist history. A magnet for the darkest forces of the colonial endeavour. A conspiracy theorist's wet dream.'

She clicked her tongue impatiently 'So when was it closed?'

'In 1963. Zaire was called the Congo then. Shinkolobwe was owned by a Belgian mining company. When the Congo was given independence from the Belgians in 1960, Katanga declared itself an independent republic. The Belgians who owned the mines there financed a puppet regime so they could carry on mining. And the Katanga army that defended them was run by a bunch of European mercenaries.'

Jesus. Jim and Don Chance. 1960. Shinkolobwe. That was where Jim had parted from Chance in 1960, he had said. She tried to trace his course in her mind, remember what he had told her, piece the fragments together. Gun-running. He had been transporting weapons across southern Africa. He must have delivered the guns to the Katanga army. But then he had been shocked by the conditions in Shinkolobwe, argued with the foreman, had his toes shot off and decided he'd had enough. He wasn't prepared to fight the Belgians' battle. He had seen the bigger, bleaker picture, had already acquired too many mercenary scars. Backed away from the precipice. Her hands were sweaty. She wiped her palms on her trousers.

'So what happened after 1960?'

'A lot of fighting. And assassinations. UN Secretary Generals dead. Prime Ministers bumped off. Anybody and everybody was involved apparently. MI6. CIA. KGB.'

'Shit.'

'Exactly. But, despite the West's efforts to keep control of the area, presumably to keep it out of the hands of the Soviets who were backing the Congolese, the Belgians were forced out and Katanga was reunited with the rest of the Congo. The Belgians filled the mineshafts with concrete before they left. 1963. Mobutu became President in 1971. That's when the Congo's name was changed to Zaire. The state took ownership of the mines. And Katanga's name was changed to Shaba.'

Shaba? Shaba Security Limited. The torn receipt in the manila envelope must have come from Shinkolobwe. Black dots started dancing in front of her eyes. She rubbed the back of her neck. Trying to clear her head, make sense of it all.

'Sam?'

'So Shinkolobwe is still closed?' she demanded.

'Officially. Heavily guarded by security companies supposedly. But, according to my mum's mate, people have carried on mining anyway. Illegally. The locals just go into the mines because they don't know the risks. Or don't care because they are so desperate for cash. They dig the stuff out by hand, would you believe, carry it out in sacks. Presumably if they survive the mines, they die horribly a few years later. Apparently uranium is found in copper ore, and that's how it's smuggled out of the country. Every now and then some border guard decides to run a Geiger counter over a copper consignment and the needle goes ballistic.'

Christ. What had Jim said? Chance had been back to Shinkolobwe. To do what? Providing security services: turning a blind eye, oiling palms, greasing wheels. Enabling illegal uranium mining perhaps? For a cut of the profits. Backhanders. She inhaled, attempting to fill her lungs. Her chest was too tight. She tried breathing through her nose. It wasn't helping. She opened her mouth wide. No oxygen.

'Sam, are you still there?'

'Yes.' Just.

'There's more.'

'More?'

'This mate of my mum's said he'd heard from one of his academic contacts in Kinshasa that there were rumours of some sort of massacre there a few months ago.'

'Massacre? What kind of massacre?'

'The story is that the locals who were going into the mine were fed up with the size of the bribes that the security guards were demanding. So some of them got together and organized a deputation to confront the guards, there was an argument, and the guards shot the lot of them. A Danish demographer was doing some research on maternal mortality in the area. But all the villagers wanted to talk about was the deaths of the men at the mine. So this researcher reported the story to an official at the Danish Embassy and it seems as if somebody there has decided to try and follow it up.'

Sam stared into space, her brain racing.

'Sam. Why do you think Jim asked us whether we knew where Shinkolobwe was?'

She was glad he couldn't see her reddening face. 'He was probably just showing off. Demonstrating his superior knowledge of geography.'

'Why don't you ask him about it?'

'I can't.'

'He brought it up. He mentioned it. So why can't you ask?'

'Because he's...' She stopped. She didn't want to tell Tom about Jim's death, didn't want to prolong the conversation.

'Look,' she said, 'thanks for telling me all this. It's very interesting. But I've got to go now.'

'Sam. Is there some connection between Shinkolobwe and something that happened in Orkney while we were there?'

'I doubt it very much. I really do have to go now. Thanks for phoning. I'll call you.'

She slammed the receiver down, sat there on the floor, turning Tom's question over in her mind. She tried to recall Jim's exact words about Shinkolobwe on the train coming back from Orkney. When Chance told him that he had been back to Shinkolobwe, he hadn't thought it was significant. And then oddly enough, he had said, something turned up in Orkney that made him think about Shinkolobwe again. A funny connection. A funny connection with what? With the Watcher and Intelligence plans to fix the miners' strike perhaps? And what had turned up in Orkney? The manila envelope of course. She pushed herself up from the floor and ran to her bedroom.

She ferreted under the bed, removed the shoebox, extracted the manila envelope and emptied its contents on the floor. She wiped her mouth with the back of her hand, concentrated, trying to comprehend all the links in the chain. She started shuffling the pieces around on the floor. On her right-hand side she placed the receipt for electrical wire, the list of bomb-making parts, the hand-drawn map of the station, the photocopy of the passport for Anthony Baines. Those were the papers, she reckoned, that gave away information about Intelligence and the strike. On her left she put the torn receipt from Shaba Security Limited, subsidiary of – whatever the missing word was – Asset Management. That piece of paper, she now knew, came from Shinkolobwe. How did it get into the envelope? How was it connected to Intelligence and the miners' strike?

She held her palm over the papers as if she were divining their hidden meanings. She shut her eyes. Opened them again. Reached for the passport photocopy. This was, she reckoned, fake ID for a man who was working with the Watcher and Intelligence, possibly as some kind of provocateur. Was he also, somehow, connected with Shinkolobwe? Was he the critical link? There was, she realized now, only one way she could find out. She would have to ask Anne Greenaway. She gathered up the pieces, stuffed them back in the envelope and placed the envelope in the side pocket of her Laurence Corner cargo trousers. She rummaged in the shoebox, glanced at Anne Greenaway's address on the purple envelope – 24 Milton House, Brixton. She would go to Brixton and talk to Anne Greenaway. And then she would work out what to do with the envelope.

She grabbed her coat, put her hand on the door handle, caught sight of the fading burn mark on her forearm, grimaced. She must be crazy to be doing this, messing with the professionals – the wet-workers, the hitmen. Her brain churned, searching for any shred of information that might help her make it through the day. Ruth's whispered words to her at the funeral floated into her head; Jim had left her a number. She dived across the room, fished around in the shoebox once more and retrieved the scrap Tom had found under Jim's bed in Nethergate. She glanced at the scribbled London phone number and added it to her pocket.

Liz was in the kitchen, standing by the sink, rubbing her hands vigorously under a gushing tap. As Sam entered, her mother's eyes darted sideways towards the holiday brochure lying open on the counter.

'Greek Islands,' Liz said. 'I'm thinking of going with Roger in September after you've gone up to college.'

Sam put one elbow on the counter, flicked casually through the pages, perusing the descriptions of the exquisite villas with their windows opening on to the Aegean. She could feel Liz watching her, nervously trying to gauge her reaction. The song of a thrush drifted in through the open kitchen window.

'Mum,' Sam said. 'You know all that stuff about chucking dust on the grave. You don't think there was a bit of a message there, do you?'

'What?'

'Was there a message for Roger in the dust-throwing? "I will show you fear." Jim getting in the final word to the Professor of English Literature.'

Liz opened her mouth, a protesting oh, and closed it again. 'Don't be ridiculous.' She gave her hands one last rinse, shook them dry. 'The dust. That was just Jim and his weird relationship with religion.'

'I don't think he had a weird relationship with religion,' Sam replied. 'He had spiritual beliefs about the world; he just didn't think much of the church. Not the Catholic Church at least.'

'Well, the dust was just one of Jim's idiosyncratic gestures.' Liz waved her hand dismissively.

Sam stared pointedly at the holiday brochure in front of her. 'Why did you stick with Jim?' she asked. 'Why didn't you leave him?'

'Relationships are complicated.' Liz was talking to the cooker. 'They're not like your beloved cryptic crosswords. You can't just work them out by parsing all the clues. The thing is; I fell in love with Jim. He was the man I wanted to marry. But it wasn't easy. His job made it difficult from the start. He was never there anyway, and when he was at home, he wasn't always pleasant company. I often felt that he was married to his job, to the bloody Commander. But sometimes you just have to stick things out. For the sake of the family.' She paused, twisted her wedding ring. 'I'm not sure he turned out to be the man I thought I'd married.'

Sam said nothing. The thrush twittered.

Liz shouted suddenly. 'God knows what he got up to when he was on his fucking secret missions.'

Sam suddenly felt awkward, uncertain what to say. Now she had provoked it, she didn't want to have this discussion, didn't want to get into the nitty-gritty of her parents' relationship.

She gabbled. 'I think he always thought he was doing things for the public good. He just wanted to repair the world.' She immediately regretted saying anything, realized she sounded completely ridiculous. Trite. She had no idea why she was defending Jim anyway.

'Repair the world,' Liz repeated scornfully.

'*Tikkun olam*,' Sam said.

'*Tikkun* what?'

'*Tikkun*... oh, never mind.'

She gazed out of the window, watched the fat thrush yanking away at a worm wedged in between the roots of the Bramley. Somewhere in the distance Liz was venting.

'Well maybe he thought he was doing things for the public good. And in the beginning, when I met him, when he was in uniform, he probably was. But at some point he threw his lot in with the Commander, who seemed to believe that there were no limits to what could be done in the name of national security.'

Sam wasn't really listening. She felt herself drifting off, a momentary emptiness, the disquieting sense of non-existence she had felt when she watched Jim with Anne in the café in Orkney. Liz was still spewing over.

'And in the end, only he can know whether he made the right decision, whether the information he acquired was worth the price. Because no one else will ever be able to prove what he did or did not do; how many people he might or might not have protected. But what makes me really cross, what I find really upsetting, is that our lives were thrown into the deal. We were taken for granted. Back-up services for Jim. Our family didn't matter. Nobody asked us if we wanted to sign up to be a silent support unit for their secret fucking operations. Our souls were just an invisible part of his contract, his totally gender-blind bloody Faustian pact.' She paused. Leaned on the kitchen counter, eyed the fridge pensively. 'Now that's an interesting angle on Marlowe's Faustus. Because, of course, Marlowe was rumoured to be a spy for the Elizabethan state...'

Sam inhaled slowly, turned to leave.

'Where are you going anyway?' Liz demanded.

'Brixton.'

'Why?' said Liz.

Because, she wanted to say, I want to find out about my father. I want to make one last effort to work out what he was doing, what he believed, whose side he was on. I want to have a final attempt at finding out about his true identity. Because if I don't know who he was, how can I know about myself?

'I'm going to buy a pair of monkey boots. There's a shop that sells them cheaply in the arcade near the station. By the way,' she said over her shoulder as she pushed open the door, 'Was Roger ever in the SAS?'

'No,' said Liz crossly. 'He wasn't in the SAS.'

'Didn't think so.' Roger, the stupid sodding plonker.

'SBS,' said Liz as Sam marched away. 'He was in the Special Boat Service. He loves the sea.'

She descended the steps from Brixton Station, turned left, the sweet scent of mangoes wafting enticingly from the market stalls of Electric Avenue and crossed over Coldharbour Lane. I will show you fear, she chanted to herself. I will show you fear in a handful of dust. Jim was right; she had been a bit half-arsed about her political opinions, a bit lazy. She'd been on the ban-the-bomb marches, shouted the slogans, but never bothered to find out where the uranium came from, never looked beyond her own horizons, never cared to find out how the ore made its way out of the earth, its alchemic transformation from natural element to lethal dust, its journey from Zaire to the States and on to Japan. Hiroshima: the beginning of the end of the age of science. How typical that Jim had seen the hidden connections, the darker histories, knew the clandestine pathways from here to there and everywhere, left his footprints trailing for her to follow.

She headed down Railton Road to the wrong side of town and instinctively buttoned her coat, stuck her hands in her pockets, fingers searching for her talisman, the raven's feather. She was walking towards the front line now: drugs, knife-crime, no-go area. No trees here. Boarded-up buildings and burned-out cars. It was too early, though, for the barrage of dope dealers who marked the road and hissed hashish as you advanced and cursed your back as you passed. The only signs of life on the street at this time of the morning were a couple of empty Red Stripe cans rolling along the road in the breeze and a tortoiseshell cat sniffing the remains of an abandoned Chinese takeaway left festering in the gutter.

Milton House was just beyond the drug dealers' stretch, visible through an archway across a dingy, sunless courtyard. She stalled as she surveyed the grimy Dickensian red-brick verandas. A robin hopped cheekily near her feet, cocked its head, winked and flew away at the sound of a door closing nearby. She took a deep breath, stepped into the gloomy stairwell. Her eye caught a movement in the dark space underneath the lowest flight of steps. She peered into the murk, saw a pile of abandoned rags rearrange itself into a man slumped on the floor underneath the heap of his grubby clothing. He grunted.

'Herroh,' he slurred.

Tramp. Sloshed.

'Hello,' she replied as she climbed the steps.

First floor. Second floor. Out on to the open veranda, the winking radio tower of Crystal Palace visible on the far horizon. She steeled herself. Stepped past a door painted badly in red and black and a window hung with grubby bedsheet curtains. A squat? Number 24 was the second door along. Through the adjacent window, she spotted Anne's dirty blonde hair dangling over a table. Anne looked up nervously, large eyes blinking warily from her puny, pale face. Sam smiled through the glass, reassuringly she hoped. No backing out now.

The front door opened. Close up, there was something slightly old-fashioned about Anne's appearance, a grown-up little match girl, skinny, sparrow-like fragility and pinched lines that suggested she was older than she had looked from a distance – mid-thirties at least, but still a familiar figure in her grungy baggy jumper and faded black jeans.

Anne surveyed her questioningly, waiting for her to speak first. Sam hesitated, unsure how much Anne knew, unclear how to begin.

'I think you know my dad—' she started and stopped. Why hadn't she rehearsed her first line? Why hadn't she worked out her story?

Anne interrupted. 'You're Chris's daughter, aren't you?'

She was momentarily bewildered. Chris? She twigged. Of course, Chris must have been his false identity. Chris was his cover. Sam tried not to smirk. Chris seemed like a singularly inappropriate name for Jim, it was so... so unmacho. She couldn't bring herself to repeat it.

'How did you know?' she asked.

Anne shrugged. 'He told me he'd got a daughter from his marriage. He's spoken about you quite a bit. You just fit the description. You and your mate were with him in Orkney, right?'

Sam nodded.

'It's Sam, isn't it?'

Sam smiled, too surprised at hearing her own name to speak.

Anne returned the smile, conspiratorially. 'Chris told me that you had been arrested for obstruction outside Greenham.'

Sam nodded again. Jim had mocked her when the letter from the magistrates' court had turned up. She couldn't quite decide now whether she should be furious or amused that Jim had used her identity, her history, as part of his subterfuge. Window-dressing. Anne beckoned her inside. And as she stepped over the threshold, it dawned on her that Jim had provided her with a backstory, a readymade cover. She could play herself.

Anne's front room was a more unkempt version of her brother's study in Orkney: a wonky bookcase haphazardly constructed from crates, clothes strewn across a collapsing armchair, an overflowing wastepaper bin, piles of paper everywhere. A poster of a man waving the flag of Anarchy was pinned on one wall. On another, a black paint board was covered in a tangle of chalked messages; calls to overturn the state running into reminders to buy oranges and onions. She couldn't quite see Jim here in this chaotic room with Anne and her messiness, her political naïveté. Although he would have approved of the efforts at recycling, Sam decided, and the obvious total lack of expenditure on what he considered to be unnecessary luxuries, like something to sit on that was actually comfortable. In fact she suspected she could see Jim's fingerprints on the cack-handed construction of the skip-retrieved crate shelving; it looked like something he might have helped to build. She rubbed her eye. She didn't want to think about it. Anyway, it couldn't be Jim's fingerprints because Jim had never been here. It was Chris. She began to feel queasy, overwhelmed by the confusion of ghosts and shadows, engulfed by the stories that mirrored the truth, turned them inside out and reflected them back at her in disconcertingly familiar forms. The room was spinning.

'Is this a squat?' Sam asked, forcing herself to focus on the basics. Facts.

'No, it's a housing co-op. We were given a short-term licence by Lambeth Council because they didn't have enough money to do them up.' Anne spoke in the nondescript monotone of middle-class London.

A housing co-op. Not quite so haphazard and disorganized as it all looked then.

'How did you find out where I live anyway?' Anne asked.

Sam hesitated, feeling dumb, caught on the back foot, not expecting to be the one answering questions.

'Did you find my address in my brother's house in Orkney?' Sam's cheeks burned.

'It was you who broke in, wasn't it? A neighbour said he'd passed two teenagers in a noisy maroon Cortina on the road that afternoon.'

Sam's brain scrambled for a rebuff but couldn't find one quickly enough.

'Chris said he didn't think you would do something like that,' said Anne. 'But I suspected he was probably covering for you.'

Sam glanced down at the floor, feeling like a naughty schoolgirl.

'I'm right, aren't I?'

She grimaced, decided there was no point denying it, nodded silently.

'To be honest, I was quite relieved to think it was only a couple of teenagers ferreting through my belongings. At least you didn't filch anything. But what were you after? What do you want anyway?' Anne asked. With hostility? Not exactly. Sam sensed Anne was more interested in finding out about her – or, at least, not her but Chris's daughter – than condemning her for breaking into Mark's house.

Sam inhaled deeply. 'I came to tell you something. I thought you ought to know. I wanted to tell you that he's dead.'

No reaction.

'I don't understand,' Anne said. Flat tone.

'My dad had a car crash on the way back from the station last weekend. Vauxhall Bridge. He missed a traffic light and hit a brick wall. The pathologist said he was over the limit.'

The shockwave rippled outwards from Anne's eyes, bewilderment, disbelief. An awkward silent thirty seconds before she registered realization. 'Chris is dead? Oh my God.'

She gripped the back of a chair, knuckles white, head down, shoulders heaving. Sam edged away, uncomfortable, embarrassed by the display of emotion, not quite certain how to react, feeling guilty for breaking the bad news. She wondered whether Chris would have just melted away in Anne's consciousness if she hadn't said anything. She shuffled around by the door for five minutes, maybe more. She was on the point of making a quiet getaway, giving up on the possibility of talking, when Anne wiped her eyes on the back of her hand, groped for a pouch of Golden Virginia lying on the table, took out the Rizlas, rolled herself one, offered the packet to Sam.

'No thanks, I only smoke—' she curtailed the sentence, changed her mind. 'Actually I will have one,' she said. Solidarity, more than anything, hoping the comradeship of shared nicotine might ease the atmosphere. She fumbled with the Rizla and managed to roll a camel-humped tube with stray baccy strands straggling from its ends. Anne passed her a flame-tarnished silver Zippo. Sam flipped the lid, flicked the flintwheel with her thumb, held the dancing flame to her limp effort, dragged, clacked the lighter's lid and replaced it on the table.

Anne shook her head. 'Chris is dead. It just doesn't seem real.' She paused. The thin skin on her forehead wrinkled. 'But you know he didn't think he would be around much longer.'

She raised her rollie to her mouth. And then her arm froze in mid-air. 'Oh my God. Perhaps Intelligence did him in. He thought they were after him.'

Sam threw her a bewildered expression. It wasn't an act. It was hard to keep up with Jim's stories. 'Intelligence? What you mean secret agents? Spies? Why would Intelligence be after him?'

'He was working on labour issues, workers' rights, for the *Black Flag*.'

'*Black Flag*?'

'Anarchist newspaper. Didn't he tell you about it?' There was a hint of suspicion in Anne's voice now, or perhaps it was a slight one-upmanship. She dragged heavily on her rollie as she eyed Sam quizzically.

'No. He never really talked about...' Sam stalled helplessly, floundering, flustered, unable to finish the sentence, convinced she'd done it now, given herself away. But Anne greeted her confusion with sympathy rather than mistrust. 'It must have been difficult when your parents split up.'

Sam stuck her hands in her pockets, shrugged, sensing the best tactics to use. 'You've probably seen him more often over the last couple of years than I have,' she said, improvising now, feeling her way towards her lines, searching for the sentences that had a certain ring of truth. 'He didn't really tell me that much about what he had been doing. All that stuff about the *Black Flag*. Intelligence. It doesn't really mean much to me.' It was easier than she had been expecting to act the part. It didn't feel like lying.

'It almost seemed like he became a different person when he left us. I feel like there's a part of my dad I know nothing about at all.' She sighed. 'It would really help me deal with my dad's death, if you could tell me what you think might have happened, what he was doing before he died.'

She felt Anne examining her face with her wide, childlike eyes. Anne was, Sam suspected, cynical about the system but gullible about people; too trusting. Anne pulled a thin, pained smile. A heavy step outside on the veranda made them both turn to the window. The robin flitted past the pane. Footsteps clattered down the stairwell. They exchanged nervous glances. Anne walked over, peered out, shook her head and draped a scarlet blanket over the glass, casting a deep red shade over the already dim womb-like room. Neither of them spoke for a moment, listening for tell-tale sounds of an external presence: a tread, a breath, a rustle. But Sam could hear nothing now apart from the blood rushing through her head. Anne stubbed the butt of her rollie out on a saucer, reached for the Golden Virginia pouch, rolled herself another, lit it, puffed a couple of times and moved to the far end of the room, perching on the arm of a rickety chair. She beckoned Sam to come closer. Sam balanced awkwardly on the other arm. Anne stared into space, eyes moist, puffing on her rollie. Sam wondered whether she had lost it again. She was beginning to feel slightly frustrated with Anne's inability to control her emotions.

But then Anne sighed, stubbed out the damp remains of her fag. 'I'll tell you what I can.'

CHAPTER 20

'CHRIS DOCUMENTED DETAILS of workplace accidents for the *Black Flag*,' Anne said. 'He had contacts in the unions, contacts all over the place in fact. He was always chasing up stories. Nobody paid him, of course; he did it in his spare time. He was really passionate about it, particularly when young people were involved. He thought teenagers were too easy to exploit, happy to do dangerous jobs because they had no idea about the risks involved.'

Anne's hands fiddled nervously with the tobacco and papers.

'It was his union contacts that told Chris about Intelligence's plans. They said that the security services were trying to use the trouble in the coal industry to expand their surveillance networks, crack down on anybody who steps out of line. Chris was trying to find out more. But he began to suspect that Intelligence was after him because he knew what they were up to. That was why he moved out of his flat in Stockwell. He decided to leave town, lie low for a while. He warned me before he left to be careful, not to trust anyone. He said Intelligence might be trying to plant someone in a squat round here to pick up on our contacts with the miners.'

She shook her head as she lifted a rollie to her mouth, lit it. 'About a week or so after Chris had left, this bloke appeared, started hanging around. Steve. South African Steve. I didn't think there was anything odd about him at first. Everybody liked him; he said he was on the run from the South African army. He had to do National Service, but he absconded after six months because he couldn't take it, hated the apartheid regime, went AWOL, headed north, working his way up through Africa doing casual labour here and there, and ended up in Brixton. I met him at the bookshop.'

Sam's brain was ticking. South African Steve, working his way north through the continent. Had he travelled through Zaire? Stopped at Shinkolobwe? Anne misinterpreted Sam's questioning expression.

'The anarchist bookshop on Railton Road,' she said. 'It's a sort of community centre. I help out there with an advisory service for squatters. Steve was looking for a place to live. I ended up inviting him to stay with me for a couple of days until he found a squat.'

Sam raised a judgemental eyebrow.

'He seemed like a genuine bloke in need of help,' Anne said defensively. 'And, you know I think I felt at ease with him straight away because he reminded me of Chris.'

Well he would, Sam thought with slight irritation: ex-military, not quite what he seems.

'Steve was very interested in all the stuff we had been organizing for the miners,' Anne continued.

'What stuff was that?'

'Oh, a bunch of us have been going up to the pits around Doncaster for years to hand out the *Black Flag*, so we know a few of the colliery workers up there quite well. When it was obvious a strike was on the cards, we organized a benefit to raise some money. Steve came with us to deliver the cash. He made friends very quickly with some of the younger blokes up there.' She paused, sighed. 'I don't know why I didn't spot it sooner. He went back there on his own almost every weekend after that. He said he was distributing copies of *Class War*.'

Sam frowned.

'Anarchist version of the *Beano*. All the men round here think it's great.'

Anne nodded in the direction of an amateurishly printed broadsheet slung on the table: a cartoon picture of a boot adorned the front cover, 'kill the bill' scrawled over the top.

'Then one evening – it must have been early May – we were having a couple of drinks outside the George Canning and Steve told me he had this plan to train some of the strikers to use explosives so they could blow up the railway lines being used to transport the coal from the stockpiles. I thought he was joking at first. Or fantasizing. Showing off. Being macho. It was such a terrible idea. But he insisted some of the younger blokes at the pit were up for it and he knew what he was doing because he'd been in the army. And he said he had a contact who could supply him with the materials.'

The Watcher, Sam noted to herself; the map with the Watcher's car registration must have indicated a pick-up point for explosives, bomb-making equipment.

'Steve said he was going to take the gear with him next time he went north. Kept going on about mercury fulminate. He said he could get hold of some, but he wasn't sure about using it because it was so unstable. That was when I began to worry that he might be serious. So I tried to talk him out of it. His plan seemed so stupid to me. Apart from the obvious danger, I just couldn't see how it could work. The tabloids were having a field day already with Scargill. Blowing up railway lines was hardly going to help the cause. It would just give the cops an excuse to come down harder on the strikers.'

Anne dragged on her rollie, let the smoke slip out of her mouth, glanced towards the covered window before she continued.

'I thought he simply didn't understand the politics because he was South African. I tried to make him see sense, but the more I argued against him the more stubborn and aggressive he became. I actually began to feel a bit scared; worried that he might turn on me. So I just backed off. The next day, when he had calmed down a bit, I told him he had to move out and find somewhere else to live. He didn't disagree. He said someone had just opened up a new squat further along Railton Road and he could move in there. He left some of his stuff here while he sorted out the room. And I went through his belongings.'

So Anne had acquired the information on Intelligence plans by rummaging in Steve's bags. Sam wondered whether she had more in common with Anne than she had first thought.

'I found some papers in a trouser pocket that seemed to confirm the story he had told me. At the bottom of his rucksack I discovered a British passport with his photo and a different name. Anthony Baines. Everyone round here knows how to get a fake passport. It's not difficult. And I knew already that he had a good reason for wanting a new identity.' She took a deep breath. 'Because he shot his commanding officer.'

'What? You mean, killed him?'

Anne nodded. 'He told me he had to shoot him to get away. He was in Angola, out in the bush. Part of the South African operation to overthrow the socialist government. He said he would be court martialled if he ever went back. Executed.'

Sam realized her mouth was open. Shut it. Felt slightly faint. South African Steve was a killer. Wet-worker, she thought. Hitman.

'Well, obviously,' Anne continued, 'if I'd known that to

begin with, I might have been a bit more hesitant about inviting him to stay. Maybe I'm not a very good judge of character.'

No, no, you're really not, Sam shouted silently in her head.

'Anyway, you can see his motivation for wanting a fake ID,' Anne said.

Sam nodded.

'But it was definitely odd that someone who had only been in the country a couple of months would be able to fix it up so quickly. The more I thought about it, the more I felt that something wasn't quite right. He was too well organized, too well set up. He had contacts and seemed really certain about what he was trying to do. That was when I put him together with Chris's warning about a possible plant trying to use our links with the miners.'

'A provocateur.'

'Right. Working for Intelligence or some other bit of the secret services, I don't know, trying to sabotage the strike by setting the miners up. I photocopied the passport and kept hold of all the other bits of paper I'd found. When Steve came back to pick up his stuff, I could tell that he realized something was wrong. He probably guessed I had been rummaging in his bags. That was when he disappeared. Left the squat. Nobody has seen him since. I was really disturbed by then, worried about what he might do. So I decided I had to give all the stuff I'd unearthed to Chris.'

'What did you think my dad could do with it?'

'He told me if he ever dug up enough information on Intelligence, he was going to hand it over to the press.'

Sam scratched the back of her head, wondered whether Jim and the Commander really had intended to leak the information he acquired from Anne. His continual carping about journalists had blinded her to that possibility.

'So I left a message with a mate of his who works behind the bar at the Chequers in Stockwell,' Anne said. 'And we arranged to meet in Orkney.'

'Why Orkney?'

'Remote. Chris thought it would be safer. The best way of avoiding anybody who might be watching him. I had planned to go up there anyway to see my brother. I knew Chris had been to Orkney before. He used to talk about it a lot – Skara Brae, Maeshowe, Viking runes. He was really interested in history, wasn't he?'

Sam nodded, not quite trusting her voice to say yes without cracking.

'In fact, that's what he told me he was trying to do,' Anne said. 'Lie low and finish a history degree he had started. Early Middle Ages, he said. History of the Norsemen. He said he was fed up with doing construction contracts, he needed to retrain, do something different.'

'He told me he was thinking about finishing his history degree too,' Sam managed to say. Her head was feeling woozy. She had hoped that meeting Anne would help her discover the real Jim, but the encounter was merely revealing another layer of Jim's existence. The edges of her father were all blurred, it was impossible to discern where his true self ended and his cover began. His identities were piled on top of one another, layer upon layer, a compression of life-stories in one body. A cross-section of an archaeological excavation. She wiped her eyes with her sleeve, uncertain whether she was on the verge of laughter or tears.

'Orkney does have a mysterious charm,' Anne said. She had a wistful gleam in her eyes. 'I'm going back in a couple of weeks. I'll probably stay up there for a while.'

'You're going to see your brother again?'

'Yes. Well, partly. But mainly to see this man I met up there. A fisherman. A skipper actually.'

Sam flushed. 'Oh,' she said. 'What's his name?'

As if she didn't know.

'Nils. He's Norwegian.'

'How did you meet Nils then?' She was trying hard not to sound peeved. Anne was too old for him anyway.

'It was quite funny really,' Anne said, voice brightening. 'He was one of the fishermen Mark talked to when he was doing his research. Somehow Nils had found out about his thesis. He turned up on the doorstep on midsummer's eve, ranting because he thought Mark should have shown him what he was going to write. He didn't want all the ins and outs of his business appearing in print, didn't want to be caught out with his tax returns. Mark apologized for not running it all by him first, offered him a beer. Anyway, he stayed and we chatted, found out we had a lot in common.'

'Right. Yes, that is quite funny. So now you and Nils...' she trailed off, plucked away the sour strands of tobacco sticking to her lip.

'So what happened to the envelope I gave to Jim?' Anne asked abruptly. 'Have you seen it?'

Sam willed herself to maintain an innocent visage; she shrugged. 'The police gave us his belongings, the things they had found at the crash. But there wasn't an envelope among them.'

Anne shouted with an unexpected flash of force. 'Fucking hell. They must have taken it. That proves it. They did him in to get hold of the information.'

'Do you really think that's possible?'

'Of course it's possible. That's the way it operates; the secret state, the security services. They know what they are doing. They can get away with murder. Assassination.'

Sam closed her eyes for a second, felt the reaction as her identities collided – fusion, explosive pressure, an urge to blow, tell Anne everything, reveal that Chris was a spy, an agent of the secret state, admit she had the envelope, enlist her help, mend the fractures, ditch the pretence, become a whole person. Solid. Genuine. She took a deep breath. She knew that way led to disaster.

'What do you think we should do about it?' Sam asked.

'Nothing. There's nothing we can do about it. Not if we don't want to end up like Chris. We have to drop it.'

'We have to do something,' Sam said, uncertain whether the urgency in her voice was real or pretence.

Anne grabbed a sheet of paper from her desk, thrust it under Sam's nose. 'This is what we should do. We can't undo Chris's death but we can fight the system that authorized it.'

Sam focused on the words printed across the page. 'Stop the City?'

'It's a protest against the military-financial complex. Against the rich jerks who make their profits from peddling weapons and destroying the planet. Against the secret state that supports them. Chris was always really enthusiastic about it. He was part of one of the groups that was planning some action there. You should go: 27th September. Just turn up. Chris would have approved.'

'Maybe I should turn up then.' Sam felt her eye twitching uncontrollably. She had to escape before it all became too much. But she still couldn't fit the pieces together. She still needed one more nugget of information. One more question. She hesitated. Felt Anne looking at her curiously. It was now or never.

'You know you said South African Steve worked his way up through Africa after he went AWOL.'

Anne nodded.

'Did he go to Zaire?

'Yes. He spent quite a lot of time in Zaire in fact.' Anne's features hardened slightly. 'Why are you asking?'

'Just curious. I was thinking about doing some volunteering work in Africa and when I contacted VSO they mentioned Zaire as a possibility.'

'I wouldn't go to Zaire. It sounded quite dangerous from what Steve was telling me. He said he'd worked for a while as a security guard at some mine or other and he said the place was awash with guns. Shaba, I think he said.'

Sam opened her mouth. The word Shinkolobwe almost slipped out.

'Maybe I won't bother with Zaire then.' She glanced at her watch. Noon. 'I'd better be moving. Thanks for all your help.'

'Okay, but promise me you'll forget about all this stuff with Chris and Intelligence. Swear you are going to drop it.'

'It's all way over my head. There's no way I'm going to involve myself in any of that. But thanks for talking to me anyway. It's really helped.' She dragged on her rollie. 'Sod it. It's gone out again.' She reached for the Zippo.

'Take that lighter with you,' Anne said. 'It's not mine anyway. It was Steve's. He left it here.'

Sam flicked the flintwheel with her thumb. Nothing happened. She flicked it again, harder this time and the flame appeared suddenly, dancing wildly, making her flinch. She turned her face to avoid being scorched and, as she did so, she caught sight of a rag thrown into a corner with a black smear on it, gasped, inhaled the scent of bike oil, pictured the rider outside the Coney's Tavern, patting his pockets for his lighter and froze. Yamaha XT500. A bike that could race across the Sahara. A bike that could be driven up from South Africa, north, across a continent. Ridden by a bloke who liked a spot of trouble. She recovered herself. She knew she had seen the face on the false passport before.

'Did Steve ride a motorbike?'

'How did you know that?'

'It was just a guess,' Sam replied, smoothly. She could really work this undercover malarkey, enjoy it even: the crack of living on your wits, the adrenalin. 'The oily cloth,' she said, nodding to the corner of the room, 'reminded me of a friend of mine. Biker. He's always leaving a trail of dirty rags behind him.'

'Yes, you're right. God, you are like Chris. He never misses anything either.'

'Missed,' Sam said, dropping the Zippo in her pocket.

'Missed,' Anne repeated. She crossed to the window, removed the scarlet blanket, let the daylight trickle in. 'Of course. Missed.'

Sam reached for the door, closed it quickly behind her. As she passed the window, she caught a snapshot of Anne's expression. Sad? Puzzled? She wasn't going to hang around to find out. She strode rapidly along the veranda.

The robin was waiting for her at the bottom of the steps, perched on the spindly branch of a manky buddleia. Sam stepped into the dank courtyard and the bird hopped off, back towards the stairwell, twisting its little head around, almost as if it were checking that she was watching. What was it trying to tell her? She peered into the dark space, the red of the robin's breast fluorescent in the gloom. She blinked. Empty space. Of course. The tramp had disappeared. She tried to recall what he looked like but all she could see in her mind was a pile of rags, the blurred outlines of a black knitted beanie and an unshaven face. She shook her head. No, that really would be just too pathetic for words.

Still, she crossed the courtyard cautiously now, under the archway, out on to Railton Road, scouting left and right. The tramp was nowhere in sight. She was being paranoid. Silly. She stood on the pavement trying to work out her next move. A warm pressure against her legs made her look down: the mangy tortoiseshell cat had abandoned its gutter meal and was rubbing round her calves, demanding attention. She squatted, tickled its chin. It nuzzled her hand. Yowled. Wandered back to the decomposing Chinese takeaway. She watched it toy with a noodle, her head elsewhere, pulling the pieces together, trying to make a coherent story.

So South African Steve was an agent provocateur. And the Watcher was his handler, contracted as a floating middleman by Intelligence. But the torn receipt in the envelope showed that South African Steve had also worked for Shaba Security in Shinkolobwe. And Shaba Security had to be another of Don Chance's businesses. So did that mean Chance was actually running Steve – and was hooked up with Intelligence in some way? Jim must have found the torn receipt in the envelope. That was why he asked her and Tom if they knew about Shinkolobwe that day in Nethergate. Was it also the reason Jim didn't leave the envelope at the Ring of Brodgar? He had real-ized that Don Chance was working with Intelligence and so Avis would destroy any evidence of that link rather than passing it on to the Commander.

She glanced at the cat with its head buried in the silver foil takeaway tray. Jim must have guessed that Chance's business activities in Shinkolobwe were extremely dodgy. So dodgy, in fact, that he would also want to destroy any information that might reveal his connection with the mine. Cover his tracks. Whatever the cost.

She put her hand in her overcoat pocket and touched the

cold metal of the Zippo, turning the pieces over and over. Her mind was beginning to feel blank, exhausted, eyelids drooping, almost dozing. Unable to see clearly. She was so lost in thought that she almost missed the soft footfall. She looked up, alarmed by the advancing tread, identified the dark coat appearing around the corner. The black beanie. The tramp.

'Jim's daughter,' he shouted. 'You're Jim's daughter.'

He lunged. She ducked. Picked up the tinfoil container holding the mouldering remains of the Chinese takeaway, chucked it in his face. Direct hit. He yelled. Rivulets of feculent sweet and sour sauce running down his cheeks. She stumbled over the bloody cat. Caught herself. The ground tilted and righted as she banked heavily. Gathered speed. Tore down Railton Road. Gasping for air. Lungs painful. Jesus. She reached the line of dope dealers who had now materialized and were blocking the pavement, glaring at her as she hurtled forwards, arms pumping, barging through the jostling, hostile bodies.

'That man,' she gasped as she pushed, 'that man behind me, the one dressed like a tramp. He's an undercover cop. He's in the drugs squad.'

Her breathless claim was greeted with suspicious muttering. Hissing. But as she scrambled free, she sensed the rank closing behind her, forming a barrier, blocking her from sight. And then voices rising. Shouting. Cursing. Giving him a bit of a kicking, she hoped.

She took her chance in the brief surveillance hole, swung left sharply, swerved right, legs nearly giving way beneath her. Left again. She was out on a main road, opposite the cupola of a dirty white church. She paused, trying to find her direction. Instinctively turned right. Weaving through the flow of pedestrians – punks, pushbikes, prams – heading for the high street. She spotted a 159 bus pulling away from the nearest bus stop.

Destination Westminster Bridge. The address on Avis Chance's business card flashed through her brain. Ventura Enterprises. 196 Westminster Bridge Road. She willed herself forward. Made a final run for it. She'd had enough. She didn't care who was on which side. Who was doing what. She just wanted to get rid of the envelope now. It wasn't worth risking her life for it. She was going to hand it over to Avis Chance.

CHAPTER 21

SHE MADE A dive for the platform at the back of the bus, hauled herself up the steps to the top deck, squished herself next to a thick-necked skinhead in a black Harrington, love and hate inked on his knuckles, and calculated that if she tipped back far enough she would be more or less obscured from the streets below. She fidgeted, glanced nervously over her shoulder as the bus chugged along at a grindingly slow stop-start pace. Down the High Street, past the cop shop, the Mecca bingo hall, the virid dome of the Imperial War Museum looming as the bus approached Westminster Bridge Road and the office of Ventura Enterprises. She needed the next stop. She swayed to the back of the bus and was about to descend when she heard the sudden crack of a motorbike engine. Single cylinder. She automatically bent down to peer through the window. Saw the black thorax of an off-road Yamaha. Jumped back. South African Steve – the rider. It had to be. She flattened herself against the wall of the bus and fingered the Zippo in her pocket nervously; he must have been tailing Jim that night at the Coney's Tavern when he stopped and asked her for a light. Dutch, of course she didn't look Dutch. She was marked as a secret policeman's daughter. The bus pulled into the kerb. Petrified, she stood as irritated passengers pushed past. What if he took a shot at her as she crossed the pavement? She tried to stop herself from panicking. Forced herself to think rationally. One, two, three, four, five, six, seven, she chanted in her head. All good children go to heaven. It didn't help. She looked through the rear window again, but she couldn't see the bike. Perhaps he had turned off at the traffic lights. She cautiously descended the steps to the back platform, wavered, too scared to leave the safety of the double-decker.

'Make your mind up,' said the conductor. 'On or off.'

'On,' she said.

He twanged the bell wire. The bus pulled away and crawled under the iron bridge carrying the trains to Waterloo. The river came into view. She clung momentarily to the pole as the bus straightened to cross Westminster Bridge, then she jumped to the pavement. Hit the ground running and hurtled down the stone steps leading to the embankment path. Off the road, safe from motorbikes. She parked herself on a bench, stared across the Thames at the grimy limestone façade of the House of Lords and tried to formulate a plan. Work out her next move.

The tide was high. Very high. The inward rushing waters were pulling at the dangling branches of the sycamore trees. Nothing but a pale stone wall keeping the river back. What if the bricks gave way? She concentrated, holding the weight of the water with the force of her mind. But the fretful slapping of the Thames against the bank filled her head. Louder and louder. Until she realized the roar was outside. External. In the distance. She squinted towards Vauxhall, trying to identify the source of the noise and saw the black outline of the rider growing rapidly larger. Realized, too late, that there were no steps at the Lambeth Bridge end of the embankment path. No barriers. Nothing to prevent a motorbike using it as a racing track. The flagstones rumbled as he tore down the path. She panicked. Turned. Turned again. Bolted back to Westminster Bridge. Up the flight of steps three at a time. The bike was bearing down on her. He had almost reached the bottom. In a distant corner of her brain she remembered hearing the sound of the single-cylinder bike engine that morning at the train station. She stumbled. He must have hidden in the back of the car. She knew there had been something wrong that morning when she had stood in the station car park, staring at the Cortina. Hijack. Two bullets. Fake the crash. She found her footing. Sprang to the top of the steps. He was her father's assassin. Behind her she heard the engine revving. Jesus wept, he was attempting to ride up the steps. She sprinted across the road. A black cab honked and swerved to avoid her. The cabbie leaned out of the window, effing and blinding as she bolted under the railway bridge, trains rumbling overhead, pigeons flapping around the shit-stained girders. She pelted down Westminster Bridge Road. The bike roared off. Heading east.

Number 196, the home of Ventura Enterprises, Avis's office. The revolving glass door moved at her touch, propelling her into the foyer. Face to face with a thug-featured security guard glaring from behind a desk. A badge bearing a yellow stitched V was attached to his shirt just below his epaulette: Ventura must be supplying heavies to man the reception. The menacing physical presence of the company nearly made her retch. But she couldn't afford to stop and think. There wasn't time for qualms. She was in over her head. Couldn't deal with it. South African Steve. Chance. Hitmen. Wet-workers. It was too much for her. She just had to dump the envelope and run. Somewhere in her head she could hear Jim's voice, see his finger jabbing. Pathetic. What was wrong with her? What the fuck was she playing at? She knew it wasn't the right thing to do. Handing the information back to a bunch of bloody mercenaries. Trigger-happy killers. Her own father's assassins.

'Can I help?' the guard asked in a way that suggested the only assistance he was likely to offer was a boot in the backside to speed her through the exit. She started to speak, stammered, stopped short. He glowered. She swallowed hard, ran her eye over the companies named in gold plastic letters on the board behind his head, spotted Ventura on the seventh floor, picked out a likely sounding organization on the fifth. Playing for time.

'I was just trying to find out about Third World Action. I applied for a job with them and I'm doing a bit of background research so I know what I'm talking about if I'm asked for an interview.'

He glared, put his hand to his hip and her throat went dry as she considered the possibility that he was carrying a gun. She tried to smile sweetly. It seemed to do the trick. He let his hand relax, gestured to a small leaflet-straggled table in a corner of the foyer. 'They might have left something there.'

She thanked him, sidled over to the table, nervously sifted through the pamphlets advertising charities, medical suppliers, market researchers, international shippers and spotted a plain white brochure with 'Ventura Enterprises' printed across the front in discreet, grey Arial. Underneath, in a slightly smaller font, the words 'security solutions'. She opened it and read:

Ventura is a private security company which specializes in problem resolution and the provision of associated consulting services. We are able to offer solutions that address a range of concerns from the most straightforward security needs to more complex situations. Ventura is a privately owned business. It maintains representative offices in London, Washington DC and Johannesburg. It is managed by a number of senior ex-military personnel from the UK and US armed forces and police services. This management team can draw on the services of a pool of consultants with extensive domestic and international expertise. Ventura personnel are highly professional, often former military, police and government employees, recruited from a number of different countries. We also have commercial, financial and legal expertise and experienced media handlers.

She flipped the leaflet, scrutinized the tiny, just legible print at the bottom of the back page. 'Ventura Enterprises is a subsidiary company of Prosperity Asset Management. Prosperity Asset Management provides management services for a wide portfolio of companies while maintaining a strategic focus on finding security solutions for domestic and international operations engaged in energy markets. Prosperity Asset Management is registered in the British Virgin Islands.'

Prosperity Asset Management. She pictured the torn receipt for services rendered and conjured up the small print: Shaba Security is a subsidiary of – missing word – Asset Management. She slipped the leaflet into her pocket and let the disparate scraps of information in her brain churn. Shinkolobwe. Shaba. Ventura. Prosperity Asset Management, security solutions. Security solutions my arse, said Jim's voice in her head, almost making her jump.

She looked over her shoulder to check whether he was lurking in some dark corner and, as her gaze swept the entrance door, she spotted a familiar figure on the far side of the road. Leather jacket, faded jeans, Converse high-tops, edging her way into the stream of traffic. Avis. Fuck it. She just had to hand over the envelope and get out of there.

She heard Jim's scornful tone in her head again: Where were her principles now? Whatever happened to *tikkun olam*? Sam wiped her mouth with her sleeve. Jesus. She was having her integrity questioned by a dead sodding secret policeman with alcohol issues and a life-long addiction to deception. It wasn't as if he'd actually provided her with any useful ideas about what she should do with the envelope. He hadn't helped her find a way out, hadn't left her with any way of contacting the Commander. He hadn't even told her his fucking name. All he had done was criticize, mock, been his usual sarcastic self. Death hadn't changed a thing. Even from beyond the grave he was still a lousy father. It was all his fault that she was in this mess anyway. She could feel herself steaming up, on the verge of storming off, handing the envelope to Avis as she left, giving the two-fingered salute to Jim.

Avis was almost across the road now, close enough for Sam to see the determination painted on her big-featured face; red lipstick, slick black eyeliner, an irritatingly attractive combination of ruthlessness and tomboyish glamour. Watch facing inward on her wrist. Her father's daughter. Just like Sam. She was her father's daughter too. Jim was proud of her because she did what was right. Didn't take the easy option. She was a Coyle. She inhaled. Felt the oxygen flowing. Made a sudden dash for the lifts at the back of the foyer, kick-starting her adrenalin, jamming her finger on the up button, staring manically at the illuminated floor numbers, urging them to shift. Stuck at four. Move. Move. The lift descended slowly. Three. Two. One. Ground. Doors open. Lift empty. She jumped in. Pressed five. The doors jerked together. Through the steel barrier, she could hear Avis barking orders at the guard.

'Stop her. We have to get her. I'm going up. You stay here. We need back-up. Call head office on the direct number. Let him know what's going on.'

Him? Don Chance? She watched the floor numbers illuminating. One. Two. Three. Four. Five. Doors open. She pressed the button for the ninth as she jumped out of the lift. The thump of footsteps pounding up the emergency exit reverberated around the stairwell. She searched around wildly for a hiding place, clocked the sign for Third World Action above a dull grey door.

She pushed and found herself face to face with a man wearing a Greenpeace T-shirt, gold metal-rimmed John Lennon NHS glasses and a smug smile.

'We're not open today,' he said. 'I'm just here to sort out some campaigning materials. You can come back on Monday.'

'But I want to help poor people in Africa.' She was trying not to sound too desperate.

He smiled condescendingly. 'Africa is a continent containing a wide diversity of countries, not all of them poor.'

'Zaire. I want to help in Zaire. I want to volunteer, do something for poor people in Zaire.'

'I'm afraid we don't support volunteer programmes. Volunteers without any specific experience to offer are not a very good way to promote development. We prefer to support locally driven community action.'

He threw her the acutely raised eyebrow of a man who was determined to give her the benefit of his superior knowledge. She could hear footsteps on the landing now and then a pause: Avis trying to work out where she had gone.

She leaned towards him. 'Right. I see your point. But what about women's rights? What do you do for women?'

He scowled, irritated by her questions. Outside the fire door creaked as it was opened and swung shut again. Avis departing.

'Thanks for your time anyway,' Sam said. Gave him a wink as she backed out through the office door, glanced anxiously right and left, saw the coast was clear, dived across the landing and through the emergency exit.

She could hear footsteps running up above her now. Avis on her way to the ninth. She tumbled down the stairs in the opposite direction, cautiously pushed the fire door open a crack, surveyed the foyer; the guard was at the reception desk, phone clamped against ear, fat finger running down a directory page, saying yes to whoever was shouting at him from the other end. She would just have to risk it. She took a deep breath. Shouldered the door. Charged across the foyer. Through the revolving glass and out into the street before the guard had a chance to work out what was going on. She skipped into the line of traffic crawling along Westminster Bridge Road. A car braked. Renault. Green. The vehicle behind it squealed to a halt and honked. Peugeot. Red. She quick-stepped between boots and bumpers. Dashed to the far pavement. Looked behind – nobody was following her. Yet. She dodged right and as she did so, her elbow caught the wing mirror of a car parked badly with its front end jutting out into the road. Rover. Black. MVF 476X .The Watcher. Shit.

She darted left into Lower Marsh Street, scurried along the pavement, keeping close to the shuttered shop-fronts, sensing the shifty spirits of south London's backstreets jostling her, tugging her coat, calling her to join them underground. She blocked out the whispering, no clear plan in her head except to escape. She lifted her eyes to check the slope of the taxi ramp up to the station. There was the Watcher striding down, cutting off her emergency exit. She glanced over her shoulder. Avis had tracked her down and was standing at the far end of the street, blocking her retreat. Only one route was open now. She would have to keep moving along Lower Marsh towards the Cut and up the far side of the station. She ran, but the Watcher ran too. She lowered her head and charged. He was there before she could reach the other side of the road. He grabbed her arm. She tried to twist free. He closed his hand around her wrist. She felt the dig of his fingernails. Inhaled the rank odour of stale smoke and Dettol.

'You're not going anywhere my little friend,' he said, fag end clenched between his teeth. 'Not until you've handed over the information.'

He stuck his hand in her coat pocket, groped around, pulled out the raven's feather, snorted with disgust, shoved it back in her pocket again. Somewhere in the distance a single-cylinder motorbike revved.

'Well, now. We know Jim picked up an envelope from his contact. But it has so far failed to materialize. So we can only conclude that he passed it to you. Correct?'

'Not exactly.'

'Come on. Come on. I don't have time for this.' He reached into her other coat pocket. 'We're not in the playground now.'

Playground; the word echoed around the street, bouncing off the narrow brick shop fronts, carried along by the wind blustering south from the river. The gust-harried clouds spread their shadow over the Watcher's face. His predatory eyes darted sideways and she momentarily glimpsed the bullied schoolboy behind the dodgy cover, the child who had never been unconditionally loved, the boy who had to make underhand deals to forge relationships. She almost felt sorry for the Watcher, a twinge of sympathy for a victim of Jim's playground bullying. And then she remembered the gleam of pleasure when he had burned her arm. His groping hand.

'Where's the fucking envelope?' he hissed in her ear as he yanked her hard against his body, squeezing out the last residue of empathy, stoking her anger. She was on auto-pilot now, running on sheer will-power.

'I left it at Ventura's offices,' she said. 'I gave the envelope to the Ventura security guard to hand over to Avis Chance.'

The Watcher plucked the cigarette from his lips, pursed his lips and blew a puff of smoke into her face. She tried not to cough. From the corner of a smarting eye she glimpsed Avis hovering warily at the far end of the street, calculating her next move. He poked his fag back in his mouth, eyes flicking between her and Avis. She thought for a moment he was about to take the bait.

'Don't try your stupid games on me.' He pushed the words out the side of his mouth.

She swallowed nervously, throat parched with anxiety and exertion. He must have noticed her falter; it set him off, he couldn't resist rubbing her face in the dirt.

'Unfortunately you've inherited your father's tendency to imagine you are a bit superior to everyone else. A bit of a hero. But you're no player. You're just a silly little copper's daughter.'

He leered at her. 'So I suggest you hand over whatever you got from Jim and go home before you irritate me further and I decide that you're a waste of space that has to be dealt with in other ways.'

Other ways. She felt the panic rising. Heard the bike revving again. The rider. The hitman. And then she sensed a prickling in her neck, a slight movement in the air. In the tail of her eye she caught a towering figure, a domineering presence emerging from the shadows: straight back, trenchcoat buttoned, trousers pressed. Lined face below the tilted rim of his trilby, the steel frames of his glasses glinting in the rays of the sinking sun. He took a step up the incline.

'Leave this to me,' he said to the Watcher. His voice was calm, educated, consonants pronounced without any audible twang. Golf-club English. It had to be the Commander. She almost cried with relief. Safe. She could hand the envelope over. He would sort the Watcher out.

The Watcher didn't budge, kept his tight grip on her arm. The Commander glowered at him.

'Let her go.' The Commander spoke with an air of tedium which suggested he didn't have much tolerance for people who disobeyed his instructions. The Watcher twitched, dug his fingers further into her flesh.

The Commander raised a greying eyebrow. 'I said let her go.'

The Watcher released Sam's arm and took a step backwards up the slope.

'I'm really not sure why Intelligence insist on using you.' There was a hint of tetchiness in the Commander's tone now. 'Everybody knows you are incapable of keeping to your mission objectives.'

He glared at the Watcher and the Watcher recoiled. 'Everybody knows you always end up following your own private agendas. Your own personal grudges. Your own... obsessions. You can't stop yourself, can you? I can only assume that Intelligence decided to hire you because they needed somebody disposable for this job.'

The Watcher's eyes were on the Commander, hypnotized, ensnared by his own inner demons, the trammels of his past. The Commander sighed impatiently. His words mingled with the crack of a bike's engine. Louder. Nearer this time. The rider appeared round the corner of the station, thundering down the slope from the taxi rank. The Yamaha drew level. Sam watched as the rider pushed his hand into his leather jacket. Pulled out a compact, metallic object. Packet of Benson and Hedges. It wasn't. He lifted his arm. Shoot position. The Watcher's face turned, expression locked, mesmerized by the barrel. Horrified, she saw death reaching out from the depths of the Watcher's eyes a moment before she heard the shot. Suspended for a split-second between life and nothing. The crack of the engine firing followed the whip of the pistol as the bike revved and sped off towards the Cut.

Pink spittle bubbled from one corner of the Watcher's mouth, the smouldering fag still clamped in the other. She gasped. He toppled to his knees, body flopping forward, his face hitting the pavement heavily, black blood quickly congealing on the curve of his cranium, head touching the gutter, the worn soles of his mock crocs upturned. In the unearthly silence that followed she inhaled the acrid scent of singed hair and burned flesh as the dead weight of his body extinguished his final cigarette.

She instinctively moved away, fearful of tripping over the invisible borderline, falling into oblivion. She looked up and saw the Commander smile.

'I don't think anybody is going to miss him.'

She returned his smile, too relieved to care about the clinical coldness of his reaction.

'You must be Sam,' he said.

She nodded.

'Jim talked about you a lot. He was very proud of you. He had a nickname for you he used all the time. Now what was it?'

She shrugged. He paused, glanced up to the sky and back. Moved on. 'I'm so sorry about Jim's death. It must be a very difficult time for you and your family.'

She felt herself warming to the Commander.

'I was very sad I couldn't join you at Jim's funeral,' he said. His face registered slight offence at the recollection and she thought she had better offer him an explanation for the prohibition.

'That was Liz really. Jim had said he wanted the funeral to be friends and family only and my mum took it a bit literally. I'm sure he didn't mean to exclude you.'

The Commander smiled again. 'No, I'm sure he didn't. We

were always very close. He always was...' he paused. 'He always was my favourite.' The end of the Commander's sentence was almost drowned out by the screeching of a couple of rooks fighting in the road over a scrap of greasy bacon. Carrion birds.

'Well, I don't want to waste any more of your time,' he continued briskly. 'I suspect you've had a long day. So perhaps you'd like to hand over anything that you might have... taken from Jim.'

She flushed slightly, embarrassed by the fact that he was clearly aware of her theft of the envelope. She looked swiftly over her shoulder, caught sight of Avis. What was she doing still standing there? Sam was slightly surprised to see that she hadn't disappeared as soon as the Commander had appeared on the scene. In fact, Avis had slipped along the road in their direction, as if she was closing in for the kill. That was odd. Something sparked in her brain. Some faulty connection. She couldn't quite grasp it. The Commander stepped closer to her now as well.

'It doesn't matter how you acquired the information. So long as you give it to me.'

The undercurrent of impatience had returned to his voice.

'You're totally welcome to it,' she said.

She dug her hand into her cargo trouser pocket and pulled out the manila envelope. She was about to hand it over to him when she caught sight of Jim's doodled feather on the back. She paused. What was it about the feather that made her think that Jim had meant her to take the envelope all along? She sighed. Some things would just remain forever unexplained. Jim and all his peculiar manoeuvres, his cryptic hints, his jokes, his pointless instructions. The ban on coppers at his funeral, for example. She could almost have thought that the very purpose of Jim's funeral instructions was to prevent her from communicating with the Commander. Stop her from handing the papers over to him. She hesitated. There wasn't any reason for Jim to try and prevent her from communicating with the Commander. Was there? Somewhere in a distant corner of her mind she heard her father's voice. You have to watch your back in this game. You can't afford to trust anybody. Not even the people you think are on your side. Especially not the people you think are on your side.

'The papers please.'

She stared at the feather, the black bars striping its barbs. Kestrel's feather. That's what it was. It had to be. A feather from a kestrel's tail. She touched the doodle with her finger and, for some reason, she found her head was spinning. She focused on the drawing, trying to find her centre of gravity, and she remembered then the kestrel's feather her father had given her that day at Tilbury. Its peculiar lightness and strength. Funny things feathers, Jim had said. Who would have thought something so flimsy could hold a bird aloft? She glanced down and realized the ground was tilting alarmingly. Everything was topsy-turvy. Getting smaller. Further and further away. She was on a rising thermal. Looping and looping. Soaring. Surveying the tower-blocks and wastelands of south London. Following the amber river towards the far horizon. And now when she looked down, everything made perfect sense, the pieces below fell into place. It was all so obvious: the repeat patterns of the landscape, the shape-shifting characters telling the age-old story. And there was Jim. Standing at the Commander's shoulder. The Commander and Jim, his right-hand man. Odin and Munin, his favourite raven spy. I fear for Hugin that he will not come back, Odin said. Yet I tremble more for Munin. Of course he was more worried about Munin, because we always fear betrayal most from those to whom we are closest. She could see Odin clearly from up high and, even though his trilby was tipped to cover his face, she could tell that he was concerned, suspected that his favourite spy would fly off, leave him, take all his dirty secrets to the other side. Concealed in the manila envelope. And so the Commander had unleashed his wild hunt, searching out the traitor, turning on his own beloved right-hand man. Stung by the treachery. Chasing down Munin. Cornering Jim. He had to go. The Commander had to get rid of him. She knew that now. He couldn't let his once-trusted raven fly free. She felt a tear trickling down her cheek and for a moment she thought she might not return to earth.

'You have to be sensible if you don't want to find yourself in serious trouble.'

She looked into the Commander's face, his thin-lipped mouth and his dead-fish eyes. And she could tell then that he had seen too much to bother with second thoughts, the benefit of the doubt. Regrets. She could sense his mind reckoning, totting up the debits and the credits, coming to unavoidable conclusions. Calculating the collateral damage. She didn't move.

The roar of the returning bike broke the deadlock. She watched the reflection of the black Yamaha advancing in the Commander's steel-rimmed glasses. The rider drew level. Feet on ground. Controlling the weight of the bike with one hand. Slipping the other into his leather jacket. Metallic flash. Pistol. Her turn to get it in the neck. Pay the price for her smart-arsery. She gasped. Closed her eyes. Squeezed tight.

Nothing.

Opened her eyes. The rider's arm was raised. Shoot position. His pistol aimed at the Commander. He jerked his head towards the station slip-road.

'Run,' he said.

She remained rooted to the spot, numbed by uncertainty. Exhaustion.

'Run.' He spoke more urgently this time. 'Go. Now. Quickly. Leave me to sort this fucker out.'

She came to her senses, allowed her limbs to obey his command, bolted up the slope. The South African accent of the rider rang in her ears, ricocheted around her mind.

'You shit. You fucker. You think you can make me do anything just because I'm on the run. Well, you're fucking wrong. There are limits to what you can tell me to do. I obeyed your fucking order to shoot her father, but I'm not going to kill a teenage girl. I've had enough of your fucking games.'

The pistol shot came as she reached the entrance to the mainline terminal. One crack. She halted in her stride. She couldn't help looking back. Staring at the corpse of the Commander, face down in the gutter, blood oozing out around his lopsided trilby. She stood hypnotized as Avis chased along the street, heading in her direction. Drawing nearer. Reaching the taxi ramp. But, just at that moment, the rider revved his bike and intercepted Avis's path. He turned and waved his pistol at Sam, gesturing, telling her to scram. She couldn't shift. She was riveted. It was like watching a film – a thriller, not real life. She wanted to know what happened next. How the story ended. A police siren wailed through the air, jolted her back to her senses. And finally, she managed to move her legs and sprint for the cover of Waterloo station.

CHAPTER 22

SHE CUT ACROSS the mainline terminal, tacking through knots of people huddled around train timetables, and headed to Waterloo East. On the far side of the station bridge she spotted a telephone box, sprinted to the door. Slumped inside. Sirens still wailing all around. She scrabbled around in her trouser leg pocket and grasped the scrap of paper with the phone number written on it, the one that Tom had found under Jim's bed. Message in a bottle. She squinted at the 01 London number. She had nothing to lose anyway; she might as well try it. She balanced a ten-pence piece in the coin slot and dialled. The phone rang. Nobody answered. Perhaps nobody was there. Perhaps it was a non-number. She was about to replace the receiver when somebody did pick up. She fumbled with the coin, jammed it into the slot.

'Hello,' said the voice at the other end. Gruff. Male. 'Hello. Russian Embassy.'

She almost dropped the phone. That wasn't what she had been expecting. Jim had assured her this wasn't anything to do with the KGB. He said he'd lost those Soviet contacts ages ago, and now it turned out he had been wandering around with the number of a direct line to the Russian Embassy all along. He was the Kim Philby of the Force, a double agent. He was directing her towards a poison-tipped umbrella. How stupid of her to think that a scrap of paper found in a whiskey bottle under Jim's bed might have been useful; that Jim might actually have somehow done what he had told Ruth he was going to do and left her a number to call in case she needed help. She should have known better.

'Hello, Russian Embassy,' said the voice again. In a distinctly non-Soviet accent. 'Garage extension,' the voice added. Garage extension? She frowned, trying to recall something Jim had said. Something about a sitting-down position. She pushed the coins into the machine.

'Chauffeur speaking,' the voice said.

She hesitated. 'Are you on diplomatic duties?' she asked uncertainly.

There was a pause at the other end now. ' Yes... Is that the third man?'

The third man. Tilbury. Everything went back to the day at the docks. It all began at Tilbury. She was the third man, Jim had said. He had made up his mind. It was her. The third man. That was Jim's nickname for Sam.

She took a deep breath. 'Yes. This is the third man. I have something for you. I need to hand it over. Urgently.'

'Are you in town?'

'Yes.'

'You know Charlie the lift-man?'

Charlie. Greenwich foot tunnel. Let's face the music.

'I know Charlie.'

'How soon can you be there?'

She glanced up at the clacking departure board above the ticket office – the Greenwich train posted and due to leave in fifteen minutes.

'About an hour.'

'I'll find you at the bottom.'

*

Distant voices drifted on the river's current. The glass dome glittered against the violet sky. The shadow of a man was leaning against the railing, staring out across the oily water. It was Jim. She was eight years old again and Jim was there by her side, holding her hand. We'll have to hurry. Or Liz will have our heads chopped off, he said. The concertina lift-gate was open and Charlie was sitting on the wooden bench reading a paper. He glanced up as she approached.

'Hello, Charlie,' she said.

He searched his dimming memory for her face. She smiled.

He nodded his head in recognition, returned an old man's toothless grin. 'Hello, princess. You've not changed that much.'

'Neither have you,' she lied.

'I heard your dad had passed. I'm sorry. He was a good bloke. So long as you were on the right side of him.'

She smiled again, unable to form words reliably in her lumpy throat.

'Going down?' he asked.

She nodded.

'Business?'

He pulled the gate shut across the cavernous lift and, as they descended, he whistled the lament for Tom Paine's bones. Jim's favourite song. The tune dawdled mournfully in the air as she stepped out into the eerie green light of the white tiled tunnel.

She paced under the Thames, stared straight ahead as the last notes of Charlie's whistle dwindled and the rushing of water echoed above her head. It was cold down here, beneath the river. Colder than she remembered. Cold and damp and clammy, the air dank with the fetid traces of the tunnel's inhabitants: late-night piss-heads, dead rats, slimy vegetation. River water seeping through. She shuddered. And when she heard the footsteps pacing up behind her, she began to fear she might have made a mistake. Jumped to the wrong conclusion. She turned sharply at the sudden weight of a meaty hand on her shoulder. Faced the hefty figure looming up behind her – cropped black hair, boxer's nose, leather bomber, trainers.

'Harry,' she said. 'Thank Christ it's you and not some nutty Russian. Do they know they've hired a cop for a chauffeur?'

'Course they do.' He smiled benignly. Moved swiftly on. 'I was half expecting you to call.'

'Were you?' She was too exhausted now to care or even to be surprised.

He dug around in the pocket of his bomber, pulled out a postcard.

'It arrived yesterday. The old bugger hadn't put the right stamp on it so I had to pay the difference.'

She examined the card. Postmarked Inverness. The Ring of Brodgar on the front and on the back Jim's scrawl danced like the scribble on a planchette, a message from the other side.

The third man may need your help. Jim.

'The third man,' he said. 'That's what Jim always called you. Family joke I assumed.'

She grimaced, too many memories stirring, thought she heard a whisper, a footfall, glanced over her shoulder. Nothing. Nobody.

'So what do you have for me anyway?' Harry asked.

She stuck her hand into the side pocket of her combat trousers, removed the manila envelope.

'Information from Jim. Everybody seems to be after it. That's why he was killed. Here. Take it. Please.'

Harry held the envelope, turned it over thoughtfully. 'Slaughter told me about the hit,' he said.

'Slaughter?'

'Kevin Slaughter. Mortuary assistant. Another of Jim's jokes. East End Borstal Boy. Jim helped him get the job. Thought it would give everyone a laugh to have a mortuary assistant called Slaughter who looked like a skeleton.'

She muttered, 'Sometimes Jim's jokes were a bit painful.'

'Everyone has to find their own way of dealing with the difficult stuff.' He rolled his bottom lip down, raised his eyebrows. 'And some people have more difficult stuff to deal with than others.'

He shrugged. 'You'd better tell me what's been going on anyway. I know the gist of it. Jim told me he was heading up to Orkney to pick up the gen on Intelligence and their funny business. I assume that's what this lot is.' He wafted the envelope in the air. 'And I've just heard over the airwaves that there's a bit of a mess down in the swampland that needs to be cleaned up before forensics start dusting the place for fingerprints. The Commander. That's certainly put everybody in headless chicken mode. Word is that the other stiff is that creep who had it in for Jim and me when we were at Tilbury; Intelligence shit worker.'

'The Watcher.'

'The Watcher? Yes. Him.' He harrumphed dismissively. 'What was he doing in Waterloo? Was he after the information?'

'The Watcher was the middleman for the Intelligence operation to fix the miners' strike. When Intelligence found out that Jim's contact had some information on the operation, they set the Watcher after him to try and retrieve it. But he didn't manage to get hold of the envelope in Orkney.'

Harry nodded. 'Jim told me that the Commander had instructed him to ask that old mate of theirs to provide a courier to pick the papers up in Orkney. American. Ex CIA.'

'Don Chance,' Sam confirmed. 'He sent his daughter, Avis. She works for Ventura, his security company.'

'So why didn't Jim pass the envelope on to her?'

'When Jim looked through the papers, he must have worked out that South African Steve, the agent provocateur hired by the Watcher, had also been employed by Don Chance through another of his companies – Shaba Security. And that made him suspect Chance was working with Intelligence in some way and would probably destroy the information rather than pass it on. But I reckon Chance also wanted the envelope because he was worried there might be something in it that linked Shaba Security to a load of shootings that took place at this mine they were supposed to be guarding. Shinkolobwe. He would obviously want to try and erase any connection to that. So when Jim failed to drop the envelope at Brodgar, South African Steve was ordered to hijack Jim's car on the way back from Kensington Olympia Station. Made him drive to Vauxhall.' She couldn't quite bring herself to recount the event. 'Faked the car crash.'

Harry took a sharp intake of breath. 'That's a bit wild west,' he said. 'Those kind of tactics are usually saved for overseas operations.'

'Well, I suppose Chance is more used to working overseas. And he's obviously a bit of a crackpot.'

'But they didn't find the information in the car?'

'Jim didn't have the envelope with him.'

Harry checked her out of the corner of his eye.

'I had it,' she said. She tried to grin in a dippy sort of way.

Harry stroked his chin. 'So it was Chance that ordered the hit on Jim.'

She hesitated; relieved that Harry hadn't asked about her own involvement, how she had ended up with the package.

And in the gap in the conversation she heard the strange sounds of the tunnel – the rushing river overhead, ghosts of the past whispering, and somewhere far away a drip, drip, drip of water, like the ticking of a clock.

Eventually she spoke. 'The Commander ordered the hit on Jim.'

Harry shook his head. 'No. Now I think you've lost the trail. Jim had his suspicions about the Commander. He was worried that he was setting him up. But he was wrong about that.'

'Why did Jim suspect him?'

'Jim started getting jumpy when the Commander directed him to Chance's company for a courier. Thought there was something funny going on. Although he couldn't quite see what. He suspected the Commander was conniving with his old dining-club mates in Intelligence, carving up the home turf, trying to ease Jim out of the frame because he was being difficult. But I'm sure he was wrong on that score. I always thought the Commander was too close to Jim to do him in. Used to piss me off, the Commander. Wanted to use the roughs and toughs, the street-wise cops, but he couldn't stomach our uneducated ways. But he loved Jim. Jim was a bit more cultured than the rest of us. Liked reading books. Understood Latin. The Commander and Jim were a team. The Commander wouldn't have turned on his right-hand man.'

Harry licked his thumb, rubbed a scratch on his leather jacket. 'Anyway, I know Jim was wrong about the Commander. He wasn't siding with Intelligence.'

'How do you know?'

'Jim asked me to find out whether the Commander was communicating with his old mates in Intelligence behind his back. Operation Asgard.'

Of course. Now Jim's edginess about Operation Asgard made sense.

'So Operation Asgard was Jim's attempt to find out what the Commander was doing,' Sam said. 'Not the Commander's operation to retrieve the information about Intelligence.'

He nodded. 'Operation Asgard. Jim and me, just like old times. Jim asked me to listen to the wires.'

'What wires?'

'The wires between the Embassy and Moscow. If the Commander was communicating with Intelligence, then the Russians would have found out about it and the Embassy would be passing the information back to their bosses in Moscow. And then I would have found out about it. But there wasn't anything. No noise. Nothing.'

'Are you sure?'

'Yes. Nothing. As far as I could make out from what was being reported back to Moscow, the only thing the Commander seemed to be concerned about was his pension pot. He was rabbiting on about it constantly.'

She fiddled with her bottom lip.

'Now that, in fact, was something that was getting a lot of interest from the third secretary,' Harry said. 'He wanted to find out all about that. The Commander's extra-curricular activity – private companies, business deals, the details of his latest wheeze.'

'What sort of wheeze is that then?'

'Oh, it's some sort of accountant's dodge; something to do with some new regulation changes. A loophole that meant he could avoid paying tax on his profits. Something about using someone who lives on some island or other to be a director of this company he helped set up.'

'Prosperity Asset Management,' she said.

'That's right.' Harry sounded slightly taken aback. 'That's the name of the Commander's company. How did you work that one out?'

She dug in her pocket, produced Ventura's brochure, pointed to the nearly invisible words on the back. 'Ventura is a subsidiary of Prosperity Asset Management.'

He held the brochure at arm's length, brought it up close to his eyes, moved it away again. 'Prosperity Asset Management. Security solutions. Domestic and international environments. Strategic focus on energy markets. Sounds like a load of old cobblers to me. What does it all mean then?'

'In Prosperity's case, I reckon it boils down to managing a bunch of dodgy companies that supply odd-jobbers to do dirty work for Intelligence and security guards to take a cut from illegal uranium mining in Zaire,' she said. 'Don Chance covers the groundwork through Ventura and Shaba Security. The Commander keeps his eye on the books through Prosperity.'

Harry's mouth drooped. The realization that he'd missed a trick, misread the signs, weighing his face down. 'So the Commander wasn't talking to his old mates in Intelligence,' he said. 'He didn't have to deal with the spooks because Chance was busy cutting the deals with them. The Commander just did the paperwork. Identified the gaps in the market, calculated the profit.'

She nodded.

He shook his head. 'The Commander was in it for the money all along then.'

'I reckon so.'

'Well, it will be interesting to see how they manage to cover all that lot up,' Harry said. 'Won't want the details of the Commander's activities spread all over the papers. That's for sure.'

He puffed his cheeks, blew a stream of air upward. 'Glad that's not my problem.' He stuck his hands in his pockets, hunched his shoulders. 'You're quite good at all this stuff. You must have learned it all from Jim. Picked up some of his tradecraft.'

'I started young. I've had a long apprenticeship.'

Ars longa, vita brevis.

'Ever thought about joining the Force yourself?'

'No way. I'm too short,' she added when she realized her reaction sounded rude.

'You should be proud of your dad,' Harry replied. A little huffily. 'Last of a breed. Tough old bastard. Smart. But not out for himself. Prepared to make the sacrifices. Put his life on the line. And what's more,' he said, 'he was incorruptible.'

'Do you really think he never did anything wrong?'

'I didn't say that. I said he was incorruptible. He was always doing things wrong, breaking the rules, but only because he was certain he was right. He never did anything because someone had offered him a backhander. He didn't care about money. Or promotion. In my book he was incorruptible.'

She winced, not quite sure how to respond, wondering about the certainty of Harry's judgement. She pictured Jim's smooth, unlined face gazing at her from the morgue table. She brushed her eye with her finger.

Charlie's whistle sounded faintly in the distance. Harry jolted, pulled himself together, waved the manila envelope in the air. 'Well, I'd better dispose of this lot then.'

'What are you going to do with the information? Do you think Jim might have been intending to leak it to the papers?'

'I'd be surprised.' He paused. 'Jim never had much time for journalists.'

'You're right. I suspect he wasn't too convinced by the power of whistleblowing.'

'And anyway, these scraps of paper, the information from his contact, it's not exactly irrefutable evidence of anything. Plausible deniability. Intelligence is pretty good at that.'

He batted his chin with the envelope, the doodled feather wafting to and fro. She followed the quill with her eyes, traced a line in her mind from the feather's tip to the tunnel wall.

'Is there a loose tile somewhere along here with a hole behind it?'

Harry nodded his head slowly. 'Now there's a thought,' he said. 'That might do the trick. I could leave it in the drop-box so it gets picked up and taken to the Russian Embassy. The analysts will pore over it, put two and two together without much difficulty, run the leads to ground and report their findings back to Moscow on the wires. And that way Intelligence will find out that the Russians know what they are up to, because they will be listening in. And if Intelligence know, that the other side know, then that will make them back off. It's not totally foolproof, but it's more likely to do the trick than some half-baked insinuations in a lefty newspaper.'

She remembered, then, Jim laughing that night in Nethergate when he mentioned the Russians and their poison-tipped umbrellas. Always three steps ahead.

'You know I have a funny feeling Jim was intending to leave the information here all along,' she said.

Harry winked. 'Wouldn't surprise me.'

She rubbed her forehead; she had the beginnings of a headache.

'But what about Chance and his international security business? Ventura Enterprises? Shaba Security? What can we do about that?'

Harry folded his arms. 'Not a lot. Take more than an envelope of dodgy papers to stop somebody like Chance, I'm afraid. His type are always pretty good at getaways. Best to concentrate on the things you can do something about.'

Harry flicked his wrist, checked his watch. 'I'd better shoot off and start the information moving. Have to pick up the third secretary. He's been at some meeting in the city. In fact he's not stopped having meetings in the city since he found out about the Commander's tax dodge. The genie is out of the bottle on that one I reckon. I need to encourage him to concentrate on the day job, persuade him to empty his drop-box. Times are changing. The spooks aren't as single-minded as they used to be, they're all looking for sidelines.'

'Really? That's interesting. Maybe it's a case of every regime producing its own gravediggers.'

He gave her a baffled look. 'Marx. *Communist Manifesto*. I could lend you Jim's copy if you like.'

'Thanks. But revolutionary literature isn't really my department.'

'So what is your department these days?'

Perhaps he didn't hear her. He turned to leave. 'Call me if you need me. You've got my number.'

She nodded. '*Do svidaniya.*'

'*Do svidaniya.*' He waved and strode off towards the Isle of Dogs. Halfway along the tunnel he stopped, reached up to the wall, dislodged a tile, dropped the envelope behind, pushed it back. Déjà vu. And for a moment she was slipping, drifting again, being pulled down by the undertow. She was brought back to her senses by a damp blast of wind barrelling down the tunnel from the north, chilling her skin as it passed, rustling the dry leaves, the crisp packets, the fag butts, the scraps of newspaper that had been trapped underground.

'Harry,' she shouted. 'Hang on a minute. I have to ask you something.'

She ran after him. 'Was Jim's codename Munin?'

He smiled, stared along the tunnel, reminiscing for a moment before he spoke. 'Munin was the codename Jim used when we were at the docks. We were always mucking about with those walkie-talkies, inventing codenames for people. And pubs. Hugin and Munin started off as one of Jim's jokes. He said they were ravens. Something to do with the Vikings. He liked the foreignness of the names. Said it would throw people of the scent. Tilbury's ravens. That's what we were. Birds of the hinterland. Shape-shifters, Jim said. Smart-arses. A raven can see the lie of the land. Fly away from trouble. More room for manoeuvre than being a god, he reckoned. He said, leave the playing God to the Commander.'

'Odin,' she said.

'That's right. Odin was our codename for the Commander.'

Of course.

'Where did Jim find the names anyway?'

'Now, where did he dig those names up from?' Harry's forehead furrowed. 'Oh, I remember now. I caught him reading a kid's book of Norse myths in the office once.'

Her jaw dropped. 'A kid's book of Norse myths? He must have nicked that from me. I thought I had lost that.'

Harry grinned. 'He was always picking up books – history, myths, detective stories, anything. Always had something on the go. So, well, now you know. That's where Hugin and Munin come from: your book of Norse myths. Probably where Asgard came from as well.'

'Yes,' she said. 'Almost inevitably.'

Harry turned and she watched him marching on again, disappearing into the strange white light of the tunnel. All she could hear now was the Thames gushing past above her head. And, for some reason, she found the rush of the water soothing.

She caught the train back to Waterloo, headed out of the station and descended to the embankment path. Heading west. The night lights of Parliament danced on the oily surface of the water. Big Ben's full moon face shining in the jaundiced urban sky. Once or twice she glanced over her shoulder to check for shadows, but she was definitely on her own now. She passed the flinty walls of Lambeth Palace, the gaudy penthouse heights of Alembic House, and reached the derelict wastelands of Vauxhall. She paused at the point where the Effra escaped its underground sewer and flowed out to greet the Thames. Bit of a hot spot, she heard Jim say. Gateway to the other side. She turned north, up the slope and sauntered slowly across Vauxhall Bridge, stopped at the midpoint, leaned over the grimy railings, breathed in the view: Battersea Power Station, the Cold Store, Lambeth Palace, St Paul's, Greenwich and, in the far distance, Gravesend. Tilbury. The black streak of a cormorant shot downstream, late-night fishing. Was it really only two weeks since she had driven north over the river with Jim? It felt like another lifetime. Once upon a time. A long time ago. She dug her hand into her overcoat pocket and found the raven's feather, held it up, the barbs glistening under the hazy street lights, twizzled it between her fingers before casting it over the railing. The black blade floated down to the eddying waters of the Thames and was caught up in the outward flowing tide and swept along with the river as it headed east, past Tilbury and out towards the sea.

CHAPTER 23

A SKEIN OF geese drew a line above the far horizon, flying east along the path of the river. The spires and cupolas of Oxford clustered behind her, the pale stone façades darkening to dusky emerald in the fading evening light. She licked the Rizla papers carefully, joined them in a fan, flicked the Zippo, burned the excess paper back to its seam, heated and sprinkled her gold resin, rolled the spliff perfectly. She tipped back against the chimney stack, lit the reefer, puffed and gazed at the first falling leaves of autumn, swirling in the crystal air. The harvest moon was rising behind the tower now, casting a golden path across the grey quad that bottomed out way below. Tom crawled forward on his hands and knees, dangerously close to the roof edge, and peered over.

'Careful,' she said. 'You might fall.'

He grinned at her over his shoulder. 'I didn't know you cared,' he said.

'I don't. It's just that I'll get sent down if we are caught on the roof.'

Death, she thought, came in threes. And there had been two deaths already that summer. First Jim and then the dog, who had keeled over, collapsed, been rushed to the vet and passed away on the operating table the week after Sam had left for college. It was, Sam had noted at the time, quite convenient that the dog had died shortly before Liz and Roger were due to set off for Greece on their two-week holiday. One man and his dog: two deaths. She eyed Tom retreating from the sheer drop and had a sudden flashback to the Watcher's assassination, the fleeting glimpse of oblivion in his eyes, and reminded herself that, of course, there had been more than two deaths that summer. She hadn't thought about Waterloo for weeks. She must have blanked it from her memory. Funny how she managed to do that so easily. She wasn't the only person who had wiped away the details. According to the report she had found hidden in the back pages of *The Times*, there were no witnesses: two bullets, two bodies, one unidentified, the other an off-duty senior police officer on the point of retirement. Nothing to do with his job, of course. The Superintendent in charge of the case had stated that they were working on the theory that it was a failed street-robbery attempt. Although they had no leads apart from an abandoned XT500 black Yamaha with false number plates which they had been able to trace – via its engine serial number – to its original owner in Durban, from whom it had been stolen the previous year. Sam did a quick body re-count. Two well-dodgy stiffs at Waterloo and Jim's uncorrupted corpse found at the Vauxhall end of the Effra. And the dog. So there had been four deaths that summer.

There was nothing like a death, she mused, to make you realize the pointlessness of bearing grudges. She had made up her mind to call Tom on her way back from Waterloo that night, after she had watched the raven's feather drift away and had decided that life was just too short to waste time being petty. She would be magnanimous. Take people at their word. Face value. She had dug out Tom's phone number. Stared at it as she had rerun events in Orkney, remembered catching him red-handed rummaging in Jim's bedroom, decided he was a total tosser after all and her original decision never to speak to him again had been the right one. So she hadn't phoned. Had dodged his calls. And then the week after she had arrived at college, when she was feeling depressed and lonely and was wondering how on earth she had managed to end up in a place where ninety-five per cent of her fellow students were public school boys, she had found a letter from Tom in her pigeonhole and it had cheered her up. She had called him and he had said he would come down to visit her in Oxford.

'Who are those blokes in the funny penguin suits?' he asked.

She squinted at the gathering flock of black-swathed figures. 'Might be the Bullingdon. Might be the Assassins.'

He raised a quizzical eyebrow.

'Dining clubs,' she said.

'What's a dining club?'

'It's a sort of secular secret society.' She groped for a better explanation. 'Junior freemasons. A trade union for toffs.'

'Are there a lot of toffs here then?'

'Yes. I somehow seem to have ended up in the worst college for that. They only started admitting women a couple of years ago and they haven't exactly embraced us with open arms.' She shrugged. 'Apparently this college has produced more prime ministers than all the other colleges combined.'

He took an Instamatic camera out of his anorak pocket, aimed it down into the quad and snapped, the flash briefly lighting up the night sky.

'What are you doing that for?'

'Never know when it might be useful to have a photo of a future prime minister up your sleeve.'

'Well, if you really want the money shot, you should come out here later tonight when they're running around, pulling each other's trousers down and exposing their bottoms to all and sundry.'

'Is that what the Bullingdon do then?'

She nodded. 'They go to a restaurant, get pissed and smash the place up. Then they come back here and perform stupid rituals like trying to knock a golf ball from this quad into the next one and dropping their trousers. And when they are bored with that, they go on the rampage. They shattered most of the quad's ground-floor windows the other week.'

'But that's criminal damage. What did the college authorities do about it?'

'Nothing,' she said. 'Boys will be boys, especially if their parents are stinking rich or a member of the aristocracy. You've got your law-abiding citizens, your criminals, your stirrers, and your upper classes who make the rules in the first place so they don't really have to worry all that much. So yes, the authorities turn a blind eye. Just like they ignore the graffiti.'

'I noticed the chalk all over the walls. "Women belong in the home not the house." What's that all about?'

'The house is the nickname for the college. It's their idea of a joke.'

She stuck her hand in the brown paper bag of cherries she had purchased in the covered market, dropped one in her mouth and then spat the stone out so it flew in an arc before plunging out of sight over the edge of the roof.

'What happens if my cherry stone hits someone on the head?' she asked.

'You get ten points,' he said. 'Twenty for an Assassin and thirty for a member of the Bullingdon.'

He grabbed the bag and peered inside. 'I reckon there's enough left to wipe out the lot of them.'

She pointed her finger at Tom. 'Your country needs you.'

He put a cherry in his mouth, spat. She took another, sent its stone hurtling into the air. It landed short. She sighed. 'It's no good anyway. You know what they say. An heir and a spare. Even if we manage to do away with this lot, there'll be another wave to take their place. We're doomed.'

She leaned back against the chimney, felt the rough surface of the bricks through her thin overcoat and stared disconsolately at the collection of dark figures clustering on the library steps like a flock of black birds. A murder. A storytelling.

'What really bugs me about them,' she said, gesturing with her arm across the quad, 'is that they are the men who in ten years' time will be preaching the value of the free market to the rest of us. We're done with the age of science and now we are heading for the age of greed and those are its prophets. And soon they'll be out there, peddling their fertility myth to the rest of us, insisting that if we believe in the invisible hand we will have limitless prosperity. Life without death.'

Tom raised a bored eyebrow, idly sent a few more cherry stones flying over the parapet.

She decided to carry on regardless. 'I mean, look at them, everything they have they've inherited. How do they square inherited privilege and wealth with free markets? How do they square free markets with the force needed to make them move? The only invisible hand operating here is the shadowy hand of the secret state doing the dirty work behind the scenes, fixing the unions, squashing protesters who step out of line, trying to have a quick grope while no one is looking, making absolutely certain that people have no choice other than to take the shitty jobs for pathetic wages in the stupid companies that make profits for their parents to cream off and use to pay their school fees.'

'Talking of the secret state,' Tom said casually. 'Do you miss your dad?'

She pursed her lips, irritated with herself for making a

tactical error, giving him an opening. She had tried very hard to avoid this conversation, vainly hoped that respect for the recently bereaved might restrain his urge to interrogate.

She took a deep breath. 'Well, it's hard to know whether I miss him. I mean, he hasn't been gone that long. And he wasn't around that much when he was alive. So, in a funny sort of way, it's the same as it always was – he's disappeared some-where without telling anyone where he's going and we have no way of contacting him. I'm still half expecting him to turn up; materialize from nowhere with a swagger, a whistle and a wave of his hand, to tell me I don't know my arse from my elbow.'

She smiled as she remembered Jim. And she thought then that what she really missed was the double-edged reassurance of his presence, the sense of danger letting you know you were alive, the lack of certainty, the doubts about what was real, what was cover, the feeling that he was more reliable, more trustworthy than the people who played it straight. Because in her heart she knew that truth was little more than fool's gold and there were no solid facts in this world, only stories and cover-ups, and if you scraped the surface all you would find were more strange tales and sleights of hand and anyone who thought differently was living in a land of make-believe.

'What exactly did happen anyway?' Tom asked.

'I told you – he was killed in a car crash. The morning we came back from Orkney, driving home from the station.'

'He looked pretty much alive when I left.'

'And then he sat in the car, drove across Vauxhall Bridge, swerved into a brick wall and died. That's how death happens. One minute you are alive. The next minute you're not. You don't necessarily receive three months' written notice.'

'It's hard to see why he might have swerved the car early on a Saturday morning when there wasn't much traffic about.'

'There was a lorry involved. And he had a high level of alcohol in his blood.'

'Yes, but that was probably the normal state of your dad's blood and I never saw it impair his ability to function. Did someone do him in? Did someone mess with the car? Tamper with the brakes or something like that?'

'No.'

'What about Shinkolobwe?'

'What about it?'

'You've no idea why he mentioned it?'

'No.'

'So you don't think it was anything to do with his death?'

'No.'

He persisted. 'Why weren't you in the car with him?'

She sighed. 'Liz asked me to go and collect a book from Foyles. So I took the bus into town.'

She spotted a ladybird edging along the hem of her over-coat. She tried to persuade the insect to crawl on to her finger. 'Aphid eater,' she said. 'Mass murderer.'

He watched her for a moment, toying with the bug. And then he shuffled closer, whispered. 'Do you think it was your mum?'

'What?'

'Do you think Liz was involved in it somehow? Persuaded Roger the Todger to do the dirty deed?'

Sam snorted. The ladybird lifted its red wing coverings and flew away.

'It's a plausible hypothesis,' said Tom. 'Domestic, most common form of murder. Jim was an unfaithful, dodgy under-cover cop with a drink problem. Who could blame Liz for wanting him out of the way? Roger the Todger couldn't stand him, obviously had his eye on your mum, wanted revenge for being humiliated by Jim over the *Ulysses* punch-up, so wouldn't take much persuading. Liz gave Roger the details of the train and made sure you were out of the way with the Foyles' errand. He fixed the brakes. There must have been dozens of men out there with a grudge against Jim. Roger the Todger knew that even if foul play was suspected, it would be hard to identify him among all the other blokes from Jim's undercover life just waiting to get him, a crow in a crowd.'

'I don't think it was Roger,' she said.

Tom nodded his head slowly. 'Well, I suppose even if it was Roger,' he said. 'You'd still have to explain the gun.'

Her head swivelled sharply. Her eyes met his. 'Gun?' she said. 'What gun?'

'The gun I found that night in Nethergate when I was in Jim's bedroom. The one that was in the drawer of his bedside cabinet. Small. Black. Handgun.'

She didn't blink. 'Oh. That gun.'

She reached for the bag of cherries, pulled it up to her face, peered into the bottom of the bag. Jesus. Jim had been so careless at times. What had he been thinking? Leaving his pistol in his bedside cabinet in a holiday cottage? Madness. She stuck her hand in the bag, rustled around. Lifted her head up. Dropped a plump black cherry in her mouth.

'That must have been Jim's starting pistol,' she said indistinctly as she squashed the juice out of the fruity flesh in her mouth.

Tom cocked his head to one side.

'Jim had this starting pistol he wasn't using any more,' she said. 'So he was going to give it to Bill. Because Bill is the chair of the local athletics club at Stromness.' She spat the cherry stone towards the edge of the roof. It missed.

'It had Walther engraved on the side of it,' Tom said.

She picked another cherry. 'So?'

'So, Walther is a manufacturer of firearms. James Bond carries a Walther.'

'Does he?' She hadn't realized that. 'Yes, but James Bond is a made-up character. Fiction.'

'And Walther is a real-life maker of handguns. Fact.'

She tilted her head back a bit this time, aimed towards the sky. The cherry stone followed a satisfying trajectory – beautiful arch, up and over. 'Maybe Walther is a maker of starting pistols too,' she said.

'Maybe,' he replied.

She focused on the Assassins in the far corner of the Quad; one of them was waving a golf club above his head and another was baying like a bloodhound. She grabbed the ends of her plimsolls in her hands, pulled the tips towards her.

Tom eyed her shrewdly. 'Go on. Tell me what you know about Jim's death.'

'I'm going to write it all down,' she said.

'Show me when you've written it.'

'Why?'

'I could help you with it.'

'I don't need your help. And anyway I can't show you.'

'Why not?'

'Thirty-year rule. State secrets.'

'Come on,' he said. 'Your secrets are safe with me.'

'Trust me,' she said. 'I'm a journalist.'

He put his hands behind his head, sagged back against the chimney.

'What are you going to do with it then?'

'I'll write it and sit on it for thirty years. Or else I'll sit on it for thirty years and then I'll write it.'

'You'll make it up. You're incapable of telling it straight.

You'll end up covering for him. You've always covered for Jim.'

'I've given up covering for Jim,' she said. 'The dead don't need any help holding on to their secrets.'

She relit her reefer with the Zippo, dragged a deep lungful of smoke. Coughed. Cleared her throat. 'How's your job going anyway?' she asked.

'It's okay.'

'So are you investigating the dark and dirty deeds of the burghers of Manchester?'

'Not yet.'

'What are you doing then?'

'I'm writing the showbiz column.'

'What's that involve?'

'It's like a gossip column that tells people bits of news about the local celebrities.'

Sam tried not to look disapproving. It didn't work. 'Celebrity is the opium of the masses.' She waved her spliff in the air. 'I might be a pothead but you're a dope-pusher. Are there any celebrities in Manchester?' She started sniggering.

'You really are a southern snob. How about you? How's the history going?'

'Okay.'

'And what are you going to do after that? What can you do with a history degree?'

'Dunno,' she said. 'Join the civil service maybe.'

'That's a bit boring.'

'Not necessarily. I could apply for the Foreign Office. Become a third secretary, something like that.'

'Not sure that would suit you. It seems a bit too... respectable.'

'I can be respectable when I want to be.' She stubbed her

357

spliff on the roof felting. 'Maybe you're right. Maybe that's not really me.' She stared over the Deanery Garden to the meadow and the Thames beyond, wrapped her arms around her knees. 'I have been thinking about taking a post-grad course in archaeology.'

He groaned. 'Oh God. Ancient ruins and High Priestesses.'

She ignored his comment. 'What are you doing next Thursday anyway?'

'Not sure. Why?'

'Fancy coming with me to Stop the City?'

'What's that?'

'Protest against the might of the military-financial complex. London. Could be a laugh.'

'Perhaps,' he said.

She shrugged, glanced at her watch.

'Why do you wear your watch on the inside of your wrist?' he asked.

'Habit.' She twisted it round to the front. And then she twisted it back.

'I'm hungry,' he said. 'Let's go and find something to eat. I saw a van selling kebabs parked just up the road when I walked down here from the station.'

'I'm not eating that crap. It's not proper food.'

He punched her on the arm. 'Chip off the old block.'

She jumped up, disturbing a trio of magpies that had been playing on the far roof edge. She watched them flapping, chattering and chasing each other round and round, spiralling into the night and off, far away. She smiled to herself, skipped over to the open skylight, turned, waved her hand dismissively at Tom, stepped backwards through the hatch, like a coney down a rabbit hole. And disappeared from view.

ACKNOWLEDGEMENTS AND AUTHOR'S NOTE

I am hugely grateful to my brilliant agent Oli Munson, and to Laura Palmer and everybody at Head of Zeus for their fantastic guidance and support. Thank you to Rosy, Sal, Mary, Bill and Katy for their friendship when I needed it. Thank you also to Shiona and everybody I work with for being so enthusiastic. Special thanks go to my mother for her wisdom and encouragement. And, above all, thank you to Andy, Eva and Rosa for being my bedrock.

I culled information about the Vikings from a number of sources, including *A History of the Vikings*, published by Oxford University Press in 1968, and Neil Price's 'Sorcery and circumpolar traditions in Old Norse belief', in *The Viking World*, edited by Stefan Brink in collaboration with Neil Price, published in 2008 by Routledge. I used Seumas Milne, *The Enemy Within. The Secret War Against the Miners,* published in 2004 by Verso, for background information about turf wars between MI5 and Special Branch during the miners' strike. Tom Zoellner, *Uranium. War, Energy, and the Rock that Shaped the World*, published in 2009 by Penguin Books, provides an excellent account of uranium mining in the Democratic Republic of Congo. The long-running anthropological debate about the 'skipper effect' – the theory that successful skippers are less technical experts than magicians who can persuade other fishing boats to follow them – is explained by Thorddur

Bjanason and Thorolfur Thorlindsson in their 1993 article, 'In Defense of a Folk Model: "The Skipper Effect" in the Icelandic Cod Fishery', in *American Anthropologist*, volume 95, number 2, pp. 371–94. Claude Lévi-Strauss points to the mythical appeal of carrion birds in his 1955 article, 'The Structural Study of Myths' in *The Journal of American Folklore*, volume 68, number 270, pp. 428–44. For information about Orkney's myths and folklore, I went to www.orkneyjar.com. All interpretations of the above sources are entirely my own.

The following books are mentioned in the novel:

Maurice Bloch and Jonathan Parry (eds), *Death and the Regeneration of Life*, Cambridge University Press, 1982

James George Frazer, *The Golden Bough. A Study in Magic and Religion*. First published in 1890 in two volumes, in three volumes in 1900, and in 12 volumes between 1906 and 1915. An abridged version appeared in 1922, but this excluded passages about Christianity. The abridged version was republished in 1994 by Oxford University Press with the controversial passages reinstated

James Joyce, *Ulysses*, Sylvia Beach, 1922

Kim Philby, *My Silent War. The Autobiography of a Spy*. The Modern Library. New York, 1968

The Orkneyinga Saga. The History of the Earls of Orkney. Translation by Hermann Pálsson and Paul Edwards, Hogarth Press Ltd, 1978

NOTES FOR YOUR BOOKCLUB

1. How reliable is Sam as a narrator? Do you think it is significant that her story is told in the third person?

2. Sam sets out to find out the truth about Jim. Do you think she succeeds? Do you think she finds what she is expecting?

3. Do you think Jim is a good or bad person?

4. This is a story about families and spies. What are the implications of putting the two together in one story?

5. If the Orkney Islands were a character, how would you describe him or her? Does the landscape tell you anything about Sam and her relationship with Jim?

6. Nature is an important theme in this book. What do you think of the way nature is used?

7. What is Tom's role? Do you think Sam treats him too harshly?

8. The book is set in 1984. It's a tipping point in British history and a turning point in Sam's life. What do you think of the way the personal and the political are combined?

9. Norse mythology plays an important part in the plot. What do you think of the way it is used?

10. There are a lot of references to old spy thrillers. All of these thrillers deal with themes of betrayal, empathy and guilt. What does this book say about these issues?

A letter from the publisher

We hope you enjoyed this book. We are an independent
publisher dedicated to discovering brilliant books,
new authors and great storytelling. Please join us at
www.headofzeus.com and become part of our
community of book-lovers.

We will keep you up to date with our latest books, author
blogs, special previews, tempting offers, chances to win
signed editions and much more.

If you have any questions, feedback or just want to say hi,
please drop us a line on hello@headofzeus.com

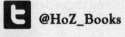

@HoZ_Books

HeadofZeusBooks

www.headofzeus.com

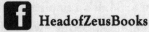

HEAD *of* **ZEUS**

The story starts here